It's A Long Way To Venice, Marco Polo . . .

An enormous scaly head rose up from the waves . . . grey-green, massively ugly, with bulging red eyes, a protruding snout, and a gaping mouth filled with irregular jutting fangs. A flaring hood, like a cobra's, shaded the head. Below the barnacle-crusted neck were two awkward little forelegs, with two short claws and one long and twitching central talon.

The grotesque head spoke in a voice like roaring surf. "The Great Naga-Khan, Basudara, Oceanic Emperor of all the Sea-Dragons, sends His Imperial greetings." The creature's breath blasted their faces like a malodorous and scorching wind. "The Naga-Khan wishes to learn the wher[illegible]bouts of a man-dragon sometimes called [illegible]' In return for this information [illegible]le Naga-Khan, Basudara, [illegible] sage to any port y[illegible]

"*Any* port?" ask[illegible]areo with eyes gone wide. [illegible]ing grant us safe passage to t[illegible]eat and Serene Port of *Venice*?"

Avram Davidson and Grania Davis

Marco Polo and The Sleeping Beauty

MARCO POLO AND THE SLEEPING BEAUTY

A Baen Books Original

Baen Publishing Enterprises
260 Fifth Avenue
New York, N.Y. 10001

First printing, March 1988

ISBN: 0-671-65372-5

Cover art by Neal McPheeters. Map © 1988 by John Westfall.

Printed in the United States of America

Distributed by
SIMON & SCHUSTER
1230 Avenue of the Americas
New York, N.Y. 10020

For Ethan Davidson and Seth Davis
#1 and #2 Sons . . .

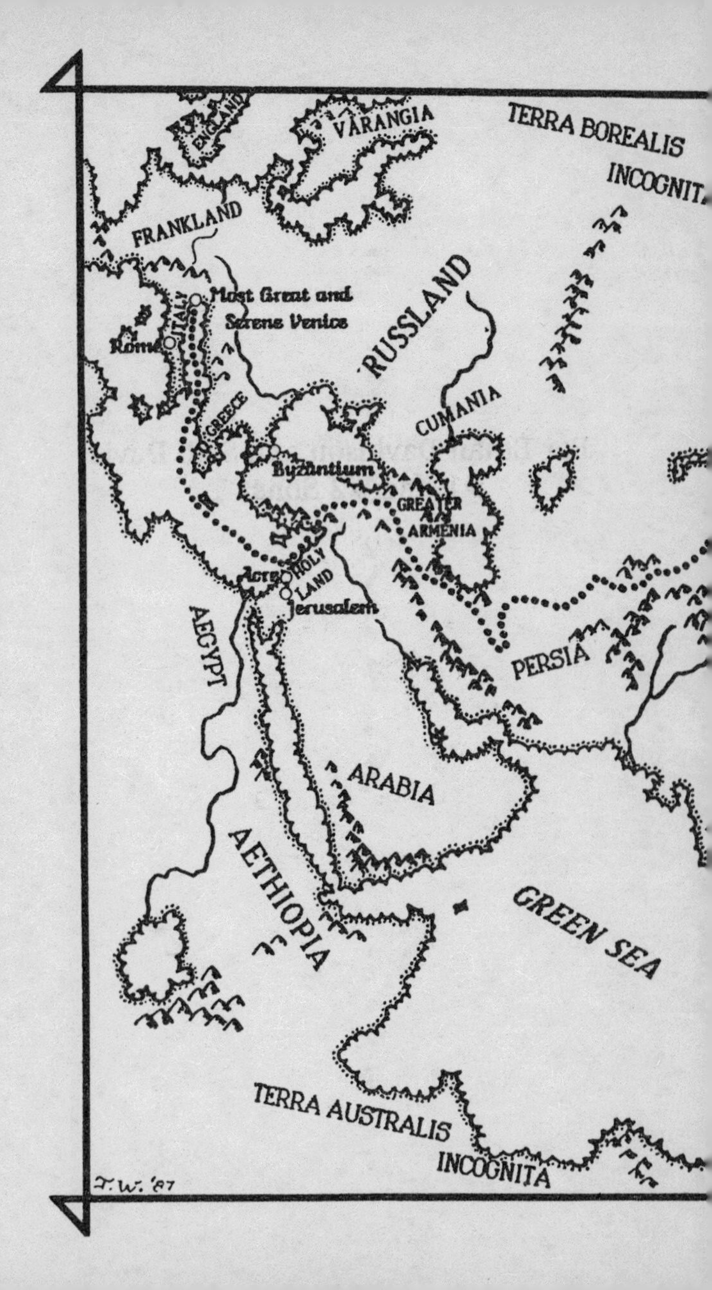
ENGLAND
VARANGIA
TERRA BOREALIS
INCOGNITA
FRANKLAND
ITALY
Most Great and
Serene Venice
Rome
RUSSLAND
GREECE
Byzantium
CUMANIA
GREATER
ARMENIA
Acre
HOLY
LAND
Jerusalem
AEGYPT
PERSIA
ARABIA
AETHIOPIA
GREEN SEA
TERRA AUSTRALIS
INCOGNITA
T.W. '87

MARCO POLO.
His Travels:
Prior to this Narrative
In this Service of the Great Khan
HYPERBOREALIS
JAPANGU
Plateau of Great Peril
Xan-du
Khanbaluc/Tai-Ting
Cloud Dancing Fairy's Cave
Grand Canal
GOBI
Great Wall
Yang-Zhau
Hangsai/Westlake
CATHAY
Yang-Tse-Kiang
Sleeping Beauty's Castle
TEBET
Kue-lin
MANZI
Ganga
BENGALA
BUR-MIEN
CHAMBA
GULF OF CHIE-NAM
GREATER INDIA
SOUTHERN SEA
ANDAMAN
JAVA
SERENDIB
PLEASURE ISLAND

—Epigraph: *This tale of Marco Polo's secret journey is, we hope, complete and entire of its own, and does not depend upon any tale ever told anywhere else, by any other person in any detail or manner. The Marco Polo of this book is not necessarily the Marco Polo of history. The Marco Polo of this book is not necessarily* not *the Marco Polo of history. The "Cathay" of this book is in an Asia of mystery, fantasy, and poesy. This is not to say that it may not be in the Asia of geography as well.*

The writers hope that the readers will accept this mystery as a book, and this book as a mystery. The readers are advised to look straightforward and straight ahead. Lastly, the readers are advised to keep a careful lookout from the corners of their eyes.

. . . "Ye Lords and Emperors, Kings and Queens, Dukes and Knights and townsfolk, and all ye who desire to know the diverse races of people and the marvels of the varied regions of the world—take this book and cause it to be read, and here ye shall find the greatest wonders . . ."

—Rustichello of Pisa; the amanuensis for *The Booke of the Travels of Messer Marco Polo.*

I
The Journey Begins

Ta Chuang; The Power of the Great. Thunder in Heaven Above. The Superior Man Treads No Turbulent Paths.

1

The very air seemed to shriek.

Who has never seen and heard a griffin attack has never really known fear. Somewhere Uncle Maffeo Polo had read those words, back when he had time to sip a good grape wine, and to read in either stuffy old Latin or melodious Italian—*how* long ago? Our Lady, *Marón*! If the entire Great Library of the Signory of the Most Serene Republic of Venice were available to him now, he could not dare the motion needed to pick even the most trifling, gossipy romance of chivalry off stand or shelf.

Face pressed to the stoney cold ground, lest its present pallor betray him to the attacker, hands withdrawn into his quilted sleeves, arms and legs and body motionless, Messer Maffeo Polo prayed that he might be mistaken for a rock or a log, and so passed by. That they *all* might be—wherever *all* might be.

The griffins had eyesight incredible; let a child of

man and woman but pout a hundred miles away, up would fly the membranes of the golden-glowing eyes. And yet, the hundred miles devoured by the massive pinions, let said son-of-man merely (*merely*!) lie face down and motionless; lo! no griffin could tell he were there.

But: *face down. And motionless.*

For the griffins ate no carrion-flesh, ate only flesh which was (at the moment before death) quick, live and moving. Not merely that if it did not move they thought it did not live. No; if it did not move they did not even see it—see what? Why, see the only meat the griff-folk ate. *Namely*? As the olden proverb put it; *nothing less good than man.*

Uncle Maffeo Polo made his corpus very still and his breath very shallow. Then of a swift sudden the stone log next to him turned, as though by sorcery, into a panicked Cathayan in a quilted blue jacket, who pounded off across the sullen slipping scree to the dubious hospit of shallow caves in the scant ravine just behind.

Angels, grant speed to his heels and soles—or soul! thought Maffeo, who made no move to follow. And then came the hoarse, harsh scream, that frightful wind-rushing from the huge wing-pinions.

The griffin fell from the sallow sky like some alien rock, all aflame, fell screaming and screeching, whistling and roaring, and the fleeing man wailed . . . once. The vast creature struck him with its cruel lion's talons, a sound like a great log rasping a lesser, and dragged him over the dusty yellow shale with skin sloughing and blood gouting and clothes rending.

The man made no more sound; the man was of course dead. The griffin it was from which proceeded those grunts and gobbles, and other hideous noises for which human-speak has no words. Those slavers and slobbers and croaks, as it broke the body into limbs and torso, torsions and sections—snapping sounds, breaking sounds, tearing sounds. Sounds unimaginable to the Venetians who daily passed the two *Grifi* columns that adorned the southern arcade of the great Basilica di San Marco in Venice.

Just as well that—just as well? *Marón*! —well that the griffin does not linger by its killing-site to digest its meal. Well that it eats quickly. And goes. *Well* and *quickly* as these things go.

All this to please the Great Khan.

All this and *more*, to please the Great Khan.

Would the Great Khan Kublai be pleased?

Our Lady, *Marón*! thought Uncle Maffeo Polo. He had better! Else—griffins or no griffins—they were all dead men's meat. Which . . . of course . . . they might well (or ill) be anyway.

Three *li* or so away, Messer Niccolo Polo heard the sound of the griffin in its screaming descent and said—rapidly and aloud—a Pater Noster and three Ave Marias for the safety of his brother, Maffeo, and his son, Marco Polo. He could not know which of them, or if perhaps both might be in danger from the great and perilous creature. It did not occur to him to pray for his own safety. He could not go in search of either brother or son; impossible even to try. Yet *woe* if they were separated in this wasteland!

He sat crouch-pressed against an unyielding rock, and was thankful it did not yield. Above him, a scant finger's length or two overhead, was another rock; and others lay narrowly on either side. Providence had clearly provided this lichen-crusted cairn for his own safety. For outside, pacing incessantly back and forth; forth and back; prowled the great beast that drove him into this scant-spaced refuge. Now and then it paused and thrust its paw between the boulders—which it could not push aside.

In size, it compared to the regular snow-leopard as the latter did to the common house-cat. Each of its spots was the size of a man's head, and its claws were long and sharp as scimitars. Already those claws had frayed the edge of Niccolo Polo's fur-lined robe, where they had tried (and were trying still! Were trying *still*!)

to gain enough hold to pluck him forth, as a Frankishman would hook a snail from its shell.

". . . *Jesus. Amen.*" Niccolo Polo concluded the third Hail Mary, and at once followed it with another prayer to the Holy Virgin Mother; "*Lily of Israel, Tower of Ivory, House of Gold* . . ." he chanted, whilst trying to recall the correct order of this litany, now accompanied by his jangled heart. The gigantic snow-leopard coughed and growled, paced and thrust, and ripped another shred of glimmering grey silk from the robe.

One had heard legend and report of this monstrous pard. One had suspended judgment and belief. Now one *knew*: it did indeed exist. As least it existed *here*, in this accursed pagan wasteland, beyond even the sheltering ruins of the Great 10,000 *Li* Wall. Doubtless a chapter on it should be added to the Bestiary; one should discuss its Christian-religious significance with some priestly scholar. Sometime.

Sometime, when back in blessed, far-off Christendom. Sometime, when one had a comfortable couch, familiar faces, and the leisure of a well-earned retirement. Sometime, *back home in sea-scented Venice*. Home being the pink marble *Palazzo di Polo*, with its emblem of four black starlings, off the Sclavonian Quay of the Grand Canal, on the lesser canal called "Of the Embassadores of the Sclavonians." Perhaps he and his pleasure-loving younger brother, Maffeo, should have ventured no farther from Venice than the land of Sclavonia, which is a proper Christian country; one rich in—rich in *what*?—in salt, prunes, timber, honey, hemp, wax—and other dull wares which took an argosy of ships to transport.

Sometimes, as the market rose and fell on the Street of the Goldsmiths off the Rialto, where Venetian merchants and bankers and jewelers met . . . ("What news on the Rialto? Hemp is up. Wax is down. Prunes are unchanged. Wax is down very much. Hemp is hardly up at all . . ."). Sometimes it was scarcely worth the effort at all.

Whereas: *jewels*!

The very thought of jewels, of gemstones, which a man might carry as a life's fortune sewn into his hems, caused his breath (as always) to quicken and thicken. The immense spotted lion-of-the-snows may have heard. It ceased its prowl. Niccolo's thoughts turned without difficulty (indeed, it was usually difficult to turn them *off* the matter) to a certain list, almost a litany, which, truth to tell—and he would have been horrified to hear it told as truth—comforted him full as much as any prayer.

Ten diamants of Golconda of the first water, sans blemish, each the size of a fine dried Sclavonian plum, such as sell at half-a-ducat an hundredweight; value of said diamants—each worth a score of hundreds of the finest horse.

Twenty-one rubies of the kind called Spider-Rubies, every one the size of the clenched fist of a lusty man-child ten days in age; value of said Spider-Rubies—

Two-score sapphires, and an half-a-score sapphires of the kind called Star-Sapphires from the Isle of Serendib or Seylaun—

An hundred and ten matched fine brown pearls of full luster, from the Archipelago of the Cynocephali or Dog-Headed Men, each pearl the size of the pap of a fine fat woman with a nursing child—

Emeraulds, a baker's dozen, and green as the hills of the Terra Firma in the rain-time—

Value—value—value—

Oblivious to his horrid cramped position, deaf to the sounds of peril and danger, indifferent to the chill-cold spreading through his crouched limbs, Niccolo Polo drew unfailing comfort from his gem-treasurer's mind. He did not note that the shifting late-winter sun now sent a slant shaft of light through the chink between two sheltering, black-veined rocks. Did the giant leopard note it? Niccolo could not know.

He next knew that the huge beast, of a sudden, threw itself at an angle against the angled rock. And he knew, instantly, that the rock moved.

K'uei; Opposition.
Fire Above the Lake.
The Superior Man Recalls His Own Nature.

2

"Rome fell," the withered friar in the tan wool cassock had told Marco, then a restless boy in baggy leggings, "because of the wrath of God. But God waits three and four generations—a metaphorical figure, my son; it might be three or four hundred generations; God being infinite, so is His patience infinite. God waits, my son, for those who hate Him to cease to hate Him; to love Him, and to keep His commandments. If, despite this loving patience, there is no improvement, *then* and then only does He visit the sins of the sinful parents upon the still-sinful children. This interpretation of the Holy Scripture, I heard from a learned rabbin of the Jewry-folk in the far off land of Samarkand, and I regard it as acceptable exegesis; so . . .

"But in worldly terms, Marco, *Rome fell because the Great Wall of Cathay was too strong.*" So said Friar Paul, with a voice as thin and dry as the rustle of an autumn oak-leaf on a gravel-path.

The ruthless barbarian nations, driving *east*, had broken their arrows in vain against the serpentine Cathayan Wall (" *'Tis the wall of Gog and Magog, Marco!*"); had next turned *west*, and did not rest until they brought the might and glory of Rome crashing down in blood and fire. But a thousand years later, the Cathayan guard having grown weak, decadent and lax, came the relentless Mongol and Tartar hordes. Driving west, they had penetrated even to the farthest dominions of the Princes of Rus and Moscovy, who now paid them tribute; and driving east, had poured through the gaps in the Great 10,000 *Li* Wall and elevated their sons and grandsons from the chieftain's saddle to the gilded Dragon Throne . . .

. . . and Genghiz begat Tului, and Tului begat Kublai: the Khan of Khans, the Great Khan who had rebuilt war-ravaged Cathay . . .

"*I swear that this Great Khan,*" Marco—son to dour Niccolo Polo, nephew to peppery Maffeo—had written in his traveler's diary; "*is not only the mightiest of earthly rulers, but is also the wisest.*"

Had Marco not grown from youth to maturity, and in good health and prosperity (along with his father and uncle) as a civil servant of the Empire of Mongol Cathay? Was not he (and were not they) among the high favorites of Great Kublai Khan?

A trio of ragged wayfarers out of the Latin West, their very rags stinking, and befouled with fleas and lice; by Kublai's favor they had come to be clothed in sables and silks. Marco had every reason to believe utterly in his Master's greatness and wisdom—and was he to doubt them now?

Not even if the Great Khan's merest whim and fancy had sent them all three hither, beyond the crumbling outer marches of the Great 10,000 *Li* Wall, whose ruined ramparts stood like jagged yellow teeth on the ridgetops. Sent them to be scattered like the sallow dust at the edge of the wild wastelands, so perilous and forlorn.

* * *

For at least an hour the flocks of birds, at first mere black dots in the sullen sky, had circled round about overhead, croaking and shrilling. Peter the Tartar, Marco's young attendant-slave, who seemed sometimes a fool and sometimes a sage, had murmured—*once*—that it was a bad omen. But black looks from the elder Polo brothers, and a gesture from Marco himself, had bade Peter be still: *Speak not the word, lest it come to pass.*

The moon-faced Mongol horsemen had muttered briefly amongst themselves, had fallen silent, had—after that—spoken only to the horses. After that, only their narrow black eyes moved under their fur-lined leather helmets: up—briefly—up. And then down.

And then again . . . up. *Up.*

"It is only an illusion," said Scholar Yen Lung-chuan; Jade-Dragon Yen. "The life of man is itself merely an illusion, no more than the flight of a bird across an empty sky. The bird itself is an illusion. The sky as well. Also the man. The unformed gives form to that which has been formless. These birds are not real; they are illusions. Therefore the superior man does not regard them."

Shortly afterwards, as the gant black crows circled and screamed, dark crimson blood began to fall like an uncertain rain. "An illusion," said Yen. Patiently. Calmly. "One pays it no heed." Almost as he finished speaking, out of each spreading bloodstain on the face of this arid region of yellow sand and stone; of scattered dead and stunted trees, scrannel and spare as skeleton-bones—wind-whipped and sand-scoured almost as ivory-white—out of each blood-red stain a writhing black serpent appeared.

"Pay no attention," said Scholar Yen, calmly adjusting his dignified black robe. "Truly they do not exist. See, look: how the horses ignore them . . ."

And indeed. The snakes hissed, but the horses plodded on.

The Great Khan Kublai, his round and ruddy face a-gleam with good will, had said in the great audience hall of his gilded winter palace at Khanbaluc; "I need not mention risks. What are 'risks,' so-called, to you you Po-los? Brave men welcome risks; else how is one to know that they are brave?

"If this matter were as easy as eating candied crab-apples off a stick, not only would I not need speak of it to you, no one would need speak of it to *me*. So." Kublai made a gesture, ever such a slight gesture; *instantly* a liveried servant knelt mutely before him and held up a jade salver exquisitely engraved with twining dragons, and under the almost-immediately-whisked-off cover, offered a steaming-hot-wet, thick-folded, soft-rough cloth of Turkish weave. The Great Khan took it and wiped his hands and face. Let it fall on the salver. Cloth, salver, mute servant: vanished. The face of the Great Khan was rosier than ever.

The word *risk* was then forgotten.

The illusion *snakes* was not forgotten. Long later and far, far away, beneath the shadows of the crumbling 10,000 *Li* Wall.

Some tainted echo of it hung, reiterating, in the breathless air. Something in Marco's ear pretended to perceive a hissing. Perhaps it was the susurration of the shaley sands as they were cast aside by the horses' hooves. The hissing grew more shrill, more piercing, more loud and piercing shrill. Something struck the sands. Something else—and something again—hissed hissing hisses. Despite himself, Marco looked up . . . looked *up*.

The birds, turned now at some sickeningly odd angle unknown to geometry which made them look thin as sticks, were circling no more. Were falling from the sky. Were hissing as they fell.

And were falling—and striking—all around.

Yen Lung-chuan, ever the dignified philosopher, called out, "Pay no attention." Then called in a slightly louder voice, "No attention pay. The birds are not real, the blood is not real, the serpents are not real, and the so-called arrows are not real either. It is all illusion. It is not real; not *real* at all. So. So—

"*Oh*—"

The last word fell a note. Another word followed fast upon it. Marco could not tell what the word was; it was not Jade-Dragon Yen's mouth which uttered it.

One of the Mongol-men of their 20-man horse-guard, appointed by the Chief Equerry of the Great Khan's Outer Guard; a young man, Marco had never learned his name. Stolid, stoney-eyed, flat-faced, hunch-slumped all day upon his horse like a part-filled sack of millet—suddenly this young Mongol began to flap and flop his arm, oddly, awkwardly. Perhaps to dislodge some pesty sting-fly or some obscene reptile of the rocks? For in a moment the arm stood still and stiff. The man—

In his arm was an arrow.

Fletched with black feathers.

But this was not the source of the horror which Marco suddenly felt come upon him; he had seen men stricken with arrows before. A man with an arrow in—merely—his arm; such a man was *lucky*. One pushed it through till the arrowhead was clear out, and one cut off the other end below the feather-fletch, and then one pulled the rest of the shaft out. Then one dressed the wound. *If* there was time, and the wounded man recovered. Often.

Now: not so at all. As Marco watched, as they all watched; grim-faced Father Niccolo worrying his best jade worry-beads, Uncle Maffeo tugging anxiously at his grizzled beard . . . all, *all*—O San Marco, his blessed namesake—the wounded man was growing! Swelling! The wounded man expanded like an inflating bladder. O God, what swift poison on that vile-sharp arrow! The young Mongol's skin turned dark red, then purple-black like an aubergine.

His skin continued to stretch and expand like a great, shiny blow-fish—until *pop*! The stressed and bruised flesh exploded like a fearsome fireworks display, spewing bits of Mongol-horseman among them.

Then *pop*—the illusion of an illusion was shattered as their shaggy Mongol ponies whinnied with terror and bolted. Scattering their score of guardsmen like storm-tossed debris, the horses raced off in every direction. Now Marco was alone in the weird and windswept wilds.

Meng; Youthful Folly.
A Spring Gushes Beneath the Still Mountain.
The Young Fool Finds Success.

3

Marco let his fleeing horse have its head. He paid no heed to companions or direction, for his mind was full-occupied by the poisoned arrows . . . if that was what they really were. Moyses and the Magicians of Aegypt had turned staffs into serpents and serpents into staffs. Could *birds* (unnatural birds as they were) be changed into arrows stiff as staves? Ordinary arrows would not *bleed.* Yet it was not the magic or the sorcery of it all which most gripped him, not the terror of being separated from guardsmen and kin; it was not even the thought which now occupied a corner of his mind, the question: *Who has done this? Why?*

It was the horrific image of that venom, poison, magical taint upon the arrows which, in a matter of moments (seconds, actually: *seconds*!) had turned the young Mongol purple-black and bloated and swollen huge—while still alive, whilst *still alive*!—and still the poisoned body had spread wide; until the engendered humors burst the festered skin apart.

—Another arrow sank, hissing, into the sand near the pony's racing hooves. Past fear *this* was; it was past terror. Marco cried out and spurred his harried horse, as images, like dream fragments, flowed through his horror-numbed mind . . .

"Why had the Pope," Kublai demanded . . . for the hundredth time . . . not sent, as Kublai had requested, an hundred learned priests to accompany the three Polos back to Cathay? "—To teach about the holy cross and the holy oil and the holy bread and the holy wine, and to build great big clocks for me and great big towers and fortresses for me and great big siege engines for me and great big ships-of-war for me? If he claims to be the universal father?" The Great Khan sighed deeply and growled a bit in his throat, which shimmied the long pearl fringes dangling from the filigreed gold of his sun-and-moon crown.

This embassy to the Pope had been the main purpose of young Marco's first and only journey (and his greying father's and uncle's second) across the endlessly varied expanse of Eurasia. Why had the Great Khan desired to establish contact with the Pontiff? Perhaps because he was genuinely curious about the Holy Father of Christendom, for his mother had been a Nestorian Christian who venerated the cross. Perhaps he wanted to cement the silken trade routes between east and west. Perhaps Kublai hoped to find western allies against the feverish expansion of the Saracens; and the restless vassal Khanates of the grasslands, led by belligerent Kaidu Khan.

No matter *why*. The journey had originally begun as a bold yet simple trading venture, when Marco was but a small boy. The Polo brothers, taciturn and chestnut-bearded Niccolo the elder, and swarthy and volatile Maffeo the younger, had traveled eastward in the Christian year 1260, to tap lucrative new markets on the broad River Volga. Instead they found fierce warfare between bickering local Khanates—which blocked their way home. They pushed ever eastward, to dusty lands that no Venetian merchant had seen, and finally joined a plodding camel caravan traveling the desert trade routes to the court of Kublai, the Great Khan of all the Mongols and Tartars—where few Europeans had ever been.

Kublai's mind was quick as a grassland racing pony and his curiosity was vast as his empire. He welcomed the shabby strangers and heard their tales of exotic Christian Europe. At last the Great Khan sent Niccolo and Maffeo Po-lo as his personal ambassadors to the Pope, carrying the imperial golden tablet that guaranteed their safe passage through all the hostile Mongol and Tartar lands. Kublai requested from the Pope a delegation of 100 learned priests, who were well-versed in the seven arts and in Christian beliefs. So the travel-worn Polo brothers journeyed to the west as emissaries of the Dragon Throne, and recrossed the entire war-ravaged Eurasian continent.

. . . And still the venomous arrows hissed hissing hisses in Marco's fear-ravaged mind . . .

In the year 1269, (according to the reckoning of western calendars) Niccolo and Maffeo finally returned to their beloved port-city: the powerful and wealthy Republic of Venice, whose splendid treasuries bulged with Byzantine baubles and crusaders' gold, and whose proud warehouses swelled with merchandise from the trading ports of all the then-known world. At last the Polo brothers beheld the pink-marble walls of their sorely missed home, the Palazzo di Polo, whose emblem bore four black starlings. Yet all was not unchanged; Niccolo was deeply saddened to learn that his wife had died during his decade of absence. But his surprised son, Marco, had grown into a sturdy lad of 15 who still awaited his father's return.

Waiting . . . waiting . . . had Marco spent all his young life waiting? Waiting stubbornly for his father and uncle to come home, though the family assumed that the wandering Polo brothers had long ago been killed. Waiting for audience with a newly elected pope, to carry out their mission for Kublai Khan. Waiting for storms and plagues and battles to pass, so they might continue their journey to remote Cathay. Waiting apprehensively to meet the Great Khan . . . and now waiting for the terrible poison arrows to stop hissing round his head so his horse might cease its sickening race for safety; as they pursued this latest mad mission for Kublai . . .

Marco well remembered his surprise on that soft-misted Venetian morn; he came wandering home from some mischievous errand along the fish-scented Sclavonian Quay of the Grand Canal, and had stopped at the dim-lit church of San Zaccaria, which held his mother's and the Doges' graves. He was a haughty student from a proud merchant family, with a jaunty pheasant feather in his cap and the first traces of curly, coppery down on his cheeks. In the outer hall of the Palazzo di Polo sat two shabby mendicants in ragged, rough-woven wool cloaks, grinning like *Punchinellos* from the street players.

Marco began to rebuke the servants for allowing such beggars beyond the rear kitchen, when the taller of the two men, chestnut-bearded and gaunt-faced, rose and enfolded him in a stable-scented embrace—and laughed and called him "*my son.*"

Marco's mother had met the angels when he was just a lad, so there was only one person in all the world who could take the liberty of addressing him thus: and Marco had cried, "*Papa*!"

Pudgy, grizzle-haired Uncle Maffeo guffawed and pinched his delighted nephew's cheeks. Then they had dined on a haunch of veal stewed with mushrooms and wine, and talked far into the lamp-lit night, exciting Marco with tales of their travels and their mission for the Great Khan.

And what was Marco to say to them? That he preferred to remain behind the comfortable pink-marble walls of the Palazzo di Polo, studying dry Latin verbs with withered Friar Paul, and learning to inventory shipments of Sclavonian prunes in the family warehouse? *No.* Marco had spoken the words of any bold Venetian boy. "Father . . . Uncle . . . *take me with you!*"

—With you to the perilous wastelands of the east, where venom-tipped arrows fly like crows, and turn young Mongol horsemen into bloated, exploding, purple-black aubergines . . .

But Marco knew nothing of such wonders and terrors in those days. He could not *imagine* the size and diversity of the world, or the vast and strange distances they would traverse. He thought perhaps they would travel a little farther than Bologna—perhaps even farther than Rome.

In Rome, the broad-minded old Frankish Pope Clement had died, and the power-hungry cardinals squabbled and haggled among themselves for three long years; while the disputed papal throne remained empty, and the Polos' mission for the Great Khan languished. The aunts and cousins and clerks of the Palazzo di Polo urged them to abandon this futile embassy; to sell Kublai's precious golden passport-tablet and remain home beneath the four-starling shield, preening like silken cats before the family hearth. Here the wine was sweet and their lives were safe, and here Uncle Maffeo could pinch the cooks' bottoms and steal hot almond cakes from the great outdoor oven.

Instead they set out for the crusaders' tawny rock-walled city of Acre, on the sun-baked Palestine coast. Perhaps to derive spiritual sustenance from the Holy Land—or perhaps because the brothers Polo seemed always driven eastward, as though by some mad wind out of the west.

As the icy wind blew the yellow dusts of the western wastes into Marco's fear-maddened eyes . . .

At the Frankish stronghold of Acre, the Polos were destined to meet the newly elected Pope Gregory, who sent his benevolent greetings to the Great Khan, and a gift of holy oil from the lamp of Christ's sepulchre in Jerusalem. In answer to mighty Kublai's request, the new Pope sent—not 100—but two; only *two* learned priests to journey with the Polos to Cathay. These two proved to be faint-hearted men, who were quickly frightened by the rigors of their journey and their task in heathen lands. Thus they turned back . . .

Leaving the weary Polos, Niccolo, Maffeo, and now young Marco, to journey eastward across wild and war-blasted Eurasia, accompanied by no learned priests at all. *None.* Not one. Not even a Friar or Deacon or a lay-brother.

All along their way they faced extreme difficulties and dangers, but none was more worrisome than the constant anxiety that clouded their minds: would the Great Khan be pleased to see them—unaccompanied by the priests? Or would Kublai be angry that their mission had failed?

Worse yet, was this hazardous journey from immensely rich Venice to even richer Cathay entirely futile? After so many years, would the Great Khan even *remember* who they were?

Now sixteen years later, early in the Christian year 1285, Marco's own chestnut-colored beard was fully grown, and they were on yet another fearsome mission for Kublai. *Would* the Great Khan be pleased? Would they ever *see* him (or each other) again? Or would Marco's sweating pony finally collapse—to leave him at the mercy of the taunting and tainted arrows?

Wu Wang; Innocence.
Thunder Bellows Below Heaven.
Thus Ancient Kings Nourished Their People.

4

The Mongol guard-captain's cry of, "*Scatter! Scatter!*" persuaded all to follow his command, though it was hardly needed. His many-thonged whip brought down with full force upon the haunches of the horses and ponies accomplished more than his words. The mounted party fled in every direction without observing which one it was. Anywhere—any way!—to escape the tainted arrows. Poison, venom, were in themselves no novelty; it was the frightful suddenness of the empoisoned or envenomed death which filled them with such urgent loathing.

Even when Niccolo's panicked horse cast him off, he remained strangely calm on noting that no black-feathered arrows fell nearby. Even when observing the swift approach of the colossal lynx-like creature, he quick-cast his eyes abroad and scuttled into the shelter of the pile of rocks (in no wise stopping to wonder if man or nature had piled them there), he stayed calm.

Grey-white and powdered with great black spots, the *gyant ownse* or giant ounce, the magnaform of the snow-leopard was merely (*merely*!) an immense cat, to which men were as mice. Though this did not make Niccolo Polo, crouched in his burrow and worrying his best jade worry-beads, less afraid of it. But he was—merely—afraid: no more.

Chance had sent Uncle Maffeo and the fussy Han-Cathayan Clerk of the Voyage galloping in the same direction; which of them had first heard the scream of the alerted griffin made no matter. They also screamed, gestured at each other, made shift swift to make their horses halt, and lay face-down upon the ground. The horses did not wait to check the truth of the report that griffins really ate not horseflesh but, heaving up their hooves, fled across the stony ground.

Whoever had first described a griffin as being part lion, part eagle, and part snake, had not only never read *The Commentary to Aristotle on the Categories*; such a one had clearly never seen a griffin either. The griffin in no way resembled any safe and familiar animal. Still the Soldan of New Babylon, or Grand Cairo, sometimes had a lion or two by his divan-throne; the Western Emperors sometimes had eagles trained as if falcons, which they used in coursing wolves. One could not really call eagle or lion *safe* or *familiar*—still, everyone had an *idea* what a griffin was.

Most folk who had looked in books with illuminations had seen anyway one picture of a griffin, fantastically unrealistic though such pictures were. It made Maffeo, thinking unexpectedly of it now, wonder how real to life the other illustrations in the *Bestiary* might be. As *real* as life in strange heathen lands . . . ?

Uncle Maffeo thought back to summery evenings seated at the arched library windows of the Palazzo di Polo, reading his illuminated Bestiary whilst munching toasted almond kernels, and sipping red wine from a Venetianware crystal goblet etched in gold with the

Polos' four-starling emblem. Ah, the smooth wines of Venice . . . the lavish Venetian banquets . . .

Ah . . . how the Italian servingmen in their gorgeous liveries (many a minor sovereign did not habitually wear clothes one-half as rich) never ceased bringing great plates of sundry foods to the marble-inlaid banqueting tables: here a huge mullet, there a quarter of a roasted ox, or hares with spiced crabapples in their bellies. Cranes, herons, and bustards came along too: and, ah! what wings! and, oh! what drumsticks! Many pigs perished (their meat was considered good enough for the servants) in order that their bones and trotters, along with the feet of the calves which provided the veal, be boiled to provide a good strong jelly. And did the jelly not taste well, mixed with crushed almonds and with the famous pink sugar of Cyprus (itself a source for several good wines)? Stiff enough—the jelly—to stand without melting when released from the very ingenious molds: castles and elephants, pyramids and ships . . .

Now it was the griffin's own banquet which was, indeed, terribly and terrifyingly real. Uncle Maffeo Polo lay with his greying beard pressed down into the grey pebbles, washed smooth by some ancient, vanished river. He was terrified, true. But he was *merely* terrified.

Marco fled beyond terror. Unlike Uncle he did not dismount; unlike Father he was not thrown off in a mad gallop. Marco had some dim notion that the horse, if given its head, would find its way to safety. But twice he felt the horse shy and, looking down, looking back, saw each time a heap of rags and rottenness. Saw, each time, the croaking crows at meat. Heard in his mind the grassland proverb: *The Mongol's coffin is the corbie's maw.* With horrified eyes he looked about, with straining ears tried to listen, but heard only the drum-tattoo of horse-hooves . . . and his own agonizing breath.

An arrow, hissing, sank into the sands . . .

Once the Great Khan had spoken to Marco, after offering him the great indulgence of accepting a rice-cake from the Imperial hand. Marco broke the cake small, and tossed the crumbles to the greedy fish in the Imperial Park's Carp Pond of Great Seclusion, at the winter capital of Khanbaluc—a task Kublai seldom allotted to others.

The Great Khan had said, with a broad gesture of a flowing green brocade sleeve, lavishly embroidered with golden lotuses and carp: "There! That one! The huge yellow carp beneath the willow, throw him a nice bit; he was here when my father came. Very old. 'Old Buddha,' they call him—I am sure I do not know why—was Buddha a fish? Never mind. I honor all religions, why not? When one is tired or sad or angry, any god makes one feel good. Marco, have you ever heard of a castle where everyone lives forever, but asleep? All know that carp live to be very old . . . if one lets them. My grandfather, Genghiz, used to consult hermit alchemists, said to have the secret of immortality. It is said that fish never sleep, but often when I observe them, they seem to be dreaming long, slow dreams . . ."

This was the first time Kublai had mentioned the *castle where everyone lives forever—but asleep.* At that time Marco had made little note of it. But observing Kublai, he did note that the old Khan had lately become more and more preoccupied with notions of immortality expounded by Taoist recluses, who had previously found little favor with the Great Khan. Indeed he once had scoffed at their magical potions, and seized and burned their books. Marco knew that this was only natural in a man approaching seventy years of age . . . even if that man were the Khan of Khans of all the Lands and Seas.

Indeed, Kublai had visibly aged since Marco had first glimpsed him more than ten years ago. Then Kublai was in the prime of his late middle years, stocky and powerfully built in the manner of Mongols; with shrewd yet benevolent eyes set in deep slits in a broad, ruddy face. As with other men of power whom Marco had met, Kublai's presence in a room was *felt* as well as seen. Now the old Khan stooped a bit, and hobbled a bit from (it was said) recurrant attacks of gout. His hair and long, fine beard were streaked with wisps of silver, and his round face bore spidery lines of age, as well as deep creases etched by Tartary's harsh climate. Yet his powerful presence was undiminished.

Marco had grown older too; from a skinny youth of barely twenty years to a well-muscled man of thirty, at the peak of his own powers. Yet well he remembered that first meeting with the Great Khan at his summer palace of Xan-du, which is ten days' journey north of the winter capital at Khanbaluc . . .

Far from forgetting the Polos, as they had feared; when Kublai's couriers brought word that his Papal ambassadors were approaching, the Great Khan sent a party of mounted escorts with sun-and-moon banners flying, to greet the travel-grimed Venetians and escort them to his summer court. Young Marco had seen many impressive palaces, both in Venice and during his travels, but Xan-du had filled him with special wonder . . .

The vast main structure was built of carved and gilded marble, and other semi-precious stones. It was surrounded by a wall which enclosed twice-ten miles of parkland, well-watered with ponds and springs and streams, planted with a variety of conifers and flowering trees and broad lawns bedecked with summer wildflowers. In this park Kublai kept herds of deer and other game animals, so he might enjoy the hunt with his questing leopards and flocks of trained white falcons.

In a grove of tall pines within the park was another imposing, dome-like structure, constructed in the manner of the Mongol *yurt* of the grasslands. This was built of bamboo canes and shingles, nailed and tied by 200 thick ropes of silk, and it stood on gilt and lacquered pillars twined with carved dragons, which supported the roof-dome. The interior of this giant yurt was decorated with elaborate carvings of mythical birds and beasts, and it was here that Kublai held his summer court.

The newly arrived Polos had bowed their heads to the ground before the Great Khan, who bade them rise, and greeted them warmly as old friends. They presented the letters and holy oil from the Pope, which Kublai received gladly. Then he questioned them in great detail about the rigors of their journey, and the many strange and wondrous sights they had beheld along their way; and about conditions in the vassal Khanates of the west, especially that of his rebellious nephew and rival, Kaidu Khan.

Marco had remained humbly silent, but he could not stop staring at this vigorous legend of a man, this autocratic and unpredictable Son of Heaven; descended from the conquering grassland barbarians, yet learned in the elegant ways of his restored Cathayan court; ruthless in war, but generous in distributing grain to the poor during times of famine. This Khan of Khans who sat upon a raised dais of carved and bejeweled ebony, robed in brocade of purple and gold.

Beside the Great Khan sat a younger, frail-looking man, robed in pale peach brocade. Marco later learned this was Kublai's ailing and favorite second son, Prince Chenghin (his *Yang* and *Yin* were rumored to be out of balance). The younger man returned Marco's gaze with a frank and friendly curiosity, beneath the pearl fringes of his golden coronet, and whispered something to the Great Khan—who finally turned his august attention upon Marco himself.

"So where are the hundred learned priests whom I requested of the Holy Pontiff?" asked Kublai. The brow imperial furrowed, then cleared. "I see only this stripling lad."

"This is my son, Marco; your liege-man . . . here to serve you, my lord," replied Niccolo, with another kowtow.

"Well, he is welcome," said Kublai with a kindly smile.

And Marco had found favor in the Great Khan's eyes, and had served him for more than ten years . . . as they both aged and changed, and as their friendship deepened and grew . . .

At first Kublai had assigned Marco a post administering the salt-tax in the rich southern province of Manzi, at the bustling port city of Yang-zhau, where the mighty east/west-flowing Yangtze Kiang River meets the Great Khan's north/south Grand Canal. Later, as Kublai gained confidence in Marco's loyalty, and unusual ability to observe and describe all he saw, the Great Khan assigned the young Venetian to special and confidential missions . . . such as this one . . .

Marco spurred his horse, as yet another poisoned arrow sang its horrid song past his aching head.

Ku; Stagnation.
Gentle Winds Blow Beneath the Quiet Mountain.
Danger; But In the End Good Fortune.

5

He could not be sure later if it was a thought he thought or a voice which he heard. *North*! it came. And it came again: *North*! It sang like plainsong in his head. *North . . . North . . . North . . .*

"O Saint Mark," he cried. "O blessed San Marco, Patron of Venice, and my namesake! Which way *is* north?"

And a voice answered, deep-deep inside his head, a deep and grumbling voice saying, "*They should have left my bones in Aegypt, the land of my preaching . . .*"

"Saint Mark; San Marco, it was *north* the Venetians took thy bones, to be buried beneath the enameled high altar of your Basilica! Which way *is* north?"

And the grumbling silence which followed the grumbling voice was in turn followed by the grumbling voice again. It said: "*Toward those hills. Peter knows their fishy shape. Namesake:* that *is north.*"

Marco's own servant, Peter the Tartar, *should* know

the shape of the hills in this land, if any of them should—though not in his country of Tartary, then at least two thousand leagues nearer it than beloved Venice!

By main force, Marco wrestled the horse's shaggy head till now he could see hills on the horizon. Three, they were, of vaguely fishy shape. He gave a sob of triumph and flogged the beast forward. "Horse!" he cried. "*Horse*! But get us there in safety and thou shalt have my ration of kumis, and I shall do without! *North! North! North!*"

"*That accursed scroll*!" was what Uncle Maffeo had called it. Niccolo and Marco could not quite agree. True, the strange map-scroll . . . was it prose? Was it poetry? Was it some immensely involved and mysterious cryptogram? The scroll it was (whatever it was) which had guided them thus far—if *guided* was not too strong a word. In the opinion of Niccolo and his son Marco, the map-scroll alone it was which could safely get them forth or back—or anywhere else.

"For the Great Khan does nothing without good reason," Marco had said.

"The Great Khan! *Marón*!" Maffeo had exclaimed with a scowl, while tugging at his grizzled beard.

Fortunate that they spoke Italian between themselves as always; who knew which of the mixed body of Mongols and Tartars, Cathayans, Saracens and Cumanians, and the Lord God knew what else—sure it was that at least one of them was a spy. *More* than one! *One* at least, for Kublai himself. At least one for Prince Temur, his grandson and heir, son of the ailing Prince Chenghin. Probably not more than one each for the other surviving sons. Impossible that the Corps of Shamans, the Corps of Eunuchs, the Senior Civil Servants, the Great Families, the Allied Foreign Cousins, should not have taken the commonplace precaution of retaining some members of the expedition to report back (somehow) to each of these rival factions. It was a consolation of sorts that "he who is boughten doth not always stay bought." Still . . .

The text of the map-scroll was a curious mixture of archaic Cathayan calligraphy, and strange and mystifying symbols. It was inscribed in the blackest ink on the finest mulberry-bark paper, and mounted on the purest white silk. The paper was bonded to cloth with paste of frankincense, which not only perfumed it and made it easier to find, but held it firm and kept away mildew, moths, and other destructive vermin.

At top and bottom, the scroll was fastened onto rollers of camphorwood. The container was of multi-colored silk threads woven into a design of a bell-shaped Buddhist stupa-temple: this was wrapped in oiled red silk, impermeable to water, and finally boxed in a casket of red lacquer and black ebony (which refinements must have been added later).

"But for all the commonsense it makes," Uncle Maffeo had growled, "it might as well be a-scribbled on common soft rice-paper of the sort which I might use to wipe my nose or my . . ."

True that no Asian spy could possibly recognize the Great Khan's name in the Italic syllables *Il Signor Grande.* But still . . .

"Uncle!" Marco had said, sharply. Blustery Uncle Maffeo had snorted, but said no more.

Marco had first seen the *accursed* scroll one day in late winter, in the twenty-first year of Zhi-Yuan—or Kublai's reign—which was the year 1284 in the calendars of the Christian west. He strolled with Kublai along the banks of the Carp Pond of Great Seclusion, on the spacious grounds of the Imperial Palace at Khanbaluc; they admired the sweet-scented white magnolias, and the scarlet-flowering quince, and the early-blooming plum trees of palest pink, which grew among the dark green cypresses and budding weeping willows. Kublai was energetically planning a grand fireworks display as an imperial gift for the surrounding city of Tai-Ting, to celebrate the Cathayan New Year.

The Great Khan and his young Venetian confidant walked slowly along the side of the pond. It was quite different here from the involved, stiff ceremonies of the Cathayan court from which it was death to deviate. Familiar acquaintance with the ritual ceremonies of the Doge's court in Venice had given the Polo family an immense advantage over those non-Cathayans of farther Asia, who were accustomed to dip their hands in another's bowl of boiled goat-flesh or clabbered mare's milk.

Kublai paused in his enthused discussion of the cunning little firecrackers made of bamboo sticks filled with heaven-shaking-thunder-powder. He flicked a finger at a deaf-mute servant, who knelt before them on the icy pathway and unbound the elaborately wrapped scroll. At one time Marco had thought that, when speaking informally, the Great Khan rambled—but he had long ago learned better, so he was not surprised at this sudden digression.

"See here, Marco," said Kublai. "This old bit of calligraphy has lately come into my possession. It cannot rival the splendid horse paintings of Chao Meng-fu of the discredited Sung imperial family—whom I hope to persuade to join my court. Yet this scroll is attractive and interesting in its own way. Is it not so, Po-lo?"

Marco nodded and listened patiently, waiting for the old Khan to make his point—whatever that point might be.

Kublai pointed to the scroll and continued. "My court scholars tell me that the scroll is a guide—or map—revealing the route to a mountain castle or stupa-temple, surrounded by thickets of thorns and brambles, where a beautiful woman lives forever—but asleep. Intriguing, eh Marco? I want you and your father and your uncle to journey to the southwest and find this mysterious woman for me. She will be a novel and interesting new concubine. Kublai and this Sleeping Beauty . . . both unique . . . a good match; is it not so, Po-lo? I am sure that my court La-mas and sorcerers can wake her from slumber, and she must know the sublime secrets of immortality. Such a woman would be both beautiful *and* useful. They say that your Pope in Rome has knowledge of eternal life; had he but sent the hundred learned scholars, as I so modestly requested, this particular costly expedition might not be necessary. I am *not* pleased with your Pope! Not so!"

Marco had been through all this (well . . . more or less . . . almost all) before. He nodded and stood patiently.

"Still, would the hundred learned scholars have been an hundred beautiful women as well?" asked Kublai with a short bark of a laugh. "I think not—and I do not wish always to find the same delicacy in my rice-bowl—nor the same concubine in my bed," remarked the greatest and wisest king on earth with a sly little smile. "So, I want you Po-los to find this marvelous and immortal Sleeping Beauty, and bring her to me!"

At the mention of the Pope in Italy, Marco felt a certain breath of hope. "When my father and uncle and I return to Venice," he said—knowing as he knew his own prominent nose that there was not the least possibility of their returning without the Great Khan giving them leave to go—they could not have gone a league or a *li* without his consent. "When my father and uncle and I return home, we hope to have audience with the present Pope Gregory, and discuss this matter of eternal life."

Kublai turned a suddenly eager face towards him. "Yes! Yes! I want you to . . . that is just what I want! You men from the west know so many things. The Pope is really not married? Exceedingly odd. Not even, ah, informally? No, eh. You Po-lo men not marrying and having no official families of your own; this is very useful to me. You are faithful to *my* interests, to *me*! Everyone else is faithful first to family. Families are faithful to factions; when factions grow powerful, friction results: neglect of necessary duty, civil disorder, calamities of men and nature follow. Were it not for the Son of Heaven on the Dragon Throne, pirates would ravage the coast, canals would fill with silt, dikes and levees would collapse, stone walls fall, enemies pour across the borders; the peasants would starve in times of famine. All know this. None want this to happen. But none would, if left alone, refrain from favoring family, forming factions, practising corruption . . ."

Marco knew it was all true. But he knew also that not he, nor his father, nor his uncle wished to spend their lives honestly assisting the Great Khan with the endless tasks of administration, which alone assured the peace and safety of the immense realm of empire.

His father and uncle were aging now, too, and had long grown weary of journeying. They spoke often of their desire to retire honorably beneath the four-starling shield, among the comforts of the pink-walled Palazzo di Polo, on the brakish banks of the Sclavonian Canal. Marco, too, was ready to return home, to tend the neglected fortunes of the Polo family warehouses—and to establish a family of his own. He and they wanted now, only and above all things, to return to live out their lives and die in their own beds . . . in the Most Serene Republic of Venice.

And only the Great Khan's leave to depart—and his golden passport-tablet—could get them there. And this golden tablet was not to be had by corruption, nor by family, nor by faction; only through loyally serving the Great Khan.

Marco sighed and said, "In regard to what your Imperial Majesty wants done . . ." Marco meant: in regard to Pope and priests and the Doctrine of Eternal Life . . .

"Yes! Yes! In regard to . . ." Kublai gestured briefly, and the deaf-mute servant rolled up the scroll, and replaced it in the woven silk container.

The well-trusted pair of brawny deaf and mute sedan-chair bearers who had silently followed seven paces behind, at once came forward; lay their litter down and, with great strength and infinite gentleness, assisted their master and lord to step inside. He, with a soft sigh, next allowed them to lift his gout-swollen and-wrapped left leg and then to set it softly down, so that the foot rested on a fox-fur support stuffed with goose down. Another brief gesture. The palanquin rose, moved slowly forward, Marco following by its side. The green willows drooped their new grey catkins down to the great reflecting pool.

"What are thickets, prickets, thorns and brambles to you three travelers?" asked Kublai Khan. "Mountains, deserts, haunted heaths? Pooh! Foh! What to you is so-called sorcery? Alleged dangers? *Actual* dangers?"

Nothing, implied the tone of the greatest and wisest king on earth, as he fondly took his young friend by the arm. "You Po-los are Westerners, Latins, Franks. That is to say: gallant . . . brave . . . courageous. You will do this thing for me—confidentially, of course—we will say that you are attending to the salt tax. You will do this thing for me, and I will reward you *royally*."

It was hardly a request. It was not even an order. It was a statement.

Marco's own sigh, so oft-repeated, was now entirely internal. Clearly what the Great Khan wanted, though it might be almost any strangeness, was one thing *not*. It was not that Marco, Maffeo, Niccolo might now—nor even very soon—have the royal permission and golden imperial passport to depart for home, forever.

"*God is very patient*," Marco's old teacher, Friar Paul, had often said.

It behooved the Polos to be very patient too. Perhaps if this mysterious mission were carried out successfully, Kublai would royally-reward them with leave and passport of gold—to return to Venice. Or perhaps this Sleeping Beauty, whoever *she* might be, might *not* have secrets of immortality . . . might merely be slothful, and not so beautiful after all. Then Marco could suggest that it was high time to consult the Pope on the Doctrine of Eternal Life. The venture held a certain promise . . .

"Hearkening and obedience, my great lord," Messer Marco Polo had said with a deep bow.

So now they were here—wherever *here* was: a place of immense and fearful peril, and increasingly proximate death.

K'un; Exhaustion.
Water Sinks Below the Dry Lake.
Motion Brings Remorse.

6

As the rock moved, Messer Niccolo Polo whispered a Hail Mary and tried to shrink yet farther into the recesses of the black-veined boulders. As he did so, two things happened. First; some splint of wood which a wind had likely blown, or likelier a rare flow of surface water after a rare rain had washed there to dessicate ever since, snapped beneath his knee. Second; something pressed painfully against his hip. He knew—remembering—that it was a large, oddly shaped lump of crystal which he had kept about him for years (no experienced gem-dealer any longer believed crystal to be petrified ice, but none had any objection to a possible purchaser's believing it). Its curious shape alone was a curiosity to show; he had come to regard it as a sort of luck-piece, and it had, as he had learned, a singular quality indeed.

The rock moved again as the gigantic grey-white and black snow-leopard heaved against it. Then the rock settled with a groan back in its former place . . . almost in its former place . . . a fraction of an inch only had it settled out of its former place. Were Niccolo so minded, he might calculate how long it might take for the rock to fall; he was not so minded. He was minded instead—as the *pad-pad-pad* of the beast's great paws indicated that it was now pacing round and round again, and not poised to attack at once again—he was minded to remove the lump of crystal which pressed painfully against his hip. And he was minded, as always, to waft a few Hail Marys heavenward.

As he dared not simply move forward to remove the crystal in a normal fashion, cramped and crouched as he was, he reached with his free hand and ripped out that part of the quilted robe from the inside; one more tear, and the odd-shaped lump had ceased to press painfully against his hip. He held it in his hand a moment, wondering as always in its strange contours and even stranger contents. Then, very cautiously, he held it out in the single thin shaft of sunlight shining through a space in the rocks a hand's length away. The beam passed through it . . . but not simply through it . . . the beam of sunlight seemed to swirl inside it, to mingle with the swirling clouds inside it; to emerge, to be sure, again—but at an angle.

And this angled beam of (somehow augmented and intensified) sunlight, Niccolo turned upon the threads, shreds, and patches of the corner of his rubbed-worn old robe, which the immense pard had ripped off and (of course) left lying where they fell. At least, he tried to. His hand trembled so.

Uncle Maffeo lay still upon his face, listening to the griffin gobbling its feed which once had been a man. He tried to remember his prayers, but found that he could only remember Venice. How the brackish waters of the Sclavonian Canal lapped lazily outside the arched window of his bedchamber when he was a rowdy youth, and how those same brackish waters still lapped lazily in his dreams. How coolly the golden mosaics of the four patron saints glimmered and dazzled the eye with their dim-lit brilliance, in the shadowy arch of the great Basilica di San Marco on a hot Venetian summer's day. And the banquets . . . ah, the lovely banquets . . .

As was the custom, the Doge was preceded into the Great Banqueting Hall of the marble Ducal Palace by a band of scarlet-robed bagpipers from the Abruzzi. It was not altogether certain whether Venice had gained this by virtue of having once conquered the Abruzzi, or whether the Abruzzi had gained it by virtue of having once conquered Venice. Neither conquest was noted in the Chronicles, so perhaps it was all a matter of taste . . .

In any event, the wailing and wheezing, once the shock had worn off, was soon drowned out by the general conversation. The Venetians, as has been observed, were not a noticeably silent people. Nor—as its Captain-General had once remarked—did Most Serene Venice deign to transport *mules* in its galleys. Therefore the bagpipers had come, mules and all, by foot (or perhaps it would be more accurate to say, by hoof) all the way from their remote region in the far south of Italy. "*Marón!*" Maffeo had said; "Are we hearing their mules, or their music?" And added, "Or is there no difference?"

The first course was of victuals from near at hand, namely water-fowl taken in the Venetian lagoons themselves, and farced with truffles—the white truffles of the Terra Firma beyond the Venetian shores, and not the black ones so dearly beloved by Spaniard and Frank. There were not as many truffles as usual, for the bells had been sounding for days in honor of the coming saint's festival; and the pigs trained to smell out the fragrant fungus had also learned to run for shelter whenever the bells rang out. For did they not also ring out as an alarm when hostile forces were at hand? These were not, of course, the same swine to which samples of every luscious dish were carefully tendered, lest there be poison in the food. There were always 33 such testing-pigs, in memory of Alexander the Great who (so legends say) was poisoned in Babylon when he was 33 years old . . .

By and by Maffeo was aware that the bagpipers were no longer there. A more familiar band had appeared; and when this music paused to allow the musicians to drain spittle from their instruments, then jesters and sundry sorts of buffoons were seen to play. Now many high-ranking folk placed without stealth in their pockets and pouches, handfuls of nuts and sweet-meats from all three continents, to take home for wives and children and favored servants. Meanwhile the several bands played on in turn. Ah, the lovely banquets . . . ah, *Venice* . . .

The threads and scraps of rag were not, probably, as dry and combustible as linen burned in a closed vessel. They were not as dry as tinder. But . . . perhaps . . . they were dry enough. Especially when augmented by chips flaked from the dark-veined boulders, of that strange soft black Cathayan stone that burns like charcoal. For a long moment Niccolo regarded the intensified beam of sunlight filtering through the lump of crystal—as though through a burning glass. And nothing happened . . .

And nothing happened.

Then, oh so faint at first, from the heap of char-stone flakes and threads and ripped-small rags a wisp of smoke arose. It increased. It faltered. Nic frantically bethought him what to do. And, fully aware of the risk, the danger, he pursed his lips and crouched his head down and forward, and he puffed. The *pad-pad-pad* stopped on the instant. Then the gigantic pard leaped forward; again the rock shifted, slipped.

Again Nic puffed—and prayed, indeed. The smoke flared into flame. Swiftly, swiftly, Niccolo seized up the stick of time-dried wood and thrust it forward into the fire. The wood was perhaps not decayed quite so flammable as punk, thus it caught fire with no slow smoulder, but with a bright and instant flame.

Messer Niccolo Polo shouted. The huge beast took three huge paces round the heap of boulders and, as a hundred times before, thrust in its sword-clawed paw. And Niccolo thrust the burning brand upon it and into it with all his might.

The gigant ounce screamed its surprise and pain. It clawed at the cairn once, twice. Then it raised its burned paw to its mouth, and—leaping, lurching, howling loud—it fled fast away, maddened by the agony it was vainly trying to out-run.

Uncle Maffeo knew what the griffin would do when it had eaten its fill. Not that he had seen what, but he had heard it described, in whispers aghast, round more than one campfire of thornbrush and char-stones and dried dung. The griffin would stretch first one huge wing and then the other, preening each in turn. It would then raise up its avian head and, flapping huge pinions, begin a lumbering canter over the ground. The griffin would next rear up on its hind, and supposedly leonine legs as it ran. The griffin would then defecate—in order, so the Mongols, Turks, and Tartars thought, to lose weight instantly—enough to become more buoyant, the quicker to fly. Then, with that terrible sound of great rushing, which seemed a savage and satanic mockery of the sweet song of the seraphs' wings . . .

Maffeo heard what he assumed to be most of these sounds. Then, partly because the noise seemed to be going away from him, and it was always said that *the griffin never looks back*, and partly because he could simply remain prone no longer; he raised his grizzled head.

What he saw brought a *Marón!* of astonishment and fear from him. Instantly he checked it; no one else and nothing else heard it. Out from some previously unnoted cleft in the gaunt rocks came dashing an immense snowy ounce or gigant snow-leopard—of which he had only heard tales.

The beast came on in a sort of limping lope, mostly on three feet, coughing and roaring loud as Cathayan thunder-powder. Now and then, out of natural and accustomed habitude, it went on all four limbs. When this happened it gave a shocking scream in an indescribably different register than the griffin-scream, and made almost as though it would bite off its left front paw.

Did the griffin not *see* this monstrous cat-creature? Did the griffin not *care*? Did the griffin have no way of stopping its headlong run?

Straight toward the gigant pard eame the griffin. Straight toward the griffin came the gigant pard. The griffin rose upon its hind legs now as it ran, simultaneously lifting aside its snakey tail and voiding its great mound of smoking, reeking dung upon the ground.

Perhaps it was the rearing of the griffin's forequarters which made the vast and massy cat think it was about to attack. Perhaps the colossus-cat was insane with pain. Leaping forward in an immense bound, it seized the griffin by the throat and wrapped itself, talons sinking deep, around and into that fierce and fabulous body. Twice the griffin, despite the weight, rose thrashing, shrieking into the air, unable somehow to bring its own writhing-climbing limbs into proper play to dislodge its attacker; twice the griffin came a-tumbling down. What shrieks then, and what screams and roars!

Maffeo was sure it could not rise a third time, and yet it did. *It did*! Who had ever before, perhaps since blind Homer harped of burning Troy, known such a mighty and terrible sight? That bloody battle raging up there aloft, in the middle of that now dusk-yellowing sky . . . which Yen Lung-chuan had said was but illusion. And, Maffeo thought, *would that it were*!

If the griffin succeeded in shaking off its murderous burthen, might yet the griffin live? If the giant leopard-of-the-snows succeeded in forcing the griffin to the ground, might yet the gigant snow-leopard live?

Round and round in a great, irregular gyre, the battle roared; beasts screamed, blood spattered as down they hurled. One great formless form struck the shuddering ground.

Became two . . .

It was suddenly very quiet.

Ts'ui; Coming Together.
The Lake Floats Above the Earth.
The Emperor Brings Great Temple Offerings.

7

The cave was small, dark and narrow. It was hardly a proper cave at all, more like a shallow depression eroded in the side of the fish-shaped hill, just about where a carp's gills would be. The cave was barely big enough to hold one man and his mount. Surely it could not contain two. Yet Marco rejoiced in the crowding when he found the cave already occupied by Peter the Tartar, his young servant and slave, who had also fled to these finny, scrub-clad hills to escape the poison arrows—as if guided by his own namesake, Saint Peter the fisherman.

The two trembling, sweating ponies stood side by side, pressed closely together, for indeed the space *was* cramped and the contact was reassuring. Marco and Peter embraced one another with hearty hugs and back-slaps for much the same reassurance.

"The others—have you seen them?" asked Marco.

The young Tartar shook his angular head; no. Peter was a comely youth whose obsidian-black hair hung below the ear-flaps of his fur-lined helmet in a shiny curtain, and framed his jutting cheek-bones and narrow black eyes. Marco had singled him from the mounted guard as his personal servant because of Peter's quick wit, and his uncanny ability to talk to angels—and devil-spirits—which ofttimes gave him a strange ability to foretell what was to come. But no angels or devil-spirits spoke to him now, to guide worried Marco and Peter to their vanished troop.

The day was growing late and, after the horses had rested and grown calm, they left their sheltering cave and climbed to the top of the fish-shaped hill. The lethal crows had disappeared—but so had their traveling companions.

"I used to play a hiding game with Prince Chenghin, among the drooping willows that surround the Carp Pond of Great Seclusion at the winter palace of Khanbaluc." Marco mused, almost to himself. "For Chenghin's health was failing even before I arrived in Cathay, and he was too weak for the vigorous hunts and sports of men . . . yet when the weather was fine and he was feeling strong, he enjoyed besporting himself as a boy. Would that this were a mere hiding game in the winter gardens of the palace."

Marco and Peter sat upon their shaggy ponies, anxiously scanning the bleak ochre horizon for signs of their band. While Marco's mind played and replayed games with frail Prince Chenghin, in the park beneath the glimmering rainbow roof-tiles of Khanbaluc.

The whitewashed outer walls of the Great Khan's winter capital were fully three *li* in length. They were surrounded by a moat and studded with battlements, storehouses, and mighty gates that led to the teeming city of Tai-Ting, which Kublai had rebuilt from the ashes of the Mongol conquest. Between this outer stone wall, and the brightly tiled inner walls which surrounded the lavish imperial apartments, were vast cobbled ceremonial courtyards and the gardens; with their stately trees, broad lawns—to remind Kublai of the Mongolian grasslands—and well-paved pathways. Among the willows and early-flowering plum and magnolia trees, deer and squirrels grazed and played.

At the northern end of the park was a hillock, where Kublai had replanted giant evergreen trees of every variety, transported by tattooed elephants from the farthest regions of his empire. This hillock was paved with slabs of green jasper and jade, and on its summit was a pavilion also of jade and jasper, with upturned eaves and green-tiled roofs mounted with jade guardian dragons—so the total effect was intensely green.

Circling the base of this Green Mount was a large artificial pond, fed by a natural stream, well stocked with carp, swans, and other fish and water-fowl, where the animals came to drink. Ornate enameled bridges crossed the pond, and led to the Green Mount and to Prince Chenghin's own palace beyond the stream. It was at this Carp Pond of Great Seclusion that Marco walked, talked, and hand-fed the old carp with Kublai, and it was here that he played at hiding games with the ailing prince.

Chenghin was an ivory-pale and slender man, a few years older than Marco, and well-talented at the pipa-lute and calligraphy brush. The features of his delicately hewn face were often clouded with pain from the wasting disease which had spread through his body. Yet Chenghin's mind was as lively and curious as Marco's own, which had drawn them into friendship. "Tell me again of your journey through Greater Armenia," the Prince would urge the young Venetian, and Marco would recount the tales of his travels to Cathay once more.

None of Kublai's La-ma sorcerers or court physicians had been able to discover a cause or cure for Chenghin's imbalance of *Yin* and *Yang*, despite divinations and exorcisms, and diagnoses of his pulses, breaths and fluids. They had tried treatments with the slender and precise acupuncture needles, the burning of moxabustion herbs upon his sallow skin, the application of pungent ointments, and the ingestion of healing mushrooms, herbal potions, and the pulverized vital organs of vigorous young beasts. Even vipers broiled to a char and boiled in the fat of mole-shrews had obtained no cure.

"Had your Pope sent the hundred learned doctors, as I requested . . ." Kublai would grumble when Chenghin was feeling poorly and confined to his couch. But Marco knew from the haunted look in the Great Khan's eyes, that he had little hope that even the Pope's doctors could help his favorite son.

Eventually all knew of the hopelessness of Prince Chenghin's condition when Kublai selected Prince Temur, Chenghin's own young son, as heir to the Dragon Throne. Thus the lad, Temur, was given apartments equal to Kublai's within the palace, and the use of the imperial seal . . . while his father, Chenghin, languished.

Yet on days when the weather was fine and he was feeling stronger, ailing Chenghin still delighted in boyish hiding games. And in sipping hot rice wine in the green pavilion, whilst practicing poetic calligraphy and horse-painting in the style of renowned Chao Meng-fu, and playing his lute while hearing of the journeys of his Venetian friend, Marco Polo. —Who now sat upon the ridge of a fish-shaped hill in the terrible wastelands of western Cathay, beyond the Great 10,000 *Li* Wall, scanning the barren yellowish horizon for his father and uncle—and wishing this *were* but a game or an exciting *tale* of adventure.

"Ser Marco, is that smoke I see in the distance?" asked Peter the Tartar, abruptly interrupting Marco's thoughts.

Smoke indeed—but smoke signifying what? Perhaps the cosy Polo campfire—or perhaps some weird new enchantment.

"What say your devil-spirits?" Marco asked Peter.

"They say that we should not remain all night upon this wind-buffeted hill. They say that we should approach the flame with stealth, to discover whether it means friend or foe."

"My sharp Italian wits could have told me as much—without any aid from your devils," grumbled Marco.

"Me thinks your sharp Italian wits *are* your devils," replied Peter with a loud slap upon his horse's flank.

But the smoke signified neither friend *nor* foe. When they finally found the source just before dusk, it signified something more ominous than either ally or enemy. For the smoke curled lazily between a jumble of black-veined boulders, and it rose from the smoldering scraps of char-stones and Niccolo Polo's old grey silk robe. All around the rock-tumble were great mounds of fresh dung from some enormous, flesh-eating beast. Yet neither beast nor Niccolo could be seen—had the creature dragged Marco's father to some remote den to savor an Italian meal?

"What speak your devils about *this*?" asked Marco with an anxious scowl upon his sun-browned face, which had gone ashy-pale.

"My devils—and your own sharp wits, if you would but heed them, say that the dung-path left by this beast is as well marked as the Great Khan's highway—and untainted by human blood. So, fine master, let us follow this turd-trail and see where it leads . . ."

They followed the beast's droppings beyond the tumble of boulders, and past the fragmented remains of the poison-arrow-slain young Mongol. About three *li* from the mysterious curl of smoke, they found a broad, gravel-floored clearing—and *the others*! Father Niccolo and Uncle Maffeo Polo, with weary faces and tattered robes, but alive . . . *alive* . . . stooped to examine the remains of the still death-twined griffin and giant pard, along with Scholar Yen and others of their band.

"*Illusion* you say? *Marón!*" Uncle Maffeo snorted, and glared at Scholar Yen.

"And such a *large* illusion." The scholar nodded agreeably and calmly tucked his hands into the sleeves of his fur-lined black silk robe. "Such a large and well-formed illusion that—were it not for my many decades of philosophical training—I, too, might believe such phantasms were real."

Alive . . . almost all alive, except for the young horseman who had burst like an overipe grape from the illusion of the poison arrows, and the poor Cathayan clerk gobbled by the griffin. Almost all alive and safe and together again, they made camp in this place for the night. They built their fire from the still smouldering char-stone flakes and the remnants of Niccolo Polo's burning brand; to which they added such fortuitously-found items as isolated shrubs of wormwood, dessicated flaps of dung from who-knew-what beasts of time ago, and the wooden parts of such pack-saddles and man-saddles as lay here and there, fallen off in the wild chase.

"We should celebrate our escape from these perils," said Uncle Maffeo, as they sipped sour mare's milk and gnawed on stringy smoked mutton, and some dried handfuls of the jujube fruit. "Let us send the servants to the marketplace at the Rialto; there to buy for us a barrel of the sweetest red wine of Tuscany, and a basket of freshly caught sardines from our own Venetian lagoons. The sardines can be grilled with fresh onions and garlic in golden olive oil, and eaten with crusty loaves of hot wheaten bread, baked in the big brick oven outside the kitchen of the Palazzo di Polo. Such a fine feast for wandering merchants returning to home and family. We could gather all the nephews and nieces around us, and tell them such exciting tales . . ."

"You make your poor brother weep," said Niccolo with a quiet sigh. "I have not tasted crusty-hot wheaten bread in *years*. Nothing but millet and gritty rice and those damn slimy noodles that slither down the throat like serpents—or worms. *Little* worms!"

"The noodles might not taste so bad if they were properly prepared with olive oil and garlic, and perhaps a bit of crumbled cheese. The Venetians might like them and pay a handsome price—let us bring some dried noodles home with us, brother—if we ever *go* home," said Uncle Maffeo, echoing his elder brother's quiet sigh with a noisier version of his own, and wrapping himself in a wolverine-pelt robe against the icy winds that blew off the dusty northwestern wastes.

"If the Great Khan ever *allows* us to go home . . ." grumbled Niccolo, while worrying his jade worry-beads (each the size of a plump pigeon's egg, and worth three full baskets of prized white truffles on the Rialto). "Now let us finish our banquet of rancid mare's milk curds and leathery meat, and these fruits which are neither figs nor dates, so we can get some sleep. Who knows what perils may come on the morrow . . . as we pursue this elusive Sleeping Beauty . . ."

"*May*, father? *May?*" asked Marco.

K'un; Yielding.
Earth Above; Earth Below.
The Persevering Mare Finds Southwestern Friends.

8

New perils could barely wait for the morrow to come. The Polos and their men still slumbered fitfully, wrapped in their verminous and musty sleeping furs and fleeces, and the dawn was just shading the sallow eastern horizon with lavender tones. Marco lay half asleep and half awake. He could never sleep comfortably on such rugged expeditions; the graveled earth was too hard and lumpy, the fleas in his sleeping fur were overly familiar with his savory flesh—and worst of all, the ghosts of the wastelands whispered into his mind like the keening winds all through the night. Thus sound sleep, if it came at all, came accompanied by fevered dreams and sudden, startled wakenings.

But sound sleep came not. Instead came buzzing, humming, droning in Marco's ear . . . and not the mind-hum of ghosts. This was the very real hum and buzz of multitudes of biting jade-green flies drawn to the swelling corpses of griffin and horsemen and giant pard. In the next moment they were *everywhere*, lighting and crawling all over Marco's face, inside his nostrils and ears, clothes and furs, and biting at his skin. Then rising and circling in green-black, droning clouds while new and hungry reinforcements dived down to attack.

"*Marón*! 'Tis the devil Balsebub, Lord of Flies!" cried Uncle Maffeo, as he scrambled out of his sleeping fur, and slapped uselessly at the swarm.

The Mongol horsemen shouted obscure grassland obscenities as they clawed at their stinging flesh. The camels sneered and snorted, and the horses screamed and pawed and tried to bolt as the buzzing black-jade agony settled on their hides. Peter the Tartar yelped as the voracious little beasts invaded his tormented eyes.

Through all the chaos and confusion, Marco's keen ears detected yet another strange sound. It was the rhythmic beating of a small hand-drum, and the monotonous chanting of those idolaters who kowtow to the Buddha, Sakyamuni. ("He would have been a very great saint for Our Lord, had he lived in Christian times," Friar Paul had said.) Then a curious figure came strolling into view . . . a very small and very shabby old man with a shaven head and the tattered maroon robes of a La-ma sorcerer.

He beat his little drum and chanted his monotonous, droning chant . . . and eyed with calm disinterest the frantic contortions of hysterical beasts and slapping, cursing men. Then he lifted his left hand and curled his fingers in an odd gesture. In a warbling voice that was thin as reeds, he began another chant that droned in tune with the droning flies, and ended with the sharp expletive, "*Phat*!"

And when he shouted *Phat*! three times, the flies abruptly disappeared.

The Mongol and Tartar horsemen all threw themselves to the icy ground in deep kowtows of thanks to their protector, while the Polos and Scholar Yen clasped their hands together and bowed low. The wandering La-ma wryly thrust out his tongue in greeting, as is the way of these highland folk. Marco's eyes were drawn to his angular face, which was smeared with rancid butter as protection from the harsh weather. Neither sooty, greasy face, nor filthy, fetid woolen robe had recently (or ever) seen a bath, thus the little La-ma exuded a musty odor, rather like a ram in rut. Yet his black eyes glittered merrily.

Marco had encountered such itinerant sorcerers before, as they wandered the narrow lanes of the sprawling capital city of Tai-Ting, catering to the superstitions of the idolaters. Often one or a few of them would invade a prosperous merchant household, claiming that protection was needed from hovering demonic forces. To the householders this was obvious; only the price of protection warranted discussion. And *much* discussion at that.

At times they took residence in spacious rooms on the sunniest courtyards for many months, and helped themselves to the choicest morsels of food, and even to the master's concubines. They usually preferred jewels and gold (rather than the Great Khan's novel paper money) as payment for their complex spells and incantations to ward off evil—and indeed, no tragedies would befall the household while they were present. Perhaps they would not dare. But Marco ofttimes wondered whether good fortune would have come in any case, and whether some of the La-mas might be fabricating demons to provide themselves cosy quarters for the biting-cold winter season.

Yet now that he had seen this sorcery at work, he confessed to himself that he was impressed. Very impressed, indeed.

"I thank you, Precious One, for relieving us of those pesty flies," said Niccolo Polo, elder and leader of their expedition. "May I offer you some refreshment from our scanty rations? I am sure there are some modest sweetmeats and wine, carefully saved for such a special occasion . . ."

"I am but a wandering monk, a maker of rain and a banisher of flies. The earth provides my sweetmeats;

the sky provides my wine. Today's sweets? Tomorrow's dung. Today's wine? Tomorrow's piddle. I need no sugared rice from any man," said the La-ma in his high, wavering voice that sang like the constant winds. "How does such a noble and sturdy band come to such ignoble and stony wastes?"

"We . . . are engrossed in the *gabelle*, the salt tax for the Great Khan, Lord Kublai," said Maffeo, still scratching at a fly sting on his broad and swarthy arm. Would this serve to convince? He himself had doubts.

"Ah yes, salt is very important to those bound to the wheel; they say that without it the food lacks taste. Lacks *taste*! One sensual illusion gives birth to another. They pay for salt, which gives them thirst, then pay for wine to quench it . . . what mirth! Well, nobody is here to pay taxes except the thornbushes—though I suppose Kublai King has learned to exact tribute even from them." The little La-ma cackled and twirled his hand-drum, which Marco noticed was made of a pair of split human skulls, joined together and covered with sooty hide, and strung with fringes of turquoise beads which rattled when the drum was whirled.

The Mongol horsemen grunted at such bold, almost treasonous words, and Scholar Yen frowned and twined his twelve-haired mustache. There was little warmth lost between the wandering wizards and the court philosophers.

"You see, Precious One, we have lost our way," said Niccolo. "We were pursued into this wasteland by a marauding griffin and a giant snow-leopard—whose corpses mayhap drew the vicious flies hither . . . and had you not come along . . ."

"*Lost*, are you?" interrupted the La-ma in his reedy voice. "Climb just over those hills to the north . . . you see that ridge of hills shaped like a school of fat carp? Just beyond those fishy hills is a market town where you might find shelter, and refreshment for yourselves and your horses and camels—and tribute for Kublai's tax-pouches." Then the tattered little La-ma wandered away, twirling his skull-drum, and chanting in a voice that sang like the ceaseless wind in Marco's ears.

"I recall no market town beyond those hills," said Peter the Tartar with a scowl. "My devil-spirits whisper that something is amiss."

"All is illusion," said Scholar Yen with (perhaps) a bit of relief to be on familiar philosophical ground again.

Despite the whispers of Peter's devils, the Polos decided to cross the fish-shaped ridge. ". . . For what harm can come of it?" asked Uncle Maffeo, a-tugging his beard as if making sure it was still attached to his face.

What harm indeed? Marco and Peter turned their horses to the north once more, back across the sinuous and sheltering hills. But Peter was right: beyond the ridge there was no market town, only the desolate and muddy expanse of a drying lake bed.

"We will travel just a little further beyond this bog," said Niccolo, fingering his second-best amber worry-beads.

"I like it not," murmured Peter.

Nor did the first horseman who entered the marsh, with his imperial sun-and-moon banner waving in a sullen breeze; like it—not at all. The horse floundered up to its shanks; up to its knees in sicky-sticky muck, while the impassive expression on the horseman's round face turned to one of fear.

"Halt! *Swampsand*!" shouted the leader of the Mongol guard.

And all halted and watched with helpless dismay as the screaming and thrashing horse sank up to its shuddering flanks, then lurched sideways in a futile attempt to gain a foothold, until its head and gaily ribboned mane were swamped by the swamp-ooze. The young rider half-slid, half-fell into the sticky soup, and tried to swim/run to solid ground. The Mongol guard-captain tossed him a length of hempen rope, and tried to pull the horseman to safety, but the mud-slicked rope slithered from his grasp and slid out of his clawing reach. Marco sickened as he saw the living sands engulf the horseman's shingled leather armor in a half-liquid embrace that dragged him downward . . . ever downward as his limbs flailed wildly and his frantic eyes went dead with despair. At length only his leather helmet could be seen, with its fur-lined ear-flaps floating haplessly upon the mire.

"The question now is, *who* has worked this great dark sorcery against us?" This was how Marco's father phrased it, as they later made their crude camp for the night.

Who had devised the eerie crows which turned to serpents and then to bloody arrows? *Who* had caused the sudden-swift and horrid death of the young Mongol horseman by some poison worse than serpent's venom? Who had brought the griffin and the gigant pard down from their immemorial lairs against them? Who had sent the treacherous La-ma sorcerer to lead them to the lethal bog—where yet another horseman met a loathsome death?

Uncle Maffeo fingered the small gold cross at his throat. "Be sure the Evil One, Brother Nic. *Satan*. The very devil."

But Brother Nic was not sure. "If we were engaged in some Christian work for a Christian king, certainly the devil would try to baffle us. It is his wont. But what are the plain facts? Our royal master is not a Christian; he is a pagan, an idolater. On what task are we bound for him now? Not one against the holy Catholic faith, I trust . . . but I cannot say it is *for* the Lord's work. I do not see *the* devil's hoof in this. But of course *some* devil is involved. Probably a whole host of them. —Eh, Marc?"

Marco slowly nodded. "Still," he mused. "Devils might be commanded by men. Often *are*. And was that La-ma a man, a wasteland ghost—or the very devil himself? So weirdly his voice sang wind-like in my ears. Yet who is powerful enough to command such sorcery? And who is also the Great Khan's enemy?"

"Prester John? Or mayhap the Old Man of the Mountains?" asked Uncle Maffeo. "*Marón!* Who can know?"

But Marco was not persuaded. "Prester John is of the Indies, *which* Indies I cannot say, but not of *here*. And does the Old Man of the Mountains work these waste places? Surely his mountains are farther west by far."

"*Kaidu Khan* would have the power to command such sorcery, *and* enmity against Lord Kublai as well," said Peter the Tartar. "Did you note that La-ma, whether man or illusion, devil or ghost, scoffed at the Great Khan's name—and questioned us closely on our mission? Mayhap he was a spy sent by Kublai's rival nephew, Kaidu of Samarkand, who is Khan of the flowing grasses and barbarian steppelands. Kaidu is also grandson of the great conqueror, Lord Genghiz; he refuses to kowtow to the Son of Heaven, and claims Kublai's own title of Khan of Khans."

"You may be right, lad," said Niccolo. "You should have reasoned this sooner . . . before we encountered that deadly bog."

Much talk. Many questions.

Few answers. No conclusions.

Marco consulted his scanty maps by the dying light of the campfire, in preparation for the morrow's journey. In addition to Kublai's highly fanciful scroll-map, he used Scholar Yen's translations of the Flying-Bird maps of Cathay. These had fairly accurate measurements of the well-charted provinces, but grew quite vague in representing the border regions.

Marco also scanned the rumpled map drawn for him on parchment by his old teacher, Friar Paul. The Polos had carried this parting gift all the way from Venice and, accurate or not, Marco treasured this map precisely because it reminded him of *home*. Friar Paul had been no great cartographer—who *had*, since the death of Great Ptolemy? But his painfully scrawled, and alas, painfully inaccurate sketches of Cathay, ("I was born, my son, under the sign of the crab, whose sidewise motion models the motion of the moon . . . I am a moonchild by birth, and the moon is lightly moving . . .") his sketches, carefully copied by Marco lest the originals might fade (they were already fading), traveled in Marco's own saddle bag. Often he consulted them for what little aid they could offer.

Friar Paul had given his own names to things, ignoring those given (when given) by earlier travelers. He had never bothered to note if *North* were at the top, or (as was equally the custom) *South*. Sometimes he had scribbled *M* for *Marsh* and sometimes *M* signified *Mountain*. Although the old friar had traveled the eastern trade routes as a wandering priest in his youth . . . so long, long ago . . . it was certain he had not gone the entire obscure route which this expedition was following, at the Great Khan's urging. Only a small part of the way eastward; and then from another direction.

Probably he had heard of this waste at the end of the civilized Cathayan world whilst traveling somewhere else. Perhaps while looking for the Tartar horde reputed to be Christians; perhaps looking for the Lost Tribes in order to convert them; perhaps looking for Prester John's kingdom or for the Terrestrial Paradise. Certainly he had not been in search of worldly treasures—or of people or places enchanted.

Marco was fairly certain that their party was presently in the area indicated on one of the map-scraps, which Marco himself had numbered with the Roman numeral *L*—the friar not having numbered them at all. In the lower left quadrant, the friar's quavering hand had scrawled *Plateau of Great Peril in* . . . and after that was a place scorched quite through. Some fragment of burning thornbush—a usefully quick fuel; good to start slower ones to smoulder here on the flowing and treeless plains—had erased the word or words which had named the *Great Peril*.

Higher up on the map-sketch the same hand had noted: *Here There be Griffins and the Gyant Ownse*. Again a scorch mark had erased writing, so the line actually read *Here There be G . . . s;* scorched place; *and the Gyant Ownse*. But later Friar Paul had neatly, in a different ink, written under that burned-out spot;

Griffins. Why then had he not re-written what was erased by fire in the *Plateau of Great Peril*?

Marco had no way of knowing. But he truly hoped that, whatever, it represented no such terrible danger For which travelers needed warning.

II
They Find a Sleeping Beauty

Wei Chi; Transition.
Fire Flares Above the Water.
The Bold Young Fox Gets His Tail Wet.

9

Their rudimentary maps had led them many a league and *li* southward, when there came a strange sound. A voice of, "Ho! Travelers!" *Pause.* "Halt!" did not at first persuade them to do so. But the call, coming from the scant shade of a clump of jujube trees, was repeated. Without saying that they would, or asking each other if they should, they did.

The man who had hailed them now stepped forth from the shadow. Though some traces of the shadow seemed still to linger upon him, likely this was but dust remnant of the road. The man was Han-Cathayan, and neither tall nor short, but very staunchly built and stalwart. Wrinkles set thickly at the corners of his narrow eyes indicated perhaps much laughter, or perhaps much squinting into sun or dust. Perhaps all of these.

A battered sword was in his belt, and he leaned upon a staff which—as he walked forward—was revealed to be a halberd, with the axe-part more prominent than the spear. Red was its pole; a deeper and sweat-stained red was the water-buffalo-leather cuirass seen beneath the travel-faded red of his tunic. Short boots of worn red leather, a loose green cotton blouse (if one might call it so) and coarse tan hempen trousers down only to the massive calves of his legs, completed the costume.

Marco had seen his like often before, roving the highways, byways and alleyways of the empire. Bands of them camped among the sheltering arches of the mighty marble bridge which entered the capital city of Tai-Ting (this broad bridge fascinated Marco because each of its many graceful columns was topped by a carved stone lion . . . and no two lions were alike).

These *yu-xia* were wandering adventurers who used their rough swords to enforce their rough-hewn code of ethics. They were the landless petty nobles and their retainers, unemployed artisans and warriors, bankrupt merchants and peasants who shared a distaste for common labor—or had not found any—and preferred the independent life of the warrior-errant. They offered their loyalty and their lives to the feudal lords who employed them, and obeyed no law outside their masters' direction, or their own keen sense of justice. With their sharp tempers and swords, they boldly (if not always wisely) defended the causes that drew their volatile sympathies, with little thought of reward or their own skins. Marco had always respected these untamed free-lancers—from a distance.

"Travelers," said the stranger, in a husky voice, "have you space in your expedition for a wandering knight?"

"What quality of knight?" —Niccolo.

"What name of knight?" —Maffeo.

"What destination, knight?" —Marco.

The man's manner was civil and calm. Marco felt he kept a certain sense of amusement subdued. "Of many qualities, this knight. A knight of princes, but no matter which ones. A knight of broad plains and narrow alleys. Sometimes called Ching K'o, Chi An, or sometimes . . . but has the wind a milk name? Call me Hou Ying, then." No one replying, the man went on. "The true knight has no destination of his own, my young sir. He goes on the dusty road as he is told, or where he binds himself to go; and if he sees a wrong, his swift sword will make it right. So it is said . . ." Said Ching K'o . . . or Chi An . . . or Hou Ying.

Scholar Yen Lung-chuan, who had sat on his horse impassively, now hawked and spat. He seemed to mean no disrespect, and the new-found knight seemed to take none; the Cathayans hawked and spat without regard to time, person, or place. Yen began to speak in the affected tones of a recitation or scholarly quote. "Though men of the knightly way have been famed since ancient times for unselfishness; of Master Ching K'o it is said that, although a man of letters, he led an unruly life. For he associated with dog-butchers and street-musicians, jugglers and other low persons, and they drank in public and sang in public; now singing, now weeping, now singing, now weeping."

"Ho, ha," said the supposed Ching K'o, indulgently.

Yen Lung-chuan stroked the dozen hairs which were his moustache, and continued. "Although knights-errant have been famed since ancient times for being trustworthy and just, and for sharing what they have; of Chi An it is said that, though altruistic, he had an arrogant, rough, and discourteous nature."

The putative knight—Chi An?—slightly shrugged. "*Mei-yo fa-dze*," said he.

Yen nodded. "*Nothing to be done*," was a Cathayan phrase well-suited to his own philosophy. He went on in his sing-song recitative. "It was observed that the wandering knight, Chu Meng, though he honored his mother, had little respect for the law or polite manners. For he enjoyed gambling games with rowdy and disheveled youths; such as the tossing of date-stones into tiny embroidered shoes removed by sing-song girls with tiny bound feet."

The knight bowed slightly and said, "Where there is no cash, I will gamble date-stones with rude companions, at the great marble Bridge-of-Many-Lions outside the city walls of Tai-Ting. Immortal Lao Tze whispers to me that *the more laws rulers devise, the more lawless people there will be.* I am surely Chu Meng."

But Yen was not yet done. "Of Hou Ying, another knight-errant famed in ancient songs and tales; it has been reported that, though once an humble gatekeeper of Wei, he exemplified the chivalrous code of loyalty, courage and honor, and gladly offered his life to the master who esteemed him."

A light wind ruffled the knight's light green blouse. "You may call me Hou Ying," said he, equitably.

Uncle Maffeo stirred restlessly. "*Marón!* I know the Han-Cathayans, of which this man appears to be, often change their names—and quite lawfully . . . but which of these four—?"

Scholar Yen politely interrupted; "Of these four, elder Sir, all four are dead."

The Polos sat perplexed upon their horses. The Mongols muttered, the Cathayans snickered, and the Tartars gaped.

Said the knight-of-many-names, "There came a mighty king from out of the west, Is-kan-da, who married Lok-shan-ah. His tutor was named Ah-lis-to-tu. Often he would say, 'Define terms.' What is '*dead*'?"

Instantly Yen replied, warming to a favorite subject, "An illusion. So is life. So Sakyamuni Buddha taught, in his compassion. So Master Kung asked, 'As one does not know life, how can one know death?' "

Niccolo gave a deep, deep sigh. He did so whenever such esoteric matters came up. Much, much rather would he devote his merchant's mind to some thought such as: *A full score of cat's-eye amethysts, each the size of a hunting-cat's orb by full moonlight*, and the like. He rubbed his nose and his jade beads.

Maffeo grumbled, then asked if they had rations enough for another man. Marco observed that if the "another man" were *this* man, he looked like the sort who would more-or-less furnish his own rations as he went along.

"You think then, Nephew Marc, that this sly and sturdy fellow should be let to join up and come along?"

Marco laughed. "I think, Sir Uncle, that he has already joined up for . . . see for yourself! . . . he is indeed coming along."

Sure enough. How long they had stopped and paused, who could say; at what point they had re-commenced their journey, who could say; how long they had been at it, who could say?

Mei-yo fa-dze. Nothing to be done.

In an easy, effortless stride, the newest member of the expedition kept pace with them all. As to who he really was (though they fell into the habit of calling him *Hou Ying*, the last name mentioned) why . . . who could really say?

Perhaps only he himself.

I; The Open Mouth.
Thunder Rumbles in the Foothills.
The Hungry Tiger Cannot Cross the Great Water.

10

In this long-lasting landscape of little water: *water*. At last.

Not to be wondered at, thought Marco. They had strayed into a vast basin which, likely, acted as a sump for all the immemorial seepage of the area. If here it were to rain but once in a lifetime, all the water which did not evaporate (most of it likely *did* evaporate) would trickle hither and collect here. Though it might take many lifetimes for any single drop of rain to ooze its way from the broad basin's brim to its bottom, filtering almost immeasurably through the almost impermeable layers of rock.

Heat and haze by day, frosted mists by night, dust and dampness and dankness—yet—water. The men raised, well, it was not a cheer; they were all too spent for that. The men raised their voices. Somewhat. There ahead was greenery, there were ponds and brooks, there . . .

"Ah, I fear it is only a mirage!" —Niccolo, worrying his worry beads.

"Why fear so?" —Maffeo, tugging at his beard.

"Why? Well . . . the horses. Camels, mules, ponies, parched beastery; why do they not lift their heads and gallop down to slake their thirst?"

For surely by now—in fact, long before now—the animals should have smelled the infinitely welcome water. Marco himself could scarcely refrain from using whip and spur to urge his mount to berm and brink. There to leap down, tear off dust-stained, sweat-stained clothes; plunge into pond and pool . . .

And yet he did not. None of them did. Save for tossing their heads and shuddering their skins against the dull buzzing of insect swarms, the beasts merely plodded on as before, ignoring the prospect of water. Until at last the sound of their splashing hooves proved that it was, at least, no mere mirage. And, thank Our Lady, no swampsand.

"It resembles the Maremma or the Pontine," said Nic, with a long sigh, naming certain notorious swamp areas of Italy.

"It does; it does," his brother said, echoing the sigh. "I fear it may be only a marsh, yet . . . stay . . . why even a marsh . . ." He did not finish.

Now there rose to their ears a croaking as of an hundred thousand frogs, providing their own echo.

No green fields, then; the green fields were an illusion created by the scum-covered surface of the stagnant fen. No ponds, no brooks, only the listless openings where some sluggish wind or current had broken the crusted skin of slime. Almost one might have wished that the mirage had *been* mirage. Almost . . .

One of the guardsmen, younger than the others; Marco might have taken him for Mongol, Tartar, or even Han-Cathayan, had he not chanced to learn some while back that the lad was from the *kuo* of the Manchu-folk. This young rider had been sitting slumped upon his horse, going where his horse was taking him. The young man's eyes were likely more than half-closed against the dust; eyes cast down and away from the monotony of the starveling plains, noticing nothing but the sallow powder settling on his mount's gaily ribboned mane . . .

This young man, having been used to the endlessly undulating grassy meadows of his native soil, had perhaps been dreaming of them. Had perhaps been lost instead in another dream, in which dust and sand and gravel and rocks went on and on . . . forever, forever . . .

Something, then, had caused his lolling head to snap upright. For an instant he stayed but staring, upon his shaggy pony. Then with half-mad shouts of, "*Water! Water! Water!*" off he galloped.

They all watched as man and mount dashed down the slope at the bottom of the natural basin, dust mingling with dank mist, one hand at the rein and one madly beating his fur-skin cap against the animal's straining side. Straight on into the shallows they went; then the fellow half-leaped, half-slid into the muck and ooze, his feet and legs breaking the crust. They saw him almost prostrate himself as he bent, heedless of his soaking legs, to dip both cupped hands and raise them, dripping, to his cracked and parched and parted lips.

The water, as the others came up to him, was still falling in droplets from his beardless chin . . .

And he raised his now-wide eyes.

"Well?" asked the wandering knight, sometimes called Hou Ying.

The young Manchu looked at them with a look in which more than mere anguish mingled with more than mere disappointment. Then, in the tone of a small child used only to sweetened wine who has been given his first taste of sour, "*This* is not good to drink!" he said. His red, red eyes accused them all.

"Oh? No? Why not? Is it stale, then?"

Still the lad crouched. "*Stale*?" he cried. "It is worse, far worse than *stale*! It is bitter and bad. It is tainted with some mineral, and—" His wandering gaze now discovered what everyone else had long since discovered—and accepted. "Why . . . look! Even the animals will not drink of it!"

Uncle Maffeo's words were blunt. "They had more sense than to try."

The party resumed its ambling pace, skirting the useless morass. After a while, the young Manchu slowly got back on his horse and dejectedly followed them.

The frogs, triumphant, continued their mocking chorus.

The triumphant frogs continued their mocking chorus. The bitter yellow dust from the tainted soil mingled with the heat-mist and haze from the marshy sump. The air turned yellow, red, and grey. The knight, Hou Ying, made a sudden sound between a snort and a sigh; gestured with his halberd, slowly.

In a dull voice not expressive of much interest, Nic said, "Now the mirages begin again." Fell silent. Again.

Even while his father was so briefly speaking, Marco observed the mist-clouds and dust-clouds darken and swell. Then out of the midst of them, far off and far away, a pair of dull-grey-green creatures crouched and lurched.

"Frogs!" he said, startled.

In the same dull tone, Niccolo Polo commented, "Those be no frogs, my son."

Marco's father was right; those were not frogs at all, not even frogs distended, distorted by mirage. Forms of men with frog-like heads, they saw, clad in dull-grey-green with tones of brown. Slowly they seemed to climb down from the very skies and clouds.

"And those be no mirages either, Father," said Marco.

The strange creatures now retreated, now advanced. Their frog-faces grimaced and they shook their limbs threateningly.

"*Marón!* What *is* this? What is *this*?" Uncle Maffeo seemed more puzzled than afraid. He made a quizzical gesture; did not complete it. His hand stayed angled, palm up.

Scholar Yen gave a preliminary throat-clearing. "Southern Sea-Barbarians," he said. "It is well known that they have webs between fingers and toes, the better to—I suppose—the better to swim. The Superior Man does not swim and does not attempt to swim, anymore than the Superior Man attempts to fly. The Master, whose name of Kung Fu-dze you Latins have corrupted into 'Confucius' —Master Kung taught, concerning the Duke of Chou—"

But Maffeo had no desire to learn what Master Kung had taught concerning the Duke of Chou. "What, 'Barbarians of the Southern Sea?' Well, truly there are dog-headed men on some of those islands, so frog-faced ones may . . . but, a thousand devils! Why are they *here*? —A thousand leagues from the Southern Sea!"

Yen said they must be rebels against the just and benignant (if sometimes just and severe . . . or even justly severe) rule of the Great Khan. "Though it is surprising that their demon-magic extends this far." He seemed not to doubt that it *was* magic and neither did, much, Maffeo. For, indeed, what other explanation was there?

"Strange," mused Yen. "This far . . . but . . . anger travels very far indeed. I have heard tales of a powerful old temple in these border regions, built to honor the Merciful Lady Kuan-yin, and to ward off marauding frog-demons, so—*Ho*!" The batrachian figures having receded into the yellow haze once more, all eyes were turned upon the (until now) impeturbable figure of Scholar Yen. He had never once (until now) so far descended to the level of common passion as to cry *Ho*! What could it mean?

In a moment he enlightened them as, once more falling into the special sing-song with which he cited quotations, Yen recited the admonition that was written in Kublai's cryptic scroll—which was supposed to guide them on their mission: "*Savor the sea, where no sea be . . .*"

And with that, the mysterious figures emerged again from the mists and clouds, only now there were more of them gaping and gesticulating. Maffeo gave a wordless exclamation. "*Savor* these hideous demons?" he cried.

"One hears that Franks eat frogs, and doubtless *they* savor them—but we? No! For all that the Saracens call all Europeans '*Franks*' we are not, so—"

But the newly-enlisted knight, Hou Ying, half-raised his halberd. "Names need wait, my good sir," he interrupted. "What cannot wait is that each man should now draw his weapon, and prepare to fight for the Great Lord under whose sun-and-moon banner he has taken service."

For now, from every side, out of the sallow clouds of mist and dust and haze, the immense frog-like figures began to emerge.

And their numbers were countless.

The croaking din of the frogs increased around them.

Afterwards, Marco could not precisely remember what weapons this unnatural and unexpected enemy had used. To be sure, they must needs have been sharp; more than one deep cut and slash bore witness to that. But it was not the cut and slash of the attack which made it memorable. He had been in battle before against knife-wielding and sword-swinging and spear-thrusting enemy, and often he could not clearly remember one encounter from another.

What made this unforgettable was, for one thing, the great size of the strange enemy-forms; for another, the multitude of them, springing out of no cover save the reedy covert of the fens, like a plague of Aegypt. For yet another, their grotesque appearance, with their bulging eyes and tapering skulls, wide mouths and warty skins, and their faces reflecting the dull grey-brown-green of their rough costume. And for much more, their rhythmic croaking war-cries.

Yet above all, and most of all for memory, it was the mucky, musty stench of them; a stink of mud and musk, as though a nest of bog-snakes had been trampled down. Though the canals of Most Serene Venice, into which thousands of privies emptied, did not exactly flow with the scent of attar of roses either. This he knew; always he would remember their demon-stench. Always.

And yet a thing or two more there had been to recollect.

And to ponder.

Towards the end of the vicious battle, he had seen a great figure in the northwestern sunset sky, and this time it was no Southern Sea-barbarian, nor frog nor toad.

"*Hou Ying!*" cried he; for it much resembled the wandering knight. The resemblance was more than (the example raised itself) the way one Venetian or Cathayan resembled another; a true similarity there was in shape and form. "*Hou Ying!*" Marco had cried, but no one heard him above the noise of the battle.

Yet in facial features and costume, there was no resemblance to any earthly knight. It seemed to Marco that this great figure . . . hovering in the dusty-red sunset sky as if trampling the yellow dusk with his mighty boots . . . also bore the face and form of one of the Guardian-Kings who stand watch at the entrance to idolaters' temples. But . . . *which* idol figure was it? He could not now think of which . . .

The ruddy-skinned figure glared and stared at the battle with bulging eyes beneath bristling brows. Long fangs jutted from his down-curled lips, and his fingers were tipped with sharp vermillion claws, which clasped a twining white serpent. Glowing, flowing robes of richly gilded brocade swirled around his massive torso, an elaborate headress haloed his wrathful red face, and his great limbs glistened with glittering gold and jewels.

It seemed to Marco . . . though for sure . . . the burning red-and-yellow sun, the dust and distorting mist, the excited and almost frenzied leaping of his horse meant he could *not* be sure . . . could *never* be sure. It seemed to Marco that the formidable figure wielded a great axe-of-war and plied it mightily against the fearsome and stinking-filthy foe. Now leaping, now swirling like a whirlwind of cloth-of-gold, with axe flashing and gems sparkling. And with each vast and flaming leap and whirl, great numbers of the gruesome enemy fell to the boggy, clotted ground.

Yet scarce had Marco tried to shield his eyes, and narrow them against the reddening sun and the blazing apparition, then the vision which much resembled Hou Ying faded. The vision had faded—but he had seen enough.

Here and there the grotesque figures ("Forms and figures," mused Scholar Yen later; "figures and forms. Forms of figures and figures of forms, and surely all are illusion . . .") —still the grotesque frog-figures crouched and leaped, and at times they overbore a man on horse or foot; but by now there were so few of the enemy that the Great Khan's men soon and swiftly rallied round to save their threatened fellows. And soon enough the demon-horde, if such it was, had vanished. Not one loathsome bog-creature remained to fight.

Hou Ying wiped his reddened face on his sweat-soaked sleeve. "I fight all who attack," he said now, still lightly panting. "But I prefer, much, to fight merely men or ghosts." *Merely!* "I doubt if *these*;" slightly he emphasized the last word and gestured, as was his way, with his halberd, from the axe-blade of which an ugly ichor dripped. "I doubt if these be more . . . or less . . . than men . . . or ghosts."

Marco thought of that other Latin exile, Ovid, and of his *Metamorphosis*, as he looked where the mysterious knight had motioned. For there on the ground, all around and round about there lay, sometimes by one and sometimes by two and three, and sometimes in heaps and hillocks and mounds—not one in body and limb lying whole—a vast army of dead and dying frogs.

Savor the sea, where no sea be . . . So it was written in the Great Khan's accursed scroll—well! Frogs were creatures of the water, true. Yes. But . . . now that Marco had time to think calmly on the matter . . . not of the sea. Thus blood had been shed, yet the scroll's mysteries had not yet been solved.

Moved by a desire to depart from this murky place before nightfall, and made supple by his fear that otherwise they might never depart at all; Marco mounted, rose in his stirrups, called for attention, obtained it.

"There is where we now shall go," he said. And he pointed to a ridge shimmering in the distant mists, which could provide them an overview of the surrounding region. "We go *there*."

Faintly (and now it seemed, far from triumphantly) the frogs croaked. The frogs croaked, but the caravan moved on.

Kuan; Contemplation.
Wind Whirls Above the Earth.
Ancient Kings Journeyed to Instruct the People.

11

They reached the ridge late the next morning, after a night haunted by eerie images and echoes. But they found no solid formation of granite. Instead there was an upthrusting of yellow-red rocks, veined with the curious black stone which burns like charcoal. The ridge had weathered into a maze of twining gorges and canyons.

"So, young sir, how do you propose that we pick our way through this barrier?" Scholar Yen asked in a bland tone.

"The horses will pick the way for us. By putting one hoof before the other, they will find the easiest route through this labyrinth."

It was not that simple. The cobweb of gorges twisted and rambled in no apparent direction, and with barely a trickle of water at the sandy base to point them to clefts in the steep rock-walls.

Glaring shafts of sunlight shone directly overhead, then at an angle as the day passed. The glinting rocks magnified the power of the sun, and combined with the choking yellow dust raised by the animals' hooves to make Marco feel giddy. An occasional striped lizard scuttled across a heated slab of sun-baked rock, but otherwise there was no sound or sign of life.

The horses picked their way, one hoof before the other, following the tangled skein of passageways from frustrating dead-ends to monolithic barricades, to abrupt rock-ledges. They back-tracked countless times, and each time found their way blocked. The beasts rambled aimlessly, until the Polos realized that they knew not the way back to the aperture which entered this riddle.

"Similarly well-marked is our way back to Venice," grumbled Maffeo, impatiently tugging at his beard. "Peter must ask his devils which direction we should take."

"Which devil, Padrone? I have many fine devils," said the young Tartar.

"*Marón*! How should I know which? One useful to us . . . and on your unbaptized head be the sin . . ."

Yet they had no need to summon Peter's devils, for a devilish looking figure appeared to them as they entered a narrow cul-de-sac. Actually, it was a perfectly ordinary figure that Marco saw through the glaring haze. It was only the oddity of its unexpected appearance, here in this isolated place, that made it seem . . . somehow . . . demonic.

The figure was man-shaped, and Marco hoped he was, indeed, human. He had the supple skin, elongated eyes, and wispy beard of a Han-Cathayan, and his long black hair was tightly wound in a fist-sized knot atop his head. He wore the tattered black silk robe of a scholar, over long, flowing black silk trousers, and soft black felt slippers. He looked thoroughly out of context in this remote place, as he rooted like an enterprising pig at the base of some jutting boulders with his ivory-handled walking stick.

Marco might have expected to find such a shabby scholar in the sunny courtyard of a rich merchant's household, seated under a flowering peach tree framed by a moon-gate; whilst reciting excerpts from the Four

Classics with the merchant's children—in return for a filled rice bowl. Indeed, he seemed to be reciting some rote-learned chant, but Marco could not understand its meaning. What was he singing and seeking . . . and why here?

As they came closer, Marco was able to comprehend the simpler parts of the song: "*Metal fells wood . . . Water quenches fire . . . Wood penetrates earth . . . Fire dissolves metal . . . Earth halts water . . . Thus is the sequence of subjugation of the five elements . . .*

"*Metal of autumn creates water . . . Water of winter creates wood . . . Wood of spring creates fire . . . Fire of summer creates earth . . . Earth of late-summer creates metal . . . Thus is the sequence of creation of the five elements . . .*"

"He is reciting the interaction of the five elements within the human body," said Scholar Yen in a low voice. Indeed, they were all moving very quietly and speaking hardly at all, for the stranger still had not heard their party of over a score of men and twice that number of beasts, somehow, and it seemed impolite to interrupt his meditation.

Finally the chanting ceased, and the strange man looked up and beckoned to them with a low bow. The three Polos and Scholar Yen dismounted and approached him, eager to satisfy their curiosity—and to find a way out of this maze, which was but a rudimentary squiggle on their rudimentary maps.

"So, honored travelers, what brings you to this desolate place?" asked the shabbily dressed scholar, showing no surprise.

"We might inquire the same of you," responded Niccolo, the elder Polo brother and leader of their group.

"I come here often to collect herbs for the humble pharmacy that I carry in this wicker basket on my back, which contains my few earthly belongings as the snail's shell contains all that the snail needs. I wander from place to place, slow as a snail, seeking the proper herbs to balance the forces of *Yin and Yang* . . . and I dispense them to those who are in need. For the Yellow Emperor has written in his great ancient treatise on medicine, the *Nei Ching*, that the principle of Yin and Yang is the core-principal of all the universe, and the source of life and death. Heaven is a manifestation of Yang, which is light; while Earth is a manifestation of Yin, which is darkness . . ."

"That is most interesting," interrupted Niccolo, rattling his best jade worry beads, and sounding not at all interested. "If you come here often, perhaps you can show us the way out of this accursed place."

"*Accursed!* Not so," said the physician-scholar. "Barren, yes, but with the stark beauty only found in places of great solitude and silence . . . and a treasure trove of blessed medicinal herbs. Here grows the very rare wasteland pomegranate, whose dried rind and bitter yellow bark cool fevers. Here also grows the tiger thistle, whose plump purple flowers relieve congestion of the womb. In sunny niches where rainwater collects, the wild hemp grows tall and strong. This beneficial plant has been known since ancient days, for the Emperor Shen-nung promoted its use at the same time that he taught cultivation of the mulberry tree and the silk-worm. The oil of hemp, or *ma-yo*, can promote sleep and relieve pain. Eating the seeds keeps the flesh firm and prevents old age. The incense of hemp flowers cures 120 diseases which I can name for you . . ." He placed the tip of one forefinger athwart another.

"*Marón*! Please spare us your lists of ailments, my good sir, and tell us the way out of this maze," pleaded Maffeo. "For we are on an important mission for the Great Khan, Kublai, and have no patience for such esoteric lore."

"Stay . . ." said Marco, thoughtfully. "The Great Khan might well be interested in seeds which can be eaten to prevent old age—for such matters worry his mind a great deal these days."

"If your Great Khan is learning that his flesh shrivels as surely as any common man's, then you must speak to the Lady who sleeps in the cavern."

"The *what*! Who *sleeps where*?" cried Niccolo, his lined and travel-worn face brightening for perhaps the first time since they had embarked on this wretched journey.

"So," chuckled the ragged herbalist, "have you been apart from womankind for so long that your cheeks flush at the mere mention of such a one? Perhaps you should hasten to the market-town beyond this wilderness. There you will find inns and livelier ladies to provide you with companionship."

"The pleasures of town can wait until *after* we have met this 'Lady who sleeps in a cavern'—who has knowledge of staying old age. For it is just such a one that Kublai has sent us to seek!" said Niccolo, looking pleased as if he had just found a bright red Bur-mienese ruby, the size of a wild wasteland pomegranate seed.

"Her resting place is over there," said the herbalist, gesturing vaguely to the west.

"Where is *there*?" asked Marco.

"There is where. . ." said the herbalist.

"*Marón*! Can these Cathayans *never* speak directions plainly?" fumed Maffeo. "It is bad enough that they sing when they speak, but even their songs have no meaning."

"I believe Scholar Yen greatly desires to learn the names of *each* of the 120 diseases which can be cured with the incense of benevolent hemp-flowers," said Marco, with a sly smile. "Please ride along with us . . . over there . . . to guide us to the cavern of this Sleeping Lady, and while we are traveling, you can teach the names of those 120 ailments to Yen."

The shabby herbalist bowed very low. "The humble scholar-physician, Hua T'o, is always eager to share his scanty knowledge with those who can benefit from it—and especially with those honored sirs who are eager to share the contents of their rice bowls with the lowly scholar-physician, Hua T'o."

Scholar Yen sighed, and gazed at them blandly.

Hsien; Attraction.
A Mountain Lake Reflects the Summit.
A Joyful Woman Brings Good Fortune.

12

The ragged herbalist, Hua T'o, guided them this way and that through the ruddy-rock labyrinth. At times he became so engrossed in his pharmaceutical discourse that he quite forgot where they were, which caused seemingly endless backtracks—and endless impatience among the Polos.

". . . Now those whose illness is under the providence of the eel, being found in places dark and narrow and slimy, should eat powder of eel rubbed with sea-kelp, and moistened with the fat of sandpipers who may be found where eels abound . . . though the winds and rain be high on every creek," explained the earnest herbalist, as Scholar Yen yawned politely behind his hand.

At last they reached the jutting ridge which overlooked the vast and sallow plain. At the summit of the ridge was a solitary pine tree guarding the narrow entrance to a cave, and on the gnarled pine branches cavorted a short-tailed monkey, whose white fur glimmered like some crystalline mineral.

"Is *this* it?" asked Niccolo, showing the barely-repressed interest he might usually reserve for a shipment of white sapphires from the isle of Serendib, each the size of a plump hummingbird's egg.

"It is this," said Hua T'o, gesturing with his ivory-handled walking stick . . . and eyeing their bulging ration-bags with equal interest, as if they contained rare and costly herbs. "But first we might take a light and restorative supper before we must part."

"Part?" asked Marco. "Why need we part just yet? I believe that Scholar Yen has merely memorized 108 diseases which may be cured by the blessed hemp flower—and we hoped you might present us to the lady."

"My young sir," said Hua T'o, "I would not *dare* approach that formidable lady . . . nor the tricky ape who guards the doorway to her cavern . . . now about that small but nourishing supper?"

After the wandering herbalist had gone on his way, happily munching the dried mutton, jujubes, and millet-wafers which the Polos found so tiresome (though Uncle Maffeo could never refuse joining in a light snack); the three Italians dismounted. They, along with Scholar Yen and Peter the Tartar, slowly approached the cave on foot.

"*Halt*! Who goes there?" called the short-tailed white ape in perfect Latin.

"*Marón!*" exclaimed Maffeo, still licking millet crumbs from his fingers. "In this heathen place men sing, rather than converse—and apes chatter in the tongue of the Pope!"

"I beg your pardon," said Scholar Yen, looking puzzled. "That monkey speaks a very refined dialect of Mandarin."

"No, he is one of *us* . . . a Tartar," said Peter. "Why else would he talk in the Tartar way."

"Is this ape yet another mirage, then?" asked Niccolo,

wearily rubbing his jade worry-beads, each the size of a ripe almond kernel.

"I am certainly no mirage," boasted the short-tailed white monkey in his singular speech which was every speech. "For a mirage seems to be less than real, and I am far more than I seem . . ."

"And both seeming and being are more or less illusions," Scholar Yen retorted.

"Who *are* you, then?" asked Marco.

"You may call me *Monkey*, if you are bold enough to call me at all," said the monkey. "I was born from a stone egg which was quickened with the power of sunlight and the grace of moonlight, until it burst open to reveal—*me*! Thanks to my clever boldness, I became King of the Monkeys, and we all lived happily in the Cave of the Water-Curtain, on the Mountain of Fruit and Flowers. Then one day I felt the icy hand of Yama, the bull-headed Lord of Death, reach out to take me. Trying to elude Yama's lethal grasp, I crossed many continents and seas in search of immortality. Finally a humble woodcutter led me to the immortal Patriarch, Su-bodi, who named me Void-Knowledge, and taught me the seventy-two magical transformations, and the secrets of enlightenment and eternal life. After that, I was called the Sage of Water-Curtain Cave . . . but you may call me *Monkey* . . . if you dare to call me at all."

"*Marón!* We Venetians risk our necks journeying in search of small profits for our ledgers, while these Cathayans—and even their *animals*—go gadding about in search of eternal life," grumbled Uncle Maffeo. "Do they think it is merchandise for heathen to chaffer about for their peculiar paper money, counted on their peculiar abacus?"

"We wish to speak to the lady who sleeps in the cave," said Niccolo, impatiently worrying his beads.

"Ha! You think The Lady is a bud-footed courtesan who receives clever callers?" laughed the white monkey. "The Lady is in deep and profound meditation. You must wait a long while if you wish to speak with her. I, myself, waited seven hundred years before she granted me even one word. Now I am waiting patiently for her second word. It has been nine hundred years, and it may be nine hundred years more . . . but well worth the wait, I assure you. If you do not disrupt my tranquility, you may pitch your tents in yonder gorge and wait here with me."

"We cannot wait even nine hundred *days*," replied Marco. "We are mere mortal men. We must enter the cave and speak to her *now*."

"I cannot allow that," said Monkey sternly. "For The Lady asked me to guard the entrance of her cavern against intruders."

"And how could she say that—if she spoke only one word?" scoffed Uncle Maffeo.

"Such a lady can say a great deal with only one word."

"How can a small monkey like yourself guard the cave against an entire company of the Great Khan's men, carrying the Great Khan's arms and the Great Khan's silver seal? Come; stop this foolishness and let us pass," demanded Maffeo, tugging at his grizzled beard as if it were the door handle of the Palazzo di Polo in mist-lit Venice.

"Ho! You think that *I*—whom the celestial Jade Emperor himself has titled *Great Saint Equal to Heaven*—am too *small* to guard the cave?" cried Monkey. "Then watch *this*!"

He plucked an iron needle from behind his ear and bellowed, "*Grow*!" At once he grew tall as a mountain, with mighty muscles like ridges, red eyes blazing like lightning, and teeth like battle-axes. The iron needle became a tremendously heavy gold-banded cudgel that grazed the sky. When the monkey laughed, the ground shook.

"*Marón!* Very impressive," nodded Maffeo, as the monkey resumed his normal size. "Still, there is only *one* of you. Our men could keep you at bay while we raced inside."

"Ha!" laughed the monkey. "I said I am skilled in the seventy-two magical transformations, including the sublime *body-beyond-body*. So watch this!"

Monkey plucked a handful of luminous white hairs from his chest, and threw them into the air. At once they changed into hundreds of little short-tailed white monkeys, who chattered and somersaulted among the gnarled branches of the solitary pine.

Then the little monkeys leapt down from the tree and cavorted among the horses' legs, far too nimble and quick for any weapon to touch. Monkeys surrounded the Polos and pulled at their robes . . . and tweaked cringing Niccolo's nose . . .

"*Stop*!" yelled Marco, barely able to suppress his laughter at the mortified expression on his father's dour face. "You *are* full of monkey tricks—but we Venetians also know a trick or two."

"We *do*?" asked his father.

"Of course we do!" said Marco. "We are powerful magicians."

"We *are*?" asked Niccolo, anxiously rubbing his beads.

"Then show me a trick," bellowed Monkey, who had changed all the little monkeys back into hairs.

"I will show you how I can disappear," said Marco. He moved beneath the pine tree which guarded the entrance to the cave, with the elder Polos, Peter, and Scholar Yen following closely behind.

"Speak not hastily, Marc," warned his father.

"Ha! That is a good trick . . . for a mortal man," said Monkey. "Show me how you can disappear."

So Marco Polo strolled inside the dark doorway of the cave—and disappeared.

"Why, I believe I can disappear too," chuckled Uncle Maffeo, and he also entered the cave—and disappeared.

"Let us *all* disappear," said Niccolo, with a shaky smile, as he ushered Peter and Scholar Yen into the cave.

"*That* is not a good trick!" called the white monkey, looking disappointed. "You did not *really* disappear—you just went inside the cave! You *all* went inside the cave. You all—*went inside The Lady's cave*!" He chattered his teeth. "*That is* not *fair*!" he wailed.

Kuei Mei; The Ardent Woman.
Thunder Stirs the Joyful Lake.
Capricious Beginnings Create Eternal Ends.

13

They found themselves inside a high-ceilinged grotto, whose arched roof was hung with icicles of phosphorescent stone. There was no sign of any life, and no light source except a curious glow from a formation of oddly twisted rocks at the rear of the cave. The heavy air had a sweet and musty odor.

Outside, they could still faintly hear Monkey jabbering and calling. "Come *back* . . . you will be sorry! *Sorry* . . ."

They walked cautiously towards the glowing and gnarled rock formation, as condensation from the stone icicles dripped coldly onto their heads. Then unexpectedly, a sweet and wordless chant filled the cavern, sung in a high-pitched woman's voice of such haunting beauty that they paused, each one caught up in a mute sense of yearning.

The song ceased as abruptly as it began, and the

same crystalline voice filled the cavern with a question. "Why do you rouse me from my eternal meditations?"

"Madam Immortal, we are lowly and humble ambassadors of the Great Khan, Kublai, requesting audience with your graciousness," said Marco with a bow, using his most polite and courtly Cathayan terms of address.

"The great *Khan*?" asked the voice from the glowing rocks, with a sparkle of laughter. "Have the grassland barbarians taken the Dragon Throne, then?"

"Yes Madam, for some time now. Since the fall of the Southern Sung dynasty on the shores of enchanting Westlake, the Mongols have held all of Cathay," said Niccolo Polo; feeling oddly hopeful that this woman, whose voice glittered like newly washed diamants of Golconda, would discuss sensible matters like politics and commerce . . . rather than mysterious oriental nonsense.

"Time has little meaning for the Cloud-Dancing Fairy," said the melodious voice. "I have not given thought to such worldly matters since the era of the Immortal Yellow Emperor."

"Of course not, Madam Fairy," sighed Niccolo, his hopes promptly dashed.

"But you do not speak in the accents of Cathay . . . nor of the grassland folk," said the voice. "Come closer so I might see who you are."

"Gladly, Madam," said Marco, eager to see this Cloud-Dancing Fairy, and somehow wishing she might resemble a buxom auburn-haired Italian wench.

"At your service, exalted Immortal," said Uncle Maffeo with a courtly bow, hoping the cloud-dancer's face and form would prove as delicious to Kublai as the music of her voice (and wishing that, perhaps, she might invite them to dine) . . .

They were all disappointed. As they moved closer, they discovered that the luminous stones were carefully, yet artlessly arranged in the manner of a traditional Cathayan rock garden. Jutting and jagged phosphorescent boulders resembled craggy hills and peaks. Water collected from the dripping stone icicles formed a quiet reflecting pool at their base. Cunning little pavilions of vermillion wood perched on the rock ledges. Their roofs were tiled with translucent green jade, with upturned eaves surmounted by mantels of miniature white jade foxes. Inside each pavilion burned a tiny stone lantern, and the reflected glow gave the convoluted rocks their mica-rich sheen.

At the summit of the diminutive rock-peak sat a seven-story octagonal pagoda carved of red cinnabar, and guarded by a pair of blue lapis foxes. The light of this toy pagoda was obscured by a thick and eerie shrouding of cob-webs. And behind those glistening webs, they saw the delicate outline of a tiny translucent figure in meditation posture.

"*Marón*! She is no bigger than my hand," whispered Maffeo. "Kublai will not be pleased at *all.*"

Her quicksilver laughter rippled through the cavern. "For many centuries I have practiced the *Way Which Lies Beyond Words.* I have taken the gold and cinnabar pill, and practiced the inner alchemy to transmute my physical form. I have played the game of White-Tiger and Green-Dragon with countless young men, to absorb their vital essence and unite the Yin and Yang. I have achieved immortality, and am like a foetus, ever undergoing rebirth. I float among the mountain peaks and sail around the moon; I have little need for a fleshy husk."

"But Kublai has need . . ." muttered Maffeo.

"Now that you have wakened me, I feel rather languid," sang the Cloud-Dancing Fairy. "It is time for me to replenish my stock of White-Tiger . . . the vital male essence. Perhaps that is why you were sent here to my bower . . ."

Marco felt a sudden strange tingling sensation, as of cold fire racing through his body. He stared at the tiny pagoda as if entranced, and it seemed to grow before his eyes. Then the cobwebs parted, and he saw a woman seated on a velvet cushion, more beautiful than any woman he had ever known. She was buxom as any Italian wench, yet with the willowy grace of a Cathayan.

Auburn tints glimmered in the shining black hair which coiled around her lithe form. She was clothed in a robe of diaphanous peach-colored silk, which highlighted the tints of her downy skin. Her glistening black eyes gazed directly at him—and seemed to beckon.

The icy fire raced through Marco's flesh and heated his mind to a boil, so he could think of nothing but the beauty of this woman—and his desire to embrace her. He stumbled forward, eager to reach the magical pagoda and its bewitching occupant . . .

"*Beware*, Master." Marco heard the echo of Peter's voice, as if from far away. "*Beware*, for this fairy may be a fox spirit, who takes the form of a beautiful young woman to drain the vital energy of men . . . suck them dry . . . and destroy them."

Yet Marco paid no heed to Peter's distant voice. He was ready to risk his vitality—or his life—for this unearthly woman's caress. Her burning black eyes seemed to draw him forward . . . to absorb him. Yet as his desire reached its peak, there came to Marco's mind the memory of a reeking battlefield . . . *and the woman who lay among the carnage winking at him* . . .

"*Stop*!" cried a high-pitched yowl. An agile little creature sprang at Marco and sent him reeling backward—breaking the hold of the fairy's gaze—and breaking her spell.

The mysterious pagoda receeded back to its web-shrouded, miniature size. And the cavern was filled with the shriek of the Cloud-Dancing Fairy's mocking laughter.

The men eyed the wee creature who had freed Marco from the fairy's hungry grasp. They beheld a tawny, catlike sphinx who perched before them on a rocky ledge, preening her silken fur. The sphinx gazed at them with a sly smile on her winsome face.

"Ho, Sphinx! You are very far from your home in the western deserts," said Niccolo Polo.

"No farther from home than you," chirped the sphinx, still busily preening her wings.

"True enough. But how come you to be here?"

"My master was a turbaned trader from the western desert sands, traveling eastward with a silk caravan. His camel was separated from the others during a blinding dust storm and, quite lost, he stumbled onto this cave. Here The Lady beguiled him—just as she would have enchanted your lad."

"And where is your master now?" asked Marco, still feeling dazed from the fairy's spell.

"That is a good riddle, for he is up there . . . with the others," said the sphinx, glancing at the arched roof of the cavern, where the stone icicles dripped their chilly rain.

"A good riddle indeed, clever Sphinx, for I see no turbaned trader clinging to the ceiling," said Marco.

"You see the fossilized remnants of the fairy's frenzied lovers," said the sphinx. "They were drained of their essence, and still bleed the last of their vital fluids."

"*Marón*! You mean those icicles are the riddled remains of *men*?" asked Maffeo, looking up and looking aghast.

Niccolo hastily crossed himself and muttered a few Hail Marys.

"Illusion, surely an illusion," said Scholar Yen calmly.

Enraged by the cloud-dancer's gruesome trickery, Marco drew a short knife from his belt, and slashed at the cobwebs which shrouded the fairy's cinnabar pagoda. Her shrill laughter became a piercing scream . . . and then she was silent. When Marco peered inside her glowing chamber, now exposed to the musty air of the cave, he found no Cloud-Dancing Fairy at all. She had dissolved into a heap of tiny dried white bones, as if some delicate bird had been buried in this place and left to decompose.

Marco shuddered—and felt suddenly wide awake. Again there came to his mind the memory of a battlefield he had seen during his journeys, where two Tartar hordes had recently clashed. It was while wandering still dazed, among the horrid battle scenes of dismembered men and even some children; here an arm or head and there a trunk, that Marco saw the black woman winking. The woman winked at him as she lay on the ground with her robe wound up around her thighs. Marco knew not of any blacks in this quadrant of the land, but as he came closer he saw that the woman was not really black, but more purple; the dark purple of an aubergine or eggplant decomposing in the sun. The purple skin had stretched over the swollen flesh, so here and there the thin integument had split and cracked, showing the yellow fat beneath. Marco had not known that human fat was yellow.

Despite the effect which had moved him to approach, dazed and confused as he was, the woman had not really winked at Marco. There were maggots moving in her eyes, and maggots in her mouth and nostrils. Thus had she seemed to wink. No arrow had intentionally shot her; merely had she strayed into the line of fire. Ill-fated she was, for she had not asked to be there, and neither had Marco asked to find her, lying dead among the scattered limbs and men of several races. And so he had moved on. Yet now he recalled how her winking eyes had drawn him . . .

"We owe you a debt of gratitude, gracious Sphinx, for saving my son from the horrible fate of being gobbled by that demon-fairy," said Niccolo Polo, with a low bow to the small feline creature. "How may we repay you?"

"I smelled the sands of the western deserts still clinging to your beards," said the sphinx. "I hoped you would take me home, where I might bask and preen in the hot sunlight again."

"Lord willing, we would be happy to take you home, though we cannot say when the fates—and the Great Khan—will permit our return to the west. Meanwhile, you are welcome to travel with us, lovely Sphinx. I have heard that your kind are good at solving riddles; perhaps you can help us unravel the maze that lies outside this terrible cave," said Niccolo, addressing the creature in properly praiseful terms, for all men know that sphinxes crave flattery.

"*Marón!* Let us quickly be gone from this dreadful place," said Maffeo, trying to avoid the droplets that rained from the icicles on the ceiling.

"You are great magicians, indeed, to reappear from that cavern unscathed," said Monkey, peering down at them from the gnarled pine with his fiery red eyes, as they emerged from the cave.

"You need no longer wait for the fairy's second word," replied Marco, slipping the web-coated knife back into his belt.

"*Ha!* The Lady is an immortal and is endlessly reborn. I have not heard her last song . . . nor have you," said Monkey, with a short bark of a laugh.

They hurriedly rejoined their party and rode away, with the little winged sphinx tucked into Marco's saddle bag. For a long while Marco could still hear the echo of the monkey's teasing laughter—and the memory of the Cloud-Dancing Fairy's enchanting, wordless song.

Chi Chi; Completion.
Fire Glimmers Below the Water.
The Superior Man Takes Arms Before Trouble Arises.

14

The obscure directions of the Great Khan's accursed scroll now steered them on a southward course beyond the labyrinthian ridges of the borderlands. Their rudimentary maps guided them along the network of rural lanes that jogged now westward to avoid an impassable mountain range, and now eastward to avoid some populous market town. For their presence might rouse the suspicions of the Cathayan townfolk who were ever watchful for the Great Khan's (ofttimes greedy) foreign tax collectors.

Many weary days later, the arid yellow wastelands of northwestern Cathay gave way to the dark and fertile soil of the moist river valleys. They paused briefly to replenish some supplies, and to refresh their animals at the rough and isolated ferry dock, nestled among rugged gorges where swallows nested. Then the boatmen rowed them across the broad and muddy Yang-tze Kiang River which marks the boundary of southern Cathay.

Some days journey further south, and the travelers found startling changes in the landscape. Here was a wide green valley, well-watered by a network of meandering streams that flowed from distant and mighty mountains to the distant and mighty river. Here were rice paddies carved into the rich valley floor, and terraced into the surrounding hillsides, whose upper slopes were overgrown with dense thickets of bamboo. Here were rough mud-walled hamlets built of wicker canes roofed with thatch, where rustic peasants lived and worked side by side with their water-buffalo brethren to till night-soil-scented fields.

There the party had halted, not so much from fatigue alone as from uncertainty about which way to go on. The relief and refreshment of a rushing mountain stream was welcome indeed. Men and mounts and pack-animals had drunk their fill; men had taken off baggage and saddles and (save for halters) harness. All had bathed and splashed for a good long while.

Some wild beasts . . . wild goat? . . . wild sheep? . . . antelope of odd design? . . . doubtless long accustomed to coming down to water here, had been unwise enough not to break the habit. Instantly a rush of arrows, of half-naked men splashing and stumbling with keen-edged knives between teeth . . .

So. Fresh meat, fresh-roasted. For a change.

Some village maids, coming down to the stream to fetch water in earthen jars, had stopped to giggle and stare at the outlandish strangers. Later, at dusk, they had returned with bright ribbons and early spring wildflowers braided into their long black hair, and with their earthen jars filled with ginger-spiced rice wine which they bartered for salt. Their high-pitched southern speech was strange as the buzzing of night insects from the reeds which lined the creek. They stayed to enjoy the grilled meat and spiced wine, and later their laughter became a musical entertainment for the weary men—for a giggling encounter among the reeds is the same in any language.

It would have been a nice place to settle. But the Great Khan had not sent them there to settle.

Marco Polo wrote in his travel diary by the flickering light of the campfire: "Indeed, the land of Cathay is so vast and varied, it is a wonder that the Mongols—or any foreign nation, however ruthless—could conquer and hold it."

The errant knight, sometimes called Hou Ying, returning from some mysterious foraging expedition of his own, paused to ask what the young sir was writing. When Marco read aloud this somewhat treasonous observation, the wandering knight sighed deeply and said in a low voice, "A wonder indeed, for although the mounted troops of the great conqueror, Genghiz, slaughtered nearly half the people of Cathay, it need not have been so."

"Indeed?" asked Marco, also lowering his voice so they would not be overheard. "I was told that the weak Sung Emperors could not raise a strong enough army to defend Cathay against the invincible Mongols."

"You hear what the scholars and aristocrats want you to hear," responded Hou Ying, with a flicker of heat in his lowered voice. "When the Jin Tartars held the northern capital of Kaifeng, a great peasant general rose up in the south. Yue Fei was his name, and on his back his mother had tattooed the characters: *Loyal Devotion to Country.* Yue Fei's mighty peasant army crushed the Jin Tarters at the battle of Yancheng, and they could have retaken all of Cathay."

"What happened?" asked Marco, glancing round about to be sure nobody was listening.

"The effete Sung aristocrats feared Yue Fei's victorious peasant army far more than they feared the Tartars—for there has ever been emnity between the scholarly nobles and the unlearned peasants of Cathay. The Sung Emperor accepted a peace treaty which made him vassal of the Jin. The Sung Prime Minister and his wife, and their two accomplices—*that cowardly gang of four*—had bold Yue Fei arrested and killed. Thus the Jin Tartars remained in control of the north, while the

Southern Sung nobles amused themselves with the pleasures of art and poetry and music, on the sublime shores of Westlake at their capital of Hangsai . . . where brave Yue Fei lies buried beneath the ancient pines. And thus did mighty Genghiz' Mongol troops find easy prey for their flaming arrows."

"And thus did Genghiz' grandson, the Great Khan Kublai, reunite and rebuild Cathay," said Marco in a loud and loyal voice (just in case they *had* been overheard). Then he abruptly changed the subject. "Indeed I have seen the thronging and splendid city of Hangsai and its beguiling Westlake, which lie south of Yangzhau on the Grand Canal; where we Polos were sent by the Great Khan to administer the salt tax. Well do I recall the noble mansions and gardens that surround the lake, and the great pleasure-barges that sail upon it; some with prows shaped like dragons and others like birds, and fully equipped for the lavish banquets which the sensual people of Hangsai so enjoy."

Uncle Maffeo joined them, and added his own voice now. "Indeed, Nephew Marc, nothing on earth offers more refreshment than a voyage on Westlake, viewing the grand and lovely city on its shores, the islands and temples, palaces and pavilions and pagodas, whilst drinking the amber-colored rice wine of the province. Listening to the sing-song girls playing their lutes, while dining upon the clay-baked fowl and sweetened-vinegared fish, the succulent little lake crabs and eels, and the wild mushrooms and honeyed fruits which are famous in that region. So let us speak of these sweet memories, friend knight—for it may not be wise to recall the bitter."

Some reasonable time they spent in restoring their travel-wasted limbs and in mending clothes and gear. At length, Niccolo Polo as eldest began to talk of whither next. "Of north and east we need not speak, having come from there, and I see no reason at this point to retrace our steps. Now, for my part, I would urge that we continue south, past that lone waterfall about half a *li* downstream." He paused, and in the space left empty by his silence, the Mongols and Tartars muttered and the Cathayans spat.

He continued; "I perceive there is a path which follows the river in its fast-flowing course from rocky basin to rocky basin. The stream at this point is fed by springs which we may see bubbling up from its bottom," he pointed; "and to go upstream, which is north, would find us tracing a mere trickle-brook. South, however, is bound to guide us to any number of places suitable for water-mills and so, of course, for settlements. Thus I urge that we go south."

Maffeo Polo paused in gnawing a haunch of roasted meat, licked his fingers and cleared his throat. "As always," he said, "I listen with attention and respect to my elder brother. I quite agree about east and north. *Not* east; *not* north. But as for *south*? I am told the Cathayans are so fond of the sound of water-wheels and fulling-hammers that they mention them often in their poems. *Use*ful things. Where there are water-wheels, there are people. Perfectly *ordinary* people, too. Staring and curious townspeople; correct?"

When the roasted haunch did not answer this query, he gave it an admonishing nip, then continued. "Well, if what we are seeking would be in a town, or near a town, or even within the ken of a town—why, we would all by now know *which* town. If I may say so, our royal master has very keen ears, and the name and knowledge of it would long ago have reached those ears." And with this perhaps not entirely correct, but entirely clear comment, he stopped.

But for a moment's thoughtful pause and another morsel of roasted meat only. "To go *west*," Uncle Maffeo said. "To go out into another wilderness of stone and sand, not knowing where they would next find water; well, it would not be pleasant."

But they had not come for pleasure.

"Yet if east and north or south are all ruled out," mused Maffeo, "what else is left? West, I reluctantly say. I say *west.*" He stared at the roasted haunch as if waiting for it to disagree; then fell glumly silent.

Softly, the moon-faced Mongols muttered, as was their wont.

It was now Marco's turn.

Although certainly he had heard his father and uncle speak, and even though he had taken note of their words, still his mind was pursuing its own thoughts. *The reedy river of the Trojan shore.* Why had that old schoolboy line come into his mind? What had the Trojan War to do with anything? —With anything now and here, that is.

Yet in some secret cavern of his mind the thought went on, following some secret thread. Entirely without considering what he was doing or why; he saddled his horse, adjusted the stirrups, mounted. He looked downstream past the waterfall into the rocky gorge beyond. He looked upstream to where the brook dwindled and was almost lost to sight in its narrow ribbon of greenery. He looked across the stream toward the silent desert, where rocks grew instead of plants.

Marco's eyes looked south, looked west, then looked at the reed-clogged marshland which lay to the southwest. '*The reedy river . . .*' His mind grew very clear.

"We are waiting for your opinion, Marco my son . . ."

"Speak up, Nephew Marc—speak up—"

The youngest Polo nodded. He raised his right hand. "Follow me," he said. His knees signaled his horse to move. The Mongols murmured. The Mongols muted their murmur.

"We go *this* way," Marco said. Without looking backward he rode on, heading neither south nor west, but south *and* west. Riding southwest in a diagonal course, across the reedy marsh and away from the stream.

He rode on, but slowly; when they had all finished saddling and loading, he was still in sight.

They followed after him through the reeds.

The way Marco had chosen eventually led to a lonely region of steeply jutting limestone hills, clothed in densely green bamboo. A swift river wound among these hills, like a demon's tongue lapping demon-teeth, and they followed its reedy course for many days.

"Demons there be in the caves within these demon-teeth hills. Thus say my devils . . ." remarked Peter the Tartar.

They heard no sound of demons or devils, only the axes of woodsmen, and the screams of magpies and monkeys; they saw few signs of settlement, for the landscape was too rugged for the plow. One day they met a surly huntsman clothed in rough hemp, and sandals and broad hat of woven straw. The man showed no eagerness to stop and chat with the Great Khan's men, but he was willing to barter some fresh-killed rabbits slung across his back for a cake of salt from their stores.

"Riddles riddle his face," said the little winged sphinx from Marco's saddlebag.

Later they came upon fishermen, poling their flimsy reed rafts from shallow pool to shallow pool; netting fat fish with the help of sharp-beaked black birds, with straw collars wound tightly round their long and slender necks. These birds obediently herded the fish into their master's waiting nets . . . and the collars stopped them from swallowing even a tasty minnow.

"Where there be fishermen, there be fish markets—and settlements," said Niccolo.

"And where there be settlements, there may be useful information about the way ahead. For a fact we must admit that our scanty maps, Kublai's damned mysterious scroll, and our own clever guesses have led us nowhere thus far—except into peril," said Marco. And with that they all agreed.

Soon enough the river broadened and small wooden sampans could be seen, ferrying produce from farming hamlets which lay in misted valleys between jutting green hills. Indeed the scene resembled a classical Cathayan landscape painting. Now Marco saw quite a bustle of traffic being poled or rowed, or towed by harnessed peasants and beasts upriver to a market town, which was just a vague mark on their vague maps.

Finally one day at sunset, the watch-tower pagoda and baked-brick walls of the town itself appeared as they rounded a riverbend. This town, shaded by the cinnamon groves which gave its name of Kue-lin, held no fame or importance in world power struggles or trade, yet it was the economic and cultural heart of this remote region.

The mud-brick town walls were surrounded by a moat, and stood several times the height of a man. The great main gate was made of thick, rough-hewn planks roofed with clay tiles of soft green, that reflected the colors of the demon-teeth hills. The tree-lined central thoroughfare wore the considerable luxury of flat paving stones; unlike the winding side alleyways of pounded earth and soggy muck, lined with walled villas and their orchards, pig-pens, and gardens.

The Polos and their men and beasts joined the throngs that entered the gates just before they closed for the night, and just as the oil lamps were lit. They wandered the main streets of the town, past dense jumbles of low structures built of whitewashed bricks, with carved wooden beams and grey clay roof-shingles. Small shops fronted the streets, while the shopkeepers' homes surrounded quieter courtyards in the rear.

Marco saw that the lamp-lit shops and stalls sold the usual assortment of Cathayan goods: bolts of cotton and silk, rice and sesame oil, fleshy melons, chives and floppy cabbages, thread and candles and incense, herbal medicines, dried and salted fish, pickled vegetables and preserved eggs, black or green tea and spiced rice wine, noodles and steamed buns, and the soft white curds, crunchy sprouts, and dark salty sauce of soy beans.

The lanes were abustle with peasants and peddlers in short blue cotton jackets and trousers, straw sandals and peaked hats, carrying goods in wicker baskets suspended from bamboo shoulder poles. Sometimes these goods were silent, but ofttimes Marco heard from the baskets an astonishing variety of squeals and grunts, cackles and barking yaps.

Merchants and local scholar-officials in loose silk robes, and felt-topped slippers and caps mingled with the peasants. Their wives rode upon soft brocade cushions in curtained sedan chairs carried by household porters . . . for their poor dainty bound feet were nearly useless for walking.

Shaven-headed Buddhist monks and nuns in grey robes chanted and thrust their begging bowls at the Polos, while Taoists in austere black cassocks and tall hats tried to sell them magical charms. Tribal folk from the hills, wearing brightly embroidered garments and filigreed bangles, watched the foreigners with wondering eyes—which were ringed with dark tattoos. Street musicians sang and played their pipa-lutes, while jugglers tossed cups and knives and fruit in the air. Children scampered everywhere, with the seats cut out of their tiny pantaloons so nature's calls might be more easily answered.

And everyone turned to stare and *stare* at the tall and round-eyed strangers, with their long noses and bushy beards, escorted by the Great Khan's mounted troops.

"*Marón!* How impudently they stare!" said Maffeo. "Yet it feels so fine to breathe city air again, and to smell the scents of commerce—and cooking."

"It smells more like the scent of nightsoil buckets to me," said Peter the Tartar.

"Unless it be the scent of demon's breath—or their human brethren," muttered the knight, Hou Ying.

Maffeo ignored the remarks of his nephew's impudent young servant and the wandering knight, as he continued to enthuse: "Indeed, brother Niccolo, I believe that—other than we Venetians—the Cathayans have the keenest commercial instincts in the world . . . excepting the Jews, of course. And the canny Cathayans produce enough *people* to buy any merchant's goods!"

The crowded streets seemed to concur with this comment, as Maffeo continued: "Let us find a good inn for the night, Marco, where we can drink and dine well, bathe and sleep comfortably, with a roof over our poor grey heads for a change, and where the horses can have fresh grain. Tomorrow we must make inquiries about the way ahead . . . but tonight my empty stomach grumbles and rumbles for a decent meal, so let us enjoy the pleasures of the town!"

"You had better take your enjoyments discreetly," said Peter in a warning voice, glancing behind them at four figures enveloped in rough sheepskin cloaks.

"What do you mean?" asked Marco. "How can we be discreet among all these curious stares?"

"I mean that my devils—and my two sharp eyes—tell me that we are not merely being observed. We are being followed," said Peter the Tartar.

Ting; The Caldron.
Fire Rises from the Kindling Wood.
The Upturned Cook-Pot is Cleansed.

15

The spacious inn and its adjoining tavern looked inviting, with its colorful curtains of peony design at the moon-shaped doorway, and its ornately carved and painted wooden beams, porches and balconies. Bright lanterns of crimson and gilt oiled paper hung in arcades between the low buildings, where tables were set among flowering plants and dwarf trees in clay urns. There laughing sing-song girls and their clients sang, and drank hot rice wine from tiny porcelain cups.

The affable proprietor, wearing a long robe of pale blue cotton and a blue cap, stood with his wife and several servant-concubines. They welcomed the Great Khan's emissaries at the moon-door with low bows, clasped hands, and broad smiles. The servants were told to lead the horses to the stables to be watered and fed, and to seat the horsemen, Peter and Hou Ying in a rear dining room for their supper. The innkeeper, himself, led the three Polos and Scholar Yen to a low table in a private room adjoining the main banqueting hall.

"The man's concubines and servants are Han-Cathayans," observed Niccolo, "but he and his wife are not—might they be Saracens?"

The proprietor placed a lavender-glazed jug of hot plum-flower wine and a wicker hamper of steamed dumplings on the table and said, "We are people of the *Hui-Hui*—the sect which teaches the book and plucks out the sinews. My humble family originally hailed from the old capital at Kaifeng, where we had a prosperous inn on Earth Market Street, near our Temple of Purity and Truth. We lost everything in a great fire that destroyed our prosperity in a single night. So we traveled along the southern Ling Canal to resettle in this remote provincial town where my uncle owned property, to try and regain our fortunes."

"In other words, you are Jews," nodded Niccolo. "I knew many of your people from my homeland in Venice—and hope I might live to see—and trade with them again. I know, for a fact, that the foods you eat are wholesome, and I may trust there is no dog meat in these dumplings." He broke open a steaming bun.

"Certainly not," said the innkeeper, wiping his perspiring forehead with a coarse towel. "We serve only the finest and freshest and tastiest mutton here."

"My tongue tells me you speak the happy truth," said Maffeo, popping a fragrant morsel in his mouth . . . and pausing to recall how happy was his tongue in the sorely missed banquet halls of Venice . . . when there came the fruit pastries, cooked with honey or the famous tinted sugars of Alexandria, and served with confit of costly ginger. And after that came slices of salted tunny fish, caught in the infamous fish-traps of Sicily, where the huge fishes were slain with harpoons; such times, it was said, the sea turned thereabouts red. And next, it having been assumed that a thirst was raised, came wine in large pewter pitchers, one pitcher for every four people. A rich bumpkin from some rural seigniory had proudly taken out his own cup at this; set with jewels it was . . .

So of course Nic had to have a look at it; just as well because the fellow's attention was diverted from the smirks and snickers produced by this naive and old-fashioned gesture. And Niccolo spoke into his ear, asking that he not embarrass the hosts by displaying a goblet "so costly and rich," which the fellow did willingly enough. Though in truth the vessel would not have bought a runt-pig. Venice was, after all, famous for its glass, but if any craftsman had attempted to sell such glass as jewels, he would not have lived to do so twice. "Which," said Nic later, "was only right . . ."

"Here you can rest easy," said the innkeeper, interrupting Maffeo's reveries. "And after dinner you can enjoy a troupe of wandering players who will perform tonight in our courtyard."

"*Before* we dine, we should learn the identity of those cloaked men who are lurking about in the street—watching us," said Marco. "Do you know them, innkeeper?"

"No, I have never seen those ruffians before, and their sheepskin cloaks seem rather excessive for such a balmy and humid spring eve. There are rough bandit gangs from the countryside lurking about these days, attacking travelers even in broad daylight. I will send the servants outside to make them state their business—or to drive them away."

"Perhaps they are neither bandits . . . nor illusions," remarked Scholar Yen. "They may be spies employed by the Great Khan's enemies, seeking to learn why we are here . . . though we, ourselves, can hardly answer that illusive question."

But when the innkeeper's servants approached the four cloaked men, they slipped away into the milling and babbling crowd. And disappeared.

The troupe of players was assembled on a low platform in the main courtyard of the inn, beneath hanging lanterns suspended from a bamboo trellis overgrown with sweetly flowering jasmine. Three musicians stood at the rear of the platform, wearing long black silk robes and caps, and green brocade sashes. Behind them was a curtain painted with a mountain-village scene.

The noisy after-dinner crowd gathered at tables ringed round the platform, and ordered their jugs of hot rice wine from the busy servants. Whilst one musician plucked the *pipa*-lute, another banged the clappers and drum, and the third played the side-blown *dizi*-flute in a manner which the elder Polos found decidedly discordant.

A large man wearing an ochre cotton coat and trousers bordered with a pattern of green leaves, and the grotesque make-up and rough hempen head-cloth of a ruffian clown, stepped to the front of the platform. He began realistically to imitate the calls of barnyard animals—rooster and pig, dog, laying-hen and horse—which drew the guffaws and the attention of the crowd. Then he recited the sing-song prologue of the play, which was based on the popular *Tales of the Outlaws of Liang-Shan Marsh*. Scholar Yen cleared his throat and explained the droll words to the Polos . . .

"They call me Tang the Ox, and to me a jug of warm wine is dearer than the body of a warm woman. My ox's thirst is hard to quench, and cash is always hard to get. Tonight I went searching for my good old friend, the respectable clerk Song Jiang, hoping to borrow a few coins for some village brew—for I heard rumors that he has come into some money."

Tang the Ox marched up and down the platform, searching for Song Jiang, then he dejectedly sang: "It seems that Mother Yan has snatched him first, for she hopes to reconcile him with her daughter Po-shi, who is Song's frosty and faithless concubine."

Tang the Ox strode off the stage. The curtain with the village scene was replaced by one showing the inside of Po-shi's bedroom, with its carved ebony bedstand hung with a red silk canopy; its clothing-rack, lacquered dressing-table, and ceramic wash-basin. The clerk Song Jiang, and his unfaithful concubine Po-shi, stood in the center of the stage—quarreling—while the discordant music played in the background.

Song wore thick make-up to emphasize his features, and a long scarlet silk robe, richly embroidered with a border of white cranes. He fluttered a round white-silk fan, and sang in an angry voice: "Your mother insisted I come to see you and drink some wine, but you are so cold to me that I am surely wasting my time."

Po-shi was a tall woman wearing a peach colored brocade robe, with flowing sleeves embroidered with peach blossoms. Elaborate ivory combs twined her thick hair into a low chignon. Her face was powdered white, with pink-rouged cheeks, and exaggerated blackened eyes and brows. Her nails were very long and tinted the color of her robe, and her fingers trembled dramatically as she sang: "Then give me back my contract of sale so I can marry the man I love!"

"I will gladly transfer your contract to that unlucky man," sang Song Jiang.

"And transfer all your property to me!" demanded Po-shi.

"What! Do you think I am a fool?" laughed Song.

"You were foolish enough to take off your sash when you sat down to drink, and I have hidden the contents of your purse; including the gold bar—and the letter from the outlaw leader of Liang-Shan Marsh—thanking you for past favors. Your employer, the honorable magistrate, will be very surprised to see them in the morning."

Now Song's fingers trembled. "I have always treated you and your mother well. You can have your contract . . . and the gold . . . but give me back that letter! Or the magistrate will exchange my lowly clerk's desk for a lowlier prison cell."

Po-shi laughed and refused to return the incriminating letter. In a panic, Song grabbed her and they tussled across the stage. They performed a series of wild acrobatic leaps and turns, until the enraged clerk drew his dagger—and slit his vindictive concubine's throat.

This, though fatal, did not prevent her from singing an accusatory lament which lasted quite a while . . .

Marco Polo sipped rice wine and watched the exotic action with fascinated eyes. He had always enjoyed the masked street-players of the commedia, as a lad in beloved Venice, and had briefly dreamed of joining a carefree wandering troupe.

Marco's eyes were especially drawn to the young woman who played Po-shi. Her features were Han-Cathayan, but her eyes and nose were more pronounced, and she was taller than most Cathayan women. Auburn tints brightened her thick black hair, and she moved with serpentine grace. Most pleasing of all, her feet were of normal size, unlike the grotesquely bound little feet of the upper class Cathayan women of the court . . . which always saddened and rather repelled him.

The set-curtain was changed for act two, and depicted the Song family temple, with a large gold Buddha on the altar. The musicians played a discordant Buddhist chant. Song Jiang was hiding forlornly in a niche beneath the altar, when a strutting constable came to arrest him for the murder of Po-shi.

As lamenting Song was led away, a black-bearded figure leapt onto the stage. It was the same bulky actor who had played Tang the Ox in the prologue, but now he was costumed as the outlaw leader, Black Whirlwind, with his bearded face painted into a fierce mask of black and white and red. He wore a black leather helmet, jacket, and trousers. His massive feet were bare, and he carried two great glittering double-edged battle axes. Black Whirlwind displayed his martial skills in a wild Kung-fu battle, bounding across the stage and twirling his axes in every direction like the whirlwinds which gave him his name. The music shrilled and the clappers clanged, as the outlaw leader freed Song Jiang and helped him escape to Liang-Shan Marsh.

Act three was set in lonely woods on misty blue mountain slopes. The musicians beat their drums with frenzied cacaphony as Song Jiang traveled alone through the eerie forest. Suddenly the ghost of Po-shi appeared, wearing a grim horned witch's mask painted with blue and green stripes. She stared with bulging black eyes and gnashed sharp wolf's fangs. Her long hair was unbound, and when she tossed her head it flew about in wild disarray. With trembling hands and superhuman strength, she dragged Song down with her to the underworld.

The fourth and final act was set in the underworld. The set-curtain showed the ten bull-headed judges of the Emperor of Death, wreathed in a halo of flames. Song Jiang stood at the gates of the underworld, pleading with the gatekeeper to release him. The gatekeeper was the same sturdy actor who had played Tang the Ox and Black Whirlwind, but now he wore a plain brown hempen robe, and the long, wispy white beard and hair of a recluse.

"My name is Hou Ying," he sang. "In life I was the reclusive eastern gatekeeper at the capital of the ancient Kingdom of Wei. I was befriended by the Crown-Prince, and told him the secret way to protect the kingdom against the evil Lord of Chao. When the prince's life was in danger, I slit my own throat—out of loyalty to a man who esteemed me—and I flew to the underworld on the back of a white crane. Thus I merely smile at your terror of this place . . ."

"*Marón!* That is the name of the wandering knight who has attached himself to our party," blurted Uncle Maffeo.

"Or at least *one* of his names," nodded Niccolo . . .

Suddenly a figure wearing a loose yellow silk blouse and trousers, and a winsome monkey-mask came leaping and somersaulting onto the stage in a brilliant acrobatic display. Marco at once recognized the actress who had played Po-shi.

"I am the Sage of Water-Curtain cave," sang the monkey, "and I demand to know the reason for this commotion . . . which has interrupted my contemplations."

"This weakling insists he does not belong here, oh Great Sage Equal to Heaven," replied the gatekeeper with a low bow.

"Have you checked your celestial ledger?" demanded Monkey. "That will tell you whether he was scheduled to arrive here today . . . or whether there was some infernal mistake."

The grumbling gatekeeper consulted his thick ledger and found that, indeed, Song Jiang's name was not among those who were scheduled to meet death that day. And so Song was released by the prancing monkey—amidst the clanging music and the cheers of the audience—to rejoin his allies, the rebellious outlaws of Liang-Shan Marsh . . .

As the cheering and the music died down, Marco summoned one of the servants with a nod and whispered, "I should like to meet that red-headed actress; perhaps for a private supper in my room."

Xiao Kuo; Small Gains.
Thunder Roars Above the Mountain.
The Singing Bird Flies Low.

16

Marco was led to a rustic tile-floored room, overlooking a rear courtyard planted with blooming plum trees. The carved wooden bedstead was furnished with a straw mattress, thick quilts, and blue silk draperies with the inn's peony design. A pewter lantern stood on a chipped red lacquered table, flanked by two matching chairs. A blue and white crockery wash-basin and rough towel lay on the wooden dressing table, beside a blue-glazed porcelain vase filled with scented jasmine. It was the most homey and comfortable room Marco had seen in a very long time, and he relaxed with a deep sigh as he removed his travel-stained leather boots and fur-lined cloak.

A servant poured hot water in the basin for Marco to wash his face, hands and feet; and laid the lacquer table with two pairs of ivory chopsticks, and two small blue porcelain wine cups. The servant departed and Marco bathed contentedly.

A short while later the servant reappeared carrying a black lacquer tray shaped like a lotus. This held a lavender-glazed jug of plum-flower wine set in a bowl of hot water to keep it warm. Little porcelain plates contained a variety of pickled vegetables, salted nuts and seeds, creamy preserved eggs, sliced cold chicken and fish, crisp fritters of minced mutton and chives, and candied fruits. The servant retreated with a bow, and a little later there was a light tap at the door, which Marco hastened to open.

The actress he had summoned stood in the doorway with downcast eyes, wearing an emerald quilted vest over a pale green silk blouse and long skirt, and green embroidered satin slippers. The lamplight played on the glints in her thick black hair, which was knotted into a chignon at the nape of her graceful neck, and held by a pair of simple ivory combs. She slipped inside, and sat shyly at the edge of a lacquer chair.

Marco poured wine for both of them; they both drank quietly and sampled the array of dishes with their chopsticks. "I enjoyed your show . . . you must be hungry after such strenuous acrobatics," said Marco, trying to break the awkward silence. "I was very amused by the monkey you portrayed . . . we recently met that rascal at an immortal fairy's cave in the northwestern dustlands."

"Many people hereabouts claim to have met Monkey—and his tricks. I have never seen him myself, though I am told my poor mimicry is clever," she said in a beautifully resonant voice. "There is a Dragon King's cave near here, lit by a single glowing pearl, where Monkey long ago stole his giant cudgel."

"I should *truly* like to see that cave!" cried Marco, quite forgetting his properly diffident Cathayan manners.

"Perhaps I can show it to you . . . sometime . . . if I can obtain my honorable master's permission," she replied, still awkward and shy.

"I am called Po-lo Mar-co, and I come from a far-off Latin land called Venice," he said. "My father and uncle are merchants who journeyed to Cathay, where the Great Khan gave us humble posts administering his salt tax."

"One calls me Su-shen," she said. "Though sometimes I am called Serpent-song because my body is so agile. I have no surname, and I come from noplace. I was born to a Cathayan slave-girl on a caravan crossing the dusty deserts of the silk-road, so I am a child of the camels' dung. They say my father was an adventurer from the grassy steppelands of the Huns, and that is why I am so tall and have this reddish hair—who knows? I was orphaned and sold to this kindly troupe of wandering players when I was yet a small girl . . . full of mischievous monkey tricks. I have lived and traveled with them ever since, refining my tricks into the acrobat's lowly art to fill my rice bowl." She bowed—very, very slightly—and held out her willowy hands for just a moment as though they held a bowl.

"So you know how it feels to have no fixed place?" asked Marco, gazing at her with wine-warmed eyes. "To belong to neither Europe nor Cathay . . . to be always the stranger, the observing outsider . . . gazing through the cane lattices into the warm lamplight of family homes, and never having a family or a home of one's own?"

"Yes, I know," she said simply. And to Marco's surprise, two tears slipped from her elongated black eyes and trailed down the ivory skin of her cheeks.

He reached a comforting hand to wipe them away, and she clasped his sun-browned skin with her lithe fingers, tipped with delicate peach-tinted nails. Her hand felt cool and silky to Marco. So did her scented lips as he bent his chestnut-haired head to kiss them. And kiss them again . . . with greater fervor. And again, as the wine-heat rose and sang its beckoning song. And again, as he saw the sadness lift and an answering heat rise in her eyes. And again, as they felt its urgent touch . . . and again . . .

Marco had known many women before, of many races, in many lands. But never was there one who matched him so closely, seeming to anticipate his every move and mood. Surely Su-shen, the lady Serpent-song, had also known many men; for a wandering actress is at any man's call, to play beneath the curtains of the stage—or the bed. Yet Marco sensed an awakening closeness in her, also . . .

Once the Great Khan Kublai had said to Marco, as they hand-fed the venerable carp in the Imperial Park's willow-lined Carp Pond of Great Seclusion; "You are a lusty young man, and your father and uncle, though not young, are sturdy and in full good health. All of you are well able to support wives, and to sustain women in all the needs which women need. Is it not so Po-lo?"

"Yes, my lord."

"Yet never have any of you mentioned being married. Are none of you married, eh?"

And Marco had answered, "No, my lord. My father was married to my mother in Venice, but she died when I was a lad."

"Ah, too bad. My own mother is beneath the burial mound too." A pause, then a deliberate shift in the imperial mood . . .

"*Pooh!*" cried his lord, a comical wry look upon his full and rosy face. "And *foh!* Almost I might swallow my ring in chagrin." —An oblique reference to the hollow behind the jewel where many a prudent man kept poison. "To think that the three of you be eunuchs unknown to me—or worse—that you, Messer Marco, would lie to me. No, no: do not protest. I understand. Po-lo Marco, Niccolo, Maffeo, all normal men; but none of the women whom you maintain are joined to you by some ceremony which *you* call . . . '*marriage*' . . . is it not so?"

"It is so, my lord."

"You see! . . you see!" The Great Khan was highly delighted with his own percipience. "I know all these things! My mother taught me; she was a Christian too, a Nestorian. No priest? No marriage as *you* call marriage. But why do you not conduct these ceremonial rites with a Nestorian Christian priest?"

Marco sighed a silent, lonely sigh at the thought of marriage to one of the childlike women with sad bound feet who hobbled about the court. Aloud he said, "Because the Nestorians are considered heretics, my lord."

The brow imperial furrowed. Then it cleared. Then he gestured. " 'Heretics;' you call the Nestorian Christians '*heretics*?' Ahah, that curious concept! Thus my mother explained it: *you* say that your great holy woman, Mariam, was the mother of your god. And *they* say that the great holy woman, Mariam, was the mother only of the body in which your god dwelt. Not so? You see, I know! I know! Also, you Franks . . . you Latins, reverence images as do the Buddhists, but the Nestorians and Moslems and Jews not so. Among the *Hui-Hui*, the Moslems eat camels but not horses; the Jews eat neither. Nor do they eat beef or mutton unless they extract the sinew from the thigh and dispose of it. Why do they not? Eating sinew makes one sinewy, is that not obvious? But they say that someone called *Mosa* is the father of their prophets, and forbids them to do so. Eh?"

Not fully understanding what he was saying, but remembering that old, old, very old Friar Paul had said it; Marco answered, "The Law of Moses was nailed to the cross and is dead and reprobate."

The face of the Great Khan, which had been pensive, now suddenly became animated. "Quick! Throw the Old Buddha Carp a great piece of rice-cake, and while he is taking it, throw two smaller pieces to the two not-as-big ones over there . . . else they shall not get any . . ."

Marco tossed bits of rice-cake to the gaping-mouthed elder fish that clustered beneath a great flowing willow tree.

The Great Khan resumed: "My mother reverenced very much the cross, and I gave her—often—gold for her priests, and incense to burn before it. What a good thing that was for me to have done! I am sure that her god was very pleased with me, whatever may be the true truth of his holy mother, Mariam. But I am *not* pleased with your Pope! Oh no! If he had sent the hundred *non*-heretic priests I asked for, I could marry you to a suitable lady—to create a suitable alliance for *me*!"

Marco roused himself from the thoughts of half-slumber, and reached his hand to caress the woman who lay beside him beneath the quilts. The first lavender light of dawn filtered through the window lattices, and he raised himself up on one elbow, smiled softly and said, "Let us dress quickly and slip away from the inn before anyone else wakens. I want you to show me that Dragon King's cave . . . without either of us having to beg for leave."

"I should not go without telling my master . . . if he finds out . . ." Then she threw back her head and laughed merrily. "Why should I fret if he finds out? It is my humble duty to entertain, and if you would find the cave entertaining, Po-lo Mar-co, why so would I!"

They dressed hurriedly in the clothes they had left scattered about during the night, and hastened to the stables to saddle Marco's shaggy pony. Just as they were about to ride off, something landed beside them with a light thud . . .

"What a *lovely* creature," said Su-shen, reaching down to stroke the winged sphinx, who had flown from the branches of a flowering plum tree, where she had been curled asleep.

"Lovely sees as lovely is," said the sphinx with an enigmatic smile. "Shall I come with you, young master?"

"Is that a riddle or a request, Sphinx?" laughed Marco.

"The caves are riddled with riddles," remarked the sphinx, leaping lightly into the saddle-bag. So they trotted away from the inn, with Marco seated in the saddle, and Su-shen perched lightly behind him with her hands clasped around his waist, and her silk-clad legs curled with serpentine grace around the horse. While the smiling sphinx poked her tawny head from the saddle-bag for Su-shen to stroke.

The Dragon King's Crystal Cave was at the northwestern end of the town, where the jutting demon-teeth hills met the dawn mists of the river, which formed part of the city moat. They tethered the pony, climbed up a steep pathway through bamboo thickets, and found the reed-choked entrance to the vast cavern.

An immense glowing pearl, fully the size of a man's head, and of a value unimaginable even to Messer Niccolo Polo, rested in a niche in the center of the cave. The shimmering pearl illuminated the pillars and spires and oddly twisted rock formations.

"Is this where that rascal Monkey stole the Dragon King's iron cudgel?" asked Marco.

"Do I hear that thieving monkey's name?" rumbled a deeply deep voice, and something impossibly huge coiled and stirred deeply deep within the cavern.

"We are mere travelers admiring the beauty of your cave, Lord Dragon," called Marco.

"Hah! Once this dank cave was part of a magnificent crystal and coral Naga-Dragon Palace in the oceanic abyss, guarded by giant prawn generals mounted on fighting crabs, who led an army of stinging jellyfish soldiers. The mother-of-pearl dome was supported by a massive iron pillar that fixed the depths of all the rivers and seas in the billion worlds. Then that tricky monkey appeared and asked to borrow some weapons. I offered him anything in my arsenal—but nothing would satisfy him but the mighty iron pillar—which he stole to use as his cudgel. When he took the sea-fixing pillar, the destroying waters flooded my castle and washed it away to dry land. Here I remain, surrounded by the petrified remnants of my army and my palace, with only a pearl resting in the niche that once held the pillar . . . to recall my former grandeur. Have you seen that wretched monkey? *Have you?* Merely telling my tale makes me angry, do you hear? *Angry!*" The dragon roared, and the walls of the cave began to tremble and shake.

"Shall we be going, young master?" asked the sphinx, as loosened rocks fell from the cave walls . . . and this time her query was clearly a request, not a riddle.

They raced out of the quaking cavern and down the

hill, and leaped onto the horse with a peal of excited laughter. "Would that our adventures could go on . . . and on forever," Marco said, as they galloped away.

"They could . . . if you really wished it," murmured Su-shen.

"How so?" asked Marco, clasping her hand which clasped his waist.

"My master—he is the burly man you saw in the play—talks of selling me as a concubine, just like poor Po-shi. He needs to raise money to pay some gambling debts, and says he can always train a new and younger acrobat; it is time to make a profit off me before my looks and strength begin to fade. I have lived in dread ever since he began to speak this way. But my tears would turn to joy—if the man who bought me were *you*!"

"Alas, life with me would be a long and strange and difficult journey," said Marco with a sigh.

"A child of camels' dung has no fear of journeys," she replied.

Marco thought for a long, long moment. A woman who could share the rigors of his travels. He had never dared hope to meet such a one—and could never hope to meet her match again. "I will do it!" he cried. "I *will*!" His hazel eyes glinted with golden exhilaration in the rising sunlight. "I will have my father negotiate with your master at once."

Then he turned in the saddle to kiss Su-shen again . . . and again.

K'un; Devotion.
Yellow Earth Above; Yellow Earth Below.
The Lively Mare Finds Southwestern Friends.

17

"No, Marco. Absolutely *not*!" said Messer Niccolo Polo to his son. "The journey is too dangerous for a woman—and she is too dangerous for us. One woman traveling among so many men is sure to cause trouble."

The three Polos stood in the courtyard of the inn watching the players rehearse. Su-shen, wearing a yellow silk jacket and trousers, her hair tied with yellow ribbons into two serpentine-tails, performed an acrobatic routine. She lay face-down on a straw mat on the platform, with her head and limbs arched upward in improbable angles. One hand carefully balanced platters, bowls, and cups filled with water onto her upraised head, feet and the other hand, until wobbling and sloshing stacks of crockery towered above her. The inn's servants, and a table full of chess-playing merchants stared and pointed and guffawed. Then with equally delicate care, she lowered each dish to the ground once more.

"*Marón!* She *is* clever," said Maffeo. "But does not her art defy the clumsy spirits—and thus provoke them? And have you not known—and enjoyed—many a winsome wench along the strange roads we have traveled?" Uncle Maffeo winked slyly and munched a handful of salted seeds.

"I have known many; yes," said Marco. "Enough to know that she is . . . well . . . special."

"Time enough to think of *special* after we have gone *home*, my son," said Niccolo with unusual heat in his voice, as he worried his jade beads. "What if Kublai soon gives us leave to go, Marco? What then? Your uncle and I are lonely men too, yet we have never burdened ourselves with wives and concubines, children and households in this heathen place. Our wealth has remained in our portative jewel-pouches, and our affections have remained in Italy, because we wanted always the freedom to return to our starling-crested home. And we are counting on you to return with us, lad—to *Venice*—where you can be matched to a Christian lady of our own station who will provide the Polo family with *heirs*. And let me remind you, Marco, that Christian ladies do *not* willingly share their households with concubines! What would you do with your pretty Cathayan actress then? Drown her in a canal? Her master will place her with an established gentleman who can provide all of her needs for all of her days. Many proud men will be eager to buy her, and to give her the finery that women crave. You do her no favor to buy her on whim . . . and then abandon her. You do your family no favor . . . nor yourself. I say *no*, Marco. No!"

Su-shen was doing a headstand on a porcelain urn, while whirling two bright rice-paper umbrellas on the soles of her bare feet. The blue and white urn was balanced on a wooden stool, which was balanced on a small red lacquer table, which was balanced on the brawny shoulders of the two actors of the troupe. When she finally landed, Marco gestured her aside.

"What did they say? I saw them examining me like a stewing hen in the marketplace," said Su-shen, with a nervous little laugh.

"They said *no,*" replied Marco sadly. "They hope to return to Europe soon, and they say the journey is too difficult for a woman. *I* know they are wrong—but I am as much my father's subordinate as you are your master's. You must leave word with the innkeeper where you will go next, and leave word at the posting station of each town that you visit with your troupe. Here: you can use one of my personal seals to sign your messages. If our mission for the Great Khan succeeds, he will reward me with anything I desire—and I desire *you,* Su-shen. I will track you through the posting stations, and summon you to Khanbaluc. Keep your master at bay just a while longer. I *will* find you again . . . I promise."

"If I have not already been sold," said Su-shen, with a little shrug, and a little laugh, and a little welling of tears in her eyes. Then she returned to the platform with a frustrated flurry of acrobatic feats. Her body light as a sparrow's, she bent her limbs into elegant contortions, then twirled and leapt, and somersaulted like a floating feather in the wind.

Marco wondered what trick of the mind or eye made places look most beautiful when leaving—and especially when leaving something—or someone behind. When they had entered this provincial town of Kue-lin, Marco had felt exhausted and confused. He and the men and their mounts needed to rest, and the Polos needed to consult and consider the way ahead. Now the men had dined well, slept indoors for several nights, and fresh mounts and supplies, and rudimentary maps had been obtained from the imperial posting station.

All of Marco's senses had been fully wakened by his encounter with Su-shen, and he felt a great wistfulness as they rode through the town, admiring its exotic beauty. Marco watched the early-morning bustle of townspeople busy with their families and chores. Vendors sold bowls of steaming rice-porridge and dumplings from cookstands along the roadway, which was lined with cinnamon trees. Grubby children in bright quilted jackets, with heads shaved save for the topknots, played at noisy games in muddy alleys where chickens and pigs poked for scraps. Here a farmer in a wide straw hat, leading his placid water-buffalo to plow, stopped to bargain with a peddler carrying fresh bamboo shoots in heavy wicker baskets hung from bamboo shoulder poles. There a skinny dog stood barking among the potted chives on the prow of a sampan, which provided both a floating home and livelihood for the fisherfolk who poled the wood-and-wicker craft into swift river currents.

None of them seemed to notice the special charm of the upturned thatched and tiled rooftops in the pale morning sunlight, nor the beauty of the surrounding hillscape. The rows of abruptly towering peaks rose like pinnacles of folded green brocade, until they disappeared into distant river mists. Yet the townsfolk did not pause to admire their beauty, for they were busy filling the family rice-bowls—and they were not leaving something—or someone behind. Marco gazed at the verdant loveliness of the town, and the gleaming river twining among the demon-teeth hills, whilst the wistfulness clouded all he beheld.

Yet even Marco had little time to enjoy such tender moods. After they passed the mud-brick city walls, and the crowds and bustle thinned, they were soon again on a lonely country pathway that ran parallel to the river through dense thickets of bamboo. Marco had lagged far behind the others to be alone with his melancholy thoughts—which were abruptly interrupted.

Four cloaked shadows slipped through a thicket. Four shadowy figures in sheepskin cloaks surrounded his pony. Iron-hard fingers clamped across Marco's mouth, as four pairs of powerful arms dragged him struggling to the ground, and shoved him into the gloom of a narrow bamboo-shaded glen.

"Who *are* you?" Marco managed to gasp, as four sharp little daggers aimed directly at his throat.

"*We* speak; *you* listen," snarled the tall and sallow man who seemed to be their leader—a Cumanian of the western steppes, by the look of his face and the embroidered blouse beneath his cloak.

"You want gold?" asked Marco.

"We want more than gold," said the Cumanian gang-leader, who spoke in the cultured accent of northern Cathay. "We want knowledge of Kublai's plans to conquer the gilded city of Pagan, in the steamy southern jungles of Bur-mien."

"I have no such knowledge," said Marco, quite truthfully. "I can only tell you what all men already know. Last year—1284 in the Latin reckoning—the Great Khan's bowmen defeated the war elephants of the Bur-mien king, Narasihapati, who fled his golden capital of Pagan. But I know of no plans to advance down the river valley to take the capital itself."

"You *say* you have no knowledge," replied the sallow Cumanian. "Yet why else would Kublai send emissaries to these southern border regions—and why else would you meet in hidden caves with jugglers and acrobats? For it is known that Kublai plans to use an army of such lowly folk in the conquest of Bur-mien, because he values their agility in jungle warfare."

"Indeed, you have more knowledge of such matters than I," said Marco. "We have merely been sent hither to administer the salt tax . . . and watched the graceful acrobats' amusing tricks." Marco thought of Su-shen, and inwardly sighed—and inwardly decided that his father had likely been right—this was no fit journey for even a bold-spirited woman.

"There is no lack of greedy officials in these parts to harass the peasants over a few grains of salt," said the sneering Cumanian. "We know you are here on some secret mission. Why else would you demand obscure maps from the posting station? You see, we have followed your every move. Now tell us your business here . . . or taste the sweet edges of our well-honed little daggers."

And to emphasize his point, the steppeland bandit traced a thin—and exquisitely searing—line of blood on Marco Polo's unhappy throat.

Feng; Abundance.
Thunder Roars Above the Lightning Flare.
The Great King Shines Like the Midday Sun.

18

But *who* . . . and *why* . . . ? Marco wondered, as the blood trickled lazily past the small silver cross worn round his neck. And his own anguished mind supplied the answer as recognition abruptly dawned. This Cumanian was no mere bandit chieftain. This was a minor official named Kutan whom Marco had known at the palace of Khanbaluc. He was the son of a beautiful Cumanian concubine and the evil and corrupt minister, Aqmat Bemaketi, who had been assassinated by Cathayan rebels several years before.

Marco well recalled the scandal which had shaken the capital. Lord-Governor Aqmat of Transoxiana was the most powerful man in Khanbaluc after the Great Khan. Some said he was a sorcerer who used the black arts of entrancement to bend Kublai to his will. Indeed, Marco recalled that Lord Aqmat's forceful black eyes cast their hypnotic spell on all who were in his presence.

Thus could he destroy any man who was his enemy and raise to power any man who was his ally; so all men feared him. Thus Aqmat could take all the beautiful women and wealth he desired, for himself and for his many sons—some of whom were *very* lustful and greedy men. He ruled for over twenty years, and finally the Han-Cathayans could endure it no longer, for he made them feel like slaves in their own land. Thus they formed a secret society and plotted to assassinate Lord Aqmat . . . *and all men wearing beards* . . . Saracens and Mongols, Tartars and Christians. For these outlanders were seen as the oppressors who stole their Cathayan empire through brutal conquest, their wealth through heavy taxation, and their daughters through rape and coercion.

On the astrologically appointed night, the conspirators lured Aqmat from his lavish mansion in the old city of Tai-ting to the winter palace, blinded him with a sudden blaze of candles, and cut off his head with their swords. The Mongol guards acted quickly to uncover the plot, and the revolt was swiftly suppressed. The ringleaders were executed, and the Cathayans retreated to their docile and mercantile ways.

Yet in a sense the revolt was successful, for the sorcerer's spell over Kublai was broken. When the Great Khan learned of the evil his governor had done, he denounced Aqmat. Marco well remembered the jeering and jostling crowds of Cathayans, gathered to watch Lord Aqmat's body thrown into the icy square outside the palace of Khanbaluc—to be torn apart by the ravening dogs.

The most evil of Aqmat's sons had been flayed alive; yet some had escaped. Among them was Kutan, who now stood before Marco fingering his bloody dagger. It was rumored that Kutan, the son of a steppeland mother, had joined forces with Kublai's haughty rival, Kaidu Khan of Samarkand . . . the bold Wolf of the Steppes.

Like Kublai, Kaidu Khan was also a grandson of the Great Conqueror Genghiz, whose mounted hordes of barbarian bowmen had plundered and burned and massacred nearly half the population of Cathay. Like Kublai, Kaidu Khan also claimed the title of *Khakhan*—Great Khan. *Unlike* Kublai, Kaidu Khan had not become a civilized and Sinicized Son of Heaven. While Kublai concerned himself with rebuilding and governing the empire, Kaidu and his followers remained faithful to the rude nomadic life of true Mongol warriors. His bold horsemen nipped and bit at Kublai's western flanks—like the howling wolves of the steppes.

Now all was clear: Kutan, the rebel son of the assassinated sorcerer, Lord-Governor Aqmat, had escaped to the flowing grasses of his Cumanian motherland to become a spy for Kaidu Khan. He hoped to extract information about Kublai's planned invasion of Bur-mien from Marco through threats and torture. The only thing that was *not* clear was what Marco should do . . .

"*Speak*; speak quickly—or one flick of my knife will make sure your silent tongue never speaks again." Kutan prodded Marco's lips with the point of his dagger . . . and again drew blood.

Marco had a painful-horrid vision of sundry tongueless beggars whom he had seen, mewling and drooling in sundry lands. With an angry twist of his fear-quickened body, and with his time-sense expanded by terror and rage, Marco wrenched free of the two cloaked spies who grasped his arms and raced down the morning-shadowed glen. The four ruffians pursued him, and Marco backlashed with his left leg and kicked the closest one in the loins. The man bent over and screamed with pain, and Marco whirled around and slammed his right foot in a leaping kick to the shoulder that knocked the traitor to the ground.

This maneuver, called Duck and Drake Feet, he had learned from his martial arts instructors at Khanbaluc. But three more cloaked rebels still pursued him—and Marco knew no tricks to escape them all.

Of a swift sudden, he heard a tremendous roar like an enraged bull elephant, and another figure burst into the glen; immensely tall and broad and golden haired, wearing a shaggy fur shirt, and wielding a mighty battle axe which he whirled above his head as if it were a weightless toy. Behind him was a lithe Cathayan wearing a red leather helmet and boots, and red leather mail over a black silk jacket and trousers, and brandishing a tri-pointed double-edged sword. The great blond bear of a man charged at Kutan with a growl and hacked at his forehead with the broadside of his axe. The Cumanian crumpled on his knees to the ground, and stared at his own dripping blood.

The slight Cathayan flourished his sword in a graceful move called Torching the Heavens, and whipped it across the chest of the nearest brigand, tearing through cloak and blouse to leave a bright red stain. The four Cumanian rebels and their daggers were clearly outmatched by Marco and his two new-found allies. They leaped up and scuttled like startled insects—their speed enhanced by fear—into the surrounding dim-lit bamboo thickets, leaving a sticky vermillion blood-trail.

"We follow?" asked the immense blond, panting with exertion.

"No," said Marco. "Let them return to their master with their mission failed. Kaidu Khan will deal with them severely, as is his brutal way—and will learn that his spies cannot take us so easily as the Bur-mienese tribes snare elephants in pits. And let me thank you for your aid, my good men."

"Saw riderless horse—saw trouble," said the blond with an abrupt nod.

"You must be very far from your homeland," said Marco.

"*Home*land?" asked the blond with a puzzled frown. "Yes, homeland very far. North. Very far north. And west. Now I wander the roads with yon mute young page. Has tongue but cannot speak."

"Come ride along with me, you and your page, further up the road to meet my father. He will want to reward you."

"Yes; now we ride along with you," said the mighty blond, and he spat into the dark blood upon the ground.

* * *

How Marco and the big Northman managed to communicate around the campfire that night might have baffled those from places where folk were of one same speech and knew no word of any other. But all Venetians began to learn other languages almost from their cradles, and not seldom—if nurses or other servants were foreign—actually *in* their cradles. German and Sclavonian one learned almost thoughtlessly at canal-and-dock side, Latin and Greek instruction with rather more care. Greek was, after all, the major language of the Venetian Overseas Territories; its foreign colonies, wrested for the most part from the wreckage of the Byzantine Empire. A knowledge of Arabic was essential for the Saracen trade. With the Turkish tide rising daily higher through the Levant, any even fractionally intelligent merchant began to learn some Turkish.

And having gotten any knowledge of any language inevitably made it easier to get knowledge of any other language.

The brawny Norseman's yellow hair was likely no yellower, his blue eyes no bluer, his ruddy face no ruddier, than those of . . . say . . . a Saxon's or an Englishman's. Yet there was a something about his yellow hair and blue eyes and ruddy face which was distinctly . . . well . . . *Norse*. Gothic Swedish. *Varangian*, as the Russ called them. How came he hither to far Cathay, a journey even longer (counting from its first beginning) than Marco's own?

Marco asked him. The Northernman thought a long time. Then, "Mostly I walk," he answered.

Why O-la-fu—for such was his Cathayan name—had "mostly walked" all the way from, at least, Constantinople (*Micklegarth*, "Great City," the Northmen called it) to far Cathay, instead of rowing or sailing (or even "mostly walked") back home to his native islands . . . forests . . . fjords, Marco did not ask. But bit by bit the younger Polo came to two conclusions. *One*: that the man had left the Eastern Emperor's Varangian Guard before his enlistment was up—and without permission. *Two*: that the man had not left his misty Northern home just to seek excitement and adventure in foreign parts.

They spoke far into the night, Marco and O-la-fu, in bits and pieces of languages fitting together not well but well enough: in the largely Italic *Lingua Franca* of the Mediterranean . . . in the extremely unclassical Romaic Greek . . . in *this* Slav tongue and *that* Slav tongue from the Balkans up and over, to the rivers and lakes of Great Russland . . . in the diminishing Eastergothic of the Crimea . . . in fragments of sundry Turkic tongues of Asia Minor and Asia Major . . . words from the Latin Mass . . . quite a few words from the Tartar tongues and even a few from the Cathayan. And if, with all this, the Venetian learned a little Varangian, and the Varangian learned a little Venetian? Good.

The Northman first said his name was *Olaf*. Then he said it was *Olavr*. So Marco fell into the habit of calling him *Oliver*, after the manner of the English. But the Asians called him *O-la-fu*—when they were not calling him Sky-Eyes, Fire-Beard, Out-land Demon, or Great-Nose. They called him these last two names behind his back. *Very* far behind his back. For Olaf/O-la-fu/Olavr/Oliver was very tall indeed, and his sun-reddled body bore many scars. *Many* scars.

The Asians did not think hand-to-hand combat, battle-axe against broadsword, showed very good sense. They thought that shooting arrows from galloping horseback showed greater sense (and greater skill)—at least until their arrows were spent. But they conceded that the other way showed great courage.

So late at night, surrounded by the circling campfires of an inner guard of Mongols, and they by the circling campfires of an outer guard of Tartars; sometimes paced, sometimes sat, oftimes scowling, never smiling: Oliver. With his mute-silent page slipping like a shadow beside him, and cradling his great battle-axe in his great battle-scarred hands.

"Are you never afraid?" asked Marco.

"*Never*. Never afraid!" answered Oliver.

"But why not? It would be natural . . . sometimes . . . axe or no axe."

Oliver gave an emphatic shake of his head, an emphatic tug at his reddish-blond beard. "Because I have which protect me better than axe."

Asked: "And what might that be?"

Oliver gave a long look away, then turned the long look back to Marco. He reached inside his shaggy shirt (*Saerk*, he called it, and said it was made of *bear*-skin; but the emphasis escaped Marco). Then Oliver pulled out a pouch on a thong. And from the pouch produced a piece of bone or stone; for sure it lacked the swirling grain of ivory.

"What odd scratchings be these?" asked Marco.

Oliver gave a bark perhaps intended for a laugh. "Not scratchings. *Ho!* Scratchings; *no!* Be futhark."

"Be—what?"

"*Runes*, some call. Some call futhark. Northern folk, like, letters. Like—how say? Like—*sanctus* . . ."

"Holy?"

"Holy. Put on gravestone, like. On rune-stick, like. Witch-mark, like. Runes. Futhark. Look . . ." His long and calloused finger pointed here, pointed there . . .

"*Fay, Rider, Ice, Thorn.*
Old, Raider, Canker, Norn.
Year, Sun, Hail, Bull.
Man, Lake, Birchrod, Wool.
Thorn, Norn; Norn, Thorn . . ."

Thorn, sang the faint echo as the sparks flew upward into the vasty dark . . . and then it was lost in the sighing winds of night.

The list went on. Sometimes the translation of these odd and angular characters was difficult to understand; sometimes it was impossible. Were the names of *things* represented by the signs? Were they the names of letters? Were they . . . ? A look at Oliver's awe-strained face decided Marco not to laugh, despite the funny sounds. Instead he asked, "What does it mean?"

Oliver turned the object over. The obverse lines of character were shorter. He was silent. Then said, "Means

. . . like . . . *'Ave Maria save Oliver from evil.'* " He gave a single great nod. Returned amulet, talisman, whatever it was, into pouch; and pouch into the bosom between his own shaggy pelt and his shaggy shirt.

"That is indeed very *sanctus*, Oliver."

One more deep, abrupt nod. A grunt. Then without farewell, Oliver was off. Summoning his wordless page, and swinging his great battle-axe from hand to hand, O-la-fu resumed his nocturnal, dutiful, relentless, loping prowl. Could he see into the dark? Could he smell man-flesh on the wind? The northman and his silent page kept guard, walking to and fro; fro and to. A-walk and a-prowl, Oliver kept guard.

Marco thought there might be more to this than met the ear. It might be more than *Maria* alone to whom the runes were writing *Ave*. The Norse were fairly new Christians, after all . . . but they had fairly old memories.

Certainly they were people much given, upon insult or jealousy or other provocation, to fall upon and smite each other, face to face and hip and thigh with their immense weapons. Whereas the more civilized and subtle and sedate Venetians would hire a silent, smiling *bravo* with a knife beneath his cloak. Or, *at least*, invite the offender down into the cellar to taste the wine . . .

Then his eyes of a swift sudden filled with tears. Ah, the wine of Venice! Ah, the fruit of Venice! How he would love to present them to Su-shen. And the sweetmeats, the alpine-snow-cooled drinks. The marble villas and palaces, the gilded paintings and tapestries, the rich-burden-laden gondolas on the splendid canals of Most Serene Venice. City sole and unique in all the world, great merchant-mart of the earth; draped with pearls, bride of the sea, and hung with cloth of gold . . .

Venice!

Then a curious thought came to Marco's mind. One of those rune-scratchings looked . . . somehow . . . familiar. The oft-repeated one which meant *thorn*. Could it be the same as the mysterious marking on Kublai's accursed scroll? Marco summoned Oliver from his prowl, and roused drowsy Scholar Yen. *Indeed*, the dancing firelight showed that the rune which Oliver called *thorn* was the *same* baffling symbol which appeared and reappeared on the scroll!

How much magic might one night hold?

Marco felt a swift surge of excitement as they compared the markings on Oliver's amulet, and those on the map-scroll which they carefully lifted from its cocoon of many-hued silken threads. This new puzzle-piece might help them unravel the complex mystery of the Sleeping Beauty's resting place. Might help them find the enigmatic location of her repose; might win them Kublai's great gratitude—which could bring Su-shen to him, and take them all home to the Palazzo di Polo beneath the four-starling shield—in beloved Venice!

Does the Sleeping Beauty rest in a place of *thorns*?

III
They Find Lively Beauties

Chieh; Escaping Danger. Thunder Above Rain Brings Release. Moving Forward Brings Buds Into Bloom.

19

The expedition had begun with a caravan of fifty horses and camels—the latter not the taller and slimmer, single-hunched ones of Arabia, but the shorter and more thick-set, double-hunched camels of Bactria (the racing-camels, the so-called dromedaries or *hajjanah*, did very well indeed in lands of hot and dry sands; but suffering as they did from ice, cold, and snow, were not favored for northern or mountainous climes). As the caravan reached more tropical zones, and as their rations dwindled, the camels were gradually left behind.

In some other parts of the world, fifty beasts might not have been considered enough, but no part of the world had such an efficient posting-system as the lands of the Great Khan. More than 10,000 posting-stations (called *yamb*) were located almost everywhere, at well-calculated intervals throughout the empire. Arriving at one, a traveler on official duty had only to hold up the slender metal tablet inscribed with imperial characters and emblems, which served as an internal passport. He would be instantly furnished with shelter, supplies, and with not only as many fresh mounts as he might need, but as many of the 200,000 imperial horses as he might demand.

Minor local officials on minor local errands carried passport-tablets of brass or bronze, good for limited supplies in limited territories. Trusted emissaries such as the Polos, traveling on vital imperial missions throughout the vassal states of the empire, carried tablets of silver. But only a tablet of gold allowed post-steeds and their riders to travel safely and without question beyond the lands of the Great Khan. Only the precious golden tablet would allow the Polos' return to the Most Great and Most Serene City of Venice.

The Polos traversed the wild lands, seemingly abandoned even by the generally genial demon-gods of Cathay, whilst riding sundry breeds. For Cathayans and Mongols—and their court artists—appreciated equine types as Messer Niccolo appreciated types of gems.

The horseflesh had ranged from the sleek and proud, barrel-bodied classical steeds of olden Han, dating perhaps from even the days of half-legendary King Wen of Chou—steeds less hairy and less heavy by far than the huge war-horses of Europe, bred to carry at a lumbering gait the ponderous weight of iron-armored knights. They ranged from the handsome long-legged horses of the Cathayan hills and valleys, to the fierce half-feral Tartar ponies; related (surely) to the savage small horses which so swiftly had carried (nigh a thousand years before) the Huns from the then-impregnable Great 10,000 *Li* Wall of Cathay, to the fields which lay before the (on that occasion) inviolable Gates of Rome.

The expedition had traveled southwest, as Kublai's accursed scroll had directed. Never due west; that was only for crows, or for the vulture-eagles no longer imperiled by the ruthless bow of Genghiz Khan. Yet sometimes the terrain had led them southeast, along the bottom of a meandering valley; sometimes northwest along a level ridge. At times their path had led due south into aboriginal tribal lands, where the ghost-like gibbons gibbered and howled in the jungles; at times north, all being terribly aware of the pale-hued snow-tiger which might stalk them (and one time did!) through the horse-high grasses of the endless rolling plains.

As they made their way southwest (a shifting way to a shifting southwest, partly determined by the shifting sun, and partly by the shifting pointer of the far-from-precise cumbersome magnetic compass)—and as Cathay and its soft sites and teeming mercantile cities waned further and farther behind, in the difficult terrains and ofttimes awful weather; one by one, and sometimes by the pair, these handsome horses of olden Cathay were left behind at the posting-stations. Fresh mounts were supplied, always a degree smaller, always a degree rougher. Always a degree more able to maintain themselves in good thrift on the scanty nutriment of the frequently bitter landscapes.

The horses and camels left behind would be well cared for and, eventually, moved on to the next posting-station north-eastward. Thence to the next. Without hurry. Then to the next. Eventually these classical horses of North Cathay would be once again in Cathay North. Sooner or later the Great Khan would learn that each had come . . . whence each had come . . . might have it all plotted for him on a map . . . might not. The Great Khan had many matters to much concern him, but his day had no more hours than the day of any other man, be he son of heaven or son of earth.

"The kingdom of Chamba is tucked like a steamy armpit between the southern provinces of Cathay and Bur-mien," said Maffeo Polo to his elder brother and nephew, as they perched in the branches of a spreading banyan tree in Six-Dragon Marsh, to escape the rising waters of a sudden monsoon flood. Uncle Maffeo glumly wiped the moisture off his grizzled beard and completed his thought: "And now the armpit sweats."

Niccolo Polo did not reply. He had pulled off a soft leather boot, and was plucking an half-score of ink-black leeches from his ankle and foot. ". . . An half-score of matched matchless rubies, each the size of a crab's eye, and worth the weight and workmanship of a set of twelve silver apostle spoons . . ." he murmured to himself, as he meditatively watched his own blood, thinned by the leeches' venom, trickle and drip-drop-drip from foot . . . to tangled aerial banyan roots . . . to flooded marsh.

Marco and the tawny little sphinx sat in a crook between two thick buttresses, which supported the wildly spreading banyan and hanging roots that drew nourishment from the soggy air. He had also removed boots to pluck off the leeches which sucked at his hide. Nasty beasts; they were essentially invisible as they clung to overhead branches in the forests, waiting for a tasty morsel of humankind to wander by. With uncanny accuracy they flung themselves onto hidden parts of the body—down the backs of blouses and inside boots—where their sting numbed the skin and liquified the blood, so they might enjoy a leisurely meal until finally discovered by disgusted hosts and dislodged.

The other members of their band were scattered among the vibrant banyan branches like a flock of nervous pigeons, while their more-than-nervous horses were tethered below in knee-deep muck and water. The Mongols and Tartars grunted with revulsion as they plucked the loathsome leeches off each other's backs. In Europe the rare and costly leeches were in great demand as blood-thinning medical aides . . . and much good that did them here and now!

One young, broad-faced Tartar was quite heavily infested. Marco watched as two of his fellows squatted beside him in the banyan branches, picking clusters of the slimy black slugs off his blood-slicked flesh. The young Tartar's face looked pale . . . almost the color of ivory, but with a yellowish hue. Marco wondered whether he had already lost too much blood to continue the journey—and if he *had,* what could they do? The red, red wine of Europe, so useful in "making blood" for the weak and ailing was, alas, a far, far world away.

How came they to be perched in such a monstrous tree, in such an uninviting place, picking such repulsive vermin from their skin . . . "obscene with reptiles," like Ulysses' hound? Once again, Kublai's damnable scroll was to be blamed—for loyal liege-men could never blame the Great Khan himself. According to Scholar Yen's vague interpretation of the tangled skein of characters and symbols which composed the vague directions in the scroll, they should journey southwest until they found "the trail of the unicorn . . ."

As with many fabulous beasts which were mere mythology in Christendom, the unicorn was a rare but very real animal in the border regions of Cathay. Its thick black horn was ground to powder, and sold as a remedy for flagging virility to wealthy older men throughout the empire. For as the apothecaries snidely pointed out, "The unicorn's horn retains the upright posture which the clients' amorous organs regrettably lack."

Yet as with many fabulous creatures, the reality was far, far different from the graceful images in European beastiaries. No delicate one-horned ponies were the unicorns of Asia. No highly refined sense of morality did they hold. No. These were great black brutes, almost as large as elephants, with armored hides even thicker and brains far smaller, who enjoyed wallowing in mud. They glared with tiny, mindless red eyes, and attacked and crushed anything that moved within their sight or scent. Unlovely creatures were these—dangerous too—yet possessing the solitary black horn on their coarse snouts that made them—indisputably—unicorns. Marco hoped the fretful beasts might be enjoying the famed "peace of the unicorn," when encountered.

It was these crude creatures which the vague scroll directed them to trail, according to the vague interpretation of Scholar Yen. The posting-stations in the southwestern provinces had advised the Polos to try the southern border marches—where they were further advised to cross the border into the Kingdom of Chamba on the Gulf of Chie-nam, where the ugly black unicorns were known to lurk in the black ebony forests, attacking anything that stirred.

Chamba was a rich country, with its own customs and language. The aged king had paid a yearly tribute of twenty large elephants and of aloe wood to the Great Khan's Empire, since his surrender to ravaging Mongol forces in 1278. Thus the silver passport-tablet was recognized, and the Polos were allowed to pursue their obscure imperial mission.

Marco perched in the exuberant aerial roots of the sprawling banyan tree, and described the dismal scene in his travel-diary: ". . . Chamba is a land wealthy in black ebony and aloe wood. As befits a country rich in unicorns, its king has 326 children, including 150 sons of fighting age. Chamba is also a land of trackless swamps and violent storms and monsoon floods—which have forced us to take refuge in this untamed tree in Six-Dragon Marsh, whilst we wait for the waters to recede. We hope they do not rise again to endanger our horses. Indeed Uncle Maffeo is correct: Chamba resembles a sweaty armpit tucked beneath the strong arm of Cathay . . ."

Marco's berry-inked quill paused above the parchment of his diary, as he recalled the first time he had heard of these fearsome unicorns. Shortly after the Polos had entered the grip of the strong arm of Cathay, his father had described their journey to the Great Khan in the informal audience hall at the summer palace of Xan-du . . . "We were fortunate, Great Lord, to find an excellent Byzantine—"

"*Byzantine*," repeated Kublai Khan, imitating with absolute perfection the Venetian pronunciation of the Greek word he had just heard for the first time. "What is *Byzantine*?"

He tossed the question, not to Niccolo Polo, but to the seemingly dozing chief scholar. A withered homunculus of a man, aged beyond aging, whose wrinkled eye-lids at once flew open as his petal-thin mouth said, "Bi-zen-ti-om, Great Lord, was called of old 'Great

Syria.' There came from thence once an embassy with, allegedly, great wealth in tribute of gold and amber, and wool as fine as silk. But they were plundered in Bur-mien of these rich tributes, and were able to offer the Dragon Throne only some betel-nuts and a unicorn's horn. It was not," he quavered, "even a very *big* unicorn's horn." His shrug combined resignation with scorn . . . and perhaps a little pride in remembering a detail which was worth remembering solely because Kublai had asked him to remember it.

The Great Khan's face grew red. "Bur-mien plundered tribute intended for the Dragon Throne!" Anger filled his narrow eyes as though the affront had occurred that noon, and not a thousand years ago. Then his face convulsed and broke into a thousand lines of laughter. "Traveled, how far, countless *li* . . . and had nothing to offer but betel nuts and a unicorn's horn? Ah oh, hah how . . . !" The next moment all was grave. "But such a horn is good pharmacy. It is excellent pharmacy—especially for men of a generation much, *much* older than myself."

Kublai glanced all around, and as all minds recalled the chief use of unicorn horn by aged (but still optimistic) gentlemen, the instant response of all was, "Of course, Great Khan, of course . . ."

Of a sudden, Marco's thoughts were interrupted as the horses tethered beneath the great banyan thrashed and screamed . . .

Po; The House Is Falling Apart. The Mountain Rests on Solid Earth. Yet Ripe Fruit Remains Uneaten.

20

At the moment the horses screamed, the Mongol and Tartar riders who were clinging to the tree yelled and pointed. Scholar Yen—who was rarely given to shouting—shouted, "Look! A rising thunder-dragon!"

All looked over flooded Six-Dragon Marsh and saw, not six, but anyway one dragon ascend from the boggy mire. The knight, Hou Ying—who was rarely given to groaning—groaned aloud. For all Cathayans know that dragons are the harbingers of rainstorms, and more rain was precisely what they did not need or want. Even the Son of Heaven beat upon the thunder-voiced dragon-skin drum only in times of drought.

Marco stared in awe as the great iridescent-scaled creature flew upward. Black storm-clouds flecked with lightning gathered round its reptilian head, and rainbows streamed from its sinuously coiled tail. Unlike the grotesque unicorns, the real dragons of Asia were far more magnificent than their static images in European beastiaries. Their multicolored forms shimmered and rippled as they ascended, so they faded in and out of sight like a barely audible sound fades in and out of hearing.

"*Marón*! It is impossible to know whether the heathen creature is real . . . or whether my aging eyes and mind are failing," cried Maffeo, tugging at his beard to verify its familiar reality.

"We may be pleased that the beast is rising . . . not falling," said Scholar Yen blandly. For all Cathayans know that a dragon's fall to earth signifies great ill-fortune and terrible disasters: famines and wars and plagues. "This is merely a flying storm-dragon, who will bring only the illusion of rain—and more rain—to the already flooded marsh."

And with a great blast of lightning and crack of thunder, the sudden assault of the previously tepid monsoon rain began to pound down upon their heads. Marco's excitement at beholding a dragon changed to dismay, as he saw the flood-waters slowly creep up the agitated horses' legs.

"Kublai would not allow such flooding in *his* kingdoms," said Marco to Oliver and his mute page, who sat astride a nearby branch with rainwater beating on their worried faces.

The great blond northman grunted in reply.

Indeed, Kublai was ever concerned about matters of drought and flood, which might destroy the hard-won prosperity of his restored empire. Marco recalled an early spring day in the great audience hall of Khanbaluc; that high-roofed chamber which could hold more than six thousand persons within its gilded walls, so richly painted with all manner of beasts and birds and scenes of battle.

During a rather routine audience, the jingle of an unmounted courier's bells was heard from the great marble staircase of the palace. Courier stations were located at three-mile intervals along the main roadways of the empire, as part of the Great Khan's posting system. The runners wore bells attached to their belts, and carried important messages—or even baskets of fresh fruit for the emperor. They swiftly covered the three-mile distance, then passed their burden to the next runner at the next station, all carefully noted by a clerk. Thus the Great Khan could very quickly receive news (or produce) from all the far-flung reaches of his empire. The panting figure of the courier crouched at the broad and ornate threshold, which was raised to thwart demon-spirits who might enter the doorway.

"You may come forward. *Come.*"

The voice of the Great Khan, which had been half-drone and half-chant, changed abruptly to an everyday tone. At this last *come* there came forward, head bowed low and on his hands and knees, the Chief of Couriers. When he had come so far as protocol required, and no farther, he—still crouching—produced a rolled paper and began to read aloud. All knew, and the Great Khan knew best of all, the list of honorifics with which the man began, but not a word of it might be omitted. No, not even if the Great Palace itself were afire. The Chief of Couriers paused for a breath, and for a breath he tarried; then he read on.

"It is reported to the Son of Heaven that the rains which the Dragon Throne will never allow to fail are falling early; falling steadily, falling unfailingly from the Western Heavens, and thence upon the Western Jade Mountains. The rainwater in the Great Measuring Basin in the Temple of Willows in the Western Jade Mountains has reached the mark of six—and is still rising. Perhaps it may be that the Son of Heaven has words to speak to his vassals, servants, and slaves . . ." There was more, but the more was once more mere ceremony. The practised voice of the official runner sank to a murmur, and no one listened to his further words.

All waited for the words of the Son of Heaven, he who sat upon the elaborately carved Dragon Throne, wearing a ceremonial robe of sky-blue brocade embroidered with rainbow-hued dragons . . . throne and robe of dragons . . . who make the rain. The long pearl fringes of his tall filigreed-gold sun-and-moon crown shivered as he spoke. "Let the horns be blown and the bells be rung and the gongs be beaten—not the drums; let no one beat a drum—let the signal fires be lit, and let messengers be ready to set forth by horse and by foot. And this shall be the message:

"The work of growing grain is to continue; all other work is to stop at once, save this: Where there are sluices, strengthen them; where there are dikes, lengthen them; all levees to be made higher, all channels to be made deeper. Buckwheat and millet shall be issued from the tax-stores to feed those engaged in the work; and where there is not enough of either, let wheat be issued in the north and rice be issued in the south. Where cooking fuel is in short supply, private stores of fuel shall be taken at once, and at the highest local market price in compensation . . .

"Incense and all customary offerings shall be offered without stint in all places of worship, and all manner of prayers to all manner of gods shall be said without cease. Other orders may follow; let these be issued without delay. *Go*!"

The scribes who had been noting all this, their ink being ever kept wet in their ink-stones, departed, scuttling backwards.

"Each man to his post; *At once*!" said the Son of Heaven. "Summon my elephants; *Now!* I would that I had not that gout which disables me from mounting the horse-stirrup. Forward, my chair-bearers; *Come!*"

At times whilst saying this Kublai had spoken with greater emphasis. At no time had Kublai raised his voice.

In a moment not one entire man was left in the vast chamber. The motion of going had the effect of a great sweeping fan, and set all the huge candles to fluttering and guttering their heavy wicks in their scented wax. There remained of living creatures only the older eunuchs of the lower rank—they being not entire men—and they, with hands which sometimes trembled but never fumbled, began to trim the glowing and glowering coals.

From near and far, from tower and temple, hill and wall and fort, the sounding of gongs and the tolling of bells and the blowing of horns was heard in every varying degree of sound. But no drum-beat was heard. The Great Khan had—wisely—ordered that no one beat a drum, for the drum would rouse the dragons. The sound of drum was dragon-sound; that noise was thunder-and-lightning-noise, and dragons flashed lightning and boomed thunder. For the dragons made rain, and there was already rain enough. One prayed: not more than enough.

Thus did the Great Khan avert floods. But Kublai—and even his imperial posting-stations—were now very far away, while the monsoon flood rose ever higher in the tangled waterways of Six-Dragon Marsh in the vassal kingdom of Chamba. For the rains were no man's vassal.

Marco sat in the branches of the vast banyan tree, and watched in fear as the murky water lapped at the frenzied horses' thighs. His father was mumbling something to himself about two-score turquoises, each the size of a Saracen's thumb. His uncle was sighing for Italy—where plump pigeons, not men—roosted in trees. The Mongol and Tartar horsemen were grumbling amongst themselves, as they continued to pick leeches from their bleeding flesh. Scholar Yen . . . the wandering knight, Hou Ying . . . Peter the Tartar slave . . . Oliver and his mute page . . . all crouched among the aerial banyan roots looking drenched and dismayed.

The little sphinx, whom they had rescued from the Cloud-Dancing Fairy's eerie cave, perched on a sinuous branch and preened her water-logged golden fur with a lazily lapping tongue. "*Sphinx!*" cried Marco. "You are good at riddles, lovely sphinx, and it is far too wet here for a creature of the desert sun. Our powerful weapons and swift steeds, our strong arms and silver passports cannot help us now. Tell us how we might be safely gone from this soggy place."

Lap-lap, went the sphinx's otherwise silent tongue. And then she spoke . . .

Lu; The Wandering Stranger.
Fire Flares on the Mountain;
Good Fortune for Stubborn Travelers.

21

"Ask the banyan to help us quit this dreadful deluge," replied the sphinx, as she lazily preened her tawny-gold fur. Then she gave an enigmatic shrug.

"*Marón!* In this godforsaken place we must perch in trees like the bedraggled pigeons of our Venetian Terra Firma—and we must *talk* to trees like madmen as well," said Maffeo. "I, for one, have no intention of chatting with this overgrown shrub."

"Nor I . . . with you . . ." came a sound like softly sighing wind.

"Now you have insulted the sheltering banyan. We shall be lucky if we do not drown," said the sphinx with a pout.

". . . Drown . . ." echoed the sighing voice of the offended banyan tree.

"Not a word of sense from any of them," grumbled Maffeo, sensibly tugging his beard. "And meanwhile the horses—and the men—grow frantic at being trapped in this morass!"

Marco eyed the turbulent flood waters and recalled hearing his grandfather tell him the account, which his grandfather had told *him*, of what had followed after a servant of the Doge Marcello had—in defiance of all known science, tradition, wisdom and logic—allowed the plant called *thunder-thistle* to be cleared from the leads along the rooftop of the Ducal Palace during the summer: how the sky had almost immediately darkened, how there had come blast after blast of thunder, and torrents and torrents of rain. Pregnant women, mares and ewes, had all aborted. Everywhere the milk had turned suddenly and immediately sour, and spoiled the cheeses of the Terra Firma adjacent to Venice for that whole season.

Those rash enough to have installed the newly-fangled panes of glass (a substance generally used only for vessels by those rich enough to do without mere earthenware, and a craft for which Venice was justly famous) in their windows, had seen them shattered by the first blast of thunder. By the third, the globe-like bubbles at the end of the glassblowers' pipes had cracked into dust finer than sand. By the fourth crash, all the glassblowers were on their knees and singing *Dies Irae . . . dies illa . . . teste David cum Sibylla*, sure that *the* day of wrath had finally come.

The new wine had rushed frothing, like newly-shed blood, from vats and pipes and casks; and that which was left had turned bitter and sour, and the very slaves in the Arsenal had threatened mutiny rather than drink of it. The Adriatic, lashed to fury, had breached the dikes along the Lido. The sea had rushed in like a herd of mad horses, and with the clashing sound of an army at war, had drowned all the craft on the lagoons.

Fortunately the ill-conceived slave had been observed, and dragged before the Doge. Who, without daring to take time to summon the Senate, had ordered the dolt to be at once put to death. And there, on the very edge of the roof where he had sat—the fool!—dangling his legs and laughing as he slashed the stalks of thunderbloom, his body was propped up.

He was left to hold his grimacing severed head in his own lap.

The thunder gradually died down, with ever-diminishing growls. And all over the Republic of Venice, and even as far into the Terra Firma as inland Asola, mothers of any sense had dragged their children, yelling, from beneath the feather-beds where they had hidden in terror. And made them each down at least three drams of the famous and sovereign Theriacle of Venice, good for everything except the Black Death, and containing 365 separate ingredients, including the flesh of poisonous vipers.

Indeed, such were the far-reaching effects of this unheralded thunderstorm, that several merchants had actually lost their places as they were casting up their accounts. *Lost their places! Made mistakes in their accounts!* This, of Venetian merchants never known to lose their heads even when Tartars were shooting swollen corpses into their Overseas trading-posts with catapults.

The trade of Venice was long in recovering from this misadventure. Agate and carnelian, Indian muslins and cloths of mallow, and both varieties of spikenard; all went down in price by so much as a groat in the ducat. And long or yellow-pepper, belladonnium and lycium, singing-boys, copper of Cabul, silk gauze (both the spun-fine and unravelled), as well as lead for adulterating forged coinage, could scarcely be afforded by even the richest for months afterwards.

All this for neglecting due obedience to the laws of plants. Had not old Friar Paul dutifully tutored Marco in Elder Pliny's words? "The wilderness is one vast apothecary-shop." And should not Marco caution his rash Uncle Maffeo to beware of further offending the powerful banyan on which they perched . . . ?

"Perhaps you clever foreign magicians know some good *escaping* tricks!" Marco's memories were interrupted by a chattering voice from the highest branches of the tree.

The sphinx looked upward, waved her leonine tail—and frowned.

"Who speaks up there, Sphinx?" asked Marco.

"An old adversary of yours; the monkey who guards the Cloud-Dancing Fairy's cave."

"He is very far from his post. Perhaps the impish Lady will finally speak to him after so many centuries, and he will fail to hear her immortal words."

"Distance has no meaning for the Great Sage of Water-Curtain Cave—and my hearing is keen as my mind," chittered the white, short-tailed monkey, doing flip-flops down the sinewy branches until he finally bounced into view.

"What brings you to join us in this backwater, Monkey?" called Marco.

"Duty brings me. The Lady is newly and gently reborn, and lonely. The cloud-dancer wishes the sphinx to return to her cavern—for she misses its vain and amusing prattle."

"I am *not* vain, nor do I prattle," said the sphinx, still carefully grooming her silken fur. "And I do *not* wish to return to that gruesome cave."

"The reborn Lady's mood has become velvety as a butterfly's. Or would you prefer to perch with puny mortals on a sodden sapling?" snorted the monkey.

"We are *not* puny mortals," growled the knight, Hou Ying, gesturing with his halberd.

". . . Nor sodden saplings . . ." sighed the banyan.

"Our Lady, *Marón!*" snorted Uncle Maffeo.

Marco thought: This is like a scene from the Cathayan opera. Everyone is pirhouetting and piping, whilst the magic general stalks around taking practice swipes with his battle-axe. But this time they were *not* at the opera.

"Listen to you all!" cried Monkey. "Do you realize who I am? Do you know that the Celestial Jade Emperor himself calls me 'Equal of Heaven'? Do you know that I can out-battle and outwit the most terrible and clever demons, star-spirits, and plant-headed ogres?"

"Nonetheless, you may not take the little sphinx against her will," said Marco.

"Do you know who I *am*?" ranted Monkey, his voice growing shrill with excitement. "I sit by the Jade Emperor's side facing the door, at the heavenly Peach and Cinnabar Banquet. I know the Inside and Outside Transformations. I am so strong that I can easily carry *all* of you to the Lady's cave—where she could suck you dry like a spider sucks at moths, had she not undergone a gentler rebirth."

"Perhaps you can carry puny mortal men—but I doubt if you could carry the men *and* the horses," said Marco with a shrug.

"Nobody doubts the Great Sage of Water-Curtain Cave who is Equal of Heaven!" screamed Monkey. His fiery red eyes flashed angrily, as he inhaled the wind and grew tremendously large—with a vast number of powerful white-furred arms which scooped up sphinx, men, and horses. Then he leapt onto a passing storm cloud, and carried them *all* away.

Vain were their cries of astonishment and vain their shouts of fear. And vain was the little sphinx's smile as they sailed across the overcast sphere.

The banyan tree sighed with relief, and resumed its ancient and rambling reveries.

Clutched in one of Monkey's massive arms, and riding a turbulent storm-cloud that dipped and soared swift as a wind-swept kite on a blustery day, Marco looked down with a queasy combination of hope and alarm. They had left the flooded marsh behind, and were flying over a coastal plain that seemed to be a mixture of dense forest and farmland. If only they could escape the monkey's grasp . . .

"I am hungry and cold," announced the sphinx.

"You will be warm and cozy in the Gentle-Lady's cave soon enough," rumbled the mighty monkey.

"But I am hungry and cold *now*," whimpered the sphinx. "If you do not feed me at once, I will tell the Lady that you were cruel to me . . . and I will pout and refuse to amuse her with my banter. She will be very annoyed with you and may *never* speak her second word."

"There is no food up here—you must wait," growled Monkey.

"I *cannot* wait! You must take me down to that farming village below. I see water-buffaloes at plow; where there are buffalo, there is milk . . . which is the proper food for sphinx-folk."

"*Marón!* The creatures in these lands are finicky as Frankish friars . . ." began Maffeo, but his elder brother and nephew hushed him.

"If I take you down to lap some milk—will you speak well of me to the Lady?" asked Monkey.

"I shall tell the Lady what I *truly* think of you," replied the sphinx.

"Very well then, but be quick about it," muttered Monkey. He leapt off the cloud and floated down to a newly plowed rice paddy. The farmers in their mushroom-shaped straw hats shrieked at the sight of this many-armed apparition, and scurried across the fields.

Following the farmers' example, the Polos and their men deftly wormed their way out of Monkey's monumental arms—and scattered in every direction. The sphinx flew gracefully onto Marco's shoulder as they raced away.

"*Wait!*" bellowed Monkey.

"Thanks for the ride!" called Marco over his shoulder.

Hou Ying and his halberd—seeming somehow much larger than he had ever seemed before—and Oliver with his great battle-axe and his graceful page, kept the surprised monkey busy with a flashing whirlwind of battle, while the horses and their riders escaped. The three men fought round after round with the huge, multi-armed monkey and the giant cudgel which he plucked from behind his ear; indeed they were all well-matched opponents, too swift and skilled to draw any blood.

The Mongol and Tartar horsemen shot arrows at Monkey from a distance, but he changed the arrows to flower petals which fell softly to his feet. But in fact it was difficult for Monkey to fight in such an awkward form, and he quickly grew weary.

With a tremendous belch, the Great Sage of Water-Curtain Cave exhaled the wind, and changed back to his normal simian shape and size. Chittering furiously, Monkey leapt onto a passing rain-cloud and floated away.

"Well done, Sphinx," panted Marco, as they watched the grimacing ape sail overhead, brandishing the iron cudgel he had stolen from the Sea-Dragon King—now shrunken small as a needle.

"You asked me to free you from that waterlogged log," replied the tawny sphinx with a self-satisfied smile.

"Could you not have chosen a simpler way?" asked Marco.

"We sphinx-folk do not relish simplicity, but we *do* relish lapping up warm buffalo-milk . . . so much richer than that of the goats in the lands of Greece and Aegypt!" She smacked her lips in anticipation.

Ta Kuo; Excess.
Floodwaters Rise Over the Forest.
The Sagging Beam is Weak.

22

"When I consider my provocations, I simply *marvel* at my own moderation," the Khan of Khans had once said to Marco, as he strolled one early spring day among the peach blossoms in his private courtyard at Khanbaluc, wearing a peach-colored brocade robe embroidered with gilded peach blossoms. "Hardly a year ago, did not some aboriginal tribe demur, and seriously affront a humble official collecting the very moderate fifty-percent grain tax for the Dragon Throne? Scarcely can one believe it, yet it was true. The Great Genghiz, invincible grandfather of the present Son of Heaven, would have built a tower of their heads . . . soon to become a tower of skulls; but did *We* do so? No, We did not. Naturally *Our* troops—but let us be informal, Marco, my friend: naturally *My* troops were victorious. My troops are always victorious; such is the inevitable law of nature. Yet did I have the rebels flayed or impaled, as justifiably I might? Not so at all . . .

"Merely I had them sent into exile . . . all of them . . . of course all of them; does the Son of Heaven on the Dragon Throne break up families? With my usual and utmost benevolence I allowed them, bag and baggage, to go to the Kingdom of Chamba, that land hard upon the borders of the Nam Viet; *such* an interesting place! There one may see the wild elephants playfully plucking up the crops. Often. And also one may hear the ghosts howling, even in the daytime; what are they called, Po-Yo, those ghosts which one may hear howling even in the daytime?"

" 'Spooks,' Great Lord?"

"No! *Not* 'spooks'! *Spooks*, indeed! Ah me. *Gibbons*; they are white and skinny and ghostly, and one may hear them howling in the daytime. Which surely must increase piety towards one's ancestors. 'Gibbons,' they are called. Such is my well-nigh unlimited liberality. Eh? Speak up, young man, speak up!"

Marco, who felt no desire to hear anything or anyone howling anywhere at any time, raised his voice slightly and gazed informally at the Great Khan's round and ruddy face—an act which might be punished by death in more formal audiences. "They do not call you 'Great Lord' for nothing, Great Lord," he said.

"No indeed," said Kublai Khan. "Always speak to me without fear, for I desire only to hear the truth. Doubtless a quirk, ah me . . ."

Now the peach blossoms in the imperial courtyard had long since faded. And now Marco . . . while not in exile . . . had been sent by Great Kublai to wander in that land where the ghosty gibbons howl by day—and by night as well.

The smell first told them that this bedraggled collection of straw huts, built on stilts along a dank green estuary lined with spindly Pharaoh's-nut palms, was not merely a nameless fishing village. The odor told them that they had entered the suburbs of a coastal market town: a smell of dung and spices, cooking oil and sweat, refuse and salt air—and something which had no name, but which the Polos immediately recognized as the *scent of commerce.*

Soon they entered the mud-walls of the town and found a jumble of low wood-and-wicker buildings, and dazzling temples unlike any Marco had seen before. These were shaped like great white-washed bells, with long handles or spires covered with gold-leaf that glinted merrily in the sunlight. The sonorously chanting monks wore draperies of saffron-colored silk, and their sallow skin had a golden hue. They placed fuming brass incense-braziers before huge gold idols studded with rubies and draped with scented flowers; idols which had an oddly Grecian appearance . . . perhaps an influence of early traders . . . or had the troops of great Grecian Alexander gotten this far? Not likely, thought Marco, and not important.

"Rubies the size of a Cham-Buddha's navel," murmured Messer Niccolo Polo, as he rattled his best jade beads.

Their noses led them through narrow alleys reeking of rancid cooking oil and stale urine, where naked children played, and skinny yellow dogs, scruffy chickens and pale pigs picked in the mud for scraps. The alleys finally opened onto a shallow harbor where square-sailed fishing junks leaned crazily in the brackish ooze of low-tide. Makeshift market-stalls sprawled lazily along the waterfront, selling produce and fish, greasy snacks and trader's wares. Gap-toothed Cham women squatted before piles of odd-smelling dragons'-eggs or durian fruit, wearing nothing but brightly colored cloths wrapped around their waists. They suckled their infants as they vigorously haggled with buyers. Nut-brown boys in shabby loin-and-head-cloths drove elephants with colorfully patterned hides, who plodded among the thatch-roofed stalls carrying loads of ebony logs in their tattooed trunks. And the flies and mosquitoes buzzed *everywhere* in the steamy air.

"Stay, what is this?" asked Peter the Tartar as they wandered through the market place. "My devils tell me to pay close heed to the markings on this rug." Peter pulled a worn red and gold wool carpet from a stack of miscellaneous rags piled on the ground at a vendor's stall, and examined the faded design closely.

"Are you furnishing your wedding-tent?" asked Maffeo, with a rakish glint in his eyes.

"Note the pattern of this rug," said Peter with a hint of excitement in his usually even voice. "Is this not the self-same symbol which is written in the Great Khan's scroll, and on the blue-eyed giant's amulet—the one which he calls '*thorns*'?"

The Polos crowded round the carpet and noted the pattern with considerable enthusiasm. It was not the simple carpet of the Tartar saddle-rug, with the "two buffs, one blue" or the "two blues, one buff," but the infinitely more complex weave that was found from Persian Isfahan, eastward to Mongolian Lop Nor. The oft-repeated symbol was woven in tattered golden yarn around the faded maroon border. Indeed it was the odd rune-marking which appeared on Kublai's accursed scroll and on the northman's amulet—the one which Oliver called '*thorns!*'

"Where did you get this carpet?" Marco asked the white-bearded vendor, who wore lengths of grimy white cloth tucked around his lean waist and bony head. The dark-skinned peddler was too tall, skinny and round-eyed to be of the Cham people; perhaps he was a wandering trader from Greater India.

The old man smiled toothlessly, and gestured vaguely towards the sea.

"Tell us where the carpet was made, and we will pay you a handsome price," said Niccolo, impatiently fingering his beads.

The old trader nodded agreeably, and traced a recognizable map on the muddy ground with his walking stick: southward from the Chamba coast, around the peninsula of the Lesser Indies. Then westward along the strait of Lesser Java, which lies north of Terra Incognita Australis. Thence northwest to the coast of Bengala—and inland to the wild mountains of Tebet.

There his tracing stick stopped, whilst the Polos' excitement over this newest clue almost visibly increased.

"He is describing the long sea journey from Chamba to Greater India, thence upland to Tebet. That is doubtless how the peddler and his curious carpet voyaged here. But—*if* we decide to pursue this strange lead—would it not be quicker to travel overland?" asked Uncle Maffeo, as he peeled a fragrant mango.

"What other clear direction have we to pursue?" asked Niccolo, with a grave expression on his travel-weary face.

"The overland route would be the quickest way to meet our deaths," said Marco. "For the lands between Chamba and Greater India are held by the kings of Longkok and Bur-mien. Both are bitter enemies of the Great Khan—and would welcome his emissaries only with their spears. If we wish to follow the carpet's lead, we must either backtrack through the southern provinces of Cathay, or take the old man's advice and journey by sea."

"But there are no decent ships here—only flimsy toys that will blow apart if I break wind!" fumed Maffeo.

"Marco is right; the sea route is far safer," said his elder brother, Niccolo, whose decision seemed already made. "We will sail close to shore and anchor often for fresh supplies. The winds are favorable now, so the journey should not take overlong. If we can hire a spacious and comfortable ship, my rump will welcome a respite from the saddle."

Having reached a consensus which well-suited their Venetian sea-faring minds, the Polos paid the old trader a goodly sum of cowrie shells for the strange rug—for he would not accept the Great Khan's marvelous mulberry-bark-paper currency. Then they walked down to the docks to hire the largest and fastest and most comfortably appointed vessel that could be found in the kingdom of Chamba.

They had the good fortune to find a Cathayan merchant ship of medium size, which had stopped to trade and replenish supplies while sailing from the Great

Khan's richest province of Manzi to Greater India. The four-masted vessel was well-built of a double thickness of spruce wood fastened with iron nails, and caulked inside and out with a watertight mixture of lime, chopped hemp, and wood-oil. In addition to sails, the ship was propelled by rows of oars, each manned by four seamen. Small rowboats for fishing and shallow-water landings were lashed to the outside of the ship, and the deck was lined with small but cosy cabins which promised a far more pleasant journey than the perilous overland route.

The Polos were well pleased with this vessel—but the knight errant, Hou Ying, refused to set sail with them.

"Good Sirs, I have an old quarrel with the mighty sea-dragons, and dare not venture aboard ship; lest the briny beasts launch an attack against this humble wandering knight, and cause your sturdy craft to founder. I will journey overland and meet my refined Sirs in the kingdom of Tebet."

"*If* you can survive the dangers of the journey and *find* us in Tebet, for it is said to be a wild and desolate place," grumbled Niccolo. And all the Polos looked glum, for they had grown fond of this droll and unassuming knight with four names.

"I shall find you," he said calmly. And wearing his invariable not-quite-smile, he walked off, resolute, on the journey of a thousand miles which starts with one step.

Marco watched him stride with an even pace, and cross a low hillock that rose above the sea-scented harbor. And was it a curious mental trick that made the knight seem to vanish *before* he left Marco's line of sight? Surely a trick of the eyes—for indeed Hou Ying seemed to disappear as though he had never been.

Gigant square-sailed junks lumbering o'er the muddy sea, their timbers and strakes and ropes moaning, groaning, cracking loudly. Lurching fretfully, mumbling and muttering, creaking and squeaking as they lumbered o'er the shallow South-Cathayan Sea . . .

The voyage proceeded without notable event across a numberless blur of days, as they rounded the peninsula of the Lesser Indies and sailed through the Strait of Java, which was so far south that the Pole Star could not be seen. The shifting sky caused the Mongol and Tartar horsemen some alarm, yet the journey gave men and mounts a chance to rest and mend equipment. Marco passed the time trading riddles with the sphinx and writing in his travel diary.

One hot and dreamy afternoon a small flotilla of rude black-sailed ships approached them, and the oarsmen shouted *"Pirates!"*

Yet as the dark fleet drew closer, the Cathayan captain frowned and said, "These be no ordinary brigands; they are the Cynocephali of the Andaman Islands, where men have the heads—and dispositions—of vicious dogs!"

Niccolo Polo crossed himself, but Uncle Maffeo made a swift scoffing sound. Marco peered at a swiftly pursuing pirate vessel and saw that the captain was right. It was manned by beings with human bodies—and the hairy heads, sharp teeth and lolling tongues of great and growling mastiffs.

unicorns, precious [illegible] and [illegible] as they [illegible] into the shallow South Cathayan Sea.

The seven pocket junks [illegible] across [illegible] as they [illegible] the peninsula of the [illegible] and [illegible] through the [illegible] of [illegible] which was so far south that the Pole Star could not be seen. [illegible] the [illegible] and [illegible] of the [illegible] and [illegible] a chance to rest and [illegible] equipment. Marco passed the time trading [illegible] with the [illegible] in his [illegible].

One hot and [illegible] afternoon a small flotilla of [illegible] black [illegible] ships approached them, and the [illegible] "Pirates!"

[illegible] as the [illegible] drew closer. The [illegible] "These [illegible] they [illegible] the [illegible] of the [illegible]. These men [illegible] the [illegible] and [illegible]."

Marco [illegible] himself [illegible] a [illegible] and [illegible] saw that the [illegible] was [illegible] with [illegible] and the [illegible] of great and [illegible].

[illegible] wind [illegible] the bronze at last [illegible]

Tui; Pleasure.
Water Above; Water Below.
The Superior Man Finds Pleasure in Friends.

23

The flimsy but fast pirate vessels, with their black lateen sails, chased and surrounded the sturdy merchant ship like a pack of wild dogs. The snarling creatures boarded the boat with their powerful jaws snapping and frothing, and with sharp daggers clutched in their claws. They attacked the defending Cathayan seamen and the Mongol guards like mad beasts, tearing at flesh with fangs and knives which were equally cruel. The men fought valiantly to save the ship, and Oliver and his page split many a canine skull with battle-axe and triple-edged sword. But the dog-headed pirates streamed aboard in endless numbers, and attacked men and horses with endless—and mindless—fury.

"I like not this illusion, young Sir," gasped Scholar Yen to Marco, as they cut the lashings of a fishing boat from the side of the ship, and tumbled it into the churning water.

The Cathayan crewmen kept the brutes at bay on the

blood-slicked deck of their ship, which they were sworn to protect, while the Polos and their uninjured men slid down hemp ropes into the small rowboats, carrying whatever supplies they could snatch up. The trembling sphinx flew down to them, as they made their escape in the pitching sea.

"*Marón!*" wailed Maffeo. "We are finished for sure! We will be lost in these puny tubs, with neither meat nor wine, nor even our horses. Only the blessed saints can save us now!"

"Sapphires of Serendib like pale blue stars, the tint of young strained indigo; the value of a score of she-camel all in milk and with twin foals . . ." murmured Niccolo Polo, his face gone ashy-pale as he worried his second-best amber beads.

"Even the blessed saints would flinch from our fate—for we are being followed by sea-dragons!" said Marco, as an enormous scaly head rose up from the waves.

The grey-green head was massively ugly, with bulging red eyes, a protruding snout, and a gaping mouth filled with irregular jutting fangs. A flaring hood, like a cobra's, shaded the head. Below the barnacle-crusted neck were two awkward little forelegs, with two short claws and one long and twitching central talon.

The grotesque head spoke in a voice like roaring surf. "The Great Naga-Khan, Basudara, Oceanic Emperor of all the Sea-Dragons, sends His Imperial greetings." The creature's breath blasted their faces like a malodorous and scorching wind.

It continued: "The Naga-Khan, Basudara, Lord of the Abyss, wishes to learn the whereabouts of a man-dragon sometimes called '*Hou Ying.*' In return for this unimportant information, the Unfathomable Naga-Khan, Basudara, will grant you safe passage to any port you choose. Thus speaks the Oceanic Emperor of the Sea-Dragons, Basudara."

"*Any* port?" asked Maffeo with eyes gone wide. "Will your dragon-king grant us safe passage to the Most Great and Serene Port of *Venice*?"

The scaly greenish head cleared its throat like crashing waves. "According to imperial records, the distant and minor port of Venice is regrettably not under the jurisdiction of the Great Naga-Khan, Basudara. Those who wish safe passage to the remote port of Venice must apply directly to His Lordship, the High Basilisk of Byzantium. The Unfathomable Naga-Khan, Basudara, will generously grant safe passage to any port within *His* benevolent jurisdiction. Thus speaks the wise Naga-Khan, Basudara, Lord of the Abyss."

"In that case, we have *no* knowledge of the whereabouts of a knight sometimes called Hou Ying. When last we heard, that wanderer was wandering in the highest Himalays," said Niccolo, sternly.

"The heights of the high Himalays are not within the realm or fetch of the Lord of the Abyss," the sea-dragon said with a disappointed hiss.

"Will you leave us here to drown?" cried Peter the Tartar. "For my inland feet know not how to walk on water!"

The sea-dragon hissed a sullen sigh. "The Wise Oceanic Emperor, Basudara, advises you to take refuge on yonder small but pleasantly fertile isle, for terrible dangers await the unprotected in the open seas. Thus speaks the Naga-Khan of all the sea-dragons, Basudara." Then the monstrous head sank beneath the waves.

The Polos peered in the direction the creature had indicated, and saw that although they had refused to betray the wandering knight, Hou Ying, the mysterious dragon-messenger was more gracious than it appeared. It had somehow led them to the shore of a pretty little windblown island—which had been blown off any mariner's chart.

The men called it 'Pleasure Island,' for want of any other name or seafarers' reports. Indeed it was a pleasant place, well-watered, and with spice and fruit-trees, Pharaoh's-nut palms and fish in abundance. The tawny-skinned lowland people of this isle had no knowledge of the Great Khan, nor any other proper king, and worshiped eerie serpent-headed idols. They lived like beasts—but amiable beasts—though their brethren in the mist-shrouded peaks that rose from the island's center were rumored to be rather more ferocious.

The lowlanders went stark naked, except for tiny loincloths, but had a curious custom. They had bartered for lengths of silk from passing traders, which they draped over the entrances of their simple straw huts. They did not realize that silk was meant to clothe their bodies, and saw it instead as a colorful decoration for their conical homes. They drank a powerful spiced palm-wine, and their curly-haired women sang and danced gracefully—and did not regard chastity as a virtue. Thus the men thought this was an island of pleasure, and were in no hurry to depart, and to brave the stormy seas in their tiny rowboats.

Though the flesh of the fruit and fish, the flowers and women were sweet, the Polos took no pleasure in this delay. " 'Tis the Sleeping Beauty we are after . . . *not* these lively ones," said Niccolo glumly.

Not *these* lively ones, added Marco to himself. For only one lively beauty had captured his thoughts. And that one was Su-shen.

The Polos found little pleasure in being stranded on this isolated isle, so far from the comforts and duties and business of civilized lands. The diversions of this place did not satisfy their wants or needs. They needed only to find the Sleeping Beauty, who had seemed so tantalizingly within reach after the discovery of the strange rune-carpet. They wanted only to present this novel being to the Great Khan, and to claim their reward: leave to return home to their beloved Republic of Venice (. . . *with* Su-shen, added Marco to himself).

There was something else about this island which the Polos found quite disturbing; that was the dreams. Each evening, as the men feasted and drank before the conical straw huts which they had built for themselves in native fashion, the women sang and danced for them to the sound of beating drums and long, mournful flutes. With garlands of fragrant flowers draped over their bare breasts, the women gracefully gestured and chanted the tales of their island—and whatever was the nature of their song, the men dreamed about it that very night. If the women danced a tale of war, the men dreamed of battle and woke up shouting in the dark. If the women sang of love, the men tossed and turned . . . and crept to the womens' huts. And if the women sang of serpent-headed spirits, then serpents slithered through their restless sleep.

At first the Polos assumed the palm-wine was drugged, and forbade the men to drink of it. But the weird dreams continued. Then they realized that the island was enchanted, but from whence did the enchantment come? Was it the vengeance of the sea-dragons, who had abandoned them hither when the Polos refused to reveal the destination of the knight, Hou Ying? Or did the enchantment come from the dream-spirits of the uncharted island, itself?

"Illusions take on their own life here," remarked Scholar Yen with a scowl, after an unusually fitful night. "Yet I recall no mention of such oddities in the *Analects* . . ."

"Lands, airs and waters have their own several spirits, according to Hippocrete of old," Niccolo observed gravely, "but the ancient geographers never described such bizarre realms."

"*Marón!* I dreamed of such a *grand* Venetian banquet," said Maffeo with a yawn, waking from deep slumber when the sun was already high in the sky. "There were capons boiled and broiled and roasted. For every six men, a suckling pig was provided, and within the piglet were all sorts of nice things: figs, larks and squabs. And of course there were the great meat-pies, succulent and spicy juices running down from slits cut, in various shapes, in the pie crust. Lemons and oranges were provided in abundance to be squeezed over the lovely roasted veal; and at every other elbow was a great castor of mixed spices, ground fine . . ." Uncle Maffeo yawned again, glanced at the somber faces of the others, belched softly and fell silent.

"My devils be queasy and uneasy," said Peter the Tartar.

"Can runes guard sleeping souls?" asked Oliver.

The men sank into a torpid routine of eating and drinking, and watching the women weave their hypnotic spells . . . and dreaming shadowy dreams. They soon lost all sense of time and desire to escape. Were they sated, or merely cloyed?

The Polos themselves fretted and paced on the sandy shore—and wondered how they might ever escape from 'Pleasure' Island.

Xia Jen; The Family.

Wind Rises From the Flames.
The King and His Family Fear Naught.

24

Marco sat on a windswept knoll overlooking the creamy lapis-blue sea, and wrote with a quill on the parchment sheets of his travel diary to pass the time: "The Great Khan's expeditions of conquest beyond the borders of Cathay have ofttimes met with difficulties, disasters, even defeat, despite His wise leadership and brilliant strategies."

The Great Khan was far away at the moment—but he well might ask to have Marco's diary read aloud and translated at some later time. So best to choose one's words prudently, even here on this uncharted isle. If one should falter and try to change the meaning, the Great Khan would suspect at once. As well try to fool the Holy Father on a matter of doctrine; no, no, it would *not* do. It would not do at all.

Marco dipped his quill in berry-ink and continued writing. "I believe this is due to the natures of the Mongol and Tartar warriors, themselves. For a fact, they ride like vengeful winds across the frigid steppes, yet they wilt like fragile flowers in steamy tropical jungles. There the thick leather armor bakes them like chickens in an oven . . . when they have not sense enough to take it off. And *if* they shed their armor, they are as soft and unprotected as eggs without shells.

"All know that the Great Khan's armies have not yet conquered Bur-mien, despite their spirited bow attacks against the formidable war elephants, who carry castles full of hostile troops upon their ample backs. And although the Maharajah of Chamba pays tribute to the Great Khan, the Cham rebels still lurk in the forests and nip at the heels of the imperial tribute collectors like surly dogs. Such insurrections would not be tolerated within the well-regulated borders of Cathay, nor its rich southern province of Manzi, where the steppeland horsemen can maneuver freely. I believe the hot climate saps their strength—as can clearly be seen on this wretched island."

Marco paused to brush wind-blown chestnut-colored hair from his face, and to dip his quill in berry-ink; then resumed writing.

"Nor do the Mongol and Tartar warriors fare well on the sea, thus they are reluctant to quit this godless place. Their lack of naval power was truly the Great Khan's undoing during the ill-omened invasions of Japangu, where the pearls are red as the rising sun, and palaces and temples are roofed with purest gold.

"For a fact, there were 30,000 unseaworthy Mongol troops, and reluctant Cathayan and Korean sailors stranded on an uninhabited islet off the Japangu coast, after they were routed by a mighty storm during the first invasion in the Lord's year of 1274. (Much as we are stranded on this isolated island eleven years later.) The 30,000 managed to escape by cleverly capturing a Japanese fleet which was sent to destroy them. Yet when the Great Khan launched his second invasion of Japangu in 1281, his navies fared far worse . . . as I so well recall . . ."

* * *

"It is well known," Kublai had said in the Great Audience Hall of Khanbaluc, whilst lightly fluffing his light and fluffy beard, "that all men obey me; is it not so?"

"Yes, Great Khan," all present responded . . . Niccolo, Maffeo, and Marco Polo among them. The Polo family did not consider this assent to a statement they knew to be false a lie or cowardice or hypocrisy; they considered it mere common politeness (as well as mere common sense) to say *"Yes, Great Khan"* whenever Kublai followed any statement with; *"Is it not so?"*

"All men obey me, and those who do not should. It is true that I am indulgent; I am very indulgent, and I do not absolutely require total submission and obedience from all; best though this would be for the unity, peace and welfare of the world. Thus I allow your Emperors and Popes to keep their crowns."

The Polos recalled with what comparative ease the Latin West, incomparably weaker than the Tartar East, had deposed the Byzantine Emperor. They remained still, while the Great Khan thoughtfully took a sip of spiced rice-wine from his great bejewelled drinking cup. (It was whispered that in private he preferred the fermented mares' milk of his forebears; but the privacy implied a certain touchiness on the subject. The haughty Han Cathayans regarded milk as a mere glandular secretion, fit only for barbarians or the very young. Thus these whispers were whispered very low, and very close was whispering mouth to listening ear.)

"It is not vanity," said Kublai, taking the gem-encrusted vessel from his lips (while Niccolo shrewdly appraised its immense value), "but mere accuracy which allows me, the grandson of Oceanic Emperor, Genghiz Khan, to say that a man may travel from the shores of the Yellow Sea to those of the Indian Ocean, and up to the Mediterranean in perfect safety. I say, '*may.*' "

He snapped his fingers; at once a chrysanthemum-shaped tray of black lacquer, holding hot spiced-meats in tiny shells of puff-paste appeared. The regal grandson of invincible Genghiz Khan selected a single one, ate it, gestured. The servant distributed the rest to the august civil officers at hand; curiously, there were just enough for one apiece. The elegant grandson of mighty Genghiz Khan watched them kneel and prostrate themselves at the honor, and the refined grandson of ruthless Genghiz Khan watched them as they ate.

"Merely I enjoy to show you honor," he said, "and to feed you as a father feeds his favorite sons. Lesser monarchs, fearing poison, would have you eat first. Not I. Ha!"

Another slight gesture; the hot-wet napkin appeared, and the Great Khan wiped his mouth and fingers. The mute servant bowed over the black lacquer tray inlaid with jade and mother-of-pearl, on which the cloth was dropped. Then the Great Khan watched benevolently as the servant brought napkin and tray to those whom the Khan of Khans enjoyed to honor, and the Great Khan watched them wipe their own fingers and mouths. He said he hoped they were refreshed. They knelt again and kowtowed again, and assured him they were refreshed indeed.

Kublai nodded his head, its tall gilded-felt, bejeweled cap-of-state so different from the small skin cap or leather helmet of the Mongol warpath. "In truth," he said, "there are presently but three things which I would have and which I have not. Would I have great wealth? Lo, I have it. Would I have vast power? Lo, I have it. Sons, grandsons, a realm restored and well-run? All this I have, all given me by T'ien, the Supreme Emperor of Heaven.

"And you," he named a prominent officer of state; "and you," he named another, thanking them and assuring them of the Great Khan's present and future kindness. He named them one by one; he named them all. At the last he said, "And you, Po-lo, and your younger brother and your clever son; you have helped me too, all three. You will not find me ungrateful. No.

"Three; but three things there are which I would have and which I have not. First and foremost is the blessing of *Bhaisajya-Khan*, the Lapis-Radiant Buddha-

Khan of Healing, who shall restore full health to my favorite son, Prince Chenghin, and relieve me of this painful gout.

"Next is the suzerainty of the Isles Japangu—contumacious islanders with their clannish feuds and strifes; it would be well for them to acknowledge me as their overlord. If they do not, I shall send my fleets-of-war upon them once again. Divine wind shall fill the sails, their golden cities I shall burn to dust . . . towers of skulls . . . but enough. Not yet. I must consult my astrologers at the Imperial Terrace for Managing Heaven, regarding an auspicious time for this bold naval expedition. The sun rises from those islands, as all may see, and I would rule over them—but I do not."

He gave a sound which was half sigh and half snort. The jewel-crusted cup of the Great Khan dropped noiselessly upon the priceless thick-piled carpets, gifts of his nephew the Khan of Persia. No drop ran out from cup upon silken carpets . . .

Kublai's greying head gave a brief half-nod. Snapped upright. His eyes, half-hooded a half-moment before, were now wide open. They swept the Imperial Audience Hall to see if any had marked this; none had. They all had, as custom dictated, their eyes all low cast down. A satisfied gleam shone in the Great Khan's gaze. And out of the purest politeness, he gave a magnificent wine-scented belch.

"Thirdly, I do not care always to find the same delicacy in my rice-bowl; no," said he. "I like to slumber; I have so greatly wearied myself in my arduous reign. I would slumber long. But I would wake refreshed and renewed again. Power I love; and next to power, life. Life I love, and beauty next to life. Yet where is that beauty who will rise with me, refreshed from slumber . . . ?"

As Marco had noted many times in the past, the Great Khan's speech was rambling, but never idle. In due course offerings were offered to the Lapis-Radiant Buddha-Khan of Healing. In due course the Polos, themselves, were sent on the difficult and dangerous journey to seek a new delicacy for the Great Khan's rice bowl: the beauty who slumbered long, and whom Kublai would waken to refresh and renew his own flagging strength. But before any of these, as if to prove his powers were yet undiminished, came the imperial visit to the Terrace for Managing Heaven, to consult with astrologers regarding the bold invasion of Japangu . . .

As Marco described the astrological observatory in his diary, two figures came walking down the narrow and stony beach. One was the sphinx, delicately lifting each perfect little leonine paw so the grains of sand dropped off. The other figure was Oliver's mute young page. Marco was pleased to see company and hailed them. "Page and lovely Sphinx, would you like to hear a story?" he called, addressing the sphinx in properly flattering terms.

The page looked startled, but the sphinx scampered to Marco and curled up beside him. "*Lovely riddle sees as lovely riddle is,*" the small creature murmured, as she busily preened her tawny fur. The page followed reluctantly and sat stiffly a little distance away, staring out to sea with his leather cap pulled low to shade his face.

"Let me tell you about Kublai's invasion of Japangu," said Marco.

The page stared sullenly ahead, whilst the sphinx arched her back and smiled enigmatically. Her pointed ears seemed to lift, the better to hear, and her golden eyes gleamed with intelligence somewhat more than human.

Li; Fire.
Bright Flames Above; Bright Flames Below.
The Sun Rises Twice In One Day.

25

Marco read from his travel diary to the sphinx and Oliver's mute page, who knelt beside him on the windy beach: "A grand procession accompanied the Great Khan to the Terrace for Managing Heaven, which was a stone tower in the eastern quarter of the city of Tai-Ting. Kublai and his favorite son, Prince Chenghin, rode in palanquins curtained in gold and purple brocade with imperial sun and moon designs. For the Emperor was ever troubled by the gout which kept him from his horse, and the prince grew ever weaker from his strange wasting disease. Phalanxes of Mongol horsemen guarded the Great Khan and Prince Chenghin, riding before and after the palanquins. Their ceremonial saddles and leather armor and fur-lined helmets were trimmed with silver and phoenix feathers; they carried bows and halberds, and fluttering banners with the sun and moon emblem. Drummers clashed great cymbals to warn the jostling crowds out of their way. Certain trusted generals and ministers rode with the royal party, and I was included in their number," said Marco; and the sphinx stretched her wings and nodded approvingly at this sign of royal favor.

Marco continued his account: "The observatory had been built recently to house both the soothsayers of the capital, and also the renowned astronomer and mathematician, Guo Shou-jing, and his assistants. I had visited the Terrace on other occasions to consult with Master Guo on matters of navigation, for his calendars, celestial charts and viewing instruments were far superior to any in Christendom. For a fact, he had devised an armillary sphere supported by great bronze dragons. It was composed of intersecting metal rings attached to a sighting tube, which could measure the movements and positions of the heavenly bodies in a most marvelous way. But navigation was not our concern on that day . . .

"The imperial astrologers use an almanac in which is written the movements of the planets through the constellations, for every minute of the year. These movements influence daily conditions and events, according to the laws of nature. The sages write their forecasts in little booklets called *tacuim*, which are sold for small cash to the people, so they might plan their enterprises according to the sequence of the heavens. If a man is planning an important venture, he gives the astrologers the exact minute of his birth, and his planetary influences are plotted to determine if the business will fare well or ill, and the most favorable day to begin. Those master astrologers whose predictions prove most accurate achieve the highest fame and honors."

The sphinx yawned politely, for indeed her innate knowledge of past, present and future was far beyond the crude mechanisms of astrology. Marco read on from his traveler's diary . . .

"It was just after the New Year; the sputtering fireworks and dumpling feasts had ended, and the season of Great Cold still lingered in the capital. You may be sure that the Great Khan's visit caused considerable stir among the soothsayers, who were all dressed up in their most dignified black padded-silk gowns, scholar's caps and felt slippers. The Emperor's birthtime and animal-year sign were well known to them, and they busily consulted their voluminous almanacs for the 18th year of Zhi-yuan or Kublai Khan's reign, which was the Lord's year of 1281.

"They carefully calculated the implications of the Heavenly Stems and Earthly Branches, and the movements of the Ruling Celestial Forces. Due to the importance of the Great Khan's inquiry, the yarrow stalks were also cast to determine the shifting forces of Yin and Yang, according to the venerable Book of Changes or *Yi Ching*. Finally the divination (and its accompanying rituals and honorifics) were read aloud by the Master Astrologer in a slow and sonorous voice . . ."

"Riddle, *riddle*; what did they *say*?" asked the sphinx, who paused in her preening and perked her pointed ears to listen to Marco's account. While Oliver's page continued to stare out to sea, as if deaf as well as mute.

"Their words were very strange," replied Marco, as he flipped a parchment page . . .

" 'The humble soothsayers of the Great Khan have noted the power of the hexegram *Li*, which is fire, and a disturbance in the constellation *Canglong*, the blue dragon. This suggests to the sages of the Terrace for Managing Heaven that the Middle Kingdom must swallow the Islands Japangu at the time of the summer solstice—or the insignificant Islands Japangu will someday try to swallow the Middle Kingdom. When smoke-steeds leap over the Great 10,000 *Li* Wall, Japangu will send iron-dragons flying through the air. They will rain fire upon the cities of Cathay, and the great and prosperous sphere of East-Asia. And flames shall flare like a sun rising twice in one day. Then no Son of Heaven will sit on the Dragon Throne, the Middle Kingdom will fall—*and the east will become red*. Thus speak the humble astrologers of the Khan of Khans . . .' From that time on, the Great Khan was determined to prove that his strength was undiminished by conquering Japangu," said Marco.

"Riddle, *riddle*; did his bold invasion succeed?" asked the sphinx, stretching her tawny paws langorously in the bright sunlight.

"Alas, the sorcerers of Japangu are extremely powerful. The Great Khan assembled the mightiest armada that has ever been seen, with more than four thousand ships, and 150,000 Mongol and Cathayan and Korean troops. They were well-armed with javelins, and arrows tipped with poison or exploding packets of flaming thunder-powder. They were led by courageous barons, who set sail from ports in Cathay and Koryo that spring."

"Surely such a terrible fleet could not be vanquished," said the sphinx, flicking flies off her compact wings with her leonine tail.

"The Japanese had built a massive wall at the site of the first Mongol landing, and they defended that wall fiercely with their arrows and spears," explained Marco. "The Mongol troops were unused to the sea, and the wall hampered their cavalry charges. The vassal Koreans were not entirely loyal to Kublai, and the Cathayans were not fierce warriors. So this vast army retreated back to their ships—and then the canny Japanese worked their uncanny sorcery upon them. Their devilish gods and golden idols sent a wild yet divine wind called *kamikaze*, which tore through the Great Khan's armada like a horse's hoof tears through an ant hill. The mighty ships foundered and sank, and most of the troops were drowned, or slaughtered when they tried to reach the shore. And thus ended the bold invasion of Japangu."

Marco rolled up the parchments of his travel diary as he concluded the tale: "Indeed, the astrologers were wrong, and no Japanese fire-dragons have yet appeared in Cathay's skies. But the Great Khan's strength and vigor seemed somehow diminished after this defeat, and his thoughts turned ever more to the quest for immortality—which has brought us to this enchanted isle."

The mute young page had turned his face toward Marco, and seemed to be listening intently . . .

"Do you enjoy tales?" asked Marco. He had never really spoken to the boy before, nor paid him much heed.

"Tales within tales," said the sphinx, with a mysterious smile and flick of her tail.

Oliver's page nodded abruptly, and shyly turned his head away once more.

"Ho! So your hearing and understanding are those of a normal lad—and only your tongue is lame. I must ask your master why this is so. Mayhap later we can seek a cure for you." Marco gazed at the page's face, wondering if there was any remedy for his affliction . . . perhaps the precise acupuncture needles applied just so. Of a sudden, he was struck by a certain quality in the youth's features—a certain resemblance. With a playful gesture, Marco reached over and knocked the deep-fitting cap off the page's head. A tumble of dark-auburn hair was released, and with a great rush of excitement, Marco suddenly recognized: *"Su-shen!"*

"I wondered when you would notice me—and whether you might be pleased to see me," she said, with an embarrassed little laugh.

"*Indeed* I am pleased to see you! But how come you to be here . . . and does Oliver know who you are?"

"My father and Olavr were close comrades at arms," said Su-shen, tossing her wind-ruffled hair. "And many a time each risked his own life to save the other."

The sphinx listened to this unraveling riddle with an intent gleam in her golden eyes.

Su-shen continued. "My father was mortally wounded by a poisoned arrow of the wild steppeland Cumanians—men of the same race as Kaidu's spies who waylaid you along the road, as fate would have it. When my father lay dying in Olavr's helpless arms, he asked the northman to look out for me, his only known child. Then my father died." She lowered her eyes for a moment, then raised them again.

"Olavr swore to his northern gods that he would

watch over me as my father had ofttimes watched over him. My mother had perished in childbirth, and Olavr had no means to look after a small child. So he gave me to the troop of wandering players, who promised to care for me and train my acrobatic skills. From time to time, ever since I was a little girl, Olavr would appear in some town where we were playing—quite unexpectedly—to be sure I was faring well. When he heard of my master's plan to sell me as a concubine to pay gambling debts, Olavr's face turned scarlet with rage. He urged me to escape . . . but I had nowhere to go. Solitary lowborn women do not fare well in Cathay. Then you came along, and my choice became clear. Olavr dressed me in page's gear, and we followed your horses until we found you along the roadside, trapped by men of the same breed who killed my father. And we have followed you ever since—and I will follow you evermore . . . if you will have me . . ."

"Speak not of following . . . never again will I lose you," said Marco in a voice gone deep with feeling. Then he kissed Su-shen . . . and kissed her, joyfully again.

But their embrace was interrupted by the shrill and frightened cries of the little sphinx, who leapt trembling into Su-shen's lap. Marco glanced in the direction that the sphinx's golden eyes were staring, and saw a troop of men. Strange and savage men armed with long spears, whose naked hides were painted with bands of red and white mud, whose ridged brows seemed a relic of some dim-distant time, and whose hindquarters were covered with flat and fleshy tails.

T'ai; Peace.
Earth is Supported by Gifts from Heaven.
The Princess Must Marry Below Her Rank.

26

Marco awoke from a strange dream—yet had he been dreaming? Confused images filled his mind . . . images of Su-shen dressed as Oliver's page, with dark-auburn hair tumbling from beneath her cap . . . but *why* would Su-shen appear to him now? Had she really been here, or was she just another confusing island dream-image? Like the men . . . mud-painted men with broad, flat tails . . . were they real or were they dream-spirit fragments? On Pleasure Island it was difficult to know what was real and what was dream. Had the savages *really* dragged Su-shen away from him . . . just when he had found her again? Had the mud-painted savages dragged her away as she struggled and fought? Had the sphinx snarled and snapped at their legs until they kicked the little creature aside . . . while Marco lay entranced and dreaming? *If* he had been dreaming.

"It was *no* dream," said the sphinx, busily licking at

torn golden wing-fur—and vanity—which had been bruised by brutal kicks.

"We *must* find Oliver; then we will search for Su-shen," said Marco, now fully awake.

They found Oliver some distance down the beach; perhaps he had been coming to warn them. The northman's eyes were red, and his mouth hung slack, as if his soul had been taken by the island's strange dream-spirits. For a fact, this was not the first time Marco had seen him this way. Sometimes . . . perhaps . . . he had been applying himself to a rather muddy liquid brewed from millet. Sometimes . . . perhaps . . . he had been inhaling the fumes of a sticky substance which the Cathayans called "mud," which was actually made of the sap of poppies. And sometimes . . . perhaps . . . a ghost or demon of some sort possessed him. At such times he would perhaps gaze at a semblance which other eyes did not see; or he would mutter or mumble, chant or even shout—rather like one of the heathen shamans or sorcerers: "Prophets of the devil," Uncle Maffeo called them.

Now the dream-spirits had clearly captured Oliver's mind. He seemed not to hear Marco's urgent words, nor did the northman respond to any attempts to rouse him. Then he began to talk in a rambling fashion, with many halts and pauses; sometimes looking at the Venetian and sometimes looking away, and he spoke in his own language. Then he moved into the broken speech which he and Marco had devised, but though the words—as though spoken by a mixed multitude—were understandable, their sense was not.

At length the Venetian said, "I cannot make out what you mean." And Oliver, stumbling (almost) over his own tongue, peered at him with eyes gone odd and said; "The Ruddy Rogue's fortune-favored son sought the vines across the sea . . . and thorn-laden vines be what you seek . . . but the girl-child's tendrils must stay masked . . ."

"What do you mean?" Marco enquired. But one might as well have asked clarity of some old crone babbling into her beard in the chimney-corner, or spreading her withered claws over the glowing eggs in the charcoal brazier. "Come with us to search for Su-shen, will you, Oliver?" he asked. No reply. "Ah then . . . drink a strong infusion of the herb the Cathayans call *ch'ai* to clear your brain, will you, Oliver? So that we can . . ."

Again; no reply. Slowly Oliver's massive blond head sank to the sandy ground; there into the deadened sleep of those possessed by the island's dream-spirits. His only further sound was a rumbling snore.

Then the only sound on that dismal beach was the tossing of the waves, the rustling of the wind in the nodding Pharaoh's-nut palms, and the forceful resonance of Marco's prayers. "Blessed San Marco, Lion of Venice and my name-saint, please protect her . . . so I might bring her as a gift to be baptised in your golden cathedral! Holy Mother Maria, guardian shield of all women, who glows like the moon in the midday sky . . . please help me to find her!"

At that moment something very odd happened. All the birds of the island began sailing through the air, screeching and circling as if seeking a roost for the night; while a great round shadow moved with a slow dignity across the glaring face of the sun—*like a dark moon in the midday sky*. Then the dim dusk of a solar eclipse settled on the island. Marco automatically made note of the date—June 4, 1285—and made note to mention it to Master Guo Shou-jing at the Terrace for Managing Heaven, when he returned to Khanbaluc (*if* he ever returned to Khanbaluc).

The eclipse somehow lessened the dream-spirits' hold on Oliver, and he woke abruptly. "We find her now, while wildmen fear sun be eaten," said the brawny northman, as if he already knew what had occurred.

The small island was divided into a lowland plain at the northern rim and a range of misty crags in the south. The lowlanders never ventured into the hills, for all knew that the mountain tribes were fierce hunters and cannibals, who sometimes raided lowland villages when game was scarce. Thus there was no question *where* Marco and Oliver should search for Su-shen; their fear was what gruesome plight they might find. The sphinx half-scampered and half-flew back to their camp to alert the men, while the two Europeans—one immense blond northman armed with a rugged battle axe, and one compact and chestnut-haired Italian armed with a keen silver dagger—headed into the forbidden hills on a grim mission of devotion.

The shadowy hush of the eclipse increased, and the sun was a slender light-crescent overhead, as Marco and Oliver clambered up the stony passes of the scrubby hillsides—while trying to stay awake. As they climbed higher, great waves of lethargy seemed to sweep upon them and drag them into nodding swoons. Time and again Marco prodded Oliver—or Oliver prodded Marco—awake. Nor did the powerful dream-spirits of the mountains allow them to doze off peacefully, for each lapse of consciousness was accompanied by frightful visions.

Marco cringed at the recurrent flickering dream-image of a shattered dead-white face with tangled copper hair, one bulging black eye, and a fragmented fanged mouth that sneered and hissed, "*I see her . . .*"

Then abruptly they were awakened by the sound of unearthly growled chants—or were these dream-chants? They could not be sure. They followed the sound until they came upon the mud-and-brush village of the flat-tailed, mud-painted savages, who chanted and danced as they built a great bonfire of dried twigs. Marco watched their broad flat-tails flapping, such as flap upon the rumps of the fat-tailed sheep in the land of Lesser Armenia, hard upon the *costa* of the great (and greatly distant) midland sea. Near the fire, a circle of leathery women bedecked with parrot feathers, and with bone ornaments clasped onto their broad tails, bent over a struggling creature, as women everywhere bend over a lamb being prepared for the roasting spit. But it was no luscious lamb they had snared—it was Su-shen.

"They make feast for newborn sun," said Oliver with a somber expression on his scarred and ruddy face.

"What can we do?" asked Marco. "If we attack they

will kill Su-shen before we can get near her . . , *if* we can stay awake long enough to attack . . ."

The eclipse had reached its peak, and the sun was a flaring ring around the dark disk of the moon. The cannibals paused to gaze upward at this wonder, with small eyes deeply set beneath thick-ridged brows—and at that moment Su-shen took action. With the speed and serpentine agility for which she was famed, she broke away from the circle of women and raced across the rugged hillside, with the savages—and Marco and Oliver—in close pursuit. Su-shen ran and *ran* . . . a solitary sparrow fleeing from the swift pack of shouting, flat-tailed brutes. At last she came to a rocky promontory that jutted over the tossing sea. Then she realized she was trapped; surrounded by sheer cliffs and deep waters on all three sides, with the mud-painted, spear-wielding wildmen close behind her.

"*Su-shen!*" Marco and Oliver both bellowed, but she was too terrified to hear or see them.

With a sudden graceful motion that surprised her attackers, and perhaps surprised herself, she dived off the cliff in a slow and sinuous and elegant swoop. Time—and Marco's thudding heart—seemed to pause until she hit the waves . . . and disappeared beneath the frothy water without any struggle or sound or trace.

Marco and Oliver hid behind an outcropping of boulders while the cannibals trooped dejectedly back to their rude village; perhaps to celebrate the rebirth of the sun by feasting on their usual moderate diet of toasted grubs. After they were gone, the two Europeans stood side-by-side at the edge of the steep promontory, and stared at the restless ocean for any sign of Su-shen. They saw nothing but her deep-fitting cap floating lazily out to sea . . .

The eclipse was passing, the bright sun-disk was returning from exile, and the birds began the plainchant of dawn for the second time that day. It sounded like a funeral dirge to Marco. The Venetian and the massive Northman glared at the sea in prolonged silence . . .

and who could say whether it was the salt-wind which stirred the tears from their eyes.

At length Oliver remarked; "Big, strong war-boats be tied down there . . ."

After another long silence Marco replied, "Yes, those dugouts must belong to the savages. We never came this way and noted them before. Our men can take them; they are far sturdier than our rowboats, and we can use them to escape this accursed Pleasure Island."

IV
They Find Wonders and Dangers . . .

Pi; Unity.

Water Flows Upon the Land.
The Earthen Bowl is Full.

27

Too many countless days and nights passed. The Polos and their men rowed the flat-tailed cannibals' war-boats northward across the uncharted southern seas. They knew only that the coast of Bengala in Greater India lay to the north, and from Bengala they could journey inland to Tebet. But how many endless days must they row northward before their destination was in reach?

Great was their relief when the Pole Star, and the Bear, and the other northern stars commonly used for navigation became visible in the nighttime sky once again. Peter the Tartar sang a yodeling song of his devils to celebrate their first sighting of the fixed light-point of the Pole Star:

"Mind is endless as the sky . . . with the clouds floating by . . .
Mind is vast as the ocean . . . with the waves rushing by . . .

Mind is mighty as the mountain . . . with the wind blowing by . . .
Mind is bright as the Pole Star . . . with the heavens whirling by . . ."

"Do you know any spicy love ballads like a normal lad?" grumbled Maffeo, stroking his unkempt beard.

Most of the journey was no celebration. Mostly it was tedium and hunger and thirst. With increasing desperation, the men held out their leather helmets to capture the offerings of passing rain clouds—but there was never enough to drink. *Never.* After each brief shower, the men squeezed every drop of moisture from their musty clothing into their feverish mouths . . . drip . . . drop . . . drop . . . drip. They lapped like dogs at puddles which collected on the muddy bottoms of the splintery dug-outs. Yet there was never enough to drink. *Never.*

Now they longed for the iridescent rain-dragons, and the monsoon gusts that jingled the silver wind-chimes beneath the mossy temple eaves of Chamba . . . so far away.

With increasing voracity, they set out fishing lines baited with bright-colored strips of their clothing. When they caught a hapless fish, be it large or small, they fell upon it with a frenzy; first sucking out the eye-juices, then attacking the still-living meat and guts. And many a fight broke out in those rude dug-out boats, over whose strip of shirt-cloth had lured which fish. So that squabbling and quarreling could be heard all day and night, like the snarling of beasts closely cooped in cages, which further increased the tension and misery felt by all the men.

Sometimes there were no fish at all for many a day, when the boats passed some sea-depth that inhibited their growth. Then there was only silent despair.

"This ocean is empty as the minds of Peter's devils," said Maffeo. "Do you recall, brother Nic, the Doge's sumptuous banquets in the grand marble banqueting hall of Venice? On one occasion we sat beside a grain merchant from the Overseas Territories, who was babbling on unheard until he burst out with, 'In the country of the Abbassinds there is a great plenitude of ostrich-birds, and I do assure you that these birds can eat and digest iron.' And you replied so gravely, Nic, 'Good, then you have only to imitate them and you will have no trouble with the banquet.' For you were such a finicky eater in those days, and felt that no company of cooks, however good, could do adequate justice to so many diners. Thus you stated: 'the ox-tail broth is sure to be spoiled.' But Messer Overseas did not take your point, and he replied, 'Ah, surely not, for this is our reward for our rich trade in spicery; we have such a great wealth of spices that the broth need never spoil!' And you, brother Nic, merely rolled up your eyes . . ." Uncle Maffeo rolled his own eyes as a demonstration, then hearing no response to this mildly amusing anecdote, he fell silent.

At long last, they reached the steamy coast of the Kingdom of Bengala. They entered the branching mouth of the mighty River Ganga, whose muddy waters flow from Kanchanjunga and the other sacred mountains, and remain wholly holy until they mingle with the unholy black waters of the Indoo Sea. With considerable relief, they disembarked from the wretched dugouts onto land (muddy, not dry land—in fact, quaking-bog land—but *land* nonetheless). Even the dour faces of the Mongol and Tartar guardsmen, and the worried faces of the Polos and Scholar Yen lit briefly with gladsome smiles.

The teeming Kingdom of Bengala was not subject to the Great Khan and was, in fact, allied to Bur-mien. Thus the Polos wished to pass through quickly, under the guise of private merchants. They would travel northward to Tebet along a tributary of the Ganga, by riverboat because they were horseless. In wild Tebet they would again be within the borders of the Khanate. There they would seek the home of the mysterious rune-carpet, which could lead them to the resting place of the elusive Sleeping Beauty.

They toyed with a fleeting notion of slinking westward—to Venice—but in fact they had not gold to book ship transport, nor the golden passport to guarantee safe passage through the western Khanates. Though Bengala was not subject to the Great Khan, his spies were *everywhere.* It would not do to be apprehended whilst crossing the wide realm of Persia, now ruled by the Great Khan's nephew. For despite all grumblings and rumblings, they were indeed Kublai's loyal liege-men; and their accumulated wealth was still hidden back in Khanbaluc. Well hidden there—but *there.*

The banks of the Ganga held a maze of bazaars and warehouses along the thronging docks and odorous alleyways. Marco heard a constant din of commerce in foodstuffs for the natives, and trade goods such as bales of cotton, precious spices from the southern islands, tattooed elephants, and large numbers of eunuch slaves.

Among the spice-scented bazaars were riverside temples of intricately carved pink sandstone, with gruesome idols of black death-head goddesses wreathed in flames. Stone stairways led from the towering temples to the holy dung-scented shores, where muddy river water lapped against smokey funeral pyres. Fat ravens and skinny dogs nosed among the ashes for scraps of charred flesh and bones. The strident chanting of idolaters mingled with the raucous cries of merchants and crows, and the chattering of monkeys cavorting in temple eaves. Trumpeting elephants and bellowing water buffalo, hooting conch shells and the wails of newly captured and castrated slaves created a harsh chaos in Marco's ears.

The docks were a moil and mix of pilgrims and commerce and confusion. Ragged boatmen swarmed around the Polos, offering trade-goods and transportation, supplies and slave-girls—*anything* could be bought on these docks for a price. Then a tall figure approached Marco and spoke softly and politely in trader's Latin: "I believe you will find my master's boats sturdy and comfortable for river transport."

Marco eyed the speaker and saw it was not man nor woman, but neither or both. The slender eunuch had the soft and downy skin of a woman, and the large and strong bones of a man. According to the customs of Bengala, he wore the draped-silk garments, silver wrist and ankle bangles, and black-kohl eye shadows of a woman—but his sturdy stature told of his origins as a man.

"Show us your master's boats, then," said Marco, and the tall eunuch led him along the dock.

"You are spice traders from Europe?" asked the eunuch. "I came also from the west—when I was young and whole."

"Yes, we came from Europe, and my ears tell me that you speak Latin well . . . but my eyes tell me that you have suffered a cruel fate," replied Marco.

"Indeed," said the eunuch with a long sigh. "My name is Vahan, and my father was a grain merchant from Greater Armenia, and a follower of the Eastern Church. Vahan the Elder traveled the trade routes during harvest season, buying and selling wheat, and returned home to our vineyards in the winter with his profits."

The eunuch gazed westward as though his sad eyes could still see his family's vineyards in the bright Armenian sunlight, then he spoke softly again. "Each year was much like the next, until one summer father saw that I had grown tall and strong as a man, and ready to learn the merchant's craft. After the harvest, I proudly said farewell to the younger children and my weeping mother. She gave me a knapsack filled with goat cheese and olives, black bread and dried figs, and a flask of our wine. My father complained that *he* never had such a savory parting, and mother said, 'You took your farewell gifts during the night.' Then we set off, and at first it was all a great romp, for my father was well-known and well-liked along his usual routes. All were eager to offer meat and drink—and servant girls—to the grain merchant and his newly grown son."

"But the romp did not last?" asked Marco with a shiver, as he realized how closely this story paralleled his own . . . except for its tragic end.

"Alas, no," said the eunuch, Vahan. "As we neared the far-distant River Oxus, our caravan was attacked by a band of renegade Tartars who wanted our gold and grain. My poor father was killed—and my misfortune was far worse, for I was taken alive as a slave. I was transported in shackles to the slave market of Bengala, and here I was unmanned and robbed of that joy I had so briefly known. I was tall and strong, so I was bought by a riverboat captain who paid a good price, and my master is a kindly man . . . so here I remain."

"You are not closely guarded; have you not thought of escaping back to Christian lands?" asked Marco.

"Where would a neuter find welcome in brutish Europeland?" asked the eunuch. "My voice is too rough to sing as a castrato in some choir. Here my kind is common, and we are treated with a certain gentleness. For in time we grow docile as plump geldings, gratefully eating grain from our master's hands."

"Briefly known joys are ofttimes hardest to lose," said Marco, thinking wistfully of Su-shen.

"Briefly known joys fade like half-remembered dreams," said Vahan with a shrug. "Now allow me to show you the boats."

The boats were sturdy and well-appointed, the oarsmen were well-fed and well-muscled, and the turbaned captain was a master of river navigation and lore. A bargain was struck and payment made in cowry shells. Thus did the Polos and their party travel upstream on the holy River Ganga and its jungly northeastern tributaries, until the muddy waters churned and boiled with turbulent white foam, and grew too rough for boat passage.

They bade farewell to the sad-eyed eunuch, Vahan, and his jovial master who had served them well, and set off on foot. *Li* after weary *li*, they trudged into the icy mountain passes of the Tebetan borderlands, with no guide except their skimpy maps, the wheeling stars, and the Great Khan's accursed scroll.

Kuai; Break-Through.
The Joyous Lake Ascends to Heaven.
A Man With Strong Cheekbones Walks
Alone in the Rain.

28

"*Seek the Head with a Hundred Eyes,*" Niccolo quoted thoughtfully from the Great Khan's scroll. "What can it be; what can it *be*? I have read . . . or heard, no matter, somewhere long ago, of a monster with a hundred heads . . . I *think*. And fast as Hercules cut them off, back they would grow. *Back would they grow.*"

They continued trudging wearily upward along the windswept mountain path lined with scrubby pines. Finally Uncle Maffeo replied that herculines bore an excellent fur. "Very rich and thick, and utile for tippets in cold climates like this, for the moisture in the breath does not freeze on 'em. *Herculines* also be called gluttons, which is to say *wolverines*. We are to search for a hill with a hundred wolverines, are we?"

His nephew, marveling, as often, at his uncle's marvelous non-logic, sighed. And said he thought they were looking for a door with a hundred keyholes. Or a keyhole with a hundred doors. Or . . .

Scholar Yen Lung-chuan, who had been fatigued and silent for some time, abruptly said, "*Ha*!" They all turned to look at him.

"What *Ha*!" asked Uncle Maffeo, twiddling his greying beard.

"A tale of the Blessed Ananda . . ."

"The blessed *what*?"

Marco tactfully interposed. "An Indoo sage, Uncle. He lived before the time of Our Lord; a virtuous pagan, now doubtless in Limbo and not in Hell." Privately he considered that Limbo might be preferable to this frigid bleakness where they now were climbing.

Uncle Maffeo nodded. "Virtuous pre-Christian pagan, eh?" He now had his point of reference. "Like Vergil, eh? Ahah. I, too, have studied Vergil in my time: *Arumque*, no, what am I saying? *Arma virumque cano,* which is to say, 'Of men and dogs and arms.' Vergil." As this seemed to exhaust his comments on the subject and exhaust his breath, he said no more.

Scholar Yen picked up the thread of his own discourse. "After the passing onward of Ṣakyamuni Buddha, of whom it is certainly incorrect to say that he died from eating pork, there was a great convocation of The Monks. Ananda the Disciple came to attend the convocation. But sundry of The Monks stopped him at the door, saying;" Scholar Yen cleared his throat and adopted the droning tone of a monk . . .

" 'This convocation is barred to you, O Ananda, by reason of your past assiduous devotion to the bodies of women, which is not the way of wisdom or knowledge, O Ananda!' And so saying, they closed the door in his face, locked it and withdrew the key. Whereupon, with a noise like great thunder, the Blessed Ananda entered—*through the keyhole.*"

Only the monotonous sound of their footsteps in the icy gravel broke the silence. Then Uncle Maffeo burst out in a huge guffaw. "Did you get that?" he demanded. "So much for your virtuous pagan," he snorted. "Do you take *that* meaning? Women! Knowledge! Keyhole! Ahahaha!"

His brother Nic weakly joined in the laughter. Scholar Yen allowed himself a very slight smile.

But Marco did not care for discussions of Ananda's virtue. Marco wondered where all this was leading them—or if it was leading them anywhere at all.

"My devils are singing to me, young master," said Peter the Tartar, as they climbed higher into the arid highlands.

"What is their song?" asked Marco.

"The words are too faint to grasp," said Peter.

"Then tell your damned devils to sing louder," snorted Uncle Maffeo.

They trudged ever upward beyond the treeline, until the lowland jungles and forested foothills were a distant memory below. They scrambled across a steep and narrow pass between slippery cliffs and jutting snow peaks, where earlier travelers had built rock-cairns to celebrate their safe ascent. Beyond the treacherous pass was a dry and barren plateau with weird rock formations, where a thin and dusty wind keened coldly in their ears.

"My devils are singing of fishes . . ." announced Peter.

"There are no fishes in *this* frigid desert," snapped Niccolo.

"Perhaps they are singing of the sweet sardines of Venice," said Maffeo with a sigh, "grilled with olive oil and garlic, and served with a flask of red wine. Ah, I can smell them now . . . and I can smell the canals too. These damned highlands have no scent at all! Even the occasional dung-pat is dust-dry and odorless."

"My devils sing a yodeling song, and tell us to seek the fish-shaped rock," said Peter.

"I have heard this devil-song before when we fled from the deadly crows," mused Marco. "I did well to name you after Saint Peter the Fisherman."

"So now we are to search for a fish with a hundred eyes . . . or is it a rock with a hundred fish? I am too old and weary for such puzzles," scoffed Maffeo. But when the great fish-shaped rock unexpectedly loomed before them, crowning a tumble of huge boulders that lay near their pathway, even scornful Uncle Maffeo looked wonderously surprised.

They all scrambled up the rise to the mysterious fishy rock. Indeed their wonder increased when they saw that the massive pile of rounded boulders was not solid, but was honeycombed with a network of shallow caves which resembled a mound of skulls, —or the *Head with a Hundred Eyes* as foretold in the Great Khan's scroll.

"Could we be on the track at last . . . does *she* sleep nearby?" asked Niccolo, whilst excitedly counting his old crystal rosary beads as if they were gemstones. Indeed he had mentally formulated: a rosary of rosy ruby-stones for the Hail Marys, and diamants for the Aves. Value: howsomever many years remission from Purgatory as the Holy Father shall declare . . .

They clambered among the eyelike caves and beheld an extraordinary sight. For the walls were covered with countless carvings of austere and peaceful Buddhas, and strange demons and idols of every kind. Their features and limbs were gracefully elongated, their multiple arms held mysterious implements and symbols, and their calm and furious faces were brilliantly painted. Indeed they were beautiful to behold—however spiritually misguided.

"These are old meditation caverns," said Scholar Yen. "Here the monks carved images of the tranquil and wrathful forces of the mind's memory chambers, while cultivating the inner heat that warms without flames."

"Only one thing will tranquilize *my* mind: the heat of the hearth beneath the four-starling shield, at the Palazzo di Polo in Most Serene Venice," grumbled Uncle Maffeo.

Then the amazement on Maffeo's—and on all their faces—knew no bounds when they entered a vast and dramatically carved chamber. There they found the wandering Cathayan knight, sometimes named *Hou Ying*, seated cross-legged and smiling on the ground, beneath a huge cross-legged and smiling stone Buddha.

Though the Polos and their men shivered in their

fur-lined robes, Hou Ying wore the same thin green cotton blouse, knee-britches, and hempen sandals he had last worn in the hot and humid jungles of Chamba. Perhaps he was cultivating the inner heat. He carried his rusty and trusty old halberd, and he yawned and spoke when they entered his cave. "So you have come at last . . . I had grown weary of waiting."

"*Hou Ying!* How come you to be here?" cried Marco.

"Did I not vow to join you in Tebet . . . and does not the virtuous knight keep his vows?"

"Did you walk alone in the monsoon rains—all the way from Chamba?" asked Marco.

"Ha! Such a walk would tear my poor sandals to shreds, and I have no cash to buy more. No, I did not walk alone in the rain; I rode upon a fine, fat white mule. Though her flanks have grown thin while waiting for you laggards to appear," said Hou Ying.

"How then did you get a mule and feed, if you have no cash?" asked Maffeo.

"Are my good masters not emissaries of the Great Khan?" asked Hou Ying, with an affronted expression on his high-cheekboned face. "Do my masters not carry the silver seal which entitles them to steeds and feed, provisions and supplies at any imperial posting station?"

"This is true," said Maffeo. ". . . but how did *you* obtain a mule? Not by theft, I might hope."

"*Theft!*" He loudly slapped his knee in exasperation. "Does a common thief requisition and lead an entire herd of nags—and feed and provisions and supplies—for his kind masters to use in the wild mountains of Tebet?"

"What do you mean?" asked Niccolo, nervously thumbing his beads.

"If you do not understand my meaning, refined Sirs, then look below this fish-crowned mound of skull-shaped boulders . . ."

The Polos and Scholar Yen left the cave and looked down to the ground. There they saw a herd of well-groomed and well-equipped horses (and one fat white mule) tethered to a clump of scrubby trees that grew round a trickling spring. The horses' saddlebags bulged with supplies, and the animals snorted and stamped their hooves impatiently.

"How do you suppose he did *that*?" asked Maffeo.

"Mayhap we should not ask," replied Marco.

"The wise man thankfully eats the rice offered," said Scholar Yen. "He need not know the location of the rice-paddies."

Nobody found fault with this bit of wisdom of the east.

Sun; Penetrating Winds.
Ceaseless Winds Blow Above and Below.
Grasses Bow Before Gentle Gusts.

29

The Polos and their troop, and the knight sometimes called Hou Ying, camped that night beneath the hundred-eyed boulders which held the skull-shaped Caves of Peaceful and Wrathful Memory. All were cheered by the new supplies from the strange horses' saddle bags, and the promise of respite for their sore and blistered feet.

"The horses have grown restless as crickets in a cage . . . what kept you so long?" asked Hou Ying, sipping at rice-wine heated over their feeble high-mountain campfire.

"Our ship was beset by dog-headed pirates," explained Marco. "We escaped in the rowboats, but a Naga-dragon followed us and asked where *you* could be found. When we refused to reveal your whereabouts, the sea-dragon abandoned us on an island where strange dream-spirits charmed the men—and where flat-tailed cannibals captured Su-shen."

"*Su-shen?*" asked the knight, gripping his halberd.

"Yes; she traveled with us disguised as Oliver's mute page, and . . ." as Marco and Oliver told of Su-shen's sad fate in hushed voices, Hou Ying's grip on his rusty halberd grew tighter, until his knuckles glared white in the flickering light of the sputtering campfire.

"You say she dived into the sea but *her body was not found*?" asked Hou Ying. "You were stranded on that wretched island through your loyalty to *me*. Does not an honorable knight save his humble face by repaying such benevolence?"

"You could not have known of this . . . and you have already repaid us a great deal," said Marco.

"It has been said of Hou Ying that he was willing to die for a master who esteemed him," said the wandering knight.

The feeble mountain fire died down to glowing coals, and talk was replaced by yawns as the weary travelers settled into sleep. Marco curled up in his fur-lined cloak. In that suspended space which is neither awake nor asleep, he heard a rustling sound. Marco half-opened his eyes, and saw a vague shadow outlined in the dim light of stars and embers. It was the broad figure of a man holding a halberd, who placed something in his sleeve that looked like a folded sheet of paper.

Still neither awake nor asleep, Marco watched the high-cheekboned figure pause; then carefully remove the white paper from his sleeve again—and unfold it. The convoluted paper grew larger and larger, until it assumed the size and form of a fat white mule. The shadowy figure with the halberd mounted the glistening mule just as Marco blinked his eyes. When he opened them, both man and mule were *gone*.

A silly dream image, thought Marco; I must have been sleeping after all.

A thin mountain wind whined in Marco's ears, and deep sleep would not come, though dream-fragments gusted through his mind. The soft words of the soft-faced eunuch, Vahan, hovered in Marco's thoughts: "*Briefly known joys fade like half-remembered dreams . . .*" Were these dreams or half-faded memories that filled his head and kept him from restful sleep? Marco lay curled in his fur-lined cloak beneath the Caves of Peaceful and Wrathful Memory, surmounted by the fish-shaped rock, and the winds of remembering blew ceaselessly through his mind . . .

"*Marco!*" A woman's voice was calling him. Whose voice was it? Now he recalled . . . how could he ever have forgotten? It was his ailing mother calling him from his games on the fish-scented docks of the Sclavonian Canal. She stood at the sun-heated iron gates of the Palazzo di Polo, where a thick tangle of scented pink roses grew in the tiny triangle of dry land beneath the four-starling emblem. Servants had brought the earth in baskets from the Terra Firma to suit his grandmother's fancy.

But Marco did not answer his frail mother's call, for he had no wish to go inside where it was dreary and drab, to study dry Latin and Greek with Friar Paul. He wanted to stay out in the bright sunlight, for a troupe of wandering players was calling to him . . . calling to him to see the show . . . beckoning with lively drums and flutes . . . displaying the strange masks and multicolored garb worn by the prancing jesters and fools, who called to him to watch the play. Marco ran along the muddy banks, and across the arched stone bridge of the Sclavonian Canal, with a groat-coin clutched in his sweaty little paw. And he did not answer his mother at all, for he truly wanted to see the show . . .

Yet no naughty Venetian lad could have imagined the show along the Great Khan's Grand Canal, when Marco and ailing Prince Chenghin sailed by royal barge from Khanbaluc to the rich southern province of Manzi. The Son of Heaven had named Marco a governor of the salt-tax office in Yang-zhau, and the Prince sought to escape his sick-bed by sailing with the Venetian along the restored Grand Canal. The newly redredged canal was the main artery of north-south commerce between Manzi and Cathay, and met the east-west flowing Yang-tze-kiang River at Yang-zhou. Chenghin sat on a low brocade couch on the deck of the gilded royal barge, facing the dragon-head prow. His pale and sunken-eyed face was shaded from the sun by white silk umbrellas, and he played his plaintive three-stringed lute as they watched the ever-shifting show pass by . . .

The Grand Canal was broader and deeper and far longer than any in Venice. It joined river to river and lake to lake in an aquatic highway. A roadway ran along the banks, so Marco watched divers traffic move both by water and by land. Long caravans of sampans transported rice from the rich paddies of the south to the arid capital in the north. Black char-stones traveled from the yellow dustlands of the northwest to fuel the kilns of the south. House-barges with bright potted gardens hauled huge mounds of floppy cabbages. Ragged peasants on foot carried produce and fish in heavy wicker baskets slung from bamboo shoulder-poles. Elegant gentlemen, and their ladies with tiny bound feet, enjoyed banquets and lively songs and games in phoenix-prowed pleasure-barges. Long funeral boats carried white-robed mourners whose somber chants echoed in the humid air.

Marco and the prince, wearing shimmering summer-silk robes, sailed past night-soil scented farmlands and the watch-tower pagodas of towns. They paid a royal visit to splendid Su-zhau, whose beauty much impressed Marco, for it is a city of narrow canals and arched-stone bridges that much resembles Venice. Su-zhau is called the *City of Earth*, for it has many stately mansions and gardens. Nearby is Hang-sai on magnificent Westlake, which is called the *City of Heaven*; indeed it was the grandest city (outside Most Great and Serene Venice) that Marco had seen in all the world. So the Venetian and ailing Prince Chenghin sailed along the Great Khan's Grand Canal, and watched the dreamlike show pass by . . .

Chenghin put aside his lute with a rueful sigh, and said to Marco, "It is on sweet days like this that I regret my dwindling life-span."

"But your father's empire is full of physicians of every

creed; surely the Great Khan has not exhausted all their lore," said Marco.

"It is *I* who am exhausted," said Prince Chenghin. And he resumed his wistful lute-song, for indeed he was a talented musician.

Of a sudden the prince's form shifted like rippling water, and changed into the sad-eyed eunuch, Vahan. "*Briefly known joys fade like half-remembered dreams* . . ." said the eunuch.

"*Marco, come inside . . . !*" called his ailing mother's voice.

"*No, Mother, I must watch the shifting show* . . ." said Marco.

The dreamlike winds of remembering blew also through the mind of Niccolo Polo, father of Marco, as he lay huddled in a musty fur robe beneath the Caves of Peaceful and Wrathful Memory . . .

"*You have a fine, fat son, Messer Niccolo,*" beamed the fine, fat midwife outside the massive wooden door of his bedchamber at the Palazzo di Polo. "You may give thanks to blessed San Marco that the child and your wife—although she is frail—are both well."

"I will give more than thanks," said Niccolo. "The child will be the namesake of San Marco, whose bones rest in the high altar of the Holy Basilica in our beloved Republic of Venice."

In the Lord's year 1254, Messer Niccolo Polo, a prosperous merchant of Venice, went to the Basilica di San Marco to give thanks for the birth of a son. Mist-filtered sunlight gave a sheen to the Canal Grande, and the marble paving of the great piazza which led to the mighty domed cathedral, built in the shape of a Greek cross supported by hundreds of marble columns. The interior of the basilica was always dim and shadowy, despite the glimmer of gilded Byzantine-style mosaics on the upper walls and vaulted ceilings, and the lavish jeweled enamels of the high altar where San Marco was buried. The quietude was broken only by the hushed echo of prayers. Messer Niccolo added his own voice as he counted his crystal rosary . . .

"A rope of pearls raped away from the choicest pearl-beds, where the Africk Ocean comingles its clove-pungent waters with the sandalwood-scented wavelets of the Indoo Sea. Thus fecundating with superior mer-grit the incomparably receptive and lustrous nacreous-shells of soft shell-flesh, previously unpenetrated by even a single grain. During those langorous nights beneath the Southern Cross, this tender mollusk feels the joyful descent of the slow, slowly forming, slowly dropping rain.—A double rope of such pearls, each the size of the milk-tooth of a virgin girl-child of the age to make her first communion. Such rope to double easily twice around the lace-festooned neck of such a virgin child of the Great Families who are inscribed in the Golden Book.

"Value of each rope (with clasps like tiny sharkfish of silver, well-washed with gold): one fine, fat white riding-mule of a quality fit for a Prince of the Church to ride upon, in visitations and peregrinations to whatsoever conclaves and shrines . . ."

What rosary was this? It was no proper rosary at all! The glittering arches of the cathedral shimmered and shifted, and became the lichen-crusted rock cairn where he crouched and hid from the gigant snow-leopard that paced incessantly back and forth; forth and back. And growled and thrusted with its massive paws, whilst Niccolo recited his litany of gems for comfort . . .

"The Great Khan's wine-cup; fully twice the size of the Doges' great flagon, but of purer gold. Enchased with cusps of silver filigree set with a score of bezel-star-sapphires, each the size of a mullet's eye (the very large mullets such as Cardinals have for Lent . . . farced with garlic, rosemary and figs). Each sapphire the value of a master-cook's thumb-ring of chalcedony and jet, set with three yellow diamants to symbolize the Holy Trinity, and each diamant the size of a grain of pure, plump wheat . . ."

Another shimmer and shift, and the rock-cairn and

giant pard disappeared. Now it was the Lord's year 1270, and Messer Niccolo Polo's chestnut hair and beard were already streaked with grey. He had returned to Venice with his younger brother, Maffeo, after their first triumphant journey to Cathay—only to be greeted with mistrust by the haughty Venetians who sneered at their outlandish rags.

Yet when they tore open the seams of their garments and let fall a rainbow of gems, all scoffing was replaced by wonder, and all knew that the brothers Polo had fared well in the Mongol court. Yet Niccolo's frail wife had not fared well in his absence, and the joy of his homecoming turned to sorrow when he learned of her death. Their only son was Marco, by then a strapping chestnut-haired lad of fifteen . . .

"Item: sixteen armils wrought of finest ruddy gold, inlaid with small rosettes of jasper and chalcedony, and set all about with diamants the size of the finger-joint of a new-weaned child. Value of each armil: one port-town able to receive vessels of not more than six-feet draught, its revenues between Epiphany and Saint John's day, for a two-year term . . ."

Well might Messer Niccolo find comfort in gemstones. For a man might carry a life's fortune on his own person, and unlike a man's hair and beard, their colors would not fade . . .

The chill winds of remembering whined also through the mind of Messer Maffeo Polo, gruff and grizzle-bearded younger brother of Niccolo and uncle of Marco, who also dreamed of that which gave him greatest comfort . . . *food.* He dreamed of fresh-baked wheaten bread, and tender pigeons roasted in the wood-burning oven of the Palazzo di Polo; nicely served with a good red wine, and a relish made of raisins and wild mushrooms, and the savory spices of the orient.

Ah, it was the devilish lure of the profits from those damned spices that had brought them to this heathen land. Here the rice tasted of grit, the wheat was shaped into worms, and the meat was doused with a nasty black sauce of salted soy beans . . .

"*Have you eaten yet?*" greeted the bowing and smiling Cathayan innkeeper during one of their interminable journeys for the Great Khan. "I can recommend the milky soup of goat-stomach tonight; we do not make it every night, elder masters."

"*Marón!* So tonight it is *that* kind of mutton!" grumbled Maffeo, feeling his stomach turn queasy as dreams of crisp roasted pigeons and hot wheaten bread and good red wine from the Terra Firma faded away . . .

The obliging innkeeper, not quite understanding, said that if the refined masters wished, he could have the soup prepared from sheep's tripe instead. Though most people preferred it the other way.

"You are suddenly very finicky, Brother," said Niccolo. "Yet a short while ago you would have gobbled toasted pony with relish!"

Marco reminded his uncle that—save perhaps for the flesh of he-goat in rutting season—nobody 'back home' would have turned up a nose at goat's meat. But they skipped the soup. Sometimes tripe was very tender, but ofttimes it was very tough.

The boisterous babble in the lantern-hung tea-shop, which had briefly broken off—and been replaced by stares—at the entrance of the foreigners, had begun again louder than before. The Cathayans were not, publicly, a noticeably silent or reticent people. But then, neither were the Venetians.

The usual very small boy with the shaven head and top-knot, and the seat cut from his trousers to insure that nature's calls would be quickly met, stood quietly in a corner. He was almost invisible, save when he would step forward to pat the teapot with his tiny hand, testing for loss of warmth. Then he would scamper outside to order another pot. Whilst Messer Maffeo Polo glumly ate his rice-grit and salted entrails and wheat-worms, and dreamed of roasted pigeons and fresh-baked wheaten bread.

*   *   *

Scholar Yen the Cathayan court-sage, Peter the young Tartar slave, Oliver the wandering Varangian, the small winged sphinx of the desert sands, and the Mongol and Tartar horsemen all felt the winds of remembering howling through their minds. They slept beneath the Caves of Peaceful and Wrathful Memory, crowned by the fish-shaped rock, and they creamed of their own heathen lands in their own hethen tongues. None slept entirely peacefully . . .

Xiao Kuo; The Small Are Great.
Thunder Roars Above Clouded Western Mountains.
The Flying Bird's Ancestress Sings No More.

30

They had climbed far above the treeline, to a place where nothing grew except a crumbling greyish lichen that carpeted the arid rocks. They had climbed above the clouds which swirled far below. They had climbed above the very falcs and kestrels, which gyred and circled beneath them. The sky was deep cobalt blue, and the air was extremely clear and dry. Thus their mouths and nostrils were parched, and their hair crackled with its own lightning. Had they also climbed beyond the air? For though they panted and huffed, their laboring lungs and pounding hearts drew little sustenance from the thin atmosphere.

The horses gasped and strained and balked, and had to be prodded to climb any higher. *Then the voices began.* At first they sounded like distant thunder rumbling in the glacial peaks. Then they resolved into the rumbling echoes of voices calling . . . calling to the Polos and their men.

One of the Mongol horsemen, a squat and moon-faced fellow of middle years, heard the clatter of hooves and the voices of his companions calling . . . calling him by name. Summoning him down a narrow side-trail leading away from the main pathway—to the crumbling edge of a steep ravine. There his horse, befuddled by lack of air, stumbled. Man and horse plunged into the ravine, both screaming, and disappeared forever into the foaming clouds below.

Another young Tartar horseman heard the hoofbeats and drumbeats, the clashing arms and hoarse shouts of a great band of brigands. He panicked and took flight, racing away from the track across barren rocks, until he had gone hopelessly astray and could never find his way back.

Marco and the mighty northman, Oliver, both heard Su-shen's plaintive voice calling to them from inside a dark cave. "*Su-shen!*" They plunged inside the black maze where they might have been lost for eternity, save for the aid of Peter the Tartar, who was used to the voices of devils. Peter followed after them, shouting that she was not real, and they must not venture further into the blackness. But Marco and Oliver would not heed his words, so Peter grabbed their arms and wrestled them to the icy ground—one small and wiry Tartar against two massive Europeans! At last the wrestling match broke through the enchantment, and two subdued westerners sheepishly followed Peter out of the cave.

Messers Niccolo and Maffeo Polo both heard the gruff voice of the wandering knight, sometimes called Hou Ying, who had disappeared with his white mule during the night of wind-blown memories. He called to them from behind a jumble of rocks near the trail; saying he had found a great trove of ant-gold. They followed Hou Ying's urgent summons, for indeed they had heard that ants gather gold in the mountains of Tebet. But when they reached the rocks, the voice had moved farther away. Now it echoed from behind a boulder which lay far from their trail and, as they followed the lure of the ant-gold, the voice moved further still.

"*Marón!*" gasped Maffeo, tugging his beard and looking bewildered and dazed in the rarefied air.

Then Niccolo realized it was a phantasm. He seized the reins of his confused brother's horse, and led and dragged and guided them back to the main trail; ignoring the calling voice by keeping his mind fixed on his oft-repeated litany of beloved gemstones. ". . . *An half-score of matched matchless rubies, each the size of a crab's eye, and each worth the weight and workmanship of a set of twelve silver apostle spoons . . .*"

Only the little sphinx and Scholar Yen rode effortlessly through the swirl of bewitching voices that called to them . . . called. Did a smug expression appear on the elegant features of Yen Lung-chuan's ivory-skinned face? Had he finally proved his point to the barbarian masters?

Scholar Yen calmly tucked his hands into the sleeves of his fur-lined black scholar's robe, and rode steadfastly forward on the rocky pathway, blandly ignoring the insistent voices. "*Illusion,*" he said with a dignified smile. "I believe I have often and courteously tried to teach their crude minds that all is illusion."

Then an apparition appeared on the trail that made even Scholar Yen stop and stare. It looked like a shabby man wearing the long hair and beard and nails, and the woven-leaf robe and straw sandals of a mountain recluse—though such scanty garments gave him no protection against the highland cold. His grimy face wore an eccentric expression. He carried a rough staff, and in his thin bare arms he cradled a large three-legged toad. "*Ho!*" he called, with a crazed little laugh.

"Illusions," muttered Scholar Yen, turning his head aside with a grimace of distaste.

"We meet again, esteemed Sir," said the disheveled illusion.

"I have never met with anything like you . . . even as a mirage," said Scholar Yen. His curiosity was roused despite himself, and he eyed the apparition with a haughty stare.

"Do you not recall the humble herbalist, Hua T'o, who taught you the 120 medicinal uses of the blessed hemp flower, and guided you to the Cloud-Dancing Fairy's cave?"

"I do recall such a fellow, but you have disguised yourself poorly, shade. Hua T'o wore the robes and manners of a refined scholar; not those of a mountain madman who cradles a toad as if it were a nursing child," said Yen Lung-chuan.

"Then I wore a scholar's silks, now I wear a recluse's leaves. Everything shifts and changes—yet remains the same."

"Humph," sniffed Scholar Yen. "And if you *were* the wandering physician Hua T'o—which I do not believe for one moment—then what would you be doing on this airless and ghost-infested slope?"

"If I *were* Hua T'o—which indeed I am—I would be searching for rare mountain mushrooms and black rock-salt which exist only on this high plateau, and which have peculiar healing powers."

"Peculiar, indeed," said Scholar Yen.

"And if you were the kindly physician Hua T'o," interrupted Niccolo, whilst worrying his second-best amber beads; "although Scholar Yen insists you are but a phantasm . . . and who can tell in this uncanny place? If you really *were* Hua T'o, would you know some way to guide us through this army of illusions . . . as you once guided us to the Fairy-Lady's cave in return for a well-filled rice bowl?"

"The earth and clouds now fill my rice bowl," said the recluse. "Yet if I were the humble healer, Hua T'o—which I am—then I might guide the illustrious masters once more."

"And how would the honorable Hua T'o guide us . . . if he were real?" asked Marco.

"If lowly Hua T'o were really here to guide you—which he is—then he would ring this crystal-toned bell which dispells the voices of illusion. Thus would he lead you through the bleak mountains—if he and his companion toad were real—which indeed they are."

"*Marón!* All these allusions to illusions give me headaches!" said Maffeo. "I care not whether this specter is real. If he has a bell that can guide us through this loathsome place, then let him lead on."

"If he be not some new demon who will lead us straight to hell," muttered Oliver.

"Now the barbarian masters ask *illusions* for guidance," said Scholar Yen with a resigned sigh.

Having all agreed (more or less) to follow the recluse (real or not), they let the crystalline song of his bell vanquish the spirit-voices, and lead them through the shadowed mountains.

Did the leaf-robed healer's rare mushrooms and black-rock salt perchance cure *gout*? Marco wondered, as they trudged ever upward behind the clear resonance of the bell. For the Great Khan was ofttimes troubled by an aching and swelling of the feet, and would well-reward one who brought him relief.

Marco well recalled his dour father reading to the Son of Heaven in the informal audience hall of Khanbaluc: "We were fortunate, Great Lord, to find a fine Byzantine manuscript in our small library. I shall translate: 'Salt of Saint Gregory; compounded of spikenard, ammonia, parsley, pepper and ginger. This is said to be an excellent medication for baldness, failures of the spleen, over-copious discharge of eye-rheum, the cough that comes at midnight . . .' " The face of Kublai Khan was not for long rather sour at this listing of complaints familiar to men *much* older than himself, for Messer Niccolo ended on a rather triumphant note; "and *gout*!"

"And *gout*. Ah, and *gout*!" said the Khan of Khans. "Which kind of spikenard, the lesser or the great? Which pepper; long black, green or white? Curly parsley or straight? And is the ammonia to be derived from camel dung or . . . ? Where are the chief apothecaries? Po-lo, translate this for them. They shall try all the alternatives, and when they have found the right formula, at once shall they bring it to me . . . to *me*! If I could easily mount a horse, I would go at once to the western border region round Da-tong, to see why the millet crop is less than last year. 'Tis a disaster most far-reaching; when the tax is paid in millet, how can they pay more tax if there is less millet? Shall I tax the yellow mud which they use to build their huts? This fall in crop value may mean a fall in road repair . . ." He gestured to Niccolo to rise from the polished marble floor of the informal audience hall.

The Great Khan gestured again and gave a short bark of a laugh, which shimmied the pearl fringes of his informal filigreed-gold crown. "Why are you still lurking there in your funny and rusty kow-tow? Can you compound gout medicine without your head? Tell me, Po-lo, this Saint Guleg-ah-li; he is one of your holy good spirits who dwell in the clouds? Yes? I *knew*, you see, I *knew*! Useless attempting to conceal knowledge from the Son of Heaven; not that any would dare. Master of Rites, come forward at once. You may omit six of the sixteen kow-tows. No more, or misrule would rear its head. Not fewer, or we may be here all night."

The Master of Rites had reached the foot of the informal throne (forests of ebony and cedar had gone into its making—but only small forests). The Master of Rites performed his final kow-tow.

"Attend carefully," said the Great Khan. "The foreign ghost, Guleg-ah-li, shall be given rank as a Cloud God, second class. Make him offerings appropriate to same. Go." The Master of Rites was gone. One barely remembered he had been there.

"Gout," murmured Kublai Khan. "Millet. When there is no millet, hunger is certain. Taxes . . . hunger . . . war . . ." The mutterings were reduced to a mere mumble, then to a low hum.

Marco did not think that if the Great Khan had lived in Christian lands (not having the character of Sakyamuni Buddha), he would likely have been a great saint for Our Lord.

Candles, thick as a healthy man's arm, guttered in a

thin early-winter breeze; perhaps once a wild wind from the Gobi, far west of the yellow millet fields of Da-tong. Marco shivered as he thought of those wild winds of the Gobi.

Though the court apothecaries had tried every possible recipe for 'Salt of Saint Gregory,' and though appropriate offerings were made to the newly appointed Cloud-God, second class, no remedy for the Great Khan's gout had yet been found. No remedy for the gout, nor for flagging youth and strength. And so the search went on . . . the search went on and *on*. Marco followed the singing bell across the malevolent mountains, and said a silent and short, but very sincere prayer to Saint Gregory.

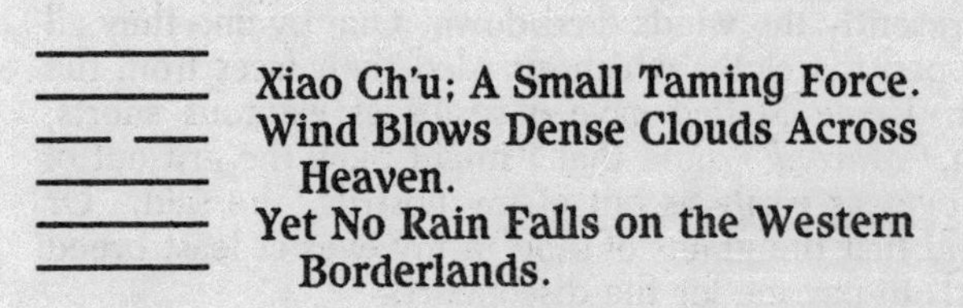

Xiao Ch'u; A Small Taming Force. Wind Blows Dense Clouds Across Heaven. Yet No Rain Falls on the Western Borderlands.

31

"Something is running through your head, my son," Niccolo said in his quiet way, so different from his brother's loud one.

Marco nodded. "Many memories; and a line from the Great Khan's scroll came running through my mind, Father, and would not go away. The one that says: '*Savor the sea where no sea be . . .*' "

Niccolo inclined his head. His angular face grew even more thoughtful than usual. "Somehow I make a connection with certain of *my* thoughts when I hid under that rock-pile from the gigantic lion-pard. Ah, what *was* it; what *is* it? Let no one speak for a while." Marco gestured to the mounted men for silence. The men fell silent. Long his father thought and brooded; brooded and thought. Then he cleared his throat and worried his best jade beads; then he shook his head.

"It has not come to me, but it will," he said. "*It will* . . ."

Now it seemed as if they had been traveling here for days . . . weeks . . . months. How long had they been following the crystal-voiced bell of the wandering herbalist, Hua T'o, through the bleak and barren mountain passes called This-La and That-La? How long had these thin, dry winds been whining in their ears, and blowing fine grit into their clothes and up their nostrils? Perhaps it had been a *day* . . . perhaps it had been a *year* that their horses had been plodding in the dusty mountain winds, while Marco's father thought upon the matter.

Presently the winds died down. One by one they all dropped the cloths which guarded their faces from the dust. Uncle Maffeo gave a series of vigorous snorts; then, "*Marón!* Would that I might blow the grit out of my eyes as easily as out of my nostrils," he said. "Or would that the grains of sand in my eyes at least breed pearls to pay me for the discomfort."

There were a few small chuckles of amusement, in which his elder brother joined. Then Niccolo's head snapped up.

A hundred and ten matched fine brown pearls of full lustre from the Archipelago of the Cynocephali or Dog-Headed men, each pearl the size of the pap of a fine fat woman with a nursing child . . . The words were from the oft-repeated inventory of precious stones which Niccolo had recited for his own immediate comfort, whilst hiding under the piled-up rocks from the gigant snow-leopard. "*Pearls!*"

They all looked up; looked over to him. "*Pearls! Pearls!* That must be the answer. The Great Kahn's scroll says, '*Savor the sea where no sea be . . . !*' What provenance have pearls? They are produced, are they not, by the rains which drop fresh water into oysters lying open in the sea? These drops fecundate them—do they not? In the sea? In the *sea*!"

Marco almost scowled his concentration; then rapidly translated his father's words. The men all looked perfectly blank. All, that is, save Scholar Yen who said, almost indulgently, "Not so, Elder Master Niccolo. It is not drops of fresh water, but flashes of lightning which engender pearls upon oysters . . . as witness our Cathayan paintings and carvings showing the heavenly dragon and heavenly pearl . . ."

Niccolo waved away this expression of eastern science. "But pearls are from the *sea*! Eh, son Marco? Brother Maffeo?"

Marco nodded. Nodded slowly. Said? Said nothing.

Not so Uncle Maffeo. His mouth worked within his grizzled beard. "The sea? Aye, the sea. Pearls? Why say 'pearls'? Why not say 'amber'? Amberjaune or ambergrise? Why not say 'cowry-shells'? Such are used for money in places remote from silver or gold, or from the Great Kahn's whimsical paper-money. Pearls, amber, ambergrise, cowries: all come from the sea, true. Yet *here* there is no sea to be seen . . ." His sunbrowned hands gestured broadly to emphasize his point.

"I see *no* sea, and I see no cowries, no amber. And I see *no* pearls. Would you seek them," Maffeo's heated voice fell silent, his dry mouth worked, his gesture encompassed all their dreadful physical world; "*here?*"

The dry and lifeless rocks stretched all around them.

Another day . . . week . . . month . . . passed as they followed the voice of the crystal bell along the mountain pathways. "What about *salt*?" Marco finally asked.

"What *about* salt?" replied his father wearily.

"Does not salt have the savor of the sea? Did not the herbalist, Hua T'o, say there were black-salt mountains in these regions?"

"Salt . . . pearls. I grow so weary of this guessing game," said Niccolo, fondling his jade beads. "Must we wander eternally in these wastelands, while our clothes turn to rags and our minds turn to dust, trying to solve the riddles of that accursed scroll?"

"I will ask the herbalist about those salt mountains; mayhap they might provide our answer—or at least a remedy for the Great Khan's gout," replied Marco, urging his breathless horse ahead and leaving his father to wearily worry his beads.

"*Riddle?*" asked the sphinx, poking her head out of Marco's saddle-bag. "Does anybody want to play riddles?"

"There are more than 2,000 remedies in my lowly pharmacy, younger sir, and among them is the highly potent black salt, found only in the rocks of these western mountains which surround us," said Hua T'o, in answer to Marco's question. "If I were really here, I would break off a bit of black rock-salt like *this* . . . for you to taste . . ."

Marco popped the bit into his mouth and tasted—the sea! "*Savor the sea where no sea be!*" he crowed. "This solves one riddle of the Great Kahn's scroll; surely we are on the right track at last."

"*Riddle* . . . would you like to play riddle?" repeated the sphinx, popping up from the saddle-bag with her small golden-furred body all a-shiver.

"Indeed, lovely Sphinx, ask me your riddle," said Marco with an indulgent chuckle, ruffling the silken fur on the creature's head.

"What causes a sphinx of the drowsy-hot deserts to shiver?" she asked.

"Well . . . I suppose it must be the cold weather," said Marco.

"It has been biting cold for many days," complained the sphinx. "Yet I have just begun to shiver *now.*"

"Are you shivering with excitement because the black rock-salt solves the scroll's sea-savor puzzle? *No?* Well then, this is an odd riddle—pray tell me the answer, charming Sphinx."

"The answer lies here in your saddle-bag," said the sphinx. "At the mention of the black-salt mountains that curious carpet, which had been my cosy nest, coiled itself like a living cobra—leaving *me* to tremble without shelter from the cold!"

"I am so sorry, sublime Sphinx, you should have *told* me!" cried Marco.

"Sphinx-folk do not *tell* . . . we *inquire.*"

Marco peered into the saddle-bag and saw that the

sphinx was not spinning tales. The faded red and gold Tebetan carpet, which bore the same thorn-rune marking as Oliver's amulet and the Great Khan's mysterious scroll, had been wrapped around the sphinx to protect her from the icy winds. But now it was coiled and tense as a quivering serpent about to strike. As Marco drew back the covering flap of the saddle-bag—it suddenly sprang *upward* into the thin air.

Then it lazily uncoiled and floated gently ahead, like a great winged butterfly dreaming it was a faded red, floating carpet. *Or did the carpet dream it had become a butterfly?*

"My devils tell me that we are very close now," said Peter the Tartar.

Awed and silent, they all followed the fluttering carpet as it glided forward. At last it led them down a slippery and obscure side-trail, which tumbled along the steep rock-face of a narrow gorge—into a green and verdant valley far below.

They slipped and slid down into the secret vale, as the air grew rich and creamy and moist. The skeletal rocks of the high passes became clothed with velvety mosses in varied shades of green. A burbling creek played happily along the valley floor, and its banks were lined with waving willows and wild apricot trees, still bearing the remnants of late-season fruit. The men paused to drink their fill of fresh, clean water, and to feast on the sour apricots, which they shared with a twittering flock of tiny yellow birds. But the floating carpet fluttered restlessly in the mild breeze, and would not wait to draw them deeper into the twisting gorge.

"I have wandered these mountains for *many* years . . . and never knew of this," said the reclusive herbalist, Hua T'o, munching a wizened apricot and gazing in wonder at the luxuriant valley. While his three-legged toad leaped from his scrawny arms and pranced merrily in the damp mosses, hunting for tasty grubs.

Then all stopped and pointed and stared. Perched on a tongue of rock, overlooking the distant mouth of the narrow gorge, was a marvelous white stone castle shaped like a curved bell with a long spire, and overgrown with brambly vines. The ramparts of the mighty castle were bedecked with faded red and gold banners tossing in the wind—which bore the throne-rune sign of the carpet, amulet and scroll!

The rune-carpet fluttered swiftly ahead . . . eager to fly home.

Sung; Conflict.
Heaven and the Abyss Go Their Separate Ways.
A Clan of 300 Must Retreat Before Mighty Foes.

32

Shouting triumphantly, and holding up his small silver cross to ward off unseen evil, Marco urged his horse into a trot. He followed the floating rune-carpet along the length of the hidden valley, with the others trailing closely behind.

As they drew closer to the glowing white stone stupa-fortress, Marco was awed by its massive size. The encircling walls rose abruptly from the rocky promontory at the valley's mouth, and were buried in a tangle of brambles and thorn-vines. The ramparts, with their fluttering red and gold rune-banners, overlooked the entire gorge. The vine-bedecked facades of the curved bell-shaped structure were windowless and blank, save for rows of narrow niches where armed warriors might stand. The immense beams were carved and inlaid with colorful designs, and supported the upturned eaves of the verandahs and their flying-phoenix crests. Ochre roof-tiles gleamed in the clear mountain sunlight, and the gold-tipped spire grazed the cobalt sky.

As they drew close to the towering stone walls of the fortress, a buzzing sound could be heard above the clatter of horses' hooves. They tethered their mounts to a clump of willows beside the swift stream, and set off on foot to explore. Then Marco realized that the castle was quite neglected and abandoned—except by humming hornets whose dried-mud nests had invaded the entire ruined structure.

Now seen from closer vantage, this was not the shining palace they had glimpsed from afar. The bell-shaped white walls were crumbling, the rune-banners were in tatters, and the ochre roof-tiles of the verandahs were cracked and shattered in many places, so they resembled a mouth filled with broken teeth. The impenetrable curtain of brambly vines sprouted and ran everywhere, threatening with long and vicious thorns that echoed and thorn-rune of carpet, banners and scroll. Rank brambles covered the broken walls and gate and ramparts, trailed from the sagging window-niches, and hung from decaying beams beneath moldering upturned eaves, which were honeycombed with a network of hornets' nests. The sleek and deadly insects swarmed round the stupa-fortress like a buzzing black cloud.

Marco explored an algae-slimed old carp pond outside the vine-shrouded gate, and wondered how they might enter. Could this ruined castle be the Sleeping Beauty's cosy bower—or had they traveled so far on a fool's errand?

Then of a sudden, the thunder of great drums and the low wail of long Tebetan horns echoed from inside the castle, and grim eyes peered from each narrow window-niche. Marco gazed upward, and saw that the eyes glared from beneath the shaven heads and brows of maroon-robed nuns of some sorcerers' sect. The three Polos and Scholar Yen hailed the nuns and bowed low in greeting, but the idolaters did not reply.

Instead there was a roaring clash of cymbals that seemed to shake the entire valley, as the nuns raised their mighty bows. The Mongols and Tartars raced to their horses to retrieve their own weapons, but before they could fit their arrows, there flew from the castle a rain of bright-hued wooden missiles shaped like flying phoenixes—with greenish smoke spurting from their plumed tails.

"*Marón!*" swore Maffeo, whilst Niccolo counted his rosary.

The warrior-nuns began a deep and sonorous sutra-chant, as they launched a hailstorm of prismatic phoenixes which descended among the shouting men. The missiles did not explode in flames like thunder-powder weapons. Instead they landed gracefully on the mossy valley floor—where they sputtered their greenish smoke in a thick, eye-stinging haze.

The men shot a round of arrows that soared upward, then fell just short of their mark. They smashed furiously at the phoenixes with their heavy felt boots. This released great clouds of rising green smoke, now tinged with purple. One by one the men staggered as if struck by a heavy blow, then fell to the ground in a deep sleep.

Marco and Peter tried to outrace the fumes, but they could not escape the valley winds carrying tendrils of sickly-sweet smoke swirling round their heads . . . swirling . . . *swirling.* The pounding drums and wailing horns, the triumphantly chanting nuns and soporific green haze swirled and echoed inside their minds—until Marco and Peter sank to the damp earth in a dream-filled swoon.

"The Great Khan . . . at times a genius without passions; at times almost a spoiled child . . ." Who had said that? Why, Marco himself had said that to his father and uncle, after an informal audience with the Son of Heaven at the slushy edge of the Carp Pond of Great Seclusion at Khanbaluc, winter citadel of the Khan of Khans; shortly before they departed for the annual springtime hunt.

The Great Khan: wise and just, cruel, generous and greedy. "I am the Son of Heaven, and like heaven not to be judged," the Khan of Khans had said one dusty and blustery day in March, as they traveled southward from the capital on the yearly hunting expedition.

The Great Khan did not travel lightly. With him were his favorite sons, barons and concubines, his many physicians and astrologers, kite-flyers, cooks and servants; all housed in splendid domed yurt-tents, lined with thick felt and tiger skins and sables, and topped with fluttering sun-and-moon banners.

Fully 10,000 falconers and keepers accompanied the imperial party, dressed in livery of scarlet and blue; indeed their line of march extended for more than a day's journey. The keepers tended the hunting mastiffs and trained lions, and leopard-spotted hunting beasts which were *not* leopards, and the 5,000 eagles and falcons, gerfalcons and peregrine falcons that provided such great sport for the Great Khan.

The Khan of Khans rode on the backs of four tattooed elephants, in an ornate wooden pavilion lined with shimmering silks and supple lion skins. He chose this form of transport due to his gout. His favorite barons and falcons rode with him as hunting companions, and on this occasion Marco had been invited to join the royal party . . .

"I grow tired of moving around from this city to that camp, and from that camp to another city, and so on," the Great Kahn had said. "Has not the Book of Analects declared that '*At forty it is time to settle in a fixed abode*'? I shall soon be forty." He gazed at Marco with his rufous eyes.

In all the east, from Byzantium to Japangu, a person who would reply to such a statement with, "Your Supremacy will never see *fifty* again,"—such a person would not merely be unwise, but dangerously insane.

"Yes, Great Lord," said Marco with a silent sigh.

Marco continued to work on the broken wing-feathers of Kublai's favorite white Manchurian falcon, which he was mending with an imping needle and white silk thread. The double blunt-ended imping needle bore the marks of the almost doll-sized hammer which had fashioned it. All of Marco's attention was required to mend the feathers without harming the white falcon's wing . . .

But why was the not-yet-healed falcon flying . . . *flying* . . . like a shimmering bird of white jade taking wing? And why had the falcon suddenly changed into a great red and gold carp with the thorn-rune symbol on its algae-crusted fins, as it glided through the air . . . *glided* . . . with Peter the Tartar riding on its back?

"The fish holds the key," laughed Peter, as he flew through the air on the rune-marked carp.

And Marco woke with a start.

Messer Marco Polo had a pounding headache that throbbed behind his temples like the echo of a great Tebetan drum. He looked around and saw the men still snoring on the ground in deep slumber. Because he had run from the soporific phoenix-missiles, he had breathed less of the fumes. Thus he had wakened sooner than the others, though his mind still lingered in a daze.

The smashed phoenixes lay still and drained of their vapors. The shaven heads and browless, glaring eyes of the warrior-nuns had disappeared from the window-niches, and their eerie music sounded no more. The red sun-globe floated low above towering snow peaks, and all was quiet and peaceful on the hidden valley floor.

Marco knew he had been dreaming, and he struggled to retrieve the dream-fragments from his clouded mind. Something about the Great Khan and smoking phoenixes . . . or was it white falcons . . . or carp? That was it! The Great Kahn had been riding a smoking carp . . . or was it Peter? Then it came to him quite clearly. Peter rode a flying carp and shouted, *"The fish holds the key!"* But what fish . . . what key? Marco glanced over at Peter, and saw that his young Tartar slave was starting to mumble and waken, but he knew it was useless to try and hurry the fog from Peter's mind. Then Marco remembered the old algae-crusted carp pond in front of the bramble-cloaked gate of the ruined castle. Could there be a connection?

Marco stumbled to the pond and peered into the green algae-slime. Could any fish still live in such stagnant water? He took a bit of barley-cake from a pocket and tossed it into the murky depth, as if summoning the venerable carp in the Pond of Great Seclusion at Khanbaluc for a tasty snack.

Of a sudden there was a great foaming and rippling in the water, which caused the green slime-crust to churn and fragment. Then from the deep emerged a huge fishy head coated with flecks of algae. "*Why wake me . . . ?*" whispered the ancient red and gold carp, with its gills flaring.

"I . . . I want the key," said Marco, staring into the carp's fathomless eyes.

"Why wake *me* for the key?" whispered the glittering red and gold carp, which had the mark of the thorn-rune on its fins.

"I thought you might have it, Sir Carp . . ."

"You must follow me if you want the key," said the ageless carp, as it abruptly dived back into the murky water.

With an impulsive leap, Marco jumped into the frigid ooze and grabbed hold of the carp's broad and flapping tail. The immense and muscular fish easily towed him down . . . down. —Just as Peter the Tartar came running to the crumbling bank of the pond, shouting, "*Master Marco!*"

Then Marco heard a bubbling splash, and felt Peter's wiry hands grab onto his ankles. The fish towed both men *down* . . . lung-bursting down through a dark aquatic channel. Flames burst in Marco's chest and shot sparks behind his eyes. He could hold his breath no longer . . . *no! longer!* He must breathe . . . *must! breathe!*

Marco opened his mouth, and was about to gasp the rancid and lethal fluid into his throat. Of a sudden the mysterious carp emerged from the black tunnel into bright green water, and shot up . . . *up* to the sunlit surface. Marco and Peter spat water flecked with bitter algae, and gasped and panted the rich and cool mountain air into their burning lungs.

Then they looked around and found that they were floating on the surface of a large pink-lotus pond—*inside* the walls of the enchanted castle.

V

The Sleeping Beauty Sleeps Soundly

Chung Fu; Inner Truth.
Gentle Wind Blows Over the Marsh.
Even Lowly Pigs May Cross the Great Sea.

33

Marco and Peter gazed round the vast courtyard of the enchanted bell-shaped castle with growing surprise. Within the thorn-grown ring, there was no evidence of the decay which was so visible from without. The impressive white-rock walls and gleaming ramparts were sturdy and free of brambles. The mighty beams of the verandahs and window-niches were brilliantly etched with heathen symbols in vermillion and gold. Perfect rows of ochre roof-tiles glittered merrily in the mountain sunlight.

There was no sign of life at all. No shaven-headed nuns glared from the windows. No greedy carp burbled in the pond. Swarms of hornets there were—but hanging suspended in mid-flight as if time had come to a halt. Marco and Peter saw that time had indeed paused in this eerie place. No clouds sailed across the cobalt sky, and no breeze brushed their cheeks. Nothing lived. Nothing grew. Nothing moved.

They climbed a steep and narrow stone stairway from the courtyard to the lower ramparts, and gazed over the wall. Outside the circle of frozen time, all was movement and life. Hornets buzzed, thorn-vines rustled on crumbling walls, and clouds wind-whirled across the sky. The men were waking from their daze and rubbing their eyes, rising from the ground and shouting to their comrades. The elder Polos were calling and searching for Marco and Peter.

"I wonder if they can hear us," said Marco. He cupped his hands around his mouth and bellowed; "*Father . . . Uncle . . . !*" There was no response. "It seems they cannot hear us—but if we go *outside* to fetch them, then how will we gain entry again?"

"We could see and hear the warrior-nuns; whether they were real or one of Scholar Yen's illusions, I cannot say. Yet they were indeed *visible* and they threw missiles *outside* the walls . . . mayhap we can throw something and be seen as well," said Peter.

"What should we throw . . . where . . . ?"

Just then Oliver came striding beneath the wall with his long and loping gait. So brawny and tall he appeared, his battle-scarred skin so ruddy and his hair and beard so fair; quite unlike the stocky and sallow Mongols and Tartars who hailed the Northman. Impulsively, Marco picked up a pebble and tossed it over the wall—so it struck Oliver's brow.

The frowning Varangian looked up, startled, and instinctively reached inside his shaggy shirt to clasp the protective rune-amulet dangling from a thong around his massive neck. Of a sudden, Marco grew as agitated as a Venetian fish-monger on a hot afternoon. He waved his arms and jumped up and down, whilst shouting; "Your *amulet*, man. *Read the spell on your amulet!*"

Oliver shaded his improbable smoke-blue eyes, and scanned the ramparts for a glimpse of his attacker. A slow smile brightened his broad face when he spied Marco gesticulating like a mad puppet at a street-fair. Then the Northman gestured helplessly at the thorn-clad walls which separated them.

"Read the spell on your amulet!" Marco shouted, and he pointed to his *own* chest, and reached inside his own leather blouse to withdraw the blessed silver cross worn around his neck . . . and gestured . . . and pointed. Until the Northman finally understood, and with a slow nod he pulled the amulet from his bear-skin shirt.

"Now *read* it . . . *read it!*" bellowed Marco, again gesturing and pointing, until at last they heard Oliver's booming voice slice through the time-stilled silence.

"Fay, Rider, Ice, Thorn.
Old, Raider, Canker, Norn.
Year, Sun, Hail, Bull.
Man, Lake, Birchrod, Wool.
Thorn, Norn; Norn, Thorn . . ."

"Break the spell, so life's reborn," Peter added in a devilish rush of inspiration.

It was ever a puzzle to Marco that pagan rune-symbols of the icy far north could retain their power over demonic forces of isolated Tebetan mountains; yet he had sensed it would be so. For are not the words of power universal, and do they not derive their strength from the All-mighty, whose speech is beyond the babble of mere humans? So Marco had sensed, and so it proved to be . . .

When Oliver finished reciting the amulet's rune-spell, there came a rumbling as of distant thunder, and the thorn-vines parted before the tall wooden gateway of the castle. Then it was a simple task for great Oliver and the troops to pry open the gates, and enter the courtyard. Marco and Peter raced down the stone stairway to greet the men, who stared in surprise at the time-frozen scene.

Nothing moved. Nobody spoke. Then the faded rune-carpet sailed majestically through the gateway—and entered the brilliantly etched portal of the castle. The sphinx gracefully took to wing and followed closely behind the carpet, while the intruders silently and cautiously trailed after the sphinx.

They entered a large and luminous chamber that shone with a soft and mysterious green light that seemed to have no source. The room was lined with tremendous idols in marvelous and grotesque postures, all carved in translucent green jade, and studded with glittering emeralds that made Niccolo's eyes bulge. The floors and walls and vaulted ceiling were lined with leaf-green marble, and all gazed in wonder at the verdant chamber.

Yet there was no time to pause, for the carpet sailed up a stairway paved with green jasper to the second level of the stupa-castle. The Polos gestured to the men to ready their arms, lest the warrior-nuns reappear; with eyes and ears alert for trouble, they followed the floating carpet.

The second level held a chamber even grander than the first, and shone with a pale and sourceless blue light. Immense effigies, carved of deep blue lapis lazuli, were studded with turquoises and sapphires of a size which made Niccolo's breath thicken and quicken. The idols were formed in male/female pairs, and entwined in embraces which made even bawdy Maffeo blush. The walls and floors and ceiling were made of peacock-blue marble, and all eyes widened at such a lavish display of azure beauty.

Onward. Up a blue marble stairway to the third level of the castle, where they found a vast hall all in *black.* The dim and shadowy light, also from some unseen source, was reflected in the faceted obsidian that studded the inky marble walls. Glowering and towering demons of polished ebony, wreathed with red cinnabar flames, glared down at them—and none wanted to tarry long in the dark chamber.

The sphinx glided behind the rune-carpet, up a somber slate stairway into the spire of the bell-shaped castle. Then she gave a shrill yelp. Marco bounded up the stairs to aid the creature, and cried out too. For the light that seared his eyes was a brilliant and blazing and blinding white. For a long and terrible moment he thought his eyes had been blasted from his head. Were those tears streaming down his cheeks—or blood?

When his vision finally cleared, he saw a soaring and

circular tower which rose above the castle, and reflected the sunlight in countless quartz crystals which covered every surface. Then Marco saw *her*.

The Sleeping Beauty reclined on a couch of milk-white alabaster in the center of the tower. Her flowing robes were of shimmering white velvet, and her glowing skin was pale as wax. Her long and silky hair shrouded her shoulders in snowy gossamer. Her eyes were closed yet she smiled softly. Her head was propped languidly on one hand, but her elegant limbs and delicate features seemed immobile—and he wondered if she even breathed.

Marco fell to his knees, without thinking why, and crossed himself as an old hymn to the Blessed Mother sprang from his lips.

"*Angels praise thee, worthy Maria, merciful and kind.*
Stainless Virgin, thy children delight in thy benevolent mind.
Look down and hear our humble voices in prayers and pleas.
You are health and healer; please relieve our miseries.
First parent, may your mighty arm protect us from all harm . . ."

Still on his knees, Marco contemplated the Sleeping Beauty, who was indeed the most beautiful woman he had ever seen. She was illuminated with an inner glory that radiated peace and compassion, wisdom and love. The others gathered behind him, still rubbing their light-seared eyes. One by one they also kneeled—or kow-towed—according to the customs of their land.

"She is Wang-ma, the *Immortal Mother who is King of the West*, and who dwells on the lofty mountain in the center of the universe," said Peter.

"Hail *Lady Isis*, Great of Magic," said the sphinx.

"I see the kindly Goddess of Mercy, *Kuan Yin*, the compassionate mother who gives sons to barren wives, and succor in time of need," said Scholar Yen with uncharacteristic fervor.

The Mongol horsemen began a deep chant in honor

of noble and victorious *Mother Drolma,* which Marco understood to mean:

"Her wisdom body smiles beautifully.
Her right hand offers long life generously.
Her left hand gestures the three jewels splendidly,
She holds a red flower with petals open delicately.
Her silken robes and flowing hair drape gracefully.
Her lotus garlands and rare ornaments shine brilliantly.
She sits on a red sun-disk throne easily.
Her rainbow light radiates infinitely . . ."

Niccolo Polo knelt and crossed himself, and began to count his crystal rosary (though he could not resist a quick and shrewd appraisal of the lady's diamant and moonstone jewelry, doubtless worth the rental of a large island in the Grecian Sea). The rune-carpet fluttered reverently around the Sleeping Beauty's couch and came to rest at her feet; whilst the sphinx perched silent and alert on its faded red and gold surface.

Only Uncle Maffeo Polo remained standing behind the others, tugging at his grizzled beard and muttering under his breath: "*Marón!* I hope the Great Khan will be pleased. She is indeed a beauty, but she looks like no *real* woman at all! Me thinks she is merely a heathen idol of some marvelous sort. A simulacrum . . . though I know not of what . . ."

Said Marco, "Paradise has infinite beauty; mayhap this be a simulacrum of something unknown and lovely in Limbo?"

Chin; Progress.
Blazing Sun Rises Over the Earth.
The Bright Prince is Honored with Regal Steeds.

34

"How, then, do we wake her?" asked Niccolo, rising stiffly to his feet.

"How, *indeed*, elder brother?" responded Maffeo. "For she has not twitched even an eyelid all the time we have been gawking and squawking in her ladyship's bedchamber."

"Perhaps Oliver's rune-spell will wake her," suggested Marco.

Oliver was roused from his musings at the Sleeping Beauty's couch. In a low, slow and rumbling voice he spoke: "When I be a sapling lad of Nordland, elders told of All-Father Odin, who wears ravens on his shoulders, and who feasts with slain heroes in the golden mead-hall of Asgard. The *Valkyrie* be Odin's mounted warrior-maidens, who select the fallen heroes of Valhalla. When the Valkyrie ride forth, their armor flashes in yon sky as nord-lights, flickering bright as this lady's face.

The rune-spell is Lord Odin's work . . . mayhap he can wake this slumbering maiden."

Ha! I suspected that weird bone amulet contained no proper prayer to the Blessed Mother, thought Marco.

Yet when Oliver thundered his rune-spell in the light-washed spire, nothing happened—nothing at all. The Sleeping Beauty did not waken, nor did she even stir.

"The Cloud-Dancing Fairy was ever diverted by my riddles," said the golden-furred sphinx, leaping lightly beside the Sleeping Beauty's left hand, which gracefully supported her brow. "Mayhap I can wake this napping lady by whispering some amusing guessing-games in her ear." But even the sphinx's *cleverest* riddles brought no flicker of interest to the Sleeping Beauty's impassive features.

"Were she *real*, she would be well awake by now," said Scholar Yen.

"Allow me to examine her pulses to determine whether she is resting or ailing, or in some other state of being," said the wandering herbalist, Hua T'o, pulling his leaf-robe tightly about his sinewy body, and allowing his three-legged toad to hop to the floor. "Will her pulses show balance or disharmony among the qualities of Great Yang, Lesser Yang and Sunlit Yang; and the qualities of Great Yin, Lesser Yin and Absolute Yin? Will her twelve internal and external pulses beat according to the interactions of the five viscera and the five seasons? Because she is a woman, and thus influenced by *Yin*, I will examine the Yin-dominated pulses of her right arm."

Hua T'o knelt beside the Sleeping Beauty's alabaster couch, gently lifted her right arm, and placed his fingertips against her translucent wrist. The herbalist listened with intense concentration as all fell silent. "My humble fingers tell me whether her pulses float lightly as a leaf on water and sound hollow as a drumbeat, or thud like a sinking stone; whether they beat slowly or quickly, regularly or erratically when compared to her breath, and whether her ch'i-energy has been touched by ill-winds," he said at last.

"Well? Get on with it, man," said Maffeo. "Have we found *something different for the Great Khan's rice bowl*—or merely something different?"

"Something *very* different, gracious Sir," said Hua T'o, bowing low and smiling, as the toad hopped back into his politely extended arms. "For the pellucid lady is neither here nor there; both there and here. She lies suspended between this world and the next; both of this world and the next; neither fully of this world nor the next. She is both woman and goddess; neither woman nor goddess. She lives, yet she does not live entirely in our realm; both in our realm and not in our realm . . ."

"*Marón!* Try to make some sense, man!" snapped Maffeo. "Can we wake her? That is the main point—*how* can we wake her?"

"*If* the humble Hua T'o were really here, he might try all the 2,000 herbs in his pharmacy, including the restorative extract of imperial Manchurian ginseng, and the musk-deer antler elixir which rouses even the most sluggish of elders."

"Good, very good," nodded Niccolo.

"He would apply his finest gold-tipped acupuncture needles, and burn moxa cones along the twelve meridians, to restore the flow and balance of Yin and Yang. But if the apologetic Hua T'o spoke frankly, he would admit that he really does *not* know how to wake the shining lady," said the herbalist with a sigh, which was echoed by Niccolo.

Would the Great Khan be pleased, wondered Marco? Or, to put it another way: would the Great Khan be *displeased*? For the Khan of Khan's displeasure was a sight no man wished to see . . .

Marco recalled a blustery November day in the jade-tiled tea pavilion, atop the hill overlooking the Carp Pond of Great Seclusion at Khanbaluc. Kublai sat with stocky hands firmly astride his knees, on a low brocade couch, with ailing and fever-flushed Prince Chenghin; surrounded by a small party of their favorite barons and retainers. They sipped hot rice wine from delicate lavender-glazed porcelain cups, and viewed the autumn-tinted trees transported from all the regions of the empire, whilst the court musicians plucked the strings of their sweet, sad *pipa*-lutes.

The Great Khan frowned and said, "Large and far away is the Isle of Serendib, also called Ceylaun, and therein is a king who has for his sceptre-staff a ruby red as fire and thick as my arm; should he not offer it to me? Do my merchant-ships not go to and from there? He should offer it to me, should he not?"

All: *"Yes, Great Khan."*

"I keep the peace of the several seas which lie between us; he must know this and be grateful. Let this be called to his attention at once—a ruby thick as my arm! Should he offer it to me, I shall offer him the life-time rents of a great city, though not of the very first class and rank, perhaps. Should he *not* offer it to me, I shall send my fleets-of-war upon him. Piles of skulls; perhaps. I *am*, after all, the grandson of Genghiz Khan!"

The Son of Heaven now slurped a cup of rice wine and spoke directly to a courtier; "Furthermore, We have ordered the 87 households of the Village of Harmonious Virtues, justly famed for its superior axe-handles, to prepare to admit 13 new households of axe-blade makers to their hamlet, so that axe and handle might sooner meet and be joined. Thus is Our inspired Imperial rule distilled into Harmonious Virtue, for is this not plainly preferable to a journey of five days to join axe and handle? Oh, what a precious example to all, that our Virtuous Harmony has also the common sense of the very fishwives. Yet you say they dare to waste Our time with frivolous prattle that '*Alas, there is no room!*' Would they bandy words with Us? —Certainly not. You are to chop off the heads of 43 of the objectors. *That* will make room, silly sons of turtle-eggs. Such wretched snobs and lazy louts; how We hate laziness and snobbery. *Read the order to me now!*"

"For failure to comply, 40 villagers: off with their heads," read the courtier, gesturing with the long and elegant nails of his long and elegant hands.

"Did We not say 43?" asked Kublai.

"Ten, Great Lord, is the number of felicity. Twenty is the duplication of felicity. Forty is the duplication of the duplication of felicity. Forty-three lifts us to the realms of metaphysics, whither the common people become confused . . ."

The Great Khan's eyes, which had begun to flicker dangerously, sank to a contented semi-closure of the lids. "Enough," said the Khan of Khans.

The courtier was observed to scuttle swiftly and silently backwards. He had saved three lives at the risk of his own, and the families of the saved would compensate him forever.

And it would now be somewhat easier and cheaper to obtain complete axes in the middle of the Middle Kingdom. Let the people think about *that* when tempted to complain.

The Great Khan's voice dropped from a low roar to a grumble. "As for my calligraphy, certain several and important subordinate kings, whose names are not worth remembering, have written to say that only the knowledge that I am far too busy prevents them from asking me to instruct their sons in calligraphy. As for my chariot-driving, it is universally exclaimed that it is above even the possibility of reproach. I would say more, save that Master Kung-fu-tse, whom you barbarians . . ." He now turned and spoke affectionately to the elder Polo brothers and to Marco, "call *Confucius* . . . risible, is it not . . . ?

"I say Master Kung informs us that chariot-driving, calligraphy, and a modest manner; all are essential to the superior man. Is it not so, you Chief Scholar?" He turned abruptly to an old man always present at such occasions; so old indeed that rumor reported he had been mummified. "Does not honorable Master Kung say so?"

Instantly the old man replied, "Frequently, Son of Heaven." He was old. He was very old. He was very, very old. But regarding the Great Khan's displeasure, he was not *that* old.

"We have tried all *our* tricks; now the Great Khan's sorcerers must wake her," said Niccolo, while anxiously thumbing his second-best strand of worry beads, which made a soothing soft click when his fingers worked them. These were made of 21 balls of amber, each the size of a jujube fruit, strung on a string of mixed linen and silk; and all together worth a yoke of strong oxen, good for plowing soil too stiff for a horse to work.

"Quite so, elder brother," replied Maffeo, twiddling his beard. "Before we departed on this mad venture, the Great Khan remarked that his magicians would find such a challenge amusing; so let us not delay their heathenish amusement. Let the men construct a bride's red palanquin from the ruddy brush-wood which grows along the creek, and let us leave this uncanny place and return directly to Khanbaluc. There the Great Khan and his court La-mas and sorcerers can toy with this novelty, whilst we graciously accept his grateful reward: the golden border-pass which will grant us safe passage to Most Serene Venice!"

"*If* the Great Khan chooses to thus reward us," Marco reminded his impetuous uncle.

The Polos lifted the Sleeping Beauty from her alabaster couch. They wrapped her cool and buoyant form in the rune-carpet, which had again grown quiescent in the presence of its shining mistress. Then they hastened away from the luminous crystal tower.

Down the narrow stairway to the black-obsidian chamber of monstrous demons . . . down another staircase to the blue-lapis chamber of embracing idols . . . down a final flight of stairs to the green-jade chamber of mighty devils and demi-gods. They paused only long enough to allow their wary eyes to adjust to the suddenly dim light, and to scan the shadowy chambers for any sign of trouble. And just long enough for Niccolo Polo to calm his nerves by scooping up (and pocketing) the occasional loose souvenir emerald and sapphire.

Finally they reached the colorfully etched portal to the courtyard, and gladly left the enchanted stupa-castle. They trooped into the late afternoon sunlight, carrying their precious burden. *But something had changed.* What . . . ? Their eyes and ears told them the hornets had changed. The vicious black creatures no longer hovered in a silent state of suspended animation. No; unlike the Sleeping Beauty, the hornets had *wakened.* They were now very awake. Their droning buzz eloquently spoke their rage at this despoiling of their time-frozen castle, as they arranged themselves in airborne battle formation—and prepared to attack.

Chien; Growth.
The Tree Grows Slowly on the Sunny Summit.
Wild Geese Fly to the Maiden's Mountain.

35

The guardsmen's quick reflexes told them to reach for their weapons, and to stand in a tight phalanx as they faced the entrapping circle of enraged hornets. But their minds told them these were futile gestures—for how could the weapons of men fight a swarm of deadly insects? Then a young Mongol horseman grunted a grassland curse and pointed up to the window niches. Marco's eyes followed the gesture and saw that the shaven-headed heathen nuns had reappeared, and were glaring down at the men with their glittering, browless eyes. Arrows were fitted into hastily drawn bows, as the cornered men prepared to fight.

They shot the first volley up toward the window-niches, but despite their flawless aim the arrows clattered uselessly to the ground. While the hornets encircled the troops in a buzzing black death-ring that moved closer . . .

Then from the brightly patterned entrance of the castle came lurching the monstrous demons of the black chamber—somehow awakened. They were wreathed in flickering red flames that scorched the ornate beams of the doorway. They had multiple heads with bulging eyes and jutting fangs, and multiple arms with ugly claws holding long obsidian daggers. They wore garlands of human skulls around their scaly necks, and they exuded a foul stench. The ground rumbled at each enormous footfall, and from their blood-stained mouths came rumbling snarls.

"*Marón!*" cried Maffeo, as the trembling sphinx scrambled into his arms. "I must have been killed and sent to the Arch-fiend's inferno!"

"We have somehow succeeded in waking every illusion in this castle . . . *except* the lady," said Scholar Yen, flapping his white silk fan at a circle of hornets that ominously orbited his head.

Then Marco looked up and saw something odd approaching in the distant sky; something *very* odd. It looked like a flock of migrating geese flying in wedge-shaped formation. Yet even from a distance it was clear that these great shimmering birds, with their streaming and scintillating tail-feathers, were no ordinary geese. And was someone perched on the gleaming back of the foremost bird?

The luminous wedge-shaped formation drew closer (as did the ensnaring hornets and dark demons), until the enormous birds were circling above (as hornets buzzed round their heads and swooped at their eyes). The men shouted and pointed (whilst dodging hornets and demons, and keeping their weapons trained on the glaring warrior-nuns in the windows). Indeed there was a great swirl of noise and confusion.

Mighty Oliver confronted the multi-limbed demon chief in hand-to-hand combat, swinging his great battle-axe like a windmill, and slicing off a scaly arm here and a fanged head there. The flame-wreathed monster swiped and drew red Nordic blood with his keen obsidian blades. Marco swatted at hornets that dived at his face, and felt a nasty sting on his hand and another on his neck. He dodged a huge demon that came lurching toward him, and peered at the hovering wedge overhead: was it friend or enemy or illusion?

The great flock descended into the chaotic courtyard of the castle, and Marco saw not geese, but *phoenixes* of translucent white jade. On the back of the grandest phoenix, with the longest streaming tail-feathers, rode the clip-tailed white monkey-sage with the fiery red eyes.

Messer Niccolo Polo buried his head in his fur-lined cloak to escape the hornets—then he peeked out to stare in awe at the white-jade birds. Then he groaned aloud when he saw Monkey . . . then he buried his face in his cloak again.

The white monkey stood atop the magnificent jade phoenix and shouted, "I am the Great Sage who is Equal to Heaven. I have eaten the Celestial Peaches of Immortality and drunk Lao Tzu's Elixir of Long Life. I have sipped the Wine of Paradise with the Jade Emperor, and my body has grown hard and indestructable as a diamond. The Cloud-Dancing Lady of the Cave sends her respects to the Shining Lady of the Castle. The gently reborn Cloud-Dancer has sent me to fetch you foolish and irresponsible mortals, for she fears the beguiling sphinx is in danger. I have taken a flock of white-jade phoenixes from the Heavenly Hall of Mysterious Mists, which will bear you to safety."

The Polos and their men needed no further invitation. They quickly clambered atop the cool and luminous phoenixes; while hornets darted, demons staggered and bellowed, and shave-pate nuns glared with hostile eyes. "We will deal with the boastful ape later," muttered Maffeo, as the Polos carefully lifted the carpet-shrouded Sleeping Beauty onto the back of their jade bird.

"What are you carrying in that carpet?" shouted Monkey, as the glimmering flock lifted off the ground.

"Just some baggage," replied Maffeo. "And what about our horses and the rest of our supplies?"

"*Easy!*" called Monkey, bellowing with laughter. "I will carry them in my sleeves—that is how they came here, after all."

"What do you suppose he meant by *that*?" asked Maffeo, as they flew swiftly over the castle wall, with the hornets trailing far behind.

"Who knows what *anything* means in this godless place?" Niccolo grumbled, fingering his second-best amber beads and muttering under his breath to sooth his increasingly frayed nerves: "*A rope of twelve-and-twenty matched carnelians, each as red and glowing as the eye of a bear by a hunter's torch in the night. Value: the worth of a Venetian gondola of the first class, well wrought, with all its apparel, and supplied with silvern bells.*"

They cleared the wall of the enchanted castle, and Marco saw that the exterior still appeared as a crumbling and thorn-girt ruin. They flew low over their startled horses, which were still tethered to the willows alongside the creek. Then Marco saw something which astonished him, even in this astonishing place. The monkey's white forepaw grew extremely large and reached down to the ground, where it crumpled the horses like wads of rice-paper—and stuffed them into a sleeve in Monkey's short purple brocade robe.

"*Marón!* The accursed ape mashed all our horses!" wailed Maffeo.

Then Marco remembered the night at the Caves of Peaceful and Wrathful Memory, when a shadowy figure (who might have been the missing knight, sometimes called Hou Ying) had carefully unfolded a white-paper mule drawn from his sleeve . . .

"Your blustery knight has more than one trick up his ragged sleeve," chortled Monkey, as if reading Marco's thoughts.

"*Wait!*" called the leaf-clad herbalist, Hua T'o, as they began to ascend again. "Since I have never really been here, I hope the gracious Sirs will not object if I take my humble leave now, for I wish to explore this hidden valley and seek the healing mountain mushrooms." Then he and his three-legged toad leaped nimbly off a phoenix and landed abruptly on the ground, where they bowed their farewells to the astounded Polos.

"Where are you taking us?" shouted Maffeo, as they soared through the air with the translucent tail-feathers of the jade phoenix flowing behind them.

"I am taking the sphinx back to the safety of the Cloud-Dancing Fairy's cave, for the Lady is gently reborn and lonely, and longs for the sphinx's diverting riddles. Indeed it is sure that *you* cannot properly care for such a precious creature. As for *you* . . . well, if you do not trouble me with your man-tricks, I suppose I can *drop* you anywhere along the way." As if to emphasize his words, their phoenix suddenly dropped with a sickening lurch, and Monkey howled with laughter.

"No; please do not *drop* us!" shouted Marco. Then to the sphinx he said, "And what is your desire, little one?"

The sphinx yawned and preened her golden fur, then smiled enigmatically. "When is a sphinx not a sphinx?" she asked. Then hearing no response, she answered her own riddle with a giggle. "When it is *a-sleep!* I have grown weary of scurrying about with you mortals, whose life-spans are so brief that you must always be in a rush. It will yet be a long and troublesome while before you can return me to the hot desert sands of my homeland, and meanwhile I wish to sphinx-nap . . . in the peace of the gently reborn Lady's cave."

"So be it," said Marco, fluffing the soft fur on the sphinx's head. "When at last we are allowed to journey to our own land of Venice, we will send a messenger to summon you to join our caravan. In the meantime, we will miss your riddles and guessing-games, lovely Sphinx."

"I shall await your summons . . . and I will miss your

Italian flattery," said the sphinx, preening her ruffled fur.

Marco shouted to the monkey who flew just ahead, "The sphinx will rest in the Lady's cave . . . for a brief while. And you can drop us—but gently—someplace where we can quickly return to civilized Cathay."

They flew like kites across cobalt skies, and mist-swirled skies, and storm-churned skies. They flew from the icy and barren highlands of Tebet, and soared like eagles over the green and populous foothills and lowlands of the Middle-Kingdom.

Messer Niccolo Polo, looking down, felt like an eagle. He recalled that not many eagles nested within the most Serene Republic of Venice, but of those few which did, two had their nests along the top of a ruined tower which (it was said) the birds had mistaken for a crag. Some said, scoffing at the architects and owner, that it was indeed ugly enough.

Watchmen were appointed to report when the eagles had finally seen their aiglons fledged, and able to fly and take prey for themselves. When the eagles were reported absolutely to have left that nest for that season, those who had bid the highest for the privilege would have men both clever and worthy of trust pour oil in the rusting key-hole of the tower door, and ascend the ruinous stairs. Their custom was to pause at the last landing and to say not more than a decade of the Our Father, and to sing not more than two verses of the old hymn (now fallen into disuse elsewhere) hailing the great pagan prophet and sorcerer, Vergil Magus. Then, following the advise of said Vergil (found long ago by an eremitic scholar in some scrap of palimpsest) they ascended the last few gaping steps and looked long into the eagles' nest. They were not permitted to do more than gently probe it with a willow-wand cut at the mouth of the Po River, much loved by Vergil who had much-loved most rivers (save only that Styx upon whose banks the ferryman's hag-wife hangs up the shrouds she takes for fare when the dead's friends have not provided a coin beneath the tongue).

And some seasons it came to pass, and some seasons it came not to pass, and all seasons, good or ill, were inscribed in a book with never-used pages of the very best vellum, with some lines as might be: *In the year when Fulano was Doge of Venice, the stone named* Aeitos *was found in the eagle's nest of the ruined tower.* As for the virtues of said stone, these were never listed; for those who had paid to know already knew, and those who knew not had no need to know. Suffice it to say that the stone was generally worn lightly linked to a light gold chain, loosely fitted through loops in the undertunic, upon or just slightly below the navel.

When it had been such a year that the stone *Aeitos* (sometimes called the stone *Stamopetra*) had been found, then the families whose men had found it (limited, by decree of the Senate, only to those decayed but noble households whose heads had lost their right hands in war-service for the Republic—*the left hand would not do*)—such families were well honored. They would give, according to custom, a great feast of roasted lambs and mutton (instead of the veal more commonly preferred), prepared with sage, an excellent pharmical herb which makes the sheepsflesh taste better too. For the sages always dress their meat with sage; as learned Theophrasto had written; 'Hardly one need die who hath sage growing in his garden.'

And one year there was a friar, doubtless mad, who urged that the Great Families invite the poor to said feast; but who listened? For as brother Maffeo had said, "*Marón!* The rich must always aid the rich; for if not, who will aid them—the poor?"

Then all looked down and saw the shining band of a broad river. The white-jade phoenixes descended and hovered just above the ground while the laughing monkey tossed a handful of wadded rice-paper from his sleeve—which immediately reformed as the Polos' horses and supplies. The men gaped, then quickly scrambled off the backs of the bright birds. All bowed low to Monkey and the sphinx, who bowed their own farewells as the luminous flock rose again into the sky.

The Polos looked around at a landscape of misted crags and reeds and countless river-boats, and saw they had reached the banks of the busiest waterway in the world: the *Yang-tze Kiang*. And with them, in her mysterious carpet-cocoon, was the precious Sleeping Beauty.

Ching: The Well.
The Tree Draws Up Cool Spring Water.
The Pitcher May Leak But The Well Is Unchanged.

36

Messer Marco Polo wrote in his travel diary: "The muddy Yang-tze Kiang is a river wide as a sea, and its traffic exceeds all the rivers and seas of Christendom put together. The main stream flows through sixteen provinces, and more than 200 well-populated cities perch on its craggy banks, which overlook many rocky islands holding idolators' temples. The Great Khan collects customs on over 200,000 craft which travel this river each year, ranging from rafts to substantial single-masted, cane-rigged ships. They carry salt and coastal goods upstream, and char-stones and up-country produce to the coast. Teams of horses are ofttimes employed to tow these ships upstream, for the current is very swift . . ."

The Polos soon learned that they had landed where the mighty river enters the prosperous southern province of Manzi. Here it would be a simple matter to commandeer a sturdy ship, through the imperial system of post and customs stations, and to sail downstream to Yang-zhau. There the Yang-tze Kiang meets the Great Khan's Grand Canal; that restored engineering marvel which lies between the rich land of Manzi and the winter capital at Khanbaluc.

"Then we will present the Sleeping Beauty to the Son of Heaven and his sorcerers, as a novel addition to the royal harem . . . ask for leave to depart as our gracious reward . . . and we will be on our way home! Oh, I can taste the red wine and warm wheaten bread already," exclaimed Maffeo, rubbing his hands together.

"First we must *get* to Khanbaluc . . . then we must *get* the Great Khan's leave . . . then we must *get* home," sighed Niccolo, worrying his best strand of jade beads.

"*First* we must get a ship," Marco reminded them.

So they sought and got a ship, using the silver tablet stamped with the Great Khan's internal pass instead of payment. And did the full-bearded Cumanian official at the customs station stare at them with a very long and odd look? And did he whisper something to a fair-skinned Cumanian sub-official? Well, considering the Polos' travel-worn appearance, this was no cause for special alarm.

They boarded the single-masted river-boat with all their horses and supplies, and marveled at the spacious comfort of the appointments after so many months of hardship. The boat set sail, moving swiftly downstream, whilst Messers Niccolo, Maffeo and Marco Polo strolled around the wooden deck, noting with approval the great variety of commercial river traffic. They enjoyed the luxury of having their underclothes and bodies washed, and their beards and hair neatly trimmed by the Cathayan captain's servants.

"For we must not look—nor smell—like barbarians when we reach the Great Khan's court," said Niccolo, as a plump maid-servant soothed his wind-chapped skin with scented oil and amused them with prattled tales.

"Indeed the river teems with stories, refined Sirs," she said, as she massaged Niccolo's brow. "Once the captain took on a barge-load of char-stones, which were to be dropped in a remote town beside an old canal.

Well, it was no proper canal at all, for it had a current flowing. The captain tied up the barge that night, and when he woke at sunrise, the boat and water were gone! Nothing was left but a pile of char-stones in the dust beside a rotting dock, and the captain's cargo and crew! To put it simply, my lords, they had sailed up a ghost-river, and why not? Every person, place and thing has a spirit which may come alive. Sometimes a ghost takes the form of a man, and this one took the form of a river. That is to say, once there was a river there, and from time to time it returns to flow for a single day and night."

"But what about the boat, my good woman?" asked Niccolo.

"The boat? Ah, the boat . . ." but the maid-servant merely smiled a bit and shrugged.

That evening they dined well on freshly caught fish steamed with ginger and young bamboo shoots, noodles in broth, and hot rice wine that made even finicky Maffeo smack his lips with pleasure. That night they watched the craggy riverbank by moonlight; nor were they alarmed when Peter remarked that a small craft seemed to be following their ship. For Peter came from landlocked Tartary and was no sailor, thus he did not understand that in a crowded waterway one craft must necessarily follow another. Later they slept soundly as contented babes in the unexpected luxury of the tiny cabins which lined the deck.

Each cabin held two low couches, and Niccolo and Maffeo bedded down together—though each grumbled that the other snored. In the adjoining cabin slept Marco and the Sleeping Beauty, still unmoving and wrapped in the faded rune-carpet, and tenderly placed on the softest couch. Peter was posted outside the door as guard. Though Marco wished that the lady beside him were Su-shen, he knew nothing could keep his weary mind and body from slumber.

Until deep in the night, when loud shouts and pounding footfalls roused him. Marco leapt from his bed and hurried to the door. Peter no longer dozed in the doorway, and the moonlit deck was a confused tumult of shouting and scuffling and shoving Cathayan sailors, Mongol horsemen—and bearded strangers in steppeland clothes.

Then a burly and bearded figure with a glittering blade rushed at Marco, caught him off guard, shoved him inside the cabin, and slammed the door behind them both. The rocking movement of the boat had caused the carpet to slip away from the Sleeping Beauty's luminous face, so the cabin was filled with her unearthly glow. In this strange light Marco recognized his attacker and cried out his name, "*Kutan*, son of fiendish Lord Aqmad!"

Marco saw it was indeed the son of the Great Khan's former corrupt minister, who had been assassinated by outraged Cathayans. Before Marco stood the same cruel ruffian who had waylaid him and accused him of spying on the Bur-mien border—and threatened to cut out his tongue. This was no welcome visitor; it was the Cumanian rebel-chief who served the Great Khan's enemy, Kaidu Khan, the steppe-wolf who worried Kublai's western flanks. The two panting men stood facing each other for a long moment in the tiny and quiet cabin.

Of a sudden, the burly Cumanian rebel lunged and grabbed Marco's arm, twisted it roughly behind his back, and held the gleaming dagger menacingly at the Venetian's throat. Marco struggled and writhed to free himself from Kutan's powerful grasp, but he was unarmed and outmatched—and fear of the dagger stilled his voice. The Cumanian swiftly and efficiently lashed Marco's arms to an overhead beam, with a length of sturdy hempen twine that bit and burned the wrists.

"So, Po-lo, you recognize your old palace friend, Kutan," he sneered. "I bear the name of the great Cumanian chief who was robbed of his steppeland kingdom by the Mongol horde. My mother was a Cumanian harem slave, stolen by the Mongols and given to my heartless father, Aqmad, like a pet dog. The Cumanians have been driven from their father's burial mounds, and scattered like the desert sands . . . by the Mongols.

My people have lost everything, and their name is a fading memory . . . thanks to the Mongols. Thus do I serve Kaidu Khan, the enemy of my enemy Kublai, to weaken the Mongols. My master wants to know more of your mysterious mission . . . as do I. If you are not spying on Bur-mien, then what *are* you doing—and what is the strange glow that fills this room?"

He shoved Marco's bound body aside, moved to the couch where the Sleeping Beauty rested, and gazed down at her. "*Pretty*, where came she from?" he asked, turning again in the tiny cabin to prod at Marco's jugular with the sharp tip of his blade.

"From a nameless vale in Tebet," replied Marco truthfully. For this knowledge could not aid the Great Khan's enemies nearly so much as that probbing dagger could harm his own throat, should he cry out or refuse to speak.

"From Tebet, eh?" growled Kutan. "All know that the most powerful sorcery comes from Tebet. So this is your mission, then, to fetch this maiden for Kublai? Though she appears to sleep, she radiates great power . . . and her lovers must partake of that power. This explains why Kublai is so eager to fetch her; but she is not under his protection . . . yet. She is here with *me*—and I shall enjoy her power."

Kutan turned his attention back to the Sleeping Beauty, who lay aglow on her couch. "Pretty, so pretty," he murmured as he slowly unfolded the carpet, and drew it away to view her reposing form. "Lovely, yes, lovely," he whispered, staring down at her with entranced eyes that seemingly had forgotten Marco and the battle that raged outside the cabin. He knelt beside the couch as if bewitched. "You shall be my bride," said Kutan, stroking the hand which languidly propped her lucent brow. Then he impulsively buried his bearded face in her shining neck. Of a sudden his body went rigid, as he dropped the Sleeping Beauty and drew back with an agonized cry.

Marco stared with horrified eyes as the greyish pallor of frostbite spread across Kutan's features. The Cumanian spy rose to his feet and staggered stiffly towards the door, with his face twisted and blue. Then he lurched and stumbled and fell to the floor, where he thrashed a bit and moaned a bit until he grew still.

With painful effort, Marco twisted his hands free of their bonds. He quickly groped for his own knife which lay beside his couch. He knelt to examine Kutan; then he realized that the Cumanian's flesh was quite frozen and icy to the touch. His breathing had ceased, and his frost-twisted face looked as bitter in death as it had in life. Kutan, son of evil Lord-Governor Aqmad, would menace the Polos no more. Marco covered the rebel's corpse with his frosty sheepskin robe.

The Sleeping Beauty lay unmoving on her couch, but as Marco bent to wrap her with the rune-carpet, he thought he spied just a hint of laughter on her gleaming lips—though it likely was an illusion. Then with knife drawn, he raced outside the glowing cabin, to the deck where the battle with Kaidu Khan's rebellious spies still raged.

Huan; Diffusion.

Wind Blows Across the Water. The Guardian King Sends Gifts to Ancestral Temples.

37

The sounds of battle are indeed jarring, thought Marco, as he stood for a moment outside the doorway of his cabin, rubbing his burning wrists. There were the clashing sounds of weapon striking weapon, and the thudding sounds of flesh striking flesh. There were battle cries and enraged cries, and cries of anguish when a weapon found its mark. As Marco rushed out, all at once the chaotic sounds of battle ceased. Cathayan sailors, Mongol horsemen, and Cumanian rebels all stared and pointed at a great whirling apparition that soared across the moonlit sky.

The figure wore glittering vermillion and gold battle-armor that clung like serpent-scales to his massive form. His skin was ruddy and his scowling black eyes had a reptilian glow. His powerful hands held a tremendous halberd, which he twirled like the spoke of a chariot-wheel. His log-like legs stood upon a flying banner of glimmering silk. Marco was reminded of the images of guardian-kings which stand at the gates of idolaters' temples.

A curious creature was coiled around the shoulders of this lofty figure. It had the face and flowing hair of a woman, and wore a woman's loose jacket of soft peach-colored silk. But it had the lower-body of a serpent, with iridescent scales which flashed and sparkled as the creature sinuously twined around the warrior like a wreath.

Scholar Yen appeared at Marco's side, with his hands tucked into the sleeves of his quilted black robe and said; "My disbelieving eyes behold the Guardian-King of the North Pole Star, and one of his serpent-spirits. He and his brothers, the Guardian-Kings of the South, East and West, protect the Celestial Jade Emperor's doctrines of truth and illusion."

The strange figures hovered above the ship, until their floating silk banner glided down to the deck. His menacing halberd whirled so fast that it became a lethal blur, as the Guardian-King of the North deftly drove the rebels overboard, where they howled and splashed in the dark river currents until they reached their small craft—or floundered and drowned.

Messers Maffeo and Niccolo crept from the doorway of their cabin and bowed low. "We wish to thank you, mighty sir, for ridding this ship of loathsome bandits . . . and might we ask your honorable name?" inquired Niccolo.

"Scholar Yen calls him Guardian-King of the North Pole Star. Perhaps he does not like to be questioned, father," murmured Marco.

The great warrior chuckled with a deep rumbling sound and said, "You may call me by that lordly name. Indeed, you may call me by *many* names. At times I am even called by the lowly name *Hou Ying*."

Marco stared closely at the fierce Guardian-King, and saw it was indeed the affable—"*Hou Ying!*" Then Marco looked intently at the serpent-woman, with her flowing auburn-tinted hair, and a shock-wave rippled through him; for the creature wore the face of—"*Su-shen!*" Then Marco's eyes and throat choked with feeling, and he could stare and speak no more.

The serpent-woman partly uncoiled from around Hou Ying's shoulders and slithered toward him. "I came to say farewell, dearest Marco," she said in Su-shen's soft voice. "For I had to recall my original serpentine form in order to save my life."

"How came this to be . . . ?" stammered Marco.

Su-shen recalled that accursed day when the flat-tailed cannibals of Pleasure Island pursued her, until she was forced to dive from a cliff into the frothing sea.

"I think of that wretched day often, with sorrow, for I thought you had drowned," said Marco.

"I would surely have drowned, if I had been entirely of human-kind . . . as we both thought," she replied. "But I was not."

Su-shen told them she had sailed off the sheer cliff-face, expecting to land in the arms of *Yama*, the bull-headed Lord of Death. Then a dim memory arose of her deceased mother cradling her infant body in arms which were not arms—but serpent's coils. When she hit the churning water, the ancestral memories flooded her mind. Suddenly she knew how to twist and turn and twine beneath the waves, and she felt her legs grow longer. *Much longer*. Until she looked back and saw a sinuous serpent's tail. Then Su-shen knew that she and her mother were descended from the *shen*, the nature-spirits who sometimes mate with men, and whose children so closely resemble mortals that none can tell them apart—until some moment of crises recalls their true shen-form.

"*Marón!* I knew no ordinary woman could move with such unnatural grace," said Maffeo.

"So you swam beneath the waves until today . . . ?" asked Marco.

"No; for a passing Naga-dragon found me and lured me to the underwater kingdom of Naga-Khan Basudara, Lord of the Abyss. There I saw the pagoda-towers of a splendid city built of black and red coral, inlaid with glowing pearls."

Messer Niccolo eyed her with sudden interest. "Did you happen to bring any . . . ah . . . samples, honorable miss?" he asked.

Su-shen laughed softly and plucked a hair ornament from the nape of her neck; it was a comb of black coral studded with a crescent of perfectly matched pearls the size of quail's eggs. This she handed to the eldest Polo, who accepted the gift with a smile of pleasure and a low bow.

Su-shen continued her story; saying she had found favor in the sight of Lord Basudara. He accepted her as an acrobat in his royal theatrical troop, and she passed the timeless time performing to the music of conch shells.

". . . Much as I have always done, except I was not happy in the sea-dragon realm. I was treated as a slave, and though my new form is even more supple than my old, I missed the warmth of human-kind . . . for the sea-serpents are cold-blooded creatures."

"As I missed you . . ." said Marco sadly.

"As I will *always* miss you," replied Su-shen with lowered eyes.

At last the wandering knight, Hou Ying, guessed her whereabouts from Marco's tale of her disappearance. Suddenly he appeared in the audience hall of the Coral Court, now revealed as a Guardian-King. He demanded Su-shen's release. At first she did not recognize this noble warrior, but the Naga-dragons knew him at once, for he was an old enemy of theirs.

"The cobra-hooded Nagas have tricky ways, and are cruel to the gentle shen-folk," said Hou Ying, pounding the staff of his halberd onto the deck for emphasis. "Besides, after accompanying you slow-paced mortals, I was as itchy for a good fight as a man wearing tight wool pants."

"And a good fight it was . . ." said Su-shen.

The Naga-dragon soldiers attacked and slashed with their razor-sharp claws, but swaggering Hou Ying was a match for them all. He whirled his halberd wildly, and leaped and kicked with locust-leg moves, and punched his way to the giant clam-shell stage.

"He snatched me up in a great armored arm, and still whirling and fighting he leaped upward, out of the Coral Court into the tossing sea," she said. "Then into the sky . . . so we might meet one last time . . ."

"Is it truly the last time?" cried Marco. "Can you never regain your human form? Where will you go . . . what will you do?"

"Alas, I will not regain my human form in this lifetime, and shen have long lives," she said. "But do not grieve overmuch for me; it is a great honor for a shen-spirit to become a squire of the Northern Guardian-King. I will wander evermore with Hou Ying, aiding those we meet along the way."

"I go with you, god-daughter," said Oliver, who had been listening quietly with his great scarred hands resting on his great rusted battle-axe.

"Did you know about . . . this?" Marco demanded of Oliver.

"I know only her father say her mother be different than all women, but all men who love say such," replied the Northman.

"Dear god-father," smiled Su-shen. "You have always cared for me as if I were your own daughter. Now what is your wish?"

Everyone listened as Oliver spoke in a slow and thoughtful voice. "You say yon knight now be King of North. I be also northman, growing old . . . weary . . . beard turning grey, scars and bones ache. Now I wish only to drink mead with All-Father Odin in yon golden mead-hall of Asgard. I fear bright Valkyrie never find me here in such far lands. Can you carry me north . . . *far north* . . . to Valhalla?"

"We will take you to the golden mead-hall lit with northern lights, where you may feast in honor with the fallen heroes," said Hou Ying. He rummaged through a sleeve in his vermillion armor, and tossed aside a woman's tiny brocade slipper and some scraps from former meals. Finally he withdrew a slip of black rice-paper, and slowly unfolded a great black-paper raven as Oliver's steed.

"So *that* is how he does it," whispered Maffeo.

Oliver saluted the Polos and mounted the shining raven. As they ascended into the moonlit sky, the Guardian-King called out, "If you need the aid of a wandering knight who is sometimes called Hou Ying, and his supple young squire, fix your mind on the North Pole Star . . . which does not move or change."

"Farewell, dearest Marco, perhaps our dreams will touch again," called Su-shen, as they circled the river-boat, then whirled upward and disappeared into the night sky.

"Did your devils know about this?" Marco demanded of Peter the Tarter, who stood silently beside him.

"Perhaps they knew; perhaps they did not. But had I told you, would you have believed me?" asked Peter.

Ken; Stillness.
Mountains Above; Mountains Below.
When Back and Mouth and Mind Are Still; No Error.

38

"I can smell the *sea!*" said Messer Niccolo Polo, and a smile broke across his usually solemn face like a sun-ray on a somber day.

The Polos stood on the deck of the river-boat, after a breakfast of steaming rice porridge flavored with preserved eggs and ginger, and bracing hot tea. The shorescape had changed markedly during the night, from gorges forested with pine and bamboo to the populous and fertile wetlands of Manzi, whose great cities stand among myriad lakes and streams and canals. Soon their voyage on the muddy Yang-tze Kiang would reach its finish, when the vast river met the Great Khan's Grand Canal, which led all the way to Khanbaluc. There the journey would end until another began; perhaps (Lord God and Lord Kublai willing) a journey home to beloved Venice.

"For a fact, father, this province of Manzi pleases me more than any in the Middle Kingdom," said Marco.

"As I wrote in my travel diary: 'There is shipping and commerce everywhere, and the fields and rice-paddies and orchards yield abundantly. The hills are full of game, the waterways are full of fish, and the cities are full of refined people who enjoy dainty dishes and every sort of artful pleasure. The cities of Manzi are the most delightsome I have seen outside of Italy; Su-zhau, the canal-side City of Earth, and Hang-sai, the lake-side City of Heaven. Both, with their branching waterways adorned with thousands of arched stone bridges, remind me much of splendid Venice!' "

"It is good to hear you speak zestfully again, my son," said Niccolo. "For you have been quiet and downcast since your graceful lady took her leave. Perhaps we shall tarry a short while here in Manzi, before we journey along the Grand Canal to Khanbaluc. The Great Khan can wait a few days more, and his slumbering lady seems comfortably at rest. The pleasures of a grand city will restore the color to your pale cheeks."

"Why not linger in Su-zhau for a brief while?" asked Maffeo. "Our clothes need mending before we return to court, and that city of gardens and canals is known for its silks . . . and silken-skinned women. Indeed, let us exercise the horses on the road to charming Su-zhau . . . which most resembles Venice!"

"Indeed you are right," said Marco, smiling for the first time in rather a while. "We all need a pause before we return to court, and Su-zhau much amuses me. For the bridges are often adorned with multitudes of carved stone lions, much like the grand span outside the capital of Taì-ting; but unlike the noble winged lion of San Marco, each Cathayan lion is different . . . each and every one! Besides, the ponies grow restless and surely need a run, for the Great Khan is ever concerned about the welfare of the imperial horses . . ."

None had required more imperial concern than the famous "blood-sweating dragon-steeds"—*dragon* at least by courtesy of poetic license—which (many believed) had perhaps come long ago from Ferghiana. Monarchs of the previous dynasties . . . T'ang and Sung . . . had loved much to sit upon silken-padded seats shielded by brocade umbrellas from the hot sun, and to watch these marvelous animals being galloped round and round the lavish paddock of the Imperial Stud—till their white sides turned blood-red with their singular sweat.

Genghiz Khan and his son, Tului, Kublai's father, had no time for such effete diversions; the one being concerned with conquering a vast empire, and the other with consolidating that conquest. Genghiz, to be sure, sometimes relaxed in lighter moments by shooting vulture-eagles, but the first Khan-of-all-the-Seas passed this off as "practicing archery for battle."

Kublai Khan had watched the splendid spectacle of the white horses turning blood-red with their ruddy sweat. He had watched once with keen interest in his keen black eyes; he had watched a second time, impassively, whilst stroking the snowy feathers of his favorite Manchurian hunting-falcon. Then he had spoken.

"They are indeed most curious creatures," said the Great Khan. "They are delicate and require costly cosseting, do they not?"

"Yes, Son of Heaven," replied the Chief of the Imperial Stud. He was ready to list the horse-leeches and farriers in attendance on each beast and to recite the formula of the feed, which included barley and choice wine, raisins, jujubes, and a pharmacopoeia of highly-priced addiments; when his master spoke on.

"The substance of the Empire must not be consumed maintaining costly toys. Begin presently to distribute them as valuable gifts to client-kings and to certain high chieftains of the frontier marches."

"Yes . . . but . . . *yes*, Son of Heaven . . ."

No need to point out that the more it cost some bumpkin border-baron to maintain a "blood-sweating dragon-steed" in its accustomed style, the less he would have available to spend for war. Which was to say, rebellion.

No one, of course, ventured to give a direct *do not* to the Emperor. But the most venerable of the Corps of

La-mas and Shamans, much favored by Kublai Khan, ventured a sort of sigh; then added, "The dragons of the clouds will seek such mares in vain at the accustomed trysting-places, Son of Heaven."

"Let them make rain," said Son of Heaven shortly; an oblique reference to the dragon-engendered lightning which emptied the clouds of moisture, and to the game of *making clouds and rain* as a euphemism for the amorous practices of the disciples of immortal Lao T'zu.

Then the Great Khan gathered up his gorgeous garments-of-state, today embroidered with three dragons in golden thread on a background of vermillion silk. He got himself gone from the precincts of the royal paddock, with the alert white falcon perched on his imperial wrist. For all knew that, like his ruthless grandfather Genghiz, the Great Khan Kublai made every occasion an occasion for the hunt.

The mighty Yang-tze Kiang River swept past the lofty Purple Mountains, now lit with autumn leaves, and past the watch-tower pagodas of the port city of Nanking. Here they disembarked; intending to travel on horseback, and join the Grand Canal at the lovely city of Su-zhau. Indeed, the faces of all the men reflected relief at being once more among *real* people and settlements—rather than among dream-spirits and monsters, phantasms and illusions.

They rode away from the bustling river-port at a good pace, and reached a low range of misted hills where an autumn-scented breeze blew rusty leaves from the trees. There they saw something very strange . . .

"Not another damned illusion," Maffeo grumbled, as they halted their horses and stared toward the spur of wooded hills which rose before them.

"It appears to be an entire Mongol *horde* blocking our way," said Niccolo in a grim voice, and he began to worry his jade beads.

Marco gazed with wordless surprise at the mighty army that marched directly towards them. He saw squadrons of mounted archers and crossbowmen, wearing plated black leather armor and spiked helmets, and troops of armored foot soldiers carrying short pikes and long swords. These men sang Mongol battle-songs in deep and resonant voices, accompanied by the melancholy trilling of steppeland fifes. Marco was relieved to hear no booming of drums—yet—for among the Mongols, only the drumbeat announces the signal to attack.

In the center of this fearsome army, Marco saw a swaying ebony watchtower, carried on the backs of four tattooed elephants clad in mail worked with gold. The towering pavilion was guarded by ranks of huge mastiffs and trained lions, held by foot soldiers with sturdy chains. Above the watchtower flew a great black banner—with no identifying emblem at all.

"Has Kaidu Khan, the hungry wolf of the steppes, sent an army of renegade Mongols and Cumanian rebels to attack us?" cried Scholar Yen, cringing in his saddle.

"Our venerable scholar does not speak so smugly of illusions when his throat is about to be slit," Maffeo observed.

Then Marco saw a flash of white in the clouded sky above, which resolved into the graceful form of a white hunting-falcon that circled above his head. Marco extended his arm in the manner of falconers, and the well-trained Manchurian bird landed obediently on his wrist and eyed the Venetian alertly. Marco carefully examined the falcon, and saw the spot where he himself had mended a broken wing-feather with an imping needle. Then Marco flung his arm and tossed the snowy bird into the air. The falcon flew off in ever-widening circles as it continued to hunt.

For all knew that Kublai Khan made every occasion an occasion for the hunt . . .

"I believe the Great Khan is nearby," said Marco Polo softly.

plated black leather armor and gilded helmets, and troops of armored foot soldiers carrying short pikes and long swords. There must have been [illegible] battle-drums in deep and resonant voice, accompanied by the [illegible] [illegible] [illegible] [illegible] [illegible] [illegible] only the drumbeat announces the signal to attack.

In the center is the [illegible] army. Marco sees a [illegible] [illegible] [illegible] [illegible] [illegible]. The [illegible] [illegible] [illegible] [illegible] [illegible] with [illegible] [illegible] [illegible] [illegible] [illegible].

The Kublai Khan, the [illegible] [illegible] [illegible] [illegible] [illegible] [illegible].

On [illegible] of the [illegible] [illegible] [illegible] [illegible].

Then Marco saw a flash of [illegible] [illegible] [illegible] [illegible] [illegible] [illegible] [illegible] [illegible] [illegible] [illegible] [illegible] [illegible] [illegible] [illegible].

[illegible]

[illegible]

[illegible] cloak to protect her from the cold [illegible]

Lu; Cautious Treading.
Heaven Floats Over the Lake.
He Treads the Tiger's Tail; Yet It Does Not Bite.

39

"So, Po-los, did I surprise you?" beamed the Great Khan from the ebony watchtower. His ruddy face was aglow with immense good humor and delight, as the ominous blank banner was replaced with his sun-and-moon emblem. "Rise up! No need to kowtow in the mud."

"Indeed you did, Great Lord," said Niccolo Polo, his fingers still atremble over Kublai's surprise as he rattled his beads.

"I thought to travel incognito with my small personal guard, so as not to alarm the populace," said Kublai. "Whispered rumors reached my vigilant ears at Khanbaluc that you have found a choice new morsel for my rice bowl, and I could not wait. No, I just could *not* wait to embrace the lovely lady. You see, I have brought a bride's vermillion palanquin for her to ride upon . . . and the most precious brocade, embroidered with peonies in pure golden thread for her robe . . . and a sable cloak to protect her from the chill autumn winds . . .

and hair ornaments set with precious gems . . . and . . . but allow the lady to see these trinkets for herself. Where is the shy little ginger-blossom hiding?"

"She is here, Great Lord," said Niccolo. He indicated the rough hempen litter slung between two shaggy ponies, where the Sleeping Beauty lay wrapped in the faded rune-carpet.

"You carry my new bride like a *sack of rice*?" demanded the Son of Heaven, as a cloud passed over his beaming face.

"Please recall that the lady you requested is *sleeping*, Great Khan," said Maffeo Polo, with a low bow.

"Tell her to wake up *now*," frowned Kublai. "Her lord and husband has come to claim her!"

"It is not so easy to rouse her, Great Lord," said Marco. "She sleeps very soundly."

"Is she ill, then?" asked the Khan of Khans, a darker cloud passing across his now less jovial face.

"She does not seem ill, Son of Heaven; she seems *enchanted*," said Marco.

The great frown on the Great Khan's brow relaxed. "Ah, well then, my sorcerers will soon have her up and about, and wrestling like a Mongol milkmaid; eh, Chenghin?" said Kublai, nudging his pale and sickly favorite son, who sat in feeble silence beside his imperial father in the elephant-borne ebony watchtower.

The eldest and most powerful and most wizened members of the Corps of La-mas and Shamans gathered around the litter in a flurry of musty maroon-wool robes. They unwrapped the rune-carpet, and stared at the glowing Sleeping Beauty with mutters of occult appreciation, and gurgles of unabashed shamanistic delight.

The wizards circled the litter like an excited flock of maroon-tinted geese. Frail men they were; often sickly and malformed and strange-minded. Yet when they performed their shamanistic feats and incantations at the Great Khan's Councils of War, they seemed larger and stronger to Marco than the mightiest of heroes . . .

* * *

Marco had attended many sessions of the Councils of War. Often they mixed and melded in his mind, and afterwards he could not always recall one from the other. Perhaps some deluded barbarian tribe beyond the Great 10,000 *Li* Wall had risen in revolt. The Pax Romana had never for long been uninterrupted by revolt along its far-extended borders—why should matters be different with the Pax Tartara?

First reports from officials nearest the scene were read. Complaints were cited . . . usually that taxes were too high. Then those officials headquartered in the capital, who were in ultimate charge of the border marches, made comments: generally that taxes were *not* too high, but errors might have been made in their collecting by the local tax-official, who was usually a scholar-official exiled for incompetence (a notion which always made Scholar Yen shudder).

The Cathayan high-sages in their dignified black-silk robes next spoke in well-worn philosophical terms: "Disobedience to the Dragon Throne is against the Mandate of Heaven. A wise ruler never breaks his subjects' rice-bowls . . ."

There followed the advice of the Imperial Warlords, all practical men of military experience in the field: "The direct-most way to the *Mo* or *Lo* (or whatever rebellious district) winds up a narrow path through bewitched swamp and haunted forest, and should be avoided."

The invariable decision in regard to rebellion was that rebellion must be put down. The Great Kahn was invariably pleased to agree with this invariable decision. Then, just as invariably, came the last scene; one which never failed to fascinate Marco.

The maroon-robed wizards were summoned and the prescribed question put to them: *Shall the forces of the Great Kahn who is Son of Heaven meet with victory?* The word "defeat" was of course never mentioned. It would have been an omen. A *dangerous* omen.

The La-mas and shamans, like all sorcerers and oracles, were unshakably prolix. No oracle in the history of the world had ever been known to answer simply YES or NO. But eventually, after the chanting and dancing, the censing and droning; the Chief Shaman, his hair worn in an elaborate top-knot, came forward with two curious staves, pale-gold in color, one in each hand. His voice a barely intelligible shriek, he announced that one staff served Kublai Khan, the Great Khan of Khans who is Son of Heaven. "And this other lowly staff," he shrilled, shaking it—and by the supple way it moved Marco realized that both had been plaited from rushes—"This one serves the rebel savages, dirty and base."

To emphasize the baseness and dirtiness, he dipped it in the ashes of the open bronze incense-burner and smeared it around; in a moment the staff turned grey. At once the wizard dashed it to the ground, and stooped to place the other staff alongside it.

He stepped back, thin arms out-stretched. In the background, a sort of uncouth band began to play on uncouth implements—tapping clay pots for drums, clicking bundles of deer-hooves, blowing raw reed whistles, jingling scraps of metal on wires—it was marvelous how quickly this discordant noise became the jarring sounds of battle. Marco heard shouts and screams of men, the sounds of galloping and charging horses, the clash of arms . . .

But this marvel he was hearing was as nothing to the marvel he was seeing. For somehow the golden staff or wand of woven rushes, supple and pliant as it must have been—the wand of Kublai Khan—had twisted itself into the shape of a man, buckled itself into the semblance of a horse, whipped itself about and when the writhing ceased; lo! It was the shape and semblance of an armed man on horseback!

Thus: the pale-gold staff.

Thus: the smeared-with-ashes.

Now, who could say how long a time they fought?

They fought. They charged repeatedly with thrusting lances. *They fought!*

At last, sometimes slowly, sometimes swiftly, one of the mock-combatants was beaten to the ground; was trodden and spurned by the other. Never, in Marco's experience, had it been the pale-gold figurine which lay motionless on the ground. Always, in Marco's experience, it had been the dirty ash-grey figurine which lay motionless on the ground.

A silence followed.

The gaunt-eyed Chief Shaman, in a voice dry, cracked, exhausted—but now a man's voice—broke the silence by announcing, "Unto Kublai, the Son of Tului, the Son of Genghiz—unto the Great Khan of Khans of All the Seas who is Son of Heaven—unto him and his expedition is proclaimed the *victory*!"

This last word, *victory*, the Chief of La-mas and Shamans cried out in almost a shout. At this there was from every throat a catch of breath in relief. And after *this* there came a greater shout and cry from all: "*Victory! Victory! Victory!*"

It might have been a victory over Prester John, or over the Old Man of the Mountains, or over the Grand Turk himself; not over the windswept mud village of some barbarian clan in the yellow dustlands beyond the Great 10,000 *Li* Wall. Unto Great Kublai Khan and his expedition was invariably proclaimed the victory.

Now these same La-mas and shamans danced around the luminous Sleeping Beauty's litter in the autumn-tinted forest, with their maroon robes all aflutter and their top-knots jouncing up and down. They chanted strange and eerie chants in strange and eerie voices, accompanied by thudding drums made of human skulls and wailing horns made of human thigh-bones. They whirled wands with streaming ribbons of every hue. They anointed the Sleeping Beauty's brow with stimulating potions and delicate yet potent ointments. They jumped and shouted, leaped and grunted, knelt and barked and howled like wild dogs.

All to no avail. The Sleeping Beauty slept peacefully through it all, with her head propped languidly on one hand. At last the sorcerers bowed their heads and fell into a long silence.

"Well?" demanded the Great Kahn, a scowl on his broad-cheeked face.

The Chief La-ma raised his head, cleared his throat, and spoke in a sing-song voice. "It seems the Shining Lady is not well-suited for the honor of the Son of Heaven's harem, for she is no mortal lady at all . . . but a resplendent though minor goddess who dwells suspended in her own ethereal realm."

"A *goddess!*" exclaimed Kublai, his face brightening like the sky after a storm. "You say she is a *goddess*? This inflames my ardor even more, for who knows what secret knowledge lies within that peach-soft brow? Surely there is *some* way to rouse her. I *insist* upon it! What says the scroll, you Scholar Yen?"

Yen Lung-chuan adjusted his dignified scholar's robe, and waited until all eyes were firmly fixed upon him. Then he slowly and ceremoniously lifted the curious scroll from its red-lacquer and ebony casket, thence from the inner container of woven multi-hued silk yarn. He unwrapped the oiled-silk wrappings, unrolled the silk-mounted paper from its camphorwood rollers, fanned himself as he scanned the exquisite calligraphy, and finally cleared his throat as he prepared to read aloud.

The Great Khan frowned and drummed his fingers on the ebony couch of the towering pavilion, which Yen well knew was the signal to be done with ceremony and get on with the matter. So he got on with it . . .

"The calligraphy is archaic and difficult to comprehend . . ." began Scholar Yen.

"That is why I retain and *feed* scholars . . ." snapped the Great Khan impatiently.

"Indeed. If my humble understanding of the scroll is correct, the only hint of wakening is this phrase: '*Slumber melts in the kiss of regal spring; but beware the frost which brings the royal fall.*' "

"That *must* be the answer!" beamed the Great Khan, playfully nudging ailing Prince Chenghin, who wore a look of inner pain on his wan face. "You say she was found in the snowy peaks of barbarous Tebet. She must be *hibernating*—and only the springlike warmth of my royal kiss can rouse her!"

The Great Khan stood up gingerly on his gout-swollen legs, and extended his hands to the elephant-drivers. "Help me down," he demanded. "I must kiss my lovely bride awake . . ."

"*No!* That might not be wise, Great Lord . . ." interrupted Marco. All turned to stare in surprise at the bold young Venetian.

Uncle Maffeo gestured frantically at Marco to be silent, whilst Niccolo turned pale and began to mumble his rosary.

"You dare to suggest that the Son of Heaven is not *wise*?" growled Kublai.

"The Khan of Khans is ever wise," said Marco hastily. "But it is my humble duty to warn my Great Lord of danger, just as the scroll warns of the frost which brings the royal fall. The lady slumbers—yet she is very powerful. When the Cumanian rebel-chief attempted to embrace her, he fell *frozen* to his death!"

"So you think a goddess cannot distinguish between the loathsome embrace of a lowly rebel—and the royal kiss of the Great Khan?" demanded Kublai, glaring at Marco as he stiffly and carefully descended from the ebony watchtower, borne by the four tattooed elephants. "Do *not* contradict my words if you wish to remain in my favor, young Po-lo. I do *not* like to be thwarted. My bride *will* be roused by my regal kiss!"

"*Wait, father!*" cried Chenghin. And Marco had never seen him looking so weak and wasted—yet so commanding and determined—like a true Mongol prince.

Sui; Following.
Thunder Rumbles in the Marsh.
At Dusk the Prince Rests Peacefully.

40

Prince Chenghin, favorite and ailing son of Kublai Khan, rose unsteadily from the couch in the ebony pavilion and signaled to the elephant drivers to help him to the ground. The prince and his imperial sire stood facing each other before the litter, slung between two shaggy ponies, where the Sleeping Beauty rested. "Wait, father," Chenghin repeated. "I cannot let you risk yourself . . . or the empire."

"So you agree with young Po-lo that it is dangerous to embrace her?" demanded Kublai. "How, then, shall my bride be wakened . . . and how will I learn her secrets?"

"*I* will kiss her, father," said Chenghin. "For her beauty stirs my own regal warmth. I am close to death now. *Very* close. Each day of life brings nothing but pain. You invited me to greet the shining lady, with the hope that she has healing powers. So now let us see.

My own royal kiss will wake her, and we will learn if she cures—or kills."

"Very well, my son," nodded Kublai. "I will stand aside and let you act as the Crown Prince you were meant to be. For it is true that I must not rashly risk the Mongol Empire, and truly your declining health concerns me more than any other matter. The sight of the slumbering lady gave you strength to speak up to me like a true great-grandson of Genghiz Khan. Perhaps the power of her touch will restore the strength of your body as well. And if she prefers your youthful embrace to mine, then it is the will of the Lord of Heaven, who is called Tengri by the steppeland nomads and T'ien by the nobles of Cathay . . . but who rules our fates by any name."

A great hush fell in the autumn-scented forest, and even the wind grew still. The musicians began a lilting Mongol wedding song as Prince Chenghin slowly knelt, and gently kissed the lips of the radiant Sleeping Beauty. Time seemed to coil in the indigo void like the changeless serpent with its tail in its mouth. Time seemed frozen in a timeless and shimmering instant . . .

Chenghin gazed up at his father and said, "I feel much better now." Then he crumpled to the ground in a deep and deathlike swoon.

Yet Marco saw that his friend, the prince, no longer wore his usual tense expression of pain. Now his face had relaxed into a soft and peaceful smile. And the luminous Sleeping Beauty also seemed to be smiling gently . . .

Silence fell again, and all knelt to the ground. The court physicians examined Chenghin's pulses, and announced that the prince still lived, but could not be wakened; he would soon waste away to a peaceful death. As the physicians lifted the prince's body into a covered litter, the court La-mas began the sonorous Buddhist chant for the dying . . . "*Gone, gone; gone to the far shore of the bitter sea of life and death* . . ."

"My *son*!" cried Kublai, looking distraught. "Truly it is best that his end will be peaceful, but how shall I mourn him? Shall I wear sackcloth and wail in a straw hut for three full years, as the Cathayan nobles mourn their heirs? Shall I carry his body to the holy mountain of Altai, where the descendants of Great Genghiz are buried in conical mounds? Shall I slash my own flesh and kill all whom I meet along the way, like an unwashed steppeland chief, so blood will mingle with my tears? How shall the Son of Heaven mourn his favorite son?"

The Great Khan gazed at the Sleeping Beauty. *"You!"* he shouted. "You have done this, and you know the answers to all that troubles me."

Niccolo Polo began to nervously count his amber beads. "I fear she does *not* please the Great Khan," he murmured to Maffeo.

Marco had ofttimes seen the Khan of Khans move quickly and decisively in a crisis, and he had often seen Kublai move stiffly and painfully due to his gout. Now Marco saw the Great Khan move both quickly and painfully, as the Son of Heaven mounted the first of the pair of tandem ponies carrying the Sleeping Beauty's litter, and trotted off with her into the dense forest.

"Where is he going?" asked Marco.

Peter the Tartar stood beside his master and replied, "He is following the old Mongol custom of kidnapping the bride and wrestling her into submission. Usually it is merely a game, which both the lad and maiden enjoy. At times there is a real battle, when there is enmity between families; or if the maiden is like Kaidu Khan's warrior-daughter, Bright Moon. This princess is so powerful that she has offered to marry any young nobleman who will wager 100 horses that he can wrestle her to the ground. Bright Moon remains unmarried, for no man can vanquish her, though many have tried, and she has collected over 10,000 fine horses. I hope the Great Khan has an easier time of it. My devils suggest that we follow and observe . . ."

The Great Khan led the Sleeping Beauty's litter, slung between the two ponies, to a misty clearing in the forest. There he halted and stiffly dismounted, and sat beside her on the mossy forest floor. He gazed at her for a long, long while.

Finally he spoke. "How can I wake you, my glowing bride? For I would speak with you . . . I have so many questions to ask; even the Son of Heaven is perplexed by countless puzzles. Must I don a wrestler's deer-hide and fight you like Bright Moon, Kaidu's stalwart daughter? Do I dare wager the hard-won Mongol empire for the risky pleasure of your icy embrace? Do I dare even *touch* you, my bride, or will I fall into a frozen sleep?"

The Great Khan extended a stocky arm from beneath his sable cloak, held his broad hand just above the Sleeping Beauty's brow and said, "Yet if I have grown too soft for risks and dares, like the effete Cathayans who preceded me on the dragon-throne, then am I still fit to be called Khan of Khans, grandson of invincible Genghiz?" A resolute expression crossed his round and ruddy face, and his hand gently caressed her wax-pale forehead, languidly supported by one delicate palm. A great shudder seemed to pass through him and Kublai toppled backwards . . . then righted himself again.

The Sleeping Beauty opened her glimmering eyes, gazed full upon him and spoke; "I sensed you and your son calling to me . . . summoning me from the peak of the celestial mountain in the center of the universe, where I sip sweet nectar from the fruit of the tree of eternal life, and dance with immortals among light and shadows. This form you see, which pleases you so, suits me like a suit of clothes when I wish to visit your realm. I can only stay with you a brief while. How may I serve you, my Lord?"

"What has become of Chenghin . . . what will become of me? I grow old and full of doubts. My bones ache and I can feel my powers diminish. Chenghin is dying, and Temur, his eldest son and now my heir, is still but a lad. The full burden of Great Genghiz' mighty empire rests upon my weary shoulders, and I know not how long I will have the strength to support it. In my dreams I see my grandfather shooting at eagles, and I hear him calling, *'Prepare for conquest . . . prepare for war!'* Yet I know not if I still have the power to answer his savage summons. You speak of immortality, Shining Lady . . . please teach your secrets to me."

"Prince Chenghin was doomed to a painful death, and the kiss which roused me was the kiss which sealed his doom . . . with peace. No kiss will wake him, yet he was a brave man, for he offered his life to protect the Dragon Throne. Now give me your hand . . . if you are courageous enough to embrace me, my Lord."

"Gladly, my bride," said Kublai. He slowly extended his hand, and boldly prepared to receive her frosty touch. Their hands met and clasped, and the Great Khan was visibly startled by a tremendous jolt that flashed through him. His skin turned icy pale, his eyes closed, and he seemed to fall into a swoon. Then a large and luminous moonstone fell from her ring into his palm, and he woke with his face aglow with vigorous warmth and strength.

"Thank you, my bride," said Kublai, gazing at the empowering moonstone in his hand. But the Sleeping Beauty did not reply, for her glowing eyes had closed in slumber again.

The Great Khan rose up from the ground; rose briskly and energetically, with no trace of stiffness in his limbs. The Khan of Khans mounted the lead-horse vigorously, with no hint of weakness or pain, and trotted through the autumnal forest to rejoin his men. In her litter, slung between the two shaggy ponies, the Sleeping Beauty slept peacefully. Marco, and Peter with his devils followed them . . .

All marveled at the sight of Kublai Khan riding his pony like a Mongol youth, without stiffness or pain. "Truly, the Great Khan's gout has become as one of his gorgeous robes, which he dons or doffs as he sees fit," whispered Maffeo to Niccolo Polo.

Great Kublai Khan, wearing a sable cloak, leather battle garb, and a silver-tipped helmet, sat upright in the saddle of an armored war-horse like a Mongol chieftain. He gathered all his men around him and spoke in a booming voice. "We will return directly to Khanbaluc, and prepare the final conquest of rebellious Bur-mien. On the Green Mount overlooking the Carp Pond of Great Seclusion, I will construct a stupa-pavilion of purest white jade, which will be the tomb of my beloved son Chenghin, when he must don his golden death-mask. Nearby, I will build a bell-shaped white stupa-temple as a peaceful resting place for my slumbering bride, and for the curious map which led us to her. For I have had all sorts and nations of women, but she is indeed like none other."

"Yes, Great Lord!" shouted all the courtiers and generals, falconers and physicians, kite-flyers and La-mas and underlings; and all kowtowed as the sun-and-moon banners snapped in the breeze.

"*Marón!* I am confused," muttered Maffeo to Niccolo. "Does the valuable icon-lady *please* him . . . or does she not? Will his Lordship reward us with treasure and a golden passport home . . . or will he not?"

Messer Niccolo fingered his amber beads and mumbled under his breath, while anxiously awaiting the Great Khan's words. "*Item; a torque of turquoise-stones of heaven-blue flecked with green, and bound about with wire of gold: the value of a ten month lease on the octroi revenues of a small walled town, large enough to contain a basilica and at least five guilds . . .*"

At last the Great Khan's gaze turned to the three Polos, Niccolo, Maffeo, and Marco, and he spoke directly to them. "A man upon whom an Empire depends has no right to risk his life unneedfully. It is a very great, an immensely great honor that I trusted you Po-los with this risky venture in my place. I am told you wish to leave. You *shall* leave, as you wish; you *shall* go, and you shall go in peace and honor. It is the golden pass which you need to leave, according to our custom and our law, and it is the gold which I shall give to you . . ." The Great Khan gestured, and a courtier brought an elaborately carved jade tray to him. The

Great Khan gestured again, and signalled for the Polos to come forward.

The Polos approached slowly, with many bows and kowtows, according to the ways of court. They were a-tremble for a glimpse of the golden tablet, which would grant them safe passage through all the kingdoms and realms of the Khanates. Yet when finally they reached the Great Khan, seated upon his great war-horse, they saw that the jade tray contained *no* golden passport at all. Instead it held a large number of large and gleaming golden coins, and circlets studded with blemish-free rubies, the color of ripe pomegranate kernels. To speak of the gold tablet was impossible under court politesse. Indeed it was against court etiquette to speak at all. So, with many bows and prostrations, the three Polos accepted the jade tray of glittering gold set with rubies, and ceremoniously withdrew.

"So it is with even the greatest of kings. They give much without giving," said Niccolo Polo, when the three Venetians were again gathered among themselves at the edge of the great throng.

"No matter. The Son of Heaven *will* give the golden passport, as he has said," replied Marco.

"*Marón!* he had better; before my untimely death—or before our regal patron must untimely wear his golden death mask," snorted Maffeo. "How I long to see the four starlings of the Polo family shield above our blossom-laden balconies in Most Great and Serene Venice."

Just then four black birds darted across the sky, flying westward. Were they starlings? —Perhaps.

"We shall leave when it pleases the Great Khan," said Messer Marco Polo.

Epilogue from the Realm of History:

In January of the historical year 1286, Prince Chenghin, favorite son of Kublai Khan, died peacefully.

In 1287, Kublai's armies successfully invaded and plundered the splendid Burmese capital of Pagan.

Kublai's reign lasted until his death at age 79, in February, 1294. He was succeeded by his grandson Temur, son of Chenghin. Among Kublai's monuments was a white stupa-temple in the old section of Beijing, where a hidden map wrapped in colorful silk yarn was recently found.

Early in 1292, Kublai at last allowed the Polos to depart by sea, to escort a young princess as a bride for Arghun, Khan of Persia. After many hardships they finally reached Venice in 1295.

In 1296, Marco Polo commanded a galley in the war between Venice and Genoa, and was taken prisoner for about a year. His fellow prisoner was a popular romance writer, Rustichello of Pisa, who collaborated on *The Travels of Messer Marco Polo.* Most observations in *The Travels* have been verified by Chinese and other sources, but some romantic flourishes may have come from the pen of Rustichello. Despite some disbelief, their book was highly successful and influenced later explorers, for it introduced the wonders of eastern Asia to Europe.

After 1299, Marco Polo settled down beneath the four-starling shield as a merchant of Venice, until his death at age 70. His will was dated 9 January, 1324. He divided his substantial property among his wife, Donata, and three daughters. He also granted full freedom to his loyal slave, Peter the Tartar.

Deo Gratias. Amen.

DAHUT, Book III
Dahut is the daughter of the King, Gratillonius, and her story is one of mythic power . . . and ancient evil. The senile gods of Ys have decreed that Dahut must become a Queen of the Christ-cursed city of Ys while her father still lives. 65371-7 $3.95

THE DOG AND THE WOLF, Book IV
Gratillonius, the once and future King, strives first to save the surviving remnant of the Ysans from utter destruction, and then to save civilization itself as barbarian night extinguishes the last flickers of the light that once was Rome! 65391-1 $4.50

ANDERSON, POUL
THE BROKEN SWORD
Come with us now to 11th-century Scandinavia, when Christianity is beginning to replace the old religon, but the Old Gods still have power, and men are still oppressed by the folk of the Faerie.
65382-2 $2.95

ASIRE, NANCY
TWILIGHT'S KINGDOMS
For centuries, two nearly-immortal races—the Krotahnya, followers of Light, and the Leishoranya, servants of Darkness—have been at war, struggling for final control of a world that belongs to neither. "The novel-length debut of an important new talent . . . I enthusiastically recommend it."—C.J. Cherryh
65362-8 $3.50

BROWN, MARY
THE UNLIKELY ONES
Thing is a young girl who hides behind a mask; her companions include a crow, a toad, a goldfish, and a kitten. Only the Dragon of the Black Mountain can restore them to health and happiness—but the questers must total seven to have a chance of success. "An imaginative and charming book."—*USA Today*. "You've got a winner here . . ."—Anne McCaffrey.
65361-X $3.95

DAVIDSON, AVRAM and DAVIS, GRANIA
MARCO POLO AND THE SLEEPING BEAUTY
Held by bonds of gracious but involuntary servitude in the court of Kublai Khan for ten years, the Polos—Marco, his father Niccolo, and his uncle Maffeo—want to go home. But first they must complete one simple task: bring the Khan the secret of immortality!
65372-5 $3.50

EMERY, CLAYTON
TALES OF ROBIN HOOD
Deep within Sherwood Forest, Robin Hood and his band have founded an entire community, but they must be always alert against those who would destroy them: Sir Guy de Gisborne, Maid Marion's ex-fiance and Robin's sworn enemy; the sorceress Taragal, who summons a demon boar to attack them; and even King Richard the Lion-Hearted, who orders Robin and his men to come and serve his will in London. And who is the false Hood whose men rape, pillage and burn in Robin's name?
65397-0 $3.50

AB HUGH, DAFYDD
HEROING
A down-on-her-luck female adventurer, a would-be boy hero, and a world-weary priest looking for new faith are comrades on a quest for the World's Dream.
65344-X $3.50

HEROES IN HELL

created by Janet Morris

The greatest heroes of history meet the greatest names of science fiction—and each other!—in the greatest meganovel of them all! (Consult "The Whole Baen Catalog" for the complete listing of HEROES IN HELL.)

MORRIS, JANET & GREGORY BENFORD,
C.J. CHERRYH, ROBERT SILVERBERG, more!
ANGELS IN HELL (Vol. VII)
Gilgamesh returns for blood; Marilyn Monroe kisses the Devil; Stalin rewrites the Bible; and Altos, the unfallen Angel, drops in on Napoleon and Marie with good news: Marie will be elevated to heaven, no strings attached! Such a deal! (So why is Napoleon crying?)
65360-1 $3.50

MORRIS, JANET, & LYNN ABBEY, NANCY ASIRE, C. J. CHERRYH, DAVID DRAKE, BILL KERBY, CHRIS MORRIS, more.
MASTERS IN HELL (Vol. VIII)
Feel the heat as the newest installment of the infernally popular HEROES IN HELL™ series roars its way into your heart! This is Hell—where you'll find

Sir Francis Burton, Copernicus, Lee Harvey Oswald, J. Edgar Hoover, Napoleon, Andropov, and other masters and would-be masters of their fate.

65379-2 $3.50

REAVES, MICHAEL
THE BURNING REALM
A gripping chronicle of the struggle between human magicians and the very *in*human Chthons with their demon masters. All want total control over the whirling fragments of what once was Earth, before the Necromancer unleashed the cataclysm that tore the world apart. "A fast-paced blend of fantasy, martial arts, and unforgettable landscapes."—Barbara Hambly

65386-5 $3.50

EMPIRE OF THE EAST

by Fred Saberhagen

THE BROKEN LANDS, Book I
A masterful blend of high technology and high sorcery; a unique adventure in a world on the brink of ultimate change; a world where magic rules—and science struggles to live again! "The work of a master."
—*The Magazine of Fantasy & Science Fiction*

65380-6 $2.95

THE BLACK MOUNTAINS, Book II
East meets West in bloody conflict on a world where magic rules, but technology is revolting! "A fine mix of fantasy and science fiction, action and speculation." —Roger Zelazny 65390-3 $2.75

ARDNEH'S WORLD, Book III
The gripping climax of the "Empire of the East" series. "Ranks favorably with Tolkien. Exceptional in sheer unbridled zest and imaginative sweep." —*School Library Journal* 65404-7 $2.95

SPRINGER, NANCY
CHANCE—AND OTHER GESTURES OF THE HAND OF FATE
Chance is a low-born forester who falls in love with the lovely Princess Halimeda—but the story begins when Halimeda's brother discovers Chance's feelings toward the Princess. It's a story of power and jealousy, taking place in the mysterious Wirral forest, whose inhabitants are not at all human . . .
65337-7 $3.50

THE HEX WITCH OF SELDOM (hardcover)
The King, the Sorceress, the Trickster, the Virgin, the Priest . . . together they form the Circle of Twelve, the primal human archetypes whose powers are manifest in us all. Young Bobbi Yandro, can speak with them at will—and when she becomes the mistress of a horse who is more than a horse, events sweep her into the very hands of the Twelve . . .
65389-X $15.95

Here is an excerpt from Mary Brown's new novel The Unlikely Ones, *coming in November 1987 from Baen Books Fantasy—SIGN OF THE DRAGON:*

MARY BROWN

THE UNLIKELY ONES

After breakfast the next morning—a helping of what looked like gruel but tasted of butter and nuts and honey and raspberries and milk—the magician led us outside into a morning sparkling with raindrops and clean as river-washed linen, but strangely the grass was dry when we seated ourselves in a semicircle in front of his throne. Hoowi, the owl, was again perched on his shoulder, eyes shut, and he took up Pisky's bowl into his lap. Although the birds sang, their songs were courtesy-muted, for the Ancient's voice was softer this morning as though he were tired, and indeed his first words confirmed this.

'I have been awake most of the night, my friends, pondering your problems. That is why I have convened this meeting. We agreed yesterday that you had all been called together for a special mission, a quest to find the dragon. You need him, but he also needs you.' He paused, and glanced at each one of us in turn. 'But perhaps last night you thought this would be easy. Find the Black Mountains, seek out the dragon's lair, return the jewels, ask for a drop of blood and a blast of fire and Hey Presto! your problems are all solved.

'But it is not as easy at that, my friends. Of your actual meeting with the dragon, if indeed you reach him, I will say nothing, for that is still in the realms of conjecture. What I can say is this: in order to reach the dragon you have a long and terrible journey ahead of you, one that will tax you all to the utmost, and may even find one or other of you tempted to give up, to leave the others and return; if that happens then you are all doomed, for I must impress upon you that as the seven you are now you have a chance, but even were there one less your chances of survival would be halved. There is no easy way to your dragon, understand that before you start. I can give you a map, signs to follow, but these will only be indications, at best. What perils and dangers you may meet upon the way I cannot tell you: all I know is that the success of your venture depends upon you staying together, and that you must all agree to go, or none.

'I can see by your expressions that you have no real idea of what I mean when I say "perils and dangers": believe me, your imaginations cannot encompass the terrors you might have to face—'

'But if we do stay together?' I interrupted.

'Then you have a better chance: that is all I can say. It is up to you.' He was serious, and for the first time I felt a qualm, a hesitation, and glancing at my friends I saw mirrored the same doubts.

'And if we don't go at all—if we decide to go back to—to wherever we came from?' I persisted.

'Then you will be crippled, all of you, in one way or another, for the rest of your lives.'

'Then there is no choice,' said Conn. 'And so the sooner we all set off the better,' and he half-rose to his feet.

'Wait!' thundered the magician, and Conn subsided, flushing. 'That's better, I have not finished.'

'Sit down, shurrup, be a good boy and listen to granpa,' muttered Corby sarcastically, but The Ancient affected not to hear.

'There is another thing,' said he. 'If you succeed

in your quest and find the dragon, and if he takes back the jewels, and if he yields a drop of blood and a blast of fire, if, I say . . . then what happens afterwards?'

The question was rhetorical, but Moglet did not understand this.

'I can catch mice again,' she said brightly, happily.

But he was gentle with her. 'Yes, kitten, you will be able to catch mice, and grow up properly to have kittens of your own—but at what cost? You may not realize it but your life, and the life of the others, has been in suspension while you have worn the jewels, but once you lose your diamond then time will catch up with you. You will be subject to your other eight lives and no longer immune, as you others have been also, to the diseases of mortality.

'Also, don't forget, your lives have been so closely woven together that you talk a language of your own making, you work together, live, eat, sleep, think together. Once the spell is broken you, cat, will want to catch birds, eat fish and kill toads; you, crow, will kill toads too, and try for kittens and fish; toad here will be frightened of you all, save the fish; and the fish will have none but enemies among you.

'And do not think that you either, Thing-as-they-call-you, will be immune from this; you may not have their killer instinct but, like them, you will forget how to talk their language and will gradually grow away from them, until even you cross your fingers when a toad crosses your path, shoo away crows and net fish for supper—'

'You are wrong!' I said, almost crying. 'I shall always want them, and never hurt them! We shall always be together!'

'But will they want you,' asked The Ancient quietly, 'once they have their freedom and identity returned to them? If not, why is it that only dog, horse, cattle, goat and sheep have been domesticated and even these revert to the wild, given the chance? Do you not think that there must be some reason why humans and wild animals dwell apart? Is it perhaps that they value their freedom, their individuality, more than man's circumscribed domesticity? Is it not that they prefer the hazards of the wild, and only live with man when they are caught, then tamed and chained by food and warmth?'

'I shall never desert Thing!' declared Moglet stoutly. 'I shan't care whether she has food and fire or not, my place is with her!'

'Of course . . . Indubitably . . . What would I do without her . . .' came from the others, and I turned to the magician.

'You see? They don't believe we shall change!'

'Not now,' said The Ancient heavily. 'Not now. But there will come a time . . . So, you are all determined to go?'

'Just a moment,' said Conn. 'You have told Thingmajig and her friends just what might be in store for them if we find the dragon: what of me and Snowy here? What unexpected changes in personality have you in store for us?' He was angry, sarcastic.

'You,' said the Ancient, 'you and my friend here, the White One, might just do the impossible: impossible, that is, for such a dedicated knight as yourself. . .'

'And what's that?'

'You might change your minds . . .'

'About what, pray?' And I saw Snow shake his head.'

'What Life is all about . . .'